ONCE
UPON A
BITE

15 INCISIVE FAERIE TALES

ANNIE BELLET ✦ CHRISTINE POPE ✦ SARA C. ROETHLE
ALETHEA KONTIS ✦ SARRA CANNON ✦ JULIA CRANE
C. GOCKEL ✦ JENNA ELIZABETH JOHNSON ✦ DONNA AUGUSTINE
PHAEDRA WELDON ✦ NIKKI JEFFORD ✦ JAMIE FERGUSON
ANTHEA SHARP ✦ KAY MCSPADDEN ✦ KATE DANLEY

Fiddlehead Press

Read more fabulous fairytale retellings from these authors - available in print and digital at all online retailers!

ONCE UPON A CURSE - 17 Dark Faerie Tales

ONCE UPON A KISS - 17 Romantic Faerie Tales

ONCE UPON A QUEST - 15 Tales of Adventure

ONCE UPON A STAR - 14 SF-Inspired Faerie Tales

ONCE UPON A GHOST - 20 Eerie Faerie Tales

ONCE UPON A WISH - 17 Dreamy Faerie Tales

Join our FB group Urban Fantasy Fiends to keep up with all the news from these authors!

CONTENTS

THE BLUE FAIRY HUNTERS GUILD   1
Phaedra Weldon

Author's Note   31

SILVEREYES AND THE THREE WOLVES   32
Nikki Jefford

Author's Note   61

RIVER DAUGHTER   64
Annie Bellet

Author's Note   79

THE GIRL WHO CRIED VAMP   80
Christine Pope

Author's Note   99

THE UGLY DAUGHTER   101
Donna Augustine

Author's Note   129

SPIDER TO THE FLY   130
Kate Danley

Author's Note   143

PRINCESS OF SALT   145
Anthea Sharp

Author's Note   177

THE HUNTRESS   178
Sara C. Roethle

Author's Note   197

YELF REVIEWS FOR JAQUELINE'S BEANSTALK CAFÉ   198
Kay McSpadden

Author's Note   211

MARUSIA AND THE MONSTER   213
Jamie Ferguson

Author's Note   227

TWISTED CINDERELLA   229
Julia Crane

Author's Note   255
FAEFROST   256
Jenna Elizabeth Johnson

Author's Note   277
CAT IN COMBAT BOOTS   279
C. Gockel

Author's Note   303
BLOOD AND WATER   304
Alethea Kontis

Author's Note   325
BREADCRUMBS   327
Sarra Cannon

Author's Note   359
Other Collections   361

ABOUT THE STORIES

Fifteen tales tinged with darkness, where vampires and werewolves roam and familiar fairytales take on overtones of blood and vengeance. (Note: Some of these stories are not suitable for sensitive readers.)

The Blue Fairy Hunters Guild - Phaedra Weldon
Joining the Blue Fairy Hunters Guild is just the first step in finding the Nightshade who made him a Puppet all those centuries ago. Revenge is the goal, but lies and truths revealed show his past has a very different tale.

Silvereyes and the Three Wolves - Nikki Jefford
Werewolf reporter Justin Slinger covers the dramatic court trial of Kingdom v. Silvereyes. Will the vampire Ada Silvereyes be found guilty of first-degree burglary and property damage?

River Daughter - Annie Bellet
The tale of a woman who is the last in a long line of magical women, and the lengths a mother will go to not only to protect her child, but also her legacy.

The Girl Who Cried Vamp - Christine Pope
Hedgewitch Selena Marx is usually ready to believe six impossible things before breakfast. But even her credulity is strained when the new kid in town is full of strange stories, each one wilder than the last.

The Ugly Daughter - Donna Augustine
The Ugly Daughter follows a scarred and ridiculed girl named Winni. All she dreams of is a future where she's accepted, but her true destiny is more than she could've imagined.

Spider to the Fly - Kate Danley
"'Will you walk into my parlour?' said the Spider to the Fly." The famous poem by Mary Howett gets a lush retelling by *USA Today* bestselling author Kate Danley. Except there's vampires.

Princess of Salt - Anthea Sharp
A daughter is cast out, but can she win her way back to forgiveness through the simple art of cooking?

The Huntress - Sara C. Roethle
When an old woman is killed, a vampire hunter is sent to find the killer. Only she isn't hunting vampires. No, the lone vampire around wants a lot more from her than blood.

Yelf Reviews for Jaqueline's Beanstalk Cafe - Kay McSpadden
Everyone's a critic, especially on social media, and especially in Fairy Tale Land. Even Jacqueline's Beanstalk Cafe lives for good Yelf reviews!

Marusia and the Monster - Jamie Ferguson
Kara never stays too long in any one place, and never allows anyone to get too close to her. It's just too risky—she never knows ahead of time what the monster inside of her might make her do. But Kara didn't expect to fall in love...

Twisted Cinderella - Julia Crane
Cinderella has had it with being pushed around. Instead of taking the high road, Cinderella embraces the darkness in this twisted tale.

Faefrost - Jenna Elizabeth Johnson
When her best friend is taken by a woman the wild animals call the Frost Witch, Tegan of Eile will stop at nothing to get him back.

Cat in Combat Boots - C. Gockel
Tenryu has two big problems. The solution is very small.

Blood and Water - Alethea Kontis
A faithful retelling of Hans Christian Andersen's "The Little Mermaid," only she's a vampire. And there are pirates.

Breadcrumbs - Sarra Cannon
Despite trying to create a new life for herself after the disappearance of her brother, Gretel is pulled back into the dark world of vampire hunting when she catches sight of the man who first lured them into the woods as children.

Read more fabulous fairytale retellings from these authors - available in print and digital at all online retailers!

ONCE UPON A CURSE - 17 Dark Faerie Tales

ONCE UPON A KISS - 17 Romantic Faerie Tales

ONCE UPON A QUEST - 15 Tales of Adventure

ONCE UPON A STAR - 14 SF-Inspired Faerie Tales

ONCE UPON A GHOST - 20 Eerie Faerie Tales

ONCE UPON A WISH - 17 Dreamy Faerie Tales

Join our FB group Urban Fantasy Fiends to keep up with all the news from these authors!

THE BLUE FAIRY HUNTERS GUILD

PHAEDRA WELDON

"DANTE."

I stepped forward. "Yes."

"The opportunity for you to become a full-fledged Nightshade Hunter, under the auspices of the *Blue Fairy Hunters Guild* has come. Do you accept?"

We stood in the Guild's meeting room—a back alley warehouse full of mannequins and debris. Seventeen of us. This place had once been the warehouse to a popular retail store, abandoned to whoever could maintain a presence in it. The Guild's Lore Master, Cedrik Red, insisted this was sacred ground, a place where Nightshades and their minions could not hurt us.

I didn't believe that bit of nonsense. I mean…there was nothing in my lore books mentioning there being sacred ground within the city limits. But I'd also learned on my first-day one does not disagree with the Lore Master. He is easily triggered and will go into screaming fits before then painting you an idiot. Of course, having been branded this way by him, no one else seemed to care.

I wasn't new to hunting. My Uncle Jiminy had been a Hunter. He wasn't a blood relative, but he was the next best thing to family I had. Knowing full well what I was in my darkest hour, he picked me up, brushed me off, and taught me how to survive. He'd also been quite a lady's man, and unfortunately, he'd been turned into a cricket by a Sorceress he'd spurned, and now traveled with me. It looked like I had a bug on my shoulder. Or my head. He sat where he wanted to, and my job was not to step on him. Or sit on him.

Or swat him.

He wouldn't die. But it was painful for him when he inflated back to life.

Jiminy was also very knowledgeable in Lore. And understood what it meant to be flexible rather than rigid. Life changed. And truths...always changed. When lies were revealed.

There were two members of the Guild that always seemed to be near Cedrik. If they had names, I never knew them. They simply were known as the Cat and the Fox. No joke. I tried to discern if their chosen titles meant something. Like, if the Cat was good at stealth and could balance well in high places or the Fox was cunning and good at theft.

No.

Neither of these was true. As far as I could see they chose the names because they believed them cool. Though they were near Cedrik all the time, they never spoke against his sometimes ridiculous lore.

Which I called him out on at any given opportunity.

And thus began my love/hate relationship with the Guild that had lasted all of two months. I had proven myself worthy to be a member, bringing in more kills than anyone present. I showed them my prowess with a Wood Ratchet, my weapon of choice, enchanted to fire six rowan stakes before needing more blood to recharge. Most hunters carry standard rifles with their special mixes of bullets with holy water or cross etched on silver. But everyone knows you can't make bullets of pure silver. The metal's too soft. You can put a filling of pure silver *inside* the bullet, which is what I have in my rifle. At least Cedrik got that right. Silver was deadly to Nightshades as well as their minions.

All I have ever wanted to be, since sending my first letters of initiation into the *Blue Fairy Hunters Guild*, was the best. A real

Nightshade Hunter. You might say...it's more than a passion, but a need for revenge.

It's not the worst backstory ever told, nor is it the longest. It won't make your eyes water or your nose run in my telling it. I never share it, and I have a slight—very slight—rep of being secretive. What I don't like is sympathy, especially the looks I get when someone does learn about my past.

And then I have to kill them.

I am twenty-two by present standards, much too young to be a part of the Guild as I was first told.

The Guild's leader, a veteran hunter named Honest John, the one who addressed me in this meeting, took a chance on me. I am nice to look at, though I admit I haven't seen myself in quite a long time. I never look in a mirror, and I avoid my reflection.

But there is a caveat in all of this. A secret I will die protecting.

I am also, a Ghoul.

Modern Vampires, or Nightshades as they prefer to be called, call us Puppets.

Taken at the age I am now, I was made to drink the blood of a Nightshade and twisted into something that seeks death. I was trained to be an assassin. To be cold and calculating. To be the hammer of the most powerful of Nightshades.

Here I stood among the Hunters, a creature none of them had the comprehension to understand, least of all Cedrik Red (who believed all Puppets were zombies—but that is another story), given the opportunity to be placed in the perfect position to slay the monster who made me.

"I accept," I said solemnly.

Most of my peers cheered and raised their hands. But not Cedrik, or the Fox or the Cat. They narrowed their eyes at me and said nothing. But being what I am, I could feel their hatred and their resentment. I knew then that I not only had enemies within the Nightshades but the very Guild I would pledge my gun too.

They hate you. Jiminy sounded very thoughtful in my mind.

Yes.

I wonder why. They don't know you. They don't even know your goal. Perhaps it is jealousy?

Maybe...and maybe it is time for me to find out, lest our plans are thwarted by these numbskulls before they begin. And with that, he jumped from my shoulder and disappeared.

Honest John nodded and crossed his arms over his ample chest. He was a big man, almost a giant, with close-cropped blond hair and an air of distrust. I would never pledge my whole self to him, but I would listen for information. "For your initiation, you will be tasked to bring me the head of the Nightshade Coven in this city."

There were murmurs and the occasional "ridiculous" and "he's too young and inexperienced for that." I even caught an "Even the Fox and the Cat couldn't bring down the King!"

But I remained in the center of the storm, my icy gaze fixed on Honest John. I sensed...something else. Something unsaid, but Jiminy was not on my shoulder to tell me what it was. And I had not drunk blood in several days.

I would have to be very cautious, and take my time—

"You have twenty-four hours to complete this initiation," Honest John said. "To become a full-fledged member of the Guild."

Damn.

I called Jiminy and heard his reply. He was listening to something...and he would get back to me. That was not what I wanted to hear.

"You will meet with Cedrik to learn the lore surrounding the King—"

"I do not need Cedrik Red's help," I said, interrupting him, but keeping my voice calm. "I am well versed in the Lore."

"Are you?" Cedrik said as he folded his arms over his chest. If anyone resembled what a Nightshade would look like, it would be him. He was shorter than I, with snow-white skin and Eurasian eyes. For a mortal, he was exotic, and I believed he chose this look to hide something. I just didn't know what.

"Yes." I met his gaze with my own.

"Meet with him anyway," Honest John said. "I will not have it said that as a leader I sent an initiate into the jaws of danger without knowledge." He raised his hand and his voice filled the room. "Dante has accepted the challenge to defeat the Nightshade King. Any opposed?"

No one spoke.

Then a cheer went up and kegs were tapped. In seconds it was a party.

Honest John stepped up to me and put his hand on my shoulder. "I will admit, the moment I saw you I thought you were a girl. Only Nightshades are as pretty as you are. Didn't even think you could use a gun, much less a Wood Ratchet. That's no small feat of magic there. So I wish you good luck, Dante."

I nodded to him before he walked away. Jiminy appeared again on my shoulder and I moved to a more private area, but not before Cedrik and his shadows approached me. "Dante," Cedrik said. "Sit and listen. You'll need my knowledge to survive the Nightshade King."

I didn't sit. I just looked at him.

"I hate that stare of yours," the Cat said and flipped a knife in the air. "It's like you're looking through me."

"Yeah," said the Fox. "I want to cut your eyes out."

"Boys," Cedrik held out his hand. "It is time to educate Dante. I believe first you should know the King's real name, and who he was. He was called—"

"Gepetto," I said and crossed my arms over my chest. I knew the monster's name.

But who wouldn't know the name of one's father?

Cedrik didn't tell me anything I didn't know. I knew Gepetto was in the city and had been for some time. I just didn't know why he'd left his castle in Italy. For him to show up in the same city I had lived in for a decade was suspicious. I had taken on a new identity and gone to great lengths to hide myself. Did he know I was here?

After Cedrik finished his long, windy warning over Gepetto's abilities and the lore of the King's past, it was time to find a quiet corner and listen to what Jiminy had discovered.

He'd overheard a few of the other Hunters talking about their initiation rights not being so...well...over-reaching. Nearly all the Hunters present believed Honest John had something else in mind. And why was Dante the target?

As I went around the room asking each of them about their initiation, one of the older Hunters, a woman named Elise, motioned me to her. She was tan-skinned, with silver hair in a braid, worn leather pants, and jacket, and knee-high boots. I assumed the motorcycle I'd seen outside was hers. She stood next to her partner, Genoise, a much smaller woman with short hair and a tattoo of some tribal pattern over the left side of her face.

On a closer look, I realized the tattoo hid a scar that ran down her jaw.

"You need to be careful, Dante," Elise said as I neared. "Something seems wrong with this whole idea."

"Yeah," Genoise said and scratched at her up-turned nose. "Like, Elise and I had our initiation job together and it was simply cleaning up Cabbage Town south of the interstate. There were a lot of hell-hounds down there so it took a night and we was done."

"Right," Elise nodded. "Mallory over there was given a bounty— some thief the Division Hunter wanted to be brought in for questioning. Rights and Scotts over there—that married couple—they were given a few half-turned to murder and bring in."

I was seeing a pattern of initiations mine did not fit into. "And what about Cedrik, the Cat, and the Fox?"

Elise made a noise. I was surprised to learn Cedrik didn't have a trial. Honest John brought Cedrik in when he took over the Guild after the founder was murdered (the murderer was never caught). "Big waste of skin, that one." She shook her head. "Cedrik. Thinks he's a real lore-master, when you and me, all of us knows, it's not the lore that keeps you alive. It's your wits and your skills in working that lore to your advantage—but the lore has to be spot-on."

I couldn't argue with that. I knew lore did play a lot into my wits and skills. I knew Gepetto had no problem with the sun, but Cedrik didn't mention this. The Nightshade King wasn't taken with the Day Sleep, nor was he locked into any one location when the sun was up. This was reported to be because of his immense age.

I also knew the rumor of Gepetto never siring a Childe or making a Puppet was false, because here I was. A Puppet who escaped and found their way back home. And once changed into a Puppet, there are two possible futures. A release back to being human, or petrification and a return to ash.

Unfortunately…one worked with the other. If a Puppet lived past the age of ten and was released, turning to stone was inevitable as the body could not withstand the rush of years the Nightshade's blood had suspended.

Ashes to ashes, dust to dust, the Priests always say.

"Now, as for the Cat and Fox," Genoise said. "I think they volunteered to go after Gepetto once, and they failed. So did Honest John, but that's only a rumor."

"Honest John went after Gepetto," I said. "And failed?"

"Yeah," Genoise said. "That's why I'm a bit surprised he's sending you after him. You're greener than most of us—or I thought you were. I get the feeling…" and she narrowed her eyes at me. "You're not."

"I think it's a trap," Elise said before she narrowed her eyes at me. "You've got something under your eye," she reached into her pocket retrieved a women's compact, and handed it to me. "I don't usually touch people, so you can use this to wipe it off." She turned and looked at the trio in the corner; Cedrik, the Cat, and the Fox. "They're up to something and I'm betting Honest John's in on it too."

Neither of them was looking at me so I opened the compact and looked at the mirror and saw the same thing I'd seen since I was made a Puppet.

Nothing.

I wiped under both eyes just to remove whatever it was she'd seen and held the compact out to Elise as she turned to face me. She smiled as she took it and the hinge nicked my finger. I didn't flinch but she noticed. "Oh shit, Dante. Sorry about that. Need a bandaid?"

"No," I sucked at my finger to hide the fact the cut was nowhere to be seen. "I'm fine."

"This does seem a bit over the top," Genoise said as she scratched her head. "As far as our intel, Gepetto hasn't killed in more than a century and has kept pretty much under the radar. He's also sponsored several artists and restored some of the landmark theaters in major cities." She looked at me and then at Elise. "I am kinda surprised he's here in Atlanta of all places. Not exactly a large hub for Nightshade."

"Rumor is he's searching for something," Elise said, the compact no longer in her hand. "Or someone." She laughed. "Maybe he's looking for someone to be his childe?"

I looked at the back of Honest John's cloak as he talked with the Cat and the Fox. There was no sign of Cedrik. Their whispers seemed very urgent, almost anxious. *Jiminy?*

But he wasn't there. I hadn't noticed him leave my shoulder. Was it possible he was spying on those three?

I looked at Elise and changed the subject. "Is there something between Gepetto and the Guild Leader? Some reason he decided to send me?"

Genoise and Elise looked at one another before they looked at me. It was Elise who answered. "Bait is my guess. Gepetto killed Honest John's son, decades ago. He was your age and couldn't wait to hunt vampires with his father."

I hadn't realized the Guild Leader had a son. "So...he expects me to take his revenge. If his son died decades ago, why didn't he take his revenge then?"

"He's tried. Numerous times. And always failed." Elise shrugged. "He's faced down the old Nightshade just about every time, but there's never a fight. Gepetto just kicks him out like Monday's trash."

I could see why that might anger a veteran hunter. It was the ultimate *Ef You.* "Odd he's never assigned this to another initiate until now?"

Elise shook her head. "Oh, he has. Cedrik, the Cat, the Fox, and even the Dog."

"The Dog?" I couldn't keep the incredulous tone out of my voice.

"He was Cedrik's half-brother. He was killed by Gepetto."

Something ticked wrong. "We all know Gepetto hasn't killed in a century—" I looked at each of them. "How is it possible for Gepetto to have killed his sister? Cedrik can't be more than forty. His sister couldn't have been over a hundred."

The two of them glanced at each other before Genoise said to me, "You're right. I guess it is hard for a young one like you to notice."

"Notice what?"

"Cedrik isn't fully human, Dante." Genoise said and crossed her arms over her chest. "He's Dhampir."

Dhampir...a creature born both human and vampire. A being stuck between worlds, not accepted by either. That explained his white skin and his sallow expression. "His brother was a Dhampir as well?"

"No," Elise said. "Look, I like you. We both do. And we think something's up here. So, we're going to go with you and have your back."

"Hunters don't work together," I said as I looked at each of them, still reeling that I had not sensed a Dhampir in front of me. I could sense any supernatural creature. What had kept me from noticing?

"Usually...no," Genoise unholstered her rifle and checked the rounds. "But just think if you do pop the old geezer...and we're there, we get part of that credit."

"You can have all the credit," I looked again at Cedrik.

"You're an odd duck, Dante." Genoise said. "But an attractive one. So, let's go."

Jiminy had indeed been listening in on the conversation between the Cat, the Fox, and Honest John, but what he told me as Elise drove us to Gepetto's lair was a bit surprising.

What they said, didn't make much sense. It's like they were talking in code. I thought the Cat and the Fox were Cedrik's minions or something, but the way they talked about Cedrik to Honest John was...well...strange.

How so?

The Cat said Cedrik didn't show any outward signs of noticing, and that a Dhampir would pick up on something so obvious.

I frowned. *Huh?*

Yeah. And then the Fox said Cedrik disappeared, and they weren't sure where he went. His car was still outside.

It sounded to me like the two of them were reporting something *to* Honest John. Something about Cedrik. And what should Cedrik have noticed that he didn't? What was obvious?

I'm confused.

Me too.

That's when I noticed where we were. I scolded myself. I was usually better at paying attention to my surroundings.

I'm sure most people would imagine a Nightshade's lair would be a deep, dark cavern, as Cedrik tried to inform me. And in that cavern would be many traps and Nightshade minions there to tempt me and take my soul.

Proving once again that I believed Cedrik culled his lore from comic books and bad novels. Or worse, Hollywood depictions of vampires.

I knew Gepetto had rented out the entire top floor of the most expensive hotel in the city. He'd even advertised his presence by planning a mask later tonight.

But the hotel was not where Elise brought us. We stopped near the hotel and parked outside. She put on her Hunter parking sign and I followed them around the back to another building—something that looked like it should be condemned. I didn't see any windows. Not even a fire escape.

"Wait," I said as Genoise cracked the lock open and no alarm system rang out. Jiminy and I were both having our doubts about this building. "Why are we going in here? What is this place?"

Genoise smiled. "To be the best at Hunting, you gotta be up on the latest intel. Gepetto put out that open and very obvious mask invite a week ago, but Elise and I have it on good authority that he did that to throw us off. The Mask is actually here, in the basement of this building."

"This is the old Archive," Elise said. "No windows, no way for records to be damaged, and no sunlight for younger Nightshade."

I guess I must have looked a bit...well...skeptical. Gepetto had never been one for subterfuge. And as far back as I could remember, he'd always kept his word. If he said something, he meant it. Even when he first took me and said I would "dance as his puppet."

"Dante, trust us. Gepetto owns this building. The Mask is actually here. Now are you coming or do you want to run over to the Grand Maquis?"

My gut instinct, the one I'd trust for so many years, told me to leave. To run to the address I had written down. But these two seemed so certain, and they had been the only members of the Guild to be kind to me. And if this was some kind of trap—which I was starting to suspect it was—I didn't want them getting hurt. Or even killed. I just couldn't puzzle who was setting them up.

Dante, keep following them. I'm going to head to the Grand Marquis and see for myself.

I nodded as he jumped off my shoulder and hopped into the overgrown weeds near the door.

"Fine," I said and readied my pistol, my Wood Ratchet primed and ready on my hip, the wood spells stacked and loaded. I only used that weapon in moments of emergency because of the price it demanded. "But if we sense trouble, we surface. You have an escape route out?"

"Yep," and she pulled out her phone.

Mine pinged and I retrieved it from my pocket. I'd received a PDF of a map and a route in red. I snapshotted the map and moved it to my wallpaper. It wasn't until we were down the stairs to what was a basement and a large, open space. It looked as if there had been debris here, but it was all swept to the sides in a very large circle.

Wait...

How did she have my phone number? It was unlisted and I'd never given it to anyone. Except—

Abruptly my body betrayed me. I froze, half walking toward Elise and Genoise on the opposite side of the room. Too late I felt the rush of magic from the floor. I lost hold of the pistol and it clacked on the concrete. Symbols of white and gold flared up as silver wires rose like vipers to wrap around my ankles and yank my legs together. I nearly fell forward but more silver wires wound around my chest, up my arms, and thickened against my wrists. I screamed as the wire pulled me up to the ceiling and wound around the pipes, my arms stretching up and out as the circle beneath me pulled at my ankles. I felt as if I were being pulled apart and I screamed even louder.

"No, no, no," Elise said in a voice full of satisfaction. "Bring him down to where I can get to him."

I was lowered but still held fast by the wire. Where it touched my flesh it burned but left no mark. I threw my head back and gritted my teeth against the agony as several of those wires drilled into my back and fastened around my spine. I was being tortured by the silver as well as the circle. It was a spell that only worked on Puppets. To trap them. Bind them. And feed on them.

They knew what I was. How?

Jiminy! I cried out in my mind. But I couldn't sense him. My thoughts couldn't reach him!

Elise was in front of me, her hands on the sides of my face, forcing me to look at her. "I knew I was right. I've been around enough Puppets in my time to see the subtleties. You never look in a mirror, and cuts never show on your skin, do they, Dante? Or should I call you...Pinocchio. Anwir. Deceiver." The right side of her lips turned up in a smirk. "Your father will pay a King's ransom to have you delivered to him. And we plan on collecting. Right before we kill him...using your blood."

Genoise stood to my right. I couldn't move any other part of my body as Elise leaned my head to my left shoulder. I could see her focusing on my neck and I saw the flash of a blade.

"No..." I choked out.

I felt the sharp bite of something against my skin, the press of lips, and Genoise drank from me.

I screamed between my gritted teeth as I felt my strength drain from me.

Genoise sighed as she pulled back. "The power...this is what we need. Go ahead and drink." She came into my limited view as she wiped her mouth with the back of her hand. All she did was smear blood as I saw her eyes glow with power. She would have my strength, my enhanced senses, and my defenses for twenty-four hours.

"I'm not sure I want to," Elise said as she let go of my head and it fell forward. I hadn't the strength to lift it. Genoise grabbed my hair and wrenched my head back to my left shoulder. I couldn't keep my eyes open. My strength was draining away. "You sure this won't make us Puppets like him?"

"Positive. Puppets are how the old Hunters once hunted the Nightshade. Where did you think this spell comes from? This is how they trapped them, held them prisoner, and used their blood. Why do you think the Nightshades stopped making them? We can get the strength they have for a day but we get to stay human."

She was right. Ghouls...*Puppets*...were the Nightshade's downfall once the Hunters learned how to use them against their masters. And it was clear to me these two wanted to use me against my master.

My Father.

I managed a word...a single one on the tip of my tongue, though my voice was soft and breathless. "D-d-don't..."

"He's still conscious," Genoise said. "Go ahead and drink and he'll sink into a stupor. This spell will hold him here until we need him again. We can get rid of Gepetto and then use Dante here to fuel our rise."

Elise laughed. "Maybe even take over the *Blue Fairy Guild*. Kick old Honest John out. I didn't believe you till now." She put her lips on my neck and I felt the drawing away of my life again.

I felt something I hadn't experienced in a century.

Fear.

Real fear of being held captive here in the basement of a building that no one knew I'd been brought to. Jiminy had always been my lifeline, my rescuer when I did something stupid, and this was the crowning mistake for me—trusting someone I didn't know. But I couldn't reach him. I knew how the spell worked. It not only held a Puppet but made them invisible. I couldn't move—not while the silver dug into my spine. I was...

Helpless.

How...did...they know?

How...

...

🐐

"...can't give him that."

"...skilled with magic. Can't you..."

"No! Don't pull...ease...."

Voices yammered from somewhere in the dark. A gnawing pain brought me back to the surface. That and an overwhelming feeling of nausea. Light sparked behind my eyelids and I opened them slowly. I saw...something black in front of my nose. I realized I was on my front on a cold, concrete floor. Light filtered up in twinkling stars from a glowing circle. I blinked and tried to move.

"No...Dante...keep still. I have to get this out."

I recognized the voice. It was Honest John's.

"Can't..." I managed to breathe. "Pull... reverse the flow."

"Can you do that? He said you have to reverse the flow." I knew he was speaking to someone else.

"Aye...I think so. It's not a complicated spell, but they did lay in some rather nasty traps. All of them designed to kill anyone....ow!"

I assumed whoever belonged to that voice had encountered one of those alleged traps.

Abruptly the dull pain in my back eased and I felt a sharp snap. I made a noise and sucked in the air. Hands lifted me into a sitting position. They also propped me up. I was shirtless and was leaning against someone so my back was exposed.

"Healing that wound is going to take more magic than I've got," said the voice who warned of traps. "Or blood?"

"He'll need more Nightshade blood," Honest John said and I realized I was leaning against him, my cheek against his chest. "Dante... you should have told us who you are."

I inhaled. Knives tore at my insides. I was...dying. He was right. I needed Nightshade blood. As a Puppet I had preternatural healing abilities, I was also still dependent on the blood of the Nightshade and paid a high price for it. Most of my salary went to blood buys to keep my independence. "Not...matter..."

"I'm afraid it does matter," said the other voice again. I realized I did not recognize it, but they were friends with Honest John, whom I had assumed was an enemy. "Cedrik knew who you were. 'Said it was because he knew the lore. Do you think those bitches knew what to do? Do you think they wove the spell to bind you? *He* did it!"

I blinked and saw Honest John's arm in front of my face. I was propped against his front and I needed to see who I was talking to. To my amazement, Honest John helped me lean sideways. I still wasn't strong enough to do it on my own. I'd lost too much blood. They had stolen so much.

A familiar face sat in front of me. The voice belonged to the Cat. He smirked as he reached out and pressed against my shoulder. "Here's your cricket. That little fucker wasn't going to give up until we found you. He was the one who finally figured out the spell. He brought us here and found you literally backstabbed and caught in a web of silver. I kinda thought you were dead."

Jiminy?

I'm here...Jesus, Dante. There was a pause. *I'm so happy you're alive.*

It's a bit hard to kill me.

But it is possible.

Yeah…he was right. I wasn't immortal. I was just… a Puppet. I cleared my throat. "How…long?"

I felt Honest John sigh beneath me. "Dante—"

"How…long…" I inhaled and felt a ghost of the stabbing pain in my back, though I knew the silver had been removed. "Have I…been here?"

No one spoke. I closed my eyes. "What's happened?"

"The *Blue Fairy Hunters Guild* is no more," Honest John said beneath me. "I'm afraid those two bitches—Cedrik as well—used your blood to annihilate the other Hunters. Of the twenty-seven members we had, there is a handful left. Myself, the Cat, the Fox, and that's it. Cedrik took over and systematically killed everyone he could find. The Guild's been renamed as *Pleasure Island Hunters Guild* and they pretty much rule the hunting here in the tri-state area."

To have achieved that much…would take time. Lots of time.

"Dante…you've been here for five years," said the Cat.

Five years of my life…gone.

Used.

Hanging in the basement as I feared.

"I would say you need to take a look at yourself," Honest John said. "But I'm pretty sure you can't see yourself, can you?"

I didn't answer.

"I know…the reasons why the Nightshade do that," the Cat said. "Because they don't want you to remember who you were. That you were once human. To see yourself…could free your conscience. But I think…Dante…you've already been freed, haven't you?"

Five…years.

They fed off of me for *five years*.

And then left me here to gather dust. I could see it on my jeans, on my hands, on…everything.

I was surprised I was alive at all. Or even awake—

"Wait…" I pulled up my hands, my shoulders, and wrists, aching as I called upon strength reserves I didn't realize I had. I managed to push away from Honest John, only to fall back against a brick wall. I looked down at my hands...they were bone white. Almost smooth as marble. I was so close to being petrified. A lifeless Puppet. The ultimate fate of all Puppets. "How did you...Five years of them feeding... How was it possible that you...brought me back?"

The Cat glanced at Honest John. "Got my ways. I also know the lore. I knew youse was close to being a statue, all strung up and wired in the back like you were. Your color still ain't right. But I managed to get you blood. Took us three days down here... but we did it. You're awake. And they won't be back here."

I looked at each of them. "Why not?"

"Because I killed them," Honest John said. "Well, I killed Genoise. She was easiest. She drank so much of your blood she started to petrify. A good shove from a high roof and she shattered into a million pieces. Cedrik killed Elise when they fought over who got to keep you." He smirked. "That's when we knew what was happening, and that you were still alive somewhere. Your bug kept spying on them and finally got the location. Right under our noses!"

"And you gave me...Nightshade blood."

"Not enough though." The Cat stood. "I think we need to get him out of here. Cedrik knows where those bitches kept him and that redirect spell ain't gonna last another week."

"You're right." Honest John stood and to my surprise, lifted me off the floor with ease. I felt heavy as marble, but apparently, I wasn't. I leaned against his shoulder as the Cat tucked my heavy arms into my lap. "I'll try to keep you out of the light. But if it does touch you, don't scream. They'll know where we are."

"Where...are we going?" it was getting harder to talk and I wanted to sleep.

The final sleep.

"I'm taking you home, Dante. He's the only way you can heal fully. And when you have..." Honest John looked down at me and smiled. "We'll have a score to settle."

I don't remember how we traveled. Or how they moved me. I only knew that I was no longer a prisoner of a spell older than the first Nightshade. A necrotic magic that was banned within the magic community. And yet, Genoise had been able to use it. Thinking back, I wasn't sure it was drinking my blood that nearly petrified her, but the punishment for using that spell.

What I do remember was waking again, only this time I wasn't strung up from silver wire wrapped around my spine. I lay on my back in a bed with sheets as soft as clouds against my bare skin. I knew instinctively I was dying. I was nude. And I was...

"You are awake."

I knew the voice, the bite of an Italian accent. I slowly turned my head to the right side of the bed. He was there, sitting on a chair, arms crossed, looking at me as he always did. Only...there were cracks in his stoney visage. Something in his brilliant pink eyes had dimmed. Something I couldn't ever remember seeing before...not in my long life.

"Gepetto."

"I am *Father* to you."

"You are not my father."

"I *am* your Father in that I took you from the streets, I gave you a new life as your old one ebbed from the frail skin that failed you..." he sighed. "But these things you don't remember. The very nature of what I did to you prevents it."

I stared at him. I had not heard this before. He had told me a different story...one of my being the son of a great pianist in London so very long ago. Of how I had been disowned and pushed in front of a carriage. I recounted in my head the words he'd used, his inflections, his fascial expressions.

"I can see by your stare you are trying to process this with the background I gave you. The human mind needs...context. You couldn't forge a new identity unless you knew where you were from, and what you were. I gave you these things."

"You...lied."

"So did you. Many times, Pinocchio."

"I hate that name."

"It was the name your half-brother gave you because you were a thief, a street urchin, and a liar."

I knew the very meaning of the name was liar. What I didn't know... "I...I had a half-brother?"

"And you continued lying after I gave you new life." It was as if I hadn't asked a very important question.

"I wanted my old life back." I closed my eyes. I couldn't really move much of anything else. My reanimation was coming to an end. As was my life.

"Another lie. You couldn't remember what it was to be human. You only know what you were told."

"I *do* remember... What it was to be human. I still do. To choose my own thoughts, my own path, my own destiny and not be...a Puppet." I opened my eyes and stared the ceiling. "I wanted to be real again."

"I know," Gepetto stood and lowered his arms. "And now all those centuries are coming to a close because of a betrayal that I am afraid...is my fault."

I didn't look at him. It was getting harder to move my head, much less my eyes. "This is your eulogy? Your confession over your dying Puppet?"

"Enough...*Dante*. Such a mockery. Do you really believe you have mastered all the levels of Hell? I have much to say and very little time to say it. It was I who originally hired the *Blue Fairy Hunters Guild*— because I had a contact within their ranks. Someone I trusted. I wanted them to find you and bring you to me. It was time you came home. There...were things you needed to know and I believed I had the time to explain them to you." He paused and I managed to look over at him. His expression wasn't stone... again it was something I'd never seen on him before.

I would have almost said...regret.

"Unfortunately, my contact was betrayed by an old enemy. A nemesis of mine I had thought nothing of. I had believed them long

dead, but apparently they had used their somewhat sketchy knowledge to outwit their enemies."

I sighed. "Cedrik."

"Yes. You know he is a Dhampir...an abomination that possess
some of the power of a Nightshade but not their full strength. I did
not know he had joined the Guild, so when I approached Honest
John about finding you and bringing you to me, Cedrik saw an
opportunity."

"I thought...or I was told...that you killed Honest John's son."

"No. John and I are old friends. He was my Right Hand after..."

He didn't need to say it. "Your son...Cedrik."

"You knew?"

I looked at him. "I guessed. There had to be a reason Cedrik knew
so much. He knew about me so he laid a trap for me. Only someone
close to you would..." my breath was a bit shallow. "Know about
your...Puppet. If he were your son, born of a human, he would know
you made me."

"Yes. The women he brought in were Sorceresses and used a
forbidden spell to trap you and steal your blood. They tried to
ransom you to me."

"I see you did not pay it."

Gepetto leaned forward and down. He hovered above me, his
right hand on my left shoulder, his left to the right of my face, upon
the pillow. "I did, my son. I gave them a King's ransom and more and
still they kept you hidden from me. I have searched for you for five
years, nearly accepting they had killed you in their bid for your
blood. The only satisfaction I had was my own knowledge that
drinking too much of a Puppet's blood will eventually turn them to
stone. I knew they would crack, and they would turn to dust. Which
was the case." He straightened up and looked away from me. That's
when I saw Jiminy on his shoulder. "Jiminy finally overheard where
you were, and how to counter the spell. I was there the moment they
found you...still suspended in that trap...little more than a night-
marish statue of a young man caught in a web."

"That...was the name...of the spell," I said. It was getting harder to breathe and I had to take air in gasps. If they had left me there, I had simply fallen into a stupor and could have died peacefully. Reanimating me like this...Gepetto had condemned me to suffer as my body turned to stone and then dust.

Gepetto sat on the bed and put a hand on my chest. I couldn't feel it. I saw him do it. "I don't blame you for hating me...Dante. I misused you, trained you to be a killer, and you changed my life in so many ways. But after two centuries and allowing you your freedom...I have also changed."

He was closer and though breathing became a labored endeavor, my eye-sight was a good as ever. There really were cracks running through his skin. He was far too pale and circles hung beneath his eyes. "What..."

"I now offer you the choice I didn't before. You linger on the precipice of life and death. You will have to choose if you live, or if you die."

Live or die? I stared at him, my breathing now in little gasps. "You (gasp)...said once (gasp)...the stone (gasp)...comes...there is no (gasp)...life..."

"For a Puppet, no. There will never be a reckoning with your human soul. But there is life if you wish to be Nightshade."

My eyes widened at him. "Night...shade...you lie... not...possible..."

"It is. I can change you at that twilight place—that moment between life and death, the instant the two worlds meet. I can't guarantee you will survive it. But if you do, you will be powerful, Dante. You will have all my strength."

"You...lie..." but I wanted to cling to the possibility. The idea that a Puppet could be made a Nightshade. All of my life I had been told it *wasn't* possible. That I would live and die as a thing, no longer real.

The darkness rose over me at that point and I took in my last breath. There was pain as every part of me solidified into stone.

"Tell me Dante! Tell me!"

My answer died on my lips.

For over two hundred years I had not seen myself in a mirror. I had forgotten what I looked like. And yet…given what I was when I died in Gepetto's arms…I might not have known even then. I ran a gang. We stole, we plundered, and we robbed houses. We'd been running from a house when I was struck by a carriage out later than it should have been. I remembered Gepetto's face, his sad expression, and his tender hand on my cheek.

"You did that on purpose!"

I could just see Cedrik looking down at me. He reminded me of my mother. "No…I just…I know it was him. I wasn't thinking!"

"You fool! To kill the only blood relative you have! Help me get him into the carriage."

I remembered everything. My mother often talked of my older brother. Of how he was employed by a rich Baron or something. A title that even now seemed unimportant. My brother was making something of himself… but not me. I was a thief, and a liar, and a nothing. I was born a nothing. I was born to *be* nothing.

Cedrik knew me. He struck me with the carriage that night. Gepetto had believed he'd done it on purpose. I didn't know. My only thoughts were I would die a nothing, just as my mother said. I didn't recognize Cedrik…because I had never seen this mysterious brother. A week later I awoke utterly changed. I had no memory of a name or a life before seeing Gepetto's face.

And from that moment all of my new Father's attention was devoted to me.

And none to Cedrik. He hated me before he knew me. And he hates me now.

The face that stared back at me would forever remain that of a twenty-two-year-old man. I had a pointed chin, an upturned nose, and sarcastic mouth, raven hair, and sky blue eyes. It was my eyes that Gepetto had always loved. I pulled my lips from my teeth and saw them.

Fangs.

Sharp.

Deadly.

And I was...for the first time...hungry.

"So how long you gonna stare at yourself, boy?" Honest John was in Gepetto's private room...no, *my* private room. Gepetto now slept in the ground after making me, his only Nightshade childe. All that he owned, was mine. All that he knew, I now knew. All that he could do...

So could I.

The Cat lounged on a sofa near a roaring fire, a flatscreen television hanging overhead, tuned to the local news. "Come on. Give him a break. He literally just came back from a fate worse than death."

I looked at the Cat's reflection, then moved my eyes to the right and saw the Fox looking out the window. "He's close, Dante."

I smiled. "Yes. But first, what's happened since my unrequested...sleep?"

The Cat shrugged. "A lot and no more. Genoise, Elise, and Cedrik fed on you for five years. They did ransom you to Gepetto, and then never released you. We didn't know where you were, and that's what stayed your Father's hand. He feared they would dismember you, and if that happened, there would be no bringing you back. There was a spell on that building. No one ever noticed it. Not even the city planners, so it was never demolished and no one stepped inside, which made it easy to keep you strung up downstairs." He sat forward. "Cedrik used the power he got from you and meticulously hunted down and killed every Guild member not loyal to him—which pretty much included everybody on Honest John's payroll. Truth was, no one liked him."

"Least of all those two bitches who kidnapped you," the Fox said. He wore a long brown duster and kept a rifle at his back. He turned from the window. "You already know what happened to them. As it stands now, Cedrik owns and runs the renamed *Paradise Island Hunters Guild*. He's got a new crew working for him—I'd say there are close to twelve members now—and he pretty much stays out of sight. Especially after Elise and Genoise were offed. Last two years none of them even went into that building, thinking they'd drained you dry. Rumor has it he's been looking for you because even he couldn't remember what building you were in. Not after the bitches were gone."

I'd stood and began dressing as the three of them talked. Father had a new set of gear made for me. Gone were my usual arraignments of leather jacket, jeans, and tee-shirt. Instead, I pulled on a pair of soft leather pants, a loose white shirt with ruffles down the front over the buttons, and a calf-length leather coat, complete with assorted straps and pockets. The collar was fur-lined and there was a place on my back for my weapon.

I looked at Honest John's reflection. "Where is my Wood Ratchet?"

"Heh," the old man snorted. "Cedrik claimed that for himself. Never saw him make it work, though. He threatened many a Nightshade with it."

"I don't think he's ever fired it," the Cat said. "I think he's afraid of it."

I pursed my lips and nodded. "Interesting." Once I was finished, I looked at myself in the mirror again. It was my eyes that I saw first. So much like my Father's piercing pink...I retained my blue. "What is it you each want to accomplish?"

Honest John shrugged. "I figured you wanted revenge for what they did to you."

I looked at the Cat. He smirked. "I want Cedrik's head. And then I want the Guild back."

I looked at the Fox. He pointed at me. "Same here, but you need to run it. How badass is that with Hunters' Guild run by a Nightshade? But not just any Nightshade, the only childe of Gepetto."

I shook my head and put my hands on my hips. "I fight to retrieve my weapon. I also fight to return the Guild to its rightful owner." I looked at Honest John. "And I'll sponsor it."

"You got a deal, Dante." He pulled the stub of a stogie from his pocket and placed it between his teeth. "I suppose we'll have to stop hunting Nightshades?"

I gave him them all a half-smile. "We can talk about that later. For now, we find Cedrik."

The Fox jumped up. "He spends his nights at the underground club, *Paradise Island.*"

"Same name as his Guild? Well then," I started to the door of my high-rise apartment home, grabbing a claymore from the wall and setting it on the magnet at the back of my coat. "Let's get going."

I don't know what I thought it would be like...not being a Puppet and being like my Father. I guess like everyone else I assumed it would make me feel omnipotent.

It did not.

It made me...uncomfortable.

The sounds were too loud, for starters. The colors of the night were too vibrant and I found myself grabbing a pair of sunglasses from a local street vendor as the sun went down. The cacophony of voices was the worst. I didn't know if they were thoughts or spoken voices. And I thought I would go mad the moment I stepped outside to our waiting limo.

It was Honest John who had the answer. "Don't think about it. Your Father used to say if he didn't think of silence, he couldn't hear his own thoughts."

So I did as Honest John suggested. I concentrated on silence. It worked...intermittently. I knew I would have to practice it.

Every.

Night.

The smell was the real shocker. Pungent, sweet, foul, decadent. Those were the first words that came to mind. And I could smell blood...so much of it in the air, especially after the limo dropped us off at our destination.

There wasn't much to this *Paradise Island.* It was a warehouse... and that was it. We were allowed in immediately, no waiting in the line around the building. I don't think the door person had any idea who we were—he only let us in because we looked cool.

The four of us moved around the undulating bodies as the latest house music pumped through the speakers. I stopped in the center of the dance floor even as several women, and men, gestured for me to dance with them. One man had the nerve to touch me—and immediately slunk away, his eyes wide with fright, his body shivering uncontrollably.

I could sense Cedrik. He was the only Dhampir in the building... and he smelled...

Really bad. Was this why the Nightshade shunned them so much? They smelled like wet dogs. I hadn't noticed this as a Puppet. Good thing too. I would have suggested he shower. Every chance he got. I spotted Cedrik on a riser to the right of the stage of dancing bodies. He'd been sitting on a couch with several women and now he stood as he sensed...well...a Nightshade. I was sure he wasn't expecting *me*.

The first thing I had to do was clear the place out. I held out my hand and closed my eyes. It took about twelve minutes for everyone to leave—after receiving a sense of impending disaster if they stayed. They didn't stampede or run, but exited quietly as the only ones left in the club were us...

And Cedrik's men. They surrounded us on the dance floor. I counted seven, which matched the number of heartbeats I heard. They had their weapons drawn.

Us? Not one of us had drawn a weapon. It was Guild code. And Cedrik's people had already broken it.

"Well, well," Cedrik walked to the edge of the riser and looked down at us. "So you finally decided to get even for your little Puppet's death."

I frowned and looked at the others. They shrugged and we all looked at Cedrik as he crossed his arms over his chest. So... he thought *I* was Gepetto? Was his eyesight that bad for him not knowing I wasn't his father? Unless it was Gepetto's power. Dhampirs were attuned to Nightshades. And I was sure he'd sensed my Father's power when he'd ransomed me...and then reneged.

So stupid.

The seven members of Cedrik's new Guild closed in. I reached behind me and retrieved my claymore. It was a nice piece, forged of the hardest steel. I was pretty sure Gepetto had left it there for me to find. I turned its blade down and let a good seven inches of the tip sink into the floor, putting a pretty nasty tear into the rubber floor.

"You'll pay for that, Gepetto."

The Cat laughed.

Even Honest John snickered.

The enemy to my right was frowning. He held a pistol aimed at my head as he turned and looked up at Cedrik. "Boss...this ain't Gepetto. I saw what he looks like. This is some other guy."

"Eh?" Cedrik leaned forward and put his hands on his knees.

I smiled up at him. "It's been a long five years, Cedrik. Even longer since the first time you tried to kill me. It's time to give me my weapon back."

There was smug satisfaction in the widening of the bastard's eyes. The way he staggered back and held his arms out. I could see the Wood Ratchet at his hip. *My* weapon. "No..." he was saying. "This isn't possible. I saw what you were looking like. You were stone... I saw you... once a Puppet is stone...it's dead! It can't come back!"

"I'm not *back*," I said as I moved the claymore in an arc and cut down two of his men in one go. That action was the signal for the others to go ham.

And they did.

As I advanced to the base of the riser, still looking up at Cedrik, the Cat, the Fox and Honest John massacred the other members. Any who fled, they let them go. Witnesses you see.

I reset the claymore at my back and with a simple jump, landed on the edge of the riser next to Cedrik. He screamed and stumble back to the couches. I took my time walking forward. "If keeping me prisoner to drink my blood was your intention, you succeeded. If turning me to stone with the loss of blood was your intention, you succeeded. If it was you who taught Genoise to build the Web spell, you succeeded. It was a success in neutralizing me...for five years."

Step forward. "Five years of my life I will never see again." Step forward. "But if you were any good at Lore, you'd know a Puppet only dies when the heart is turned to stone. But take a closer look, Cedrik. What does your lore tell you about me *now*?"

He stood in front of the couch as I retrieved the claymore and pointed it at him. The tip barely reached his chest. "You are my half-brother, the only living child of my Sire. You were his right hand. You were his most trusted. Why did you run me down that day in the street? Was it jealousy? Oh yes, Cedrik. I remember everything now. You knew who I was the moment I walked through the Guild's door and you saw your opportunity, especially when Gepetto contacted Honest John because he wanted me home." I smiled at him. "Do you know why? Because it was time, Cedrik. Time for the oldest of the Nightshades to part with his wealth, his power, and his blood."

I widened my smile and allowed him to see the sharpness of my legacy.

He pointed at me...his fear quickly turning to hatred. "You are a lie! That's not fair! I should have it all! I should have inherited every-thing!" He narrowed his eyes and spit as he spoke. "Puppets cannot be made into Nightshade!"

"The dead can, Cedrik. Oh...did you not know that? So rigid in your beliefs that you can't see the cracks? You can't see the possibili-ties beyond the absolutes?" I let the claymore drop. It clanged loudly to the floor. An elegant aged weapon between us. "Keeping me in that web and solidified would keep me preserved for some time. But when Father reanimated me...it set the clock in motion and I died in his arms." I held out my hands. "And I am reborn in his image. This could have been you, you know. If you hadn't betrayed him by using me."

Cedrik was so enraged he was shaking. He pulled the weapon from his hip and pointed int me. It was a hand-held crossbow. Small-sized. But very powerful, because it worked on magic. Made by a Nightshade Hunter, it could manifest wooden stakes from the blood of Puppets—because they weren't real. A Puppet could give it an endless supply. I'd had the thing crafted for me…I knew everything about it.

"If you're really a Nightshade now, I can kill you with one stake, Dante. So you just need to back up and call your men off."

"No." I cocked my head to my right shoulder. "You are going to put my weapon down and leave this town and never come back. If you don't, I will kill you."

He held his arm out straighter. "I'll fire this!"

"Cedrik…you haven't fired it since you stole it from me. You haven't used it because you can't use it. You are not a Puppet. Only a Puppet can use that weapon."

"Then that means you can't use it either."

I held out my hand. It was simple magic, really. I just willed the thing into my hand and it was there. I tossed it, grabbed the grip, aimed, and fired it at Cedrik. The wooden stake took a second to manifest before it pierced Cedrik's heart. He made a gurgling sound and stared at me with wide eyes as he fell backward.

I stood over him, weapon in hand. "I always kept it primed and ready with my blood in the reserve, Cedrik. It's like leaving a bullet in the chamber. I knew the moment I saw it and smelled it, it was still there."

He gurgled and tears came from his eyes. Dhampirs can die the same way Nightshade do. A stake through the heart.

Within seconds he was dead and the stake vanished.

But the body remained. The human half.

I secured the Wood Ratchet at my hip and put the claymore at my back. As I turned, I called out for them to take what they wanted as we exited the building. A few took clove cigarettes and lots of lighters. On the way out, they used those lighters to torch the place before we jumped into the limo and left.

They were excited and stoked and I was relieved…if not a bit sad. When I finally understood my father, it was too late. And it might be a century before he woke…or never. Only time would tell.

"Hungry, Dante? I know a place where the drinks are cold and the blood is warm," Honest John said.

I nodded. "Tell the driver. So, the Guild is now yours again. I'll set you up new offices and a budget for hiring."

They all hesitated before the Cat said, "And what're we hunting now?"

"Whatever we get hired to hunt," I sat back and crossed my legs as the night scene whizzed past through the windows. "There are good and bad of everything." I showed them some fang and they laughed.

I turned and looked through the window at the twilight sky. *Jiminy?*

Here boss. He was there, on my shoulder, where he'd been the whole time I faced Cedrik. My best friend.

The essence of my Father.

Are you ready for a new adventure?

I got your back boss. Just...pay more attention to traps, okay?

Will do that, Jiminy. Will do.

~END ~

AUTHOR'S NOTE

The chance to write ANY vampire story will always lure me in. And the more different I can make it, the better. Trying to combine vampires and Pinocchio—on the surface it seems like a good fit. Real boy...real human...uh...not so easy. The struggle was real. So when a combination of an uncalled for verbal attack by a Lore Crazed Guild member in my favorite game caught me off guard...The Blue Fairy Hunters Guild was born.

ABOUT THE AUTHOR

Phaedra Weldon grew up in the thick, atmospheric land of South Georgia. Most nights, especially those in October, were spent on the back of pickup trucks in the center of cornfields, telling ghost stories, or in friends' homes playing RPGs. She got her start writing in shared worlds (Eureka!, Star Trek, Battletech, Shadowrun), selling original short stories to DAW anthologies, and sold her first Urban Fantasy series to traditional publishing. Currently she is working on the Paranormal Women's Fiction series, Ravenwood Hills, as well as tentatively starting her next Urban Series about...vampires. See more at phaedraweldon.com.

SILVEREYES AND THE THREE WOLVES

NIKKI JEFFORD

"All rise for the Honorable Robert Southey presiding over the case of Kingdom v. Silvereyes. You may now be seated."

"Is the kingdom's attorney ready to call her first witness to the stand?"

"I am, Your Honor. The kingdom calls to the stand Great Big Wolf."

Heavy footsteps thumped through the courtroom as a towering male stacked with muscles stalked past rows of reporters and spectators, then the jury box. His snarl as he passed Miss Silvereyes roused squeaks of dismay from more than a few attendees, while causing others to jolt against their bench seats. Miss Silvereyes showed no reaction, as though carved out of ice on display during Winter Festival. With platinum-blonde hair brushed into a sheen of fine silken strands and a white sweater dress, Miss Silvereyes had the appearance of a young woman awaiting a court marriage rather than a vampire on trial for first-degree burglary and property damage.

Once Great Big Wolf swore his oath, the kingdom's attorney, Miss Clawson, approached the bench in a navy blazer, pencil skirt, and a smooth bob of brown hair. The tips of her one-inch heels clicked like the young stenographer's fingers on her transcriber.

Clipping to a stop before her first witness, Miss Clawson turned sideways, facing the jury. "Mr. Big Wolf, please walk us through the events of the second Saturday of August of last year."

Although the wolf was in his human form, he had the mannerisms of a wild animal cornered on the stand. Thick teeth gleamed with menace as his upper lip folded into his gums. Each inhale sounded more like a predatory sniff than human breaths before, at last, his gruff words filled the courtroom.

"Me, my mate, and my pup woke up that morning and hunted one animal each in the Merry Woods, as is sanctioned by the kingdom."

The stenographer tapped along as Great Big Wolf spoke, stopping when he did.

Miss Clawson's heels clicked six times as she moved away from her client, settling near the jury. "Please explain to the court what happened after you and your family procured your kingdom-sanctioned wild game allotment?"

It became immediately apparent why Miss Clawson had removed herself from Mr. Big Wolf's personal space. Spittle flew from the male's wide mouth as he snarled.

The stenographer's hands hovered above her machine for a moment before she brought all ten fingers down at once, then tucked a long section framing her teal bob behind one ear.

"We dragged our fresh kills into our house and set them in the kitchen to cool while we went for a run through the woods. When we returned home for our breakfast, I saw that someone had bitten into my elk and drained a portion of blood. So I shifted and roared, 'SOMEBODY HAS BEEN AT MY MEAT!'"

Fur sprang over the male's thickset fingers as he gripped the edge of the stand.

The reporters all leaned forward, pencils poised over slender spiral notebooks, me included. My mind sped in anticipation, drawing up potential headlines.

VICTIMIZED WOLF ATTEMPTS TO TAKE JUSTICE INTO HIS OWN PAWS

JURORS BECOME FIRSTHAND WITNESSES IN TRIAL TURNED BLOOD BATH

FELONY ENSUES DURING COURT PROCEEDINGS

MURDER IN THE FANG DEGREE

But Judge Southey was known for the tight leash he kept over his court proceedings. The bang of his gavel cracked through the courtroom like a hoof strike.

"Mr. Big Wolf, let me remind you that there is no shifting allowed inside my courtroom," warned the judge, looking down his long slender nose at the wolf shifter. With thick dark brown hair neatly curled around a stoic face, Southey was not one for theatrics.

Jaw locked in fury, Mr. Big Wolf held on to his human form with a low growl.

"What happened next?" Miss Clawson coaxed.

Unhinging his chops, Mr. Big Wolf continued. "My mate looked at the sheep she had caught and noticed that it, too, had been bitten into and had blood missing. So she shifted and snarled, 'SOMEBODY HAS BEEN AT MY MEAT!' After that, my pup inspected his rabbit and saw that the blood had been drained entirely from his meal. So he shifted and cried, 'SOMEBODY HAS BEEN AT MY MEAT, AND HAS DRAINED IT ALL DRY!'"

"She drained my meat, as well!" a woman shrieked from the back of the courthouse. Everyone sitting in the gallery turned their heads to look at the shriveled old woman who had interrupted the proceedings. She lifted a gnarled hand in the air as she made her untimely accusation. "The vampire thief broke into my gingerbread house and drained my fresh, plump meat until all that remained was a husk."

Murmurs broke out. The Honorable Robert Southey banged his gavel. "Bailiff, remove this witch at once."

A buff man dressed all in brown grabbed the old woman by the arm and dragged her away while she struggled and cursed.

Judge Southey cleared his throat heavily. "Members of the jury, I apologize for this interruption. Disregard every word spoken by the witch. Mr. Big Wolf, please continue."

The wolf shifter frowned from the stand, his large round eyes locked on the vampire sitting beside her fancy attorney. There was no seeing Miss Silvereyes's expression from the media gallery. The accused had not bothered to turn around during the old woman's outburst.

Miss Clawson moved into Mr. Big Wolf's line of sight, blocking his view of Miss Silvereyes. "Your pup had just noticed that his meat had been drained. What happened next?"

The wolf shifter growled. "Upon seeing that someone had come into our home and drained Little Wee Wolf's breakfast, we began to look around."

"Were there more signs that an intruder had broken in?" Miss Clawson asked.

"Objection," defense attorney Mr. Bitmore sneered. The lanky vampire, dressed in a sleek black pinstriped suit, spoke into the microphone at his table with cool precision. "According to the complaint filed with the constable, the front door was left unlocked, and the windows wide open. Therefore, it is not possible that the house was broken into."

"Overruled."

Miss Clawson smiled smugly. "Please tell the court if there were additional signs of intrusion."

Mr. Big Wolf scratched the thick, tanned skin below his chin. "We made our way to the den, where I saw that my rocker had been moved away from the window and a throw blanket placed on the wooden seat, which had not been there previously."

"And what did that tell you?" asked Miss Clawson.

"That SOMEBODY HAD BEEN SITTING IN MY CHAIR! Soon after, my mate saw that the cushions were removed from her recliner and tossed on the floor. As with my spot in the den, my mate drew the same conclusion: 'SOMEBODY HAS BEEN SITTING IN MY CHAIR!' We next heard the cry of our pup as he yelped, 'SOME-BODY HAS BEEN SITTING IN MY CHAIR, AND HAS BROKEN IT!'"

The stenographer jabbed the tips of her fingers against her machine two seconds after Mr. Big Wolf finished his tirade.

"At this point, we thought we had better make further search in case it was a burglar, so we went upstairs to our bedchambers. What I found in my chamber was my blanket folded up three times and pillows stuffed beneath."

"And what conclusion did you draw from this?" Miss Clawson asked.

"That SOMEBODY HAD BEEN LYING IN MY BED!" Mr. Big Wolf roared. "We went to my mate's chamber next and discovered her comforter and throw pillows tossed on the floor. My mate, at once, reacted as I did, snarling, 'SOMEBODY HAS BEEN LYING IN MY BED!'" Meanwhile, Little Wee Wolf ran to check his room. We soon heard our pup's cry of, 'SOMEBODY HAS BEEN LYING IN MY BED—AND HERE SHE IS STILL!' Hurrying in, we saw a vampire startled awake from the narrow bed. The second she caught sight of all three of us, she sprang out of Little Wee Wolf's bed, flashed to the window, and jumped out. By the time we looked outside, she had made her getaway."

Miss Clawson's heels clicked in rapid succession as she approached the stand. "Is the intruder you found inside your pup's chamber present in the courtroom today?"

"She is," Mr. Big Wolf snarled.

"Please point her out for the jury."

Mr. Big Wolf's muscular arm shot forward as he jammed his finger in Miss Silvereyes's direction.

"Let the record reflect that Mr. Big Wolf identified Miss Silvereyes as the intruder he found inside his son's bedchamber. Thank you, sir. No further questions."

"Your witness, Mr. Bitmore," Judge Southey said.

"Permission to approach the witness." Standing tall, Mr. Bitmore clasped his hands behind his back.

"Can you keep your beast under control during cross-examination?" Judge Southey asked the witness.

"Yes," Mr. Big Wolf growled.

The attorney's body did not tremble the slightest, nor did his voice waver as he fired off his first question. "Mr. Big Wolf, you stated that a vampire woke from your pup's bed. What made you conclude that the intruder was undead?"

"She bared her fangs at my pup," Mr. Big Wolf snarled.

"Were you present during this supposed exchange?" Mr. Bitmore pressed.

"My son is no liar."

"Were you present when the female flashed her fangs? Yes or no?"

"NO!" Mr. Big Wolf roared, his anger echoing across the courtroom.

One had to wonder how his gruff voice had not woken the intruder from slumber when Great Big Wolf had first roared his outrage over his meat. It truly must have been a vampire in the bed upstairs to sleep the sleep of death, but I was here to report on the proceedings—not speculate.

Mr. Bitmore returned to his table and plucked up his legal pad before returning to the stand.

"Tell me, Mr. Big Wolf, are you in the habit of leaving perfectly good meat lying around to rot?"

"Objection!" Miss Clawson yelled. "What do my client's dining habits have to do with the intrusion?"

"Sustained," Judge Southey said.

Mr. Big Wolf's nostrils flared. "We would never waste meat. We prefer cold cuts in the summer."

Judge Southey sighed deeply. "Sustained means that you do not have to answer the question, Mr. Big Wolf."

"Do you always leave your door unlocked and windows open?" Mr. Bitmore fired off next.

"We like fresh air, and we never had reason to lock our door before," Mr. Big Wolf growled.

"So anyone who happened along could have walked in at any time, whenever they wanted," Mr. Bitmore concluded.

"No," Mr. Big Wolf growled.

"No?" Mr. Bitmore drawled.

"No one trespassed before. Not until Sneaky Silvereyes over there broke in, stole from us, and broke my pup's chair. She violated our sanctuary."

"Objection," Mr. Bitmore snapped.

"The jury will disregard Mr. Big Wolf's statement, and it will be stricken from the record," Judge Southey said.

Paper fluttered as the defense attorney flipped a page over his notepad. "In your report filed with the constable, you say that you found a female intruder in your son's bed before she promptly fled. The account you provided described the female as a petite blonde with pale skin."

"Yes, the vampire seated there—your client," the wolf shifter interjected, glaring past Mr. Bitmore in Miss Silvereyes's direction.

Mr. Bitmore raised his voice as he finished his question. "Was the woman covered by a blanket when you first joined your son inside his chamber?"

Mr. Big Wolf screwed up his face in thought before answering gruffly, "Yes, she had my pup's blanket on her."

Mr. Bitmore nodded slowly, like they were suddenly on the same side agreeing on something. "And you said the female flashed out of bed and out the window?"

"Inhuman speed, yes." The wolf shifter nodded.

"And by the time you reached the window and looked out, there was no trace of her?"

"As I said."

"So what you're telling me is that the individual you came upon in your son's bedchamber was covered in a blanket and disappeared in the blink of an eye. In other words, impossible to positively identify beyond a doubt. Thank you, Mr. Big Wolf. No further questions, Your Honor."

Snarls cut through the courtroom. Mr. Big Wolf shot up and shifted into his beastly form, knocking the microphone off the stand with a swipe of his paw as he growled on two legs, his claws digging into the wood rail in front of him.

The stenographer lifted her fingers from her machine and spread her arms wide as she cried out, "*Lupus formella homo animalis.*"

Mr. Big Wolf's snarl whimpered out as his human form reemerged and the bailiff rushed the stand to escort him from the courtroom.

"We will take a fifteen-minute recess," Judge Southey announced.

The jury filed out of their box while spectators murmured as they exited the courtroom. Pencils scrabbled across notepads from the media gallery. After finishing my notes, I stood and stretched, then made my way down the hall, passing the doors to the toilets and the cocoa machines spewing hot chocolate into paper cups. Reaching the doors of the courthouse, I passed the red and white warning sign:

NO CANDY OR GUM INSIDE THE COURTHOUSE

Once outside, I pulled out a pack of cinnamon gum, removing a piece from the foil and slipping it into my mouth. I chewed vigorously while scanning the vacant stone benches surrounded by patches of topiary trees shaped into cones and spirals flanking the shadowed side of the grand structure. Snowdrifts carpeted the wide stone stairs leading from the hall of justice to Main Street.

The doors of the courthouse opened, and a gentleman I recognized from the media gallery stepped outside in his patched-up blazer and gray wool trousers. Shaggy brown hair inched down his neck and curled at the ends. He looked somewhere on the verge of his thirtieth decade—maybe five years my senior.

The other reporter smiled when he saw me.

"Lollypop?" he asked, extracting a rainbow swirl on a stick from his wide blazer pocket.

"No, thank you," I replied, continuing to chew my gum.

"I've got suckers too." He pulled a fistful out, dropping several on the cold ground, which he bent down to scoop back up.

"I'm good with gum. Want a piece?"

"No, thanks." The man stuffed the lollypop and suckers back inside his blazer pockets, keeping one, which he unwrapped and shoved between his lips. "Kip Caster with *Wish upon a Star Tribune.*" He held his hand out.

I shook Caster's hand and stopped chewing to answer, "Justin Slinger with the *Once Upon Times.*"

"Justin Slinger," Caster repeated, his eyes lighting up an instant later. "I read your piece on corruption and inequities in the kingdom-sponsored housing program for dwarfs. Congratulations on winning a Pied Paper Prize. Well deserved."

"Thank you," I said. Winning that award had been a shining moment in my career, but the prize was nothing compared to exposing those crooks at the Kingdom Department of Dwellings and Development. I had taken special satisfaction in exposing Director Sleezy for taking funds meant to help impoverished dwarfs and using the money to build himself a seaside mansion.

"So, Slinger, what do you think the verdict will be?" Caster asked, yanking me out of my glory days.

"I think that's for the jury to decide and for us to report."

"True enough." The paper stick bobbed from Caster's lips as he sucked on his candy, hands in his pockets. "Bit of excitement this morning. Smart thing having a witch on staff, though it would have been more interesting if the stenographer had not reversed the wolf's shift."

I could not deny having similar thoughts, even though that type of beastly behavior gave my kind a bad name. I kept those opinions to myself and chewed my gum harder.

Kip lifted his wrist to look at the yellow winky-eye watch strapped on. "Better get back inside." He crunched his lollypop and headed for the doors on swift steps.

I was preparing to do the same when a feeling of being watched kicked my senses into high gear. Sniffing the crisp air, I detected nothing beyond the scent of my cinnamon gum, which indicated a vampire nearby. The undead were bland in terms of their coloring, lack of smell, and personalities. Flavorless gum, in my opinion, which my profession had trained me to keep to myself, especially since I worked for the most iron-fisted vampire of all.

Another paranormal might have missed her, blending in with the stone bench and snow-dusted topography, but my wolf gaze locked on to the wintery blue irises of Ada Silvereyes. Her lips were painted blood red and pressed together in a pout like a child put in time out.

It was lucky for Miss Silvereyes that I was not one of her jurors. I'd done my research, read up on reports of her disorderly conduct—information the jury was not privy to, since it was not related to this case. Not once had she paid for her crimes and, sadly, I doubted this case would be any different. Getting twelve citizens of varying species to all agree on a verdict was like asking Prince Charming to decide on a princess. (My colleagues working the society beat were still grousing over another winter ball come and gone without the prince showing favor to a single fair maiden in the kingdom.)

I continued chewing my gum, though it had lost its kick, waiting for Miss Silvereyes to look away first. It was not in my nature to back down.

Steely gaze in place, Miss Silvereyes rose from the bench, her moody expression never altering as she walked up the steps of the courthouse straight for me. I chewed on my gum like it was a chunk of deer meat, focused on keeping my molars intact and not breaking out into beast form like an out-of-control animal. Self-discipline kept fur from growing over my skin.

When Miss Silvereyes was three steps away from colliding into me, she veered abruptly to my left and continued toward the courthouse. I prowled after her, waiting for her to open the door, as I refused to extend that courtesy to a criminal.

No sooner had I stepped inside the foyer than a security guard stopped me, pointing to the sign:

NO CANDY OR GUM INSIDE THE COURTHOUSE

I spit my lump of gum into the foil wrapper and tossed it into the waste receptacle. When I looked up, the halls were empty. I hurried along the corridor, making it inside the courtroom just as the security guards were closing the doors.

Kip Caster turned and gave me a friendly wave as I took up my spot on the back bench of the media gallery. (A wolf always kept his sights set on everyone else.)

"All rise for the Honorable Robert Southey. You may now be seated."

"Miss Clawson, you may call your next witness to the stand."

"Thank you, Your Honor. The kingdom calls Middle-Sized Wolf."

The doors in back opened briefly, and a buxom female with thick, wavy layers of auburn hair made her way to the stand, grumbling beneath her breath all the while.

As Miss Clawson guided her next witness through the events of the second Saturday of August of last year, we listened to the same account as before, though with far more complaint, as Mrs. Middle Wolf lamented the spoilage of her meat and abuse of her possessions.

"Every wolf knows that the best meat is raw and bloody. Not drained. Not dry," she carped. "But did the intruder stop there? Oh, no. My recliner was pulled apart and cushions thrown carelessly on the floor. Upstairs, it was no better. Pillows tossed about, thrown to the ground in disarray after I made up my bed so neatly that morning. Knowing that creature had tainted our bedsheets—" Mrs. Middle Wolf shuddered. "I washed them three times, and still they did not feel clean and never will, knowing she laid her dirty head on our bedding."

When it came time for Mr. Bitmore to cross-examine the witness, he spoke in a soothing tone. "You obviously care a great deal for your cushions and pillows, Mrs. Middle Wolf. However, aside from the displacement, no damage was done, correct?" Mrs. Middle Wolf glowered at the defense attorney. "Was there any damage to your chair or bed?" he asked loudly.

"My pup's chair was broken," Mrs. Middle Wolf growled.

"I did not ask about your son's chair."

Mrs. Middle Wolf looked at Miss Clawson and pursed her lips.

"Answer the question, Mrs. Middle Wolf," Judge Southey said.

"No, there was no outward damage done to my chair or bed," Mrs. Middle Wolf grumbled.

"No further questions, Your Honor."

Little Wee Wolf was called to the stand next.

A gangly boy in his twelfth year shuffled through the gallery. He swore his oath and, with much coaxing by Miss Clawson, proceeded to share his account of events.

"After returning from our morning run, we went to the kitchen to eat our earlier kills. That's when I noticed that someone had gotten to my rabbit and drained the blood from the carcass. My parents were busy inspecting their own meat and did not notice until I shifted and yelled, 'SOMEBODY HAS BEEN AT MY MEAT, AND HAS DRAINED IT ALL DRY!'" The boy's voice cracked with puberty.

Miss Clawson nodded her encouragement, keeping the lad's attention on her. "What happened afterward?"

Little Wee Wolf swallowed. "Afterward, I followed my parents into the den, where my father and mother shouted about their chairs having been sat in, but it was mine that was broken." His voice wavered.

"Please describe your chair to the court."

"It was a wicker hanging swing chair."

"And was it broken before you left the house to run through the woods that morning?"

"No."

"What state was your wicker chair in when you returned home?"

"The chain had snapped, and the wicker basket pod was broken to bits."

"Hmm," Miss Clawson hummed in sympathy. "Did your parents notice the broken chair?"

"They did after I yelled, 'SOMEBODY HAS BEEN SITTING IN MY CHAIR, AND HAS BROKEN IT!'"

"And what did you discover next?"

Little Wee Wolf darted a glance in Miss Silvereyes's direction. "I, uh, went upstairs to my room and, um, noticed someone asleep in my bed." The lad's cheeks pinked.

With quick taps of her heels, Miss Clawson moved to block the defendant from Little Wee Wolf's line of sight.

"That must have given you quite the fright."

"It did." The lad pulled at the collar of his starched white shirt.

"Were your parents with you at this point?"

He shook his head. "They were in their rooms hollering about their beds having been laid in. So I yelled, 'SOMEBODY HAS BEEN LYING IN MY BED—AND HERE SHE IS STILL!'"

"What happened at that point? Did the intruder wake?"

Little Wee Wolf looked around the courtroom, eyeing the exits before returning his attention to Miss Clawson. "Yes," he squeaked.

"What happened when the intruder woke up?"

"She bared her fangs at me." Little Wee Wolf swallowed and looked at his attorney, waiting for her next question.

"That must have been scary," Miss Clawson said soothingly. "At this point, it would be no surprise if you feared for your life."

"Objection!" Mr. Bitmore snapped. "It's not for prosecution to tell the boy how he felt."

"Sustained," Judge Southey said.

Little Wee Wolf's head flinched back slightly as he turned rounded eyes on Miss Clawson. The kingdom's attorney clipped her way to the prosecutor's table. "Please describe the intruder you found in your bedchamber."

Little Wee Wolf's gaze darted from his attorney to Miss Silvereyes, then back. "She had white-blonde, long, straight hair, light skin, and silvery-blue eyes. And she was wearing a blue tank top."

"And is the intruder you came upon in your bed chamber on the second Saturday of August of last year present in this courtroom today?"

Little Wee Wolf's lips moved, but no sound came forth.

"Please repeat your answer a bit louder," Miss Clawson said.

"Yes." This time, the boy's answer shrilled like a high-pitched note.

"Please point her out." Miss Clawson turned around and faced the defendant with her arms crossed.

Little Wee Wolf pointed a shaky finger at Miss Silvereyes. Whatever expression she aimed back had the boy blanching.

Miss Clawson faced the stenographer. "Let the record reflect that Little Wee Wolf identified Miss Silvereyes as the intruder found inside his bedchamber." The prosecutor turned her attention back to Little Wee Wolf. "What happened after the intruder bared her fangs at you?"

"My parents came running in and she raced to the window, which was open, and jumped out."

"Did you see her again once she jumped out the window?" Little Wee Wolf shook his head. "Please answer yes or no."

"No. When we looked out the window, she was gone."

"No further questions, Your Honor." A smug smile lifted over Miss Clawson's face as she clipped her way back to her seat.

"Mr. Bitmore, you may cross-examine."

The defense attorney strolled over to the jury box and tipped his head to the side. "Finding a beautiful young woman in your bed—sounds like every young man's fantasy, does it not?"

Smiles cracked over the jurors' lips and a couple chuckled softly.

The stenographer's eyebrows lifted as she typed.

"Objection!" Miss Clawson snarled.

Judge Southey leveled a hardened stare at the defense attorney. "Save your commentary for outside the walls of justice and address your questions to the witness."

"Of course, Your Honor." Mr. Bitmore placed his hand on his chest, his willowy frame bowing the slightest bit as he backed away from the jury box. A benevolent smile settled over the attorney's face, one that did not fool me for a breath. This was not my first time watching Elijah Bitmore in action. He was a vampire, like his client, his thirst for winning only rivaled by his craving for blood and obscenely expensive suits.

"Your breakfast drained, and chair broken," Mr. Bitmore tsked. "You must have been distraught indeed."

Little Wee Wolf looked at Miss Clawson. "Objection," she huffed. "Does the defense have any questions, or is the court to be subjected to more of his exposition?"

"Counselor, do you have any questions for the witness?" Judge Southey prodded.

"Apologies, Your Honor. I was getting to them."

"Then I suggest you do so now."

Mr. Bitmore returned his attention to the boy. "Tell me, Little Wee Wolf, were you upset after finding your rabbit drained of blood?"

"Yes," the boy squeaked.

"And were you upset when you found your chair broken?"

"Yes."

"So, at this point, before going upstairs to your bedchamber, you felt overwhelmingly upset and distraught?"

"I—"

"Objection! Defense is badgering the witness. Mr. Bitmore has already established that the witness was upset."

"Sustained."

Mr. Bitmore closed in on the witness. "After finding your meat drained and chair broken, you followed your parents upstairs and proceeded to your chamber alone, where you found a young woman in your bedchamber. What was she wearing when you first saw her?"

"She— I couldn't see what she was wearing beneath the blanket."

"Hmm. So, hair color was all you really had to go on?"

"Objection. Defense knows perfectly well the full description provided by the witness." Miss Clawson huffed irritably.

"Sustained. Get to the point, counselor."

"My point, Your Honor, is that over a quarter of the vampire population has pale skin and blonde hair. Any one of these lookalikes could have been mistaken for Miss Silvereyes."

"Objection! Speculation," Miss Clawson shrilled.

"Counselor, move on," Judge Southey said gruffly.

"No further questions, Your Honor."

"The kingdom's attorney may call their next witness."

"Your Honor, the kingdom calls Little Red Riding Hood to the stand."

I was the first to scent the young human woman as she was ushered through the doors. The smell of minced meat, yeasty bread rolls, sweet jam, stuffing, and apple pie wafted from her red cape and brown plaited hair like a buffet rolling by on two legs. Saliva filled my mouth, and I reached for my pack of gum before remembering it was not allowed.

Heads lifted in the gallery, followed by distinct sniffing. My stomach rumbled as Little Red Riding Hood swore her oath and took a seat.

"Miss Riding Hood, can you tell us what you saw as you passed by the Three Wolves' house on the morning of the second Saturday of August of last year?"

Riding Hood sat up tall. "I saw a female looking through the windows before peering through the keyhole of the house."

"Let me show you a drawing," Miss Clawson handed a document to the opposing counsel, then walked a copy to the stand and held out it to Miss Riding Hood. "Is this drawing a true and accurate depiction of the house you observed that day?"

"Yes."

"I offer this drawing into evidence, Your Honor."

"Does the defense have any objections?" Judge Southey asked.

"No, Your Honor."

"The drawing will be admitted as Exhibit A," Judge Southey announced.

"Please describe the individual you saw canvassing the home of the Three Wolves that day," Miss Clawson asked next.

"She had a petite frame and smooth, white-blonde hair that was loose down the middle of her back. On the morning I saw her, she was wearing a blue tank top over bleached skinny jeans, and she had thin white arms."

"Is the female you saw outside the Three Wolves' house present in the courtroom today?"

"Yes."

"Please point her out."

Miss Riding Hood aimed a finger at Miss Silvereyes.

"Your Honor, no further questions."

Mr. Bitmore was up in a flash and pounced on the young woman at once.

"Why were you loitering outside the Three Wolves' home that morning?"

"Objection. Irrelevant."

"Overruled. Answer the question, Miss Riding Hood."

"I was on my way to my grandmother's house."

"Do you often pass by the Three Wolves' home to visit your granny?"

"She was unwell at the time. I was bringing her a basket of food."

"Would you say you were in a hurry to deliver food to your granny that morning?"

"I guess." Riding Hood shrugged and flipped the end of her braid back and forth between her fingers.

"Yes or no?"

"Yes."

"As you passed the woman outside the house, did you see the front of her face?"

"No."

"And at any point, did you see this individual enter the home?"

"No."

"Your Honor, no further questions."

As Miss Riding Hood was escorted from the courtroom, I took in a deep inhale and checked my watch. We had another hour to go before lunch, unless the counselors wrapped things up before noon.

"Your Honor, the kingdom calls its last witness to the stand: Constable Spur Spalding."

A lofty man with a ruddy beard and mustache walked up to the stand in tall brown leather boots that covered his beige trousers. He wore a gold doublet and a short purple off-the-shoulder cape edged with smooth gold trim. On the stand, he removed a wide-brimmed black hat adorned on the front with a purple strip of fabric and the golden two-headed eagle emblem of the enforcement department.

"Please state your name for the record."

"Constable Spur Spalding of District Eleven."

"Do you swear to tell the truth to the best of your knowledge?"

"I do."

"Please be seated."

Miss Clawson approached the stand. "Constable Spalding, can you please tell us what happened after the Three Wolves filed their report with you on the afternoon of the second Saturday of August of last year?"

"Certainly. Once the report was filed, I went to inspect the home of the Three Wolves." The constable's voice projected, each word as sharp as a train whistle.

"Your inspection took place the same day as the burglary?"

"That is correct. Yes."

"Can you tell us what you observed at the home of the Three Wolves?"

"There were no signs of a forced break-in, though I did not expect any, since the Three Wolves had already reported that their doors were unlocked and windows open prior to the burglary. Regardless, I performed a thorough search of the property, confirming that there were no signs of forced entry. Once my search of the outside was complete, I stepped inside and made my way to the kitchen. By this time, it was late in the afternoon and the meat that had been left out had gone rancid. I inspected the elk first, followed by the sheep, and then the rabbit. Upon examining the meat, I located puncture marks on all three carcasses."

"What did this tell you?" Miss Clawson asked.

"That a vampire had gotten its fangs into all three animals. Two had been partially drained—the elk and the sheep—while the rabbit had been entirely drained of blood. Under section two twenty, it is unlawful to consume any part of an animal belonging to another paranormal as part of their kingdom-sanctioned sustenance." Miss Clawson nodded, but Constable Spalding needed no guidance as he continued. "I proceeded to the den, where I observed displaced recliner cushions on the floor of the home and a broken hanging wicker chair. Next, I went upstairs and examined each of the Three Wolves' beds."

"Did you find anything during your inspection?" Miss Clawson asked eagerly.

"Yes. I did. I discovered a long white-blonde hair on the pillow on the smallest bed, third room down the hall."

Miss Clawson clipped up to the stand. "Was this the hair you found on Little Wee Wolf's pillow?"

Constable Spalding's chin dipped as he looked down. "Yes, that is the hair I retrieved from the house."

"I offer this strand of hair into evidence, Your Honor."

"Objections?"

"No, Your Honor."

"The hair will be admitted as Exhibit B," Judge Southey said.

"Constable Spalding, what led to Miss Silvereyes's arrest later that evening?"

"A concerned citizen reported seeing a female canvassing the home of the Three Wolves before the burglary took place that day. She detailed a petite white woman with straight long white-blonde hair wearing a blue tank top and bleached skinny jeans. That evening, a female matching the description provided by the Three Wolves and Miss Riding Hood was apprehended at the Genie Wants a Bottle tavern."

"What led you to check that particular tavern?" Miss Clawson asked.

Constable Spalding cast a vigilant look over at Miss Silvereyes. "The defendant is a regular there."

"And have you had dealings with the defendant before this case?"

"I have. Yes."

"Tell me, Constable, what was Miss Silvereyes wearing when you found her at the tavern that evening?"

"Bleached skinny jeans and a blue tank top."

"Thank you, sir. Your Honor, the prosecution rests."

Mr. Bitmore remained seated for his cross-examination, questioning the constable in a languid tone. "The puncture marks found on the meats could have been made earlier by the wolves, could they not?"

"Yes, they could have."

"And the animals could have bled out from their kill wounds while the wolves left them unattended to go for a run in the woods?"

"Unlikely."

"Are you a wolf shifter, Constable?"

"No."

"A vampire?"

"Objection. Is the defense insinuating an esteemed constable of the kingdom must be of a certain species in order to do his job?"

"Counselor, what is the relevance?" Judge Southey demanded.

Mr. Bitmore stood. "The relevance, Your Honor, is that Constable Spalding, esteemed as he is, does not possess the same sense of smell as a vampire or a wolf shifter. A human is simply incapable of determining the amount of blood remaining in a vessel."

"Very well, counselor. Overruled. Constable Spalding, you will answer the last question. Are you a vampire?"

"No, Your Honor, I am not."

"Are you human?" Mr. Bitmore asked, though it was obvious to all at that point.

"Yes, I am."

"No further questions, Your Honor."

"Miss Clawson, anything to add?" Judge Southey asked.

"Yes, Your Honor." Miss Clawson stood to address the constable.

"Constable Spalding, did the defendant, Miss Silvereyes, match the description of the burglar provided to you by Great Big Wolf, Middle-Sized Wolf, and Little Wee Wolf?"

"Yes."

"And did the clothing she was found wearing the night of her arrest match that described by Little Red Riding Hood?"

"Yes."

"No further questions, Your Honor. The prosecution rests."

Judge Southey turned his head to the jury. "I will remind the members of the jury that the fact that the defendant is not testifying cannot be considered as evidence against her at trial. The defendant is presumed innocent regardless of whether or not she testifies." The judge redirected his attention Mr. Bitmore's way. "Defense may now call their witness to the stand."

"Thank you, Your Honor. Defense calls Truzilla Germaine to the stand."

The doors flew open and a twiggy, overly tan young woman strutted into the courtroom in turquoise capri pants and a pink halter top, her long feet stuffed inside bubble-gum-pink stilettos. The young woman's brunette hair was gathered into two messy buns that topped her head like fuzzy ears tied with pink ribbons.

The wooden sound of a pencil landing and rolling across the floor stopped the woman in her clipped tracks. Rather than pick the writing utensil up and hand it to the reporter who had dropped it, Miss Germaine kicked it before proceeding to the stand, her nose lifted high.

"Please state your name for the record."

"I am Truzilla Germaine, eldest daughter of Lady Germaine."

I wrinkled my nose. A colleague had covered the misfortune surrounding Lord Germaine's untimely death shortly after remarrying and welcoming two stepdaughters into his grand estate. Many called it tragic. I found it all a little too convenient, but my editor had killed the notion with one cool purse of his lips. The rumor surrounding Lady Germaine these days was that the widow was in debt.

"Do you swear to tell the truth to the best of your knowledge?" Judge Southey asked Miss Germaine.

"I always tell the truth," she sniped.

"Please be seated."

Miss Germaine plopped down and instantly scowled, as though the chair was not up to her high standards.

Mr. Bitmore addressed her warmly, as though she was his

favorite niece. "Miss Germaine, thank you for testifying today. What is your relationship with the defendant?"

"Ada and I are close friends."

"So you know her well?"

Miss Germaine twirled the end of a pink ribbon around her finger. "I sure do."

"And did you see Miss Silvereyes on the second Saturday of August of last year?"

"Yep."

"How can you be sure of the date?"

"Because I remember my shock the following day, when I heard she had been arrested on bogus charges."

"Hmm," Mr. Bitmore practically purred. "Going back to the second Saturday of August of last year, at what time did you see Miss Silvereyes?"

"Oh, afternoon sometime."

"Where did you see her?"

"We met up at Wonderland Emporium that afternoon. They were having a blowout on summer clothes all week long—shorts, capris, tank tops, flip flops, sunglasses, tote bags, bikinis . . . all kinds of stuff."

"Did Miss Silvereyes buy anything?"

"Yeah, Ada got herself a great big pair of sunglasses that I said made her look bug-eyed." Miss Germaine snorted. "She got some other things, including a blue tank top."

"Were there many of these blue tank tops on sale at the Emporium?"

"Yeah. A whole bunch. Half off the last markdown. Peasants were swarming the sales racks like locusts."

"Was it possible that multiple young women purchased that same blue tank top during the week-long sale?"

"Objection! Calls for speculation," Miss Clawson said.

"Sustained."

Miss Germaine narrowed her eyes in the prosecutor's direction.

"Thank you, Miss Germaine. That will be all."

"Your witness, Miss Clawson," Judge Southey said.

The view of Miss Germaine was blocked when Miss Clawson planted herself before the stand.

"Tell me, Miss Germaine, did you purchase anything at Wonderland Emporium that Saturday?"

"Eww, no. I never buy stuff from that second-rate shop."

"Then why did you meet the defendant there?"

"To hang out, obviously."

"You do realize that you're under oath, Miss Germaine?"

"I'm not stupid."

"Please answer yes or no."

"Yeah, oh excuse me, I mean yes, Miss Blah Ugly Blazer, proper well-trained wolf of the kingdom."

Miss Clawson folded her arms and turned sideways, sharing her look of disapproval with the jury.

"Miss Germaine! You will show respect in my courtroom," Judge Southey bit out.

"Sorry, Your Honor. It won't happen again." Miss Germaine crossed her heart and smirked.

"Did you see the defendant purchase the tank top?"

"Yeah. I mean, yes."

"What was she wearing when you first met up?"

"Like I can remember." Miss Germaine rolled her eyes.

"And yet you claim to recall the exact color of tank top she purchased last summer."

"Objection. Leading."

"How can you be certain that the defendant purchased a blue tank top at Wonderland Emporium on the second Saturday of August of last year?" Miss Clawson insisted.

"Objection," Mr. Bitmore repeated.

"Overruled. Answer the question, Miss Germaine."

Miss Germaine leveled a crisp gaze at the prosecutor. "The reason I'm certain is because after Ada made her purchase, we went and got snow cones to cool off from the heat. I ordered lilac ice, and Ada got blueberry. As we left the counter, some idiot bumped into

Ada, knocking her ice all over her clothes. It left blue stains all over her outfit, so she ducked into the restroom and changed into the jeans and tank top she'd just bought. When she came back out, I joked about her tank top being the same color as her snow cone and that maybe she could lick herself instead." Miss Germaine giggled as though she had made a clever joke.

Miss Clawson's shoulders sagged as she sighed. "No further questions for this *witness*, your honor," she said caustically.

"Miss Germaine, you may step down," Judge Southey said. "Is the defense ready to make a closing statement?"

"I am, Your Honor." Mr. Bitmore stood and made a show of straightening his tie, which was already tidy. "Good citizens of the jury. I want to thank you for your attention and your service this morning," he said with flourish. "Have you ever mistaken one citizen for another? Have you ever thought you recognized someone, and it turned out to be a stranger? How many times? We call that mistaken identity. And you know what? That is what happened here. The Three Wolves saw someone they thought was my client. This isn't unusual; it happens every day, and it happened on the second Saturday of August of last year.

"The Three Wolves were tired from their run, they were jumpy and shaken up over the disorder in their home, and they only caught a blur of movement when they came upon the intruder. Little Wee Wolf said the woman he found in his bedchamber was wearing a blue tank top. Little Red Riding Hood also said the woman she saw canvassing the home earlier was wearing a blue tank top. The same blue tank top Wonderland Emporium was having a blowout sale on. The same blue tank top any number of customers could have purchased for an irresistible discount. The same blue tank top my client purchased later that day, *after* the burglary took place.

"Now, the kingdom has made much of the attire seen on my client, but let's take a closer look. We have a vampire who was arrested that evening and ruthlessly questioned by a human constable. Not a drop of blood was found on my client's clothing. The constable found one hair. Case closed. This was a rush judgment on his part.

"My client deserves better. The Three Wolves deserve better. They should know who really stole nourishment from their home and damaged their personal property. The kingdom has the burden of proof. That's a high burden, but it is a burden that protects us all. We ask for a verdict of not guilty. Thank you."

Mr. Bitmore took his seat. Miss Clawson got up and paced slowly in front of the jury box.

"Thank you, citizens of the jury, for your service here today. As I stated in my opening statement, this is really a very simple case. The defendant burglarized the Three Wolves' house and damaged their property. She was found inside the house.

"The defense is arguing that there was some sort of rush to judgment in this case. That somehow the constable singled the defendant out. In reality, he sought her out because the Three Wolves and Little Red Riding Hood identified her as the culprit. This is not a case of mistaken identity. The Three Wolves returned home from their morning run. All three of the wolves saw her in Little Wee Wolf's bed. The wolves were, in fact, upset. The defendant did, in fact, flee the scene fast. But four individuals identified her. The defense is asking you to conclude that the Three Wolves and Little Red Riding Hood should not believe their own eyes—that they were all hallucinating.

"The defendant's claim—that another pale, blonde, female vampire wearing the exact same clothing the defendant was apprehended in later that same day is somehow responsible for this crime —is utter nonsense.

"Now, the defense counsel argues that the constable did a poor investigation when, in fact, the kingdom's royal guard responded to the burglary swiftly, recording witness statements, searching the house, and even apprehending the suspect all on the same day that the crime was committed. This story that the defense has concocted, good citizens, is a red herring. Don't fall for it. We ask you for a verdict of guilty."

Judge Southey called for a lunch recess after closing arguments. The decision was in the jury's hands now. Hopefully, they would reach a verdict before the end of the day so I could turn the story in and move on to something less irritating.

Kip Caster joined me for lunch at Make a Sand*wish*, the café conveniently located across from the courthouse. Unfortunately, a fair number of court employees and reporters had the same idea, forcing us to wait in a line that stretched to the door.

My stomach rumbled over the din and Caster offered a lollypop, which I turned down. He shrugged and stuck one in his mouth, pulling it out each time he spoke.

"Petty crimes—not your usual beat," he noted.

"I'm covering for a colleague who had a family emergency come up in Neverland."

"What's it like working for Augustus Kensington?" Caster's casual tone might have fooled a bystander, but I knew he was fishing. My vampire boss was more cutthroat than a bull shark ripping apart a stingray. There was a reason *Once Upon Times* won an award in at least one category of the prestigious Pied Paper Awards every year. Working for the best paper in the kingdom was both a dream come true and an eternal nightmare for anyone on staff. Only the truly obsessed news junkies lasted beyond a month at the *Times*. I'd been there three and a half years and, in that time, was awarded one Pied Paper Prize. If I wanted to stay on my usual beat, and not be transferred to the society page or worse—obituaries—I needed to win another Pied Paper for the *Times* before the year was out.

"He keeps us busy," I hedged.

"I bet," Caster said, returning to his lollypop.

By the time we ordered, received food, and finished eating, notification went out that the jury had reached a verdict. Castor and I hurried back to record the outcome.

"All rise for the Honorable Robert Southey presiding over the case of Kingdom v. Silvereyes. You may now be seated."

"Has the jury reached a verdict on each count of the information?" Judge Southey asked.

A robed mage with a long white beard stood and answered from the jury box, "Yes, sir. We have, Your Honor."

"And one verdict only?"

"Yes."

"Would you hand all of the paperwork over to the bailiff please. The defendant will rise for the verdict."

Miss Silvereyes got to her feet, posing a stoic figure in white as the bailiff stood at the lectern and looked down at the paper handed over by the jury.

"Kingdom v. Silvereyes. As to the first count of first-degree burglary, we the jury find the defendant, Ada M. Silvereyes, not guilty. As to the second count of property damage, we the jury find the defendant, Ada M. Silvereyes, not guilty."

"Members of the jury, are these your unanimous verdicts?" Judge Southey asked.

"Yes, Your Honor," came the jury's collective response.

Not a single quiver of emotion passed through Miss Silvereyes as she remained in her statuesque pose—as though she'd been expecting to be let off the hook all along.

"Is there anyone on the jury who does not agree with the verdicts just read?" When no one spoke, Judge Southey continued, "Okay, citizens, your job is done. You are now free to discuss this case outside of court. Thank you for your service. Court dismissed."

Being seated at the back of the courtroom had another advantage, as I hustled out before Kip Caster could offer me another lollypop. I had no issue with Caster, or lollypops, but I was chomping on my pencil to get the outcome of this case written and submitted to my copy editor back at the *Times*.

Wendy owed me for this one. And I needed to find a prize-winning story pronto, or I would be begging Kensington for another chance at the crime beat—even petty crimes.

I dashed into a cocoa shop and ordered a mug of spicy Aztec hot chocolate so the staff would leave me alone at my table to finish scribbling notes while the case was fresh in my head.

Had the jury reached the right verdict? That was for our readers to decide.

To me, the courthouse would always be one big theater, where countless stories were told by a cast who performed their parts to new audiences with every trial.

Had justice been served today? The truth uncovered?

Truth and justice were not the work of lawyers. That's what reporters were for.

~END ~

AUTHOR'S NOTE

First off, I have a special gift waiting when you join my V.I.P. Reader List. Catch up with Justin Slinger as he sniffs out his next story. A serial killer is loose in the kingdom. Can Slinger hunt the killer down? Will he get the story he needs to win another Pied Paper Prize and secure his position as an investigative reporter at the *Once Upon Times*? Find out in *Renegade Red and the Merry Woods Strangler*, an all-new, hot-off-the-Pied-Press novella. Sign up to receive your copy here: https://nikkijefford.com/freejustinslingernovella/.

Like Justin Slinger, I have dashed back to my desk to write this author's note while the story is still cinnamon fresh in my head.

As with my previous ONCE UPON anthology stories, I selected a fairy tale (in this case, *Goldilocks and the Three Bears*), read the original, and then brainstormed my approach using the theme of the year. In this case, I read SEVEN early versions of *The Three Bears*. They were all very similar. I kept the original names of the bears from one of the early versions: Great Big Bear, Middle-Sized Bear, and Little Small Wee Bear, and replaced them with wolves. (I axed the "Small" from Wee Wolf's name because it was getting redundant enough already.) In the first versions of the fairy tale, Middle-Sized Bear was a male. I turned him into a female, as happened in later versions, and which stuck in modern times.

Another notable difference in the earliest versions of the story is that Goldilocks is not a golden-haired girl, but a silver-haired old woman who says bad words and is a vagrant who would have stolen the spoons from the bears' porridge bowls if they had been made of silver rather than wood.

All seven versions ended with either the old woman, the girl, or, in one case, a fox, jumping out the window and the author of the tale pondering whether she broke her neck in the fall or ran into the woods or was captured by the constable and sent to jail. This, the narrator could not tell, but the three bears never saw her again.

The Three Bears was first recorded in narrative form by British author and poet Robert Southey in 1837. Judge Robert Southey is a nod to the fairy tale's first creator.

As a justice-craving Libra, it bothered me that all seven versions left readers hanging. Curiosity coupled with a series of high-profile US court cases blaring over the morning news while eating my morning porridge (steel cut oats with coconut sugar and banana slices), and before long I'd built a case—or rather, plotted a court drama.

True to the original versions, the intruder still gets away with burglary and property damage. I guess even I cannot rewrite history.

Writing this story took me back to two court cases in which I served on jury, in particular a burglary that took place on the remote island community of Orcas Island off the coast of Washington State. In this instance, the woman was seen fleeing (like Goldilocks)! She nearly ran over one of the homeowners as she sped away in her car. The defense had one single witness—the woman's shady boyfriend. The sheriff had confiscated two jackets inside the woman's car matching the description of the jackets that were stolen from the couple's home. After taking the stand, the boyfriend claimed he had been with the defendant at a yard sale and pointed the jackets out in a sale box and encouraged her to buy them.

Does anyone else smell bull?

After a short deliberation, we reached a guilty verdict. With it being a small island community, the prosecutor and defense attorney joined us in the deliberation room after the ruling to openly discuss and share information they had been unable to bring forth during the proceedings—such as the defendant's criminal record and long history of run-ins with the sheriff's department. Also, her boyfriend was a felon on probation. Even her defense lawyer was laughing along as the prosecutor aired out her dirty laundry.

I hope you enjoyed this twist on the classic fairy tale. Don't miss the waggish Justin Slinger bonus novella, available for instant download by visiting NikkiJefford.com/freejustinslingernovella.

RIVER DAUGHTER

ANNIE BELLET

WIND SANG THROUGH THE CHIMES AND TOLD HA ABOUT THE THREE men long before she sank her pole into the riverbed to make the lazy turn towards her anchoring place. She laid one strong brown hand over her bulging belly and listened to the chimes. Then, with a small smile to her unborn daughter, she gave her pole another push. Her boat, painted blue many years ago by her mother's mother, slid across the wide, slow water and came to rest against a sandy bank.

Ha ignored the three strangers with their muted city shirts and sun burnt pale skin as they stood awkwardly among the blood grass and waterweeds beneath the swamp cypress lining the riverbank. She tied up her bright green cotton skirt and slipped barefoot out onto the sandbar to secure her boat to a thick trunk leaning out over the sunlit river. Only once the boat was secure did she walk towards the waiting men, who waved to get her attention, calling out in accented voices.

They were men from the North, with narrow faces and too much clothing between their skin and the warm, hazy air. They wore gold torques and had polished bone buttons on their drably colored shirts. The tallest one waved her over, licking at thin lips shadowed by a reddish moustache.

"Are you the river witch?" he asked in halting Vien, skeptically eying her pregnant belly and youthful face.

"Yes, I am Ha," she said in the trader's tongue, and shrugged, hand on hip, waiting.

The men looked between them and after a long moment seemed to come to some agreement and the tall one spoke again. He looked like an undernourished rambutan tree, with spiky red hair prickling out of a bulbous head behind large ears.

"We want to see what lies beyond the falls, in the mountains. Everyone from Thahn Phu to Yen Cai said we should seek out the river witch in her blue boat beneath the northern mountains."

Ha considered this. By custom and blood birth she was bound to ferry any who asked to the sacred pool. To refuse would mean giving up her powers and never setting foot in the river again. Her golden fish would die and none would ever again make the journey to the sacred pool beyond the falls.

She wondered if the villagers had told these strangers so, and said, "That way is difficult to pass. No boat can go there, nor will even surefooted ox take you along the river through the white cliffs. Even for a river dancer, the way is dangerous. I would need much money to put my little Truc at risk." She rubbed her swollen belly protectively.

The men turned to each other and spoke in their garbled, urgent tongue. Her stomach rumbled its desire for the evening meal and Ha sighed. She was always hungry these days, her little Truc consuming everything as soon as it entered her body and then kicking for more. She would wait, however. It had been many years since anyone sought passage through the falls. Few believed in the old powers, these days, and fewer still dared to seek out the last of the dancers in her blue boat beneath the white mountains.

Ha fished and carried occasional loads of pineapple, rambutan, sweet potatoes, and rice between villages. That is how these men would have heard of her, in the whispers over rich cold coffee and fried salt and pepper fish in the markets. She turned her head and watched water bugs dart along the surface of the river and snatched occasionally by slender silver minnows schooling in the shallows.

The men finished their conversation and moved gingerly back towards her, the other two, their hair the yellow of dried reeds, hanging behind the tall one. Now she would learn how much they knew, whether they would pay.

"How much to take us to beyond the falls and then back again when we are ready?" he asked, chin raised in the way of a person who believes he gains superiority just by staring downward.

"How long would you wish to stay beyond the falls?" Ha asked, her face smooth and expressionless. If she closed her eyes she'd see it; a clear deep lagoon dropping away between the shining walls of stone.

"How long do people usually want to stay? We have heard it is a beautiful place."

"One day to get to the base of the falls, one day to travel through them. Most wish a day or two to pray and swim. Then one day back down the falls and here again. This will not be cheap."

He nodded, too quickly. "Tell us your price."

Ha regarded the men. They had good quality clothing, but carried no bags. She thought they must be staying in Quy and wondered who had carried them to her anchorage, for they did not seem the type to walk far. Their shoes were leather and heavy, with closed toes. They had on linen and cotton, not silk, but their belts were decorated with garnets and bronze fittings. To travel so far from Rusla, where she guessed they came from, they must have some wealth.

"You pay in zu? Or gold?" she asked.

"Gold bullion," the tall one said.

"Two stones," she said, giving the gold measurement used by the silk traders. "Brought to me beforehand." It was a lot, too much, and she doubted they carried so much gold.

"We will do this. When can we leave?" The man did not haggle, and his eyes slid away from hers, pallid and slippery like the eels she fished from the mudflats. Ha placed a hand on her belly. She knew then that the men did not intend to let her keep her wage. They must have heard of the red pearls that grew in the lagoon. Pearl hunters. She shivered, wishing she could refuse them passage.

But she wanted the money, and she needed the power, the river. It was all she'd ever known. She was the last, if she lost her powers before Truc was born, Truc would never dance with the river.

The other two men shuffled nervously, their eyes also avoiding her gaze as she glanced to them. She pasted a smile on her face and ducked into a bow. She would have her gold first, and they wouldn't harm her until she'd returned them to safety. They would leave the pearls alone once they saw her power, and the place of her ancestors. If they did not, then she would see how she left them. Ha's smile turned secretive and she straightened with effort.

"Day after tomorrow. You will bring blankets to sleep on if you wish them, and provision. I must ready myself for the journey." Ha waved at the men and pretended to lose interest now that the bargain was struck. She turned away, ignoring the pale hand with its dusting of reddish hair on the back of the palm that extended towards her. She'd never understood the need to touch others when making bargains, it seemed unclean and awkward.

With a light step that belied her large belly, Ha returned to her boat and heaved herself up over the side, sliding down the blue wood to rest her feet on the smooth plank bottom. She used her little coal stove to fry up catfish and green peppers, washing it down with green tea and dried rambutan. The men had left and the wind sang to her of an ox cart that waited down the path for them to carry them back to Quy.

In her dreams the river screamed and bucked as iron blades cut into silvered shells, thick drops of blood spilling into the churning water and then sinking like pebbles into a deep chasm.

Ha woke with the sun as the morning birds sang and freed her boat from the mud bank. Today she would pole her way upriver and check on her golden babies. She hoped that one or two fish would be ready to harvest, for she would need their power to make the river dance.

Mist played along the surface like a phantom river as she pushed the heavy boat upstream. The boat was as wide as two men with a woven canopy over the middle portion that housed her cot and clothing trunk. Though the power in her blood gave her strength, her arms were corded with muscle from fifteen years poling the boat up and down the river. She stuck to the west bank, away from the deeper, faster middle.

The sun rose high and Ha paused in her movements to watch the line of trees, looking for the bent branch of the huge swamp cypress. She spied it and guided the boat towards the tree. As she came along side, the narrow passage to the side channel revealed itself, tucked away among the trees in such a way that one would have to know to look for the opening to see it from any distance away. Her blue boat slid through and out into a deep side channel bounded on all sides by thick swamp cypress and weeping fig.

The channel opened up to a small lake. Under the trees over-hanging the sides of the lake grew a garden of bones. Many were yellowed with age and coated with algae, half buried in the red mud of the lakebed. Some shone stark white in the afternoon sun. Ha smiled and bowed her head as her boat slid past the remains of an elephant. Her mother's mother had sung the mighty beast there to die when it grew too old to lead and wandered to this lake. There were other hidden channels much like this one along the river, but Ha loved this place. Elephant bones were good luck.

She leaned over the side of the boat and smiled as she spied the blade-like, golden bodies of the prang glinting in and out of the shadows beneath the surface. As the boat drew near the latest carcass sunk below the water, her smile grew wider. Here the more mature prang moved lazily around the rotting corpse.

His face was no longer recognizable after a fortnight beneath the water. She stared hard, but could see no trace of the laughing man with skin like coconut milk in coffee and shining white teeth that had flashed when he smiled, bone in sunlight. Ha laid a hand on her belly and shook her head. Lao had talked so sweetly, but as her waist thickened he'd drawn away from her. When she'd asked for gold, for things for the coming child, he'd laughed, scorned her.

She would have left him alone, but he'd crept to the river in the darkness and tried to set fire to her boat. She guessed it was one thing to be the lover of the river witch, but another to father a child out of wedlock with one of no status. When he disappeared no one had thought to ask her any questions. Or perhaps hadn't dared.

She stared into his rotting face and sighed. Her prang, her golden babies whose flesh would give her the power to make the river dance, it was only fitting they fed themselves on the strength that had given her Truc. Lao served her as his final act. She'd taken his eyes herself, burning them with chrysanthemum and saffron.

Her thoughts were broken by the appearance of a huge prang drifting out from beneath the corpse. Its body was as long as her arm and the color had gone from burnished gold to a deep reddish gold hue. Ha slid her fishing spear out of its holder along the gunnels of the boat. With a swift, practiced motion, she hooked the barbs into the prang's thick body and drew it into the boat.

She left the fish twisting and gasping on the slats and guided her boat toward a dead tree that rose out of the lake. Once the boat was secure, Ha went to the covered baskets stored beneath her cot and chose one tied with a bit of red silk. She stoked her coal fire and stripped off her clothing. Retrieving a ceramic flask of coconut oil, she slowly rubbed it over her entire body, smiling as her daughter kicked and she felt the flesh of her belly shift with Truc's strong movements. It would not be long now; her daughter would come with the rains.

Oiled and fragrant, Ha drew her bone knife and turned towards the fish that now lay quietly, no longer gasping, its deep red and gold scales glinting in the fading sunlight. Ha cut away the prang's innards and swallowed them raw.

"I take from the river, the river nourishes me. I give to the river, the river is nourished by me," she sang aloud and looked out over the water. The wind stilled but tiny wavelets started to dance on the surface of the channel. Birds and frogs, singing up until now, hushed as well as the power rose in her.

With sure movements Ha cut up the rest of the prang and ate it down bite by bite. Even Truc was calm in her belly, as though the baby could sense the importance of this ritual. The scales cut her lips, the inside of her cheeks, and tongue but she forced herself to swallow as she repeated the words, blood dripping down her chin. Finally she chewed and forced down the tail of the prang and sang the words a final time.

The boat rocked with the violence of the water as it swirled and plumes of spray leapt free of the surface to soak the boat and trees. Drunk on the power of the river, Ha stumbled to her glowing coals and in the twilight dug a handful of dried red and white chrysan-themum blossoms from the basket and tossed them onto the fire. She bent her head, letting the blood drip from her chin as she inhaled the smoke and forced the magic under control. Her skin felt too tight and her mind spun, ears full of the water music. It felt like too much and she cried out, gasping for breath as her body drowned in power.

Then Truc moved inside her and Ha's mind returned to itself. She pulled the power inward, centering herself on her unborn daughter. With a triumphant laugh she rose to her feet and the waters around her calmed instantly. The power was hers. Tomorrow she would meet with the men from Rusla.

At false dawn, as the sky turned grey and orange, Ha rose and set out, making her way downstream to her anchorage along the mudbars. When she arrived the men were already there, standing on the more solid ground surrounded by bundles of food and supplies. In the distance she saw the ox cart that had brought them driving away toward Quy.

"Good morning," the tall one said.

"I will show you were to stow your things," Ha said and nodded to the baskets and bundles beside him.

She pulled netting out from under the floor slats and helped them secure the blankets, large basket of rice, and baskets of dried fish and fruit in a way that would keep her boat balanced and a pathway clear from bow to stern. One of the blonde men, the one with smooth cheeks, brought a large bag of gold on board and grudgingly handed it over. Ha stuffed it under her cot and risked using a little of the power in her body to whisper a charm of forgetting. If the men planned to take the gold away later, they would now forget where she'd placed it.

Today the men wore long knives on their belts. Ha smiled to herself. Thick knives of iron would not protect them from the river's wrath if they decided to harm her or defile the sacred place they traveled to. A tiny pang of guilt surprised her and she breathed with it for a long moment. The source of the river was sacred, not to be shown for profit, but Ha needed the gold. It would keep herself and newborn Truc in food and shelter until the floods lessened and mother and baby were strong again. She saw no reason she couldn't earn gold from these foreigners while performing her blood born duty.

The men settled into the boat and Ha pushed off, poling it up the river. Her blue craft rode low in the water, laden with men and food but her arms never tired and the river's power sang its song in her blood. The journey to the falls was silent for the most part, the men murmured among themselves in their tripping tongue from time to time, but did not talk to Ha. Nor did they offer her their names, but she preferred that. It was her duty to ferry them there, but also her charge to protect the sacred waters from defilement. If they had ill intentions, it would make giving them to the river easier to think of them as nameless strangers.

They heard the Trai Bao falls long before they could see them. The white mountains grew closer as the day progressed until as the sun dropped low the huge pale cliffs rose around them and the river grew narrow and fast. Ha's arms strained to keep her boat pointed upriver and her passengers crowded in the bow and watched for the first glimpse of the falls.

They came around the final bend and slipped between huge rocks that jutted from the river, coated in red mud and bird droppings. Abruptly the river gave way to a large oblong basin. The falls, though they were really a series of steep, swift rapids, dropped into this basin. The water here was too deep for travel with a pole and Ha slid hers into its hooks on one side of the boat, securing it there with braided ties. She let the boat drift to one side of the current and moved to the bow, gripping a loop of rope in her hands. The boat drifted backward, turning with the flow of the water. With a practiced throw Ha looped the rope over an outcropping of rock in one of the white cliff walls. She pulled the boat in tight to the cliffs and tied it off.

"That is what we must travel up?" The tall one rose stiffly and pointed at the roiling water broken by the occasional stone.

"Tomorrow morning, yes. It is why you hired me. Only a river dancer can take you up there," Ha said and paused, her dark eyes fixing his grey ones. "And bring you safely back."

His jaw tightened and she turned away, confident he'd read her meaning well enough. She was tired and hungry, having only eaten dried rambutan as she poled them up the river. Truc was awake and kicking and Ha's lower back hurt, her breasts sore and leaking into the cotton pads she tucked inside her shirt against them.

The men made no move to help her with the evening meal but Ha decided it would be poor manners to make only enough for herself. She cooked rice and served it with salted fish and onions fried in coconut oil. It was tempting to whisper a charm to make the men sleep over the food, but Ha decided she shouldn't risk using too much power.

She ate enough for three and then left the men to the coals and their foreign conversation and lay down on her cot, one hand on the bone knife under her pillow. They eventually got out their blankets and curled up to sleep on the cramped boat as the stars shone down and a blue moon rose over the white cliffs.

Ha woke with the dawn and found all three men still sleeping. She emptied her bladder into a small clay urn, refusing to use the river so near the source. The tall one opened bloodshot eyes as she stepped past him to warm up the coals for breakfast. Slowly the men rose and ignored the clay urn that Ha used, instead pissing into the river. Ha hid her displeasure and fried up pineapple, mushrooms, and chunks of sweet potato.

The men were clearly impatient, eating without manners as they shoveled their meal into their mouths with copper spoons. Ha took her time, letting her stomach and the baby settle before she rose and put away the dishes. She made sure everything was secure on the boat before turning to the strangers.

"You must sit and hang on. Do not speak or touch me," Ha told them.

"What will you do? How does this work?" The tall one spoke and Ha wondered suddenly if the other two understood the trading language. She shrugged that thought off. Their faces shuffled through fear, curiosity, and suspicion.

"Stay quiet," she said, "and see."

She unhooked the boat and let it drift into the flow. Then Ha stood in the bow of the boat and drew her bone knife. The power inside twisted and crawled along beneath her skin. With a swift stroke, Ha brought the blade across her left palm and held her bleeding hand out over the water and began to sing.

"I take from the river, the river nourishes me. I give to the river, the river is nourished by me. I give to the river, the river obeys."

The world stilled and the water ceased to flow for one tense moment. Power rushed from Ha's bleeding fist and she felt the strength of the river within her. She bent her mind to it and dragged the water into a great wave that built up from the depths of the river and lifted the boat high beside the cliffs. Dimly she heard a gasp, swiftly stifled, somewhere behind her, but the power was in her and she paid it no mind.

With her will she pushed the boat forward, sailing on the huge and ever-cresting wave towards the falls. The water danced beneath the boat, carrying it safely up the steep and rocky riverbed. Ha's mouth was open and she sang the song of power, wordless ululations as the spray soaked her and her precious child danced within her swollen belly.

Up and up, onward for miles beneath the cloudless blue sky

between towering white cliffs they sailed the wave of Ha's song until, as the sun settled into a red western sky, the river leveled and Ha let her song fade. The boat slid forward, riding the dying wave and coming to rest on calm water. All around them the white walls of the mountains rose and the river ended ahead in a large, deep lagoon. Higher up walls were carved with the bodies of women, benevolent round faces staring down in the gloom as they approached.

The men stood and looked around in wonder, then peered over the side and exclaimed. Exhausted, Ha sank down on her cot and watched them. They spoke in excited, hurried tones and sent many wary glances her way.

She smiled to herself. Night was coming, and she guessed the strangers would not do much in the dark. Tomorrow she would have strength again and if they would not look and then leave she would force the issue. But now, exhausted, she had to sleep.

The men did not disturb her slumber, but Ha awoke with the sun to the sound of splashing. The thick blonde one with the full bearded face had stripped to a loincloth and was in the water with his knife and a bag. Ha struggled upright and winced as she forgot the cut on her hand as she gripped the edge of the cot.

"No, what are you doing? You must look only!" she cried in Vien, forgetting they would not know her tongue. She'd slept too long; her ancestors would curse her lack of vigilance.

The tall one grabbed her as she moved toward the side of the boat, clearly understanding her tone and intent. She jerked away from him and his eel eyes widened in surprise at her strength. Her pulse quickened and a shiver went up her spine. She turned and looked at the man in the water.

He dove beneath the surface of the clear pool. All along the rocks under the deep lagoon grew red shelled mussels. They gleamed in the sunlight, rippling like blood beneath the water. These were the source of the rare red pearls that sometimes washed downstream with the monsoons. Only a river dancer could reach this place, and they never harvested the pearls that were their sacred keeping.

Ha glared down at the man who now pried a mussel from its

cluster and stuffed it into the woven sack drifting out from where it was tied to his arm. It had been childish wishing to think these men might be moved by the beauty of this place, might feel its sacredness. In a painfully honest moment, Ha admitted to herself that more than the gold that would feed her and Truc, she'd wanted to feel the power, to show it off to these doubting strangers, to ride the river as it danced beneath her mother's mother's boat.

But these men had done more than look, and Ha had caused this. She'd brought them here, it was time to punish their greed, to give them to the river and atone for her own transgression beneath the watching faces of her ancestors.

The power in her blood was slow to respond, her own mortal exhaustion clung to her, but anger lent her strength. She turned as the bearded man surfaced and started to sing the song that would call these men to their deaths.

"I nourish the river, the river obeys. I give to the river ..."

The tall one leapt forward and grabbed her tight, crushing one arm against her pregnant belly and the other firmly over her mouth. She clawed at him, trying to bite his hand. They struggled and she nearly had him overpowered when the smooth-faced man joined in, raising the hilt of his knife and slamming it down on her head. Dizzy with blood pouring into her eyes, she reeled. Cloth was jammed in her mouth and tied there and then thick ropes pulled tight around her arms and then her legs. Ha twisted as she fell to the slats, trying to protect her baby. She lay on her side, breathing heavily through her nose, and glared up at them.

The tall one drew his own knife with one scratched and bleeding arm but the other grabbed him and shook his head, saying something in their tongue. The red haired man kicked her in chest and turned away. Ha blinked blood from her eyes and watched them as they too stripped down to loincloths and dove into the lagoon.

All day she curled there, bound and wounded, her heart breaking with every shell they cracked open and discarded as they collected the pearls within. Each pearl was a drop of blood, a tear, and Ha wept to see this sacred place so defiled. She knew it was her fault and she lay silent and guilty, her mind racing to find a way free from the ropes. She dared not test the knots in daylight, not with them watching her. One remained always in the boat, cracking the shells that came up.

She grew very thirsty as the day went on, but the men ignored her and she guessed they would not risk ungagging her so that she might eat and drink. The pressure of her baby within her belly sat heavy on her bladder and finally Ha gave in, burning in shame.

The men sat once evening fell and talked quietly around the coals as they made dinner. The smells of food made Ha nauseated with hunger and she forced her mind away, visualizing a small red stone dropping away into the depths of the water.

The indigo moon rose above the mountains, spilling eerie light down into the quiet lagoon. Beyond the entrance the waterfall's rush was muted and sounded very far away. Eventually, the men curled within their blankets and their breathing grew heavy and even. Wariness of her meant they'd spaced their blankets away from where she lay, with the tall one taking her cot. Ha added this trespass to his list of ill deeds, but she was happy they'd kept away from her.

They would want to leave here eventually, and needed her to sing them down. She knew they'd keep a knife to her swollen belly, keep her from singing them to their deaths. They would kill her and Truc once they were safe, unless she drowned them all on the way down.

Or unless she found a way to free herself now. Her head throbbed and her body ached, the power a tiny spark within, like the heartbeat of her unborn child. Ha summoned her strength, focusing on those sparks of life within.

Slowly, careful to make as little noise as possible, Ha pulled herself upright against the side of the boat and then twisted to lean her hands into the water. She stared down into the depths of the lagoon and sang a prayer in her mind to the source of the river. She had no voice to give it, but tugging at the side of the boat had reopened the wound on her hand and her blood drifted in a thin dark line into the water.

Up from the depths came an iridescent cloud of tiny silver bodies.

Tiny mouths picked at the ropes, tearing them fiber by fiber until finally they gave way and her hands were free. Heavy tears flowed down Ha's face and she tore the gag from her head and whispered thanks to the river and all the mothers looking down upon her.

She did not want to risk waking them with the deathsong. She looked about for her bone knife. It gleamed in the moonlight, resting on a basket near the banked coal brazier. Ha undid the bindings around her feet, listening for any change in breathing or sounds of movement from the men. Then she crept slowly forward on sore legs and picked up her knife. The bearded man lay between her and the others, so she went to him first.

Awkwardly she bent at the knees and grabbed him by the hair, forcing his chin to his chest. He woke but had no time to struggle or cry out as she plunged the blade into the side of his throat. Blood, dark and hot, spilled over her hand and she rose, leaving him to bleed out.

She moved quickly to the side of her cot and stared down at the sleeping tall man. Anger tensed her shoulders and she resisted the urge to mutilate him before she killed. If he woke the third man, she might be in danger, and she would not risk harm to her child. She laid the knife against his throat and waited until his slippery eyes opened before sliding the blade into his neck. He raised his arms, too late, and tried to scream but only blood rushed from his mouth. The tall man died staring up at her, his face frozen in fear.

With a small smile, Ha turned and edged toward the last man.

He'd stopped the tall one from harming her further, but she still felt little pity for him. The smooth-faced blonde had destroyed as many of the precious mussels as any of the others and sealed his own fate. She killed him quickly, before he could wake.

Then she rinsed her hands in the lagoon and drank her fill of water. She hauled the tall one's body from her cot and threw the blood-soaked pillow on top of it before curling up around her belly and falling into an exhausted slumber.

She awoke in daylight. Her head hurt and blood caked her kerchief and had dried in her long black hair. She gingerly probed the bruise and decided she would live. After a breakfast of fresh fruit, she used the bag of coal to weigh down the bearded man's body and hauled him over the side of the boat.

"I nourish the river, the river takes from me," she sang. She lifted the pouch of red pearls and slowly emptied it over the side. They drifted downward into the dark depths like blood or rubies, glinting until their shimmer faded into the deep.

Ha turned away and looked at the corpses in her boat. These two she would bring to the garden of bone and give their flesh to her golden babies. Their pouches had yielded more gold bullion, enough to swaddle Truc in silk. She laid her hands over her belly and smiled down at the shifting baby within.

"I will sing to you of the river, and show you how to swallow its power that it will someday dance for you. And when you are old enough I will bring you to the place where the red pearls grow and tell you of the mistake your mother made that you must never repeat." Truc kicked in response to her soft words and Ha laughed.

She turned and walked to the bow of the boat. Summoning the last vestiges of the power within her, Ha began to sing the song that would call the wave and dance them home.

~ END ~

AUTHOR'S NOTE

This story draws on the traditions of dangerous women in waterways, from the Greek myth of the Sirens to the Slavic myths of Rusalka. I wanted to twist it, and tell the story from the POV of the water witch instead of her victims, and so this story was born.

ABOUT THE AUTHOR

Annie Bellet is the *USA Today* bestselling author of *The Twenty-Sided Sorceress*, and the *Gryphonpike Chronicles* series. Her interests besides writing include reading, powerlifting, video games, comic books, table-top RPGs, and many other nerdy pursuits. She lives in the Netherlands with her husband.

Find all her books and sign up for her newsletter at her website: https://anniebellet.com/

THE GIRL WHO CRIED VAMP

CHRISTINE POPE

A Hedgewitch for Hire Story

THE GIRL LEANED ACROSS THE COUNTER OF MY SHOP AND SAID breathlessly, "Selena, I need your help."

I blinked at her. Despite the way she'd addressed me by my first name, I was pretty sure I'd never seen the young woman before. She looked barely twenty, with long, pale brown hair and big brown eyes, and had a thin, intense sort of prettiness. It wasn't hugely surprising she'd know my name, though; since I'd opened Once in a Blue Moon, my New Age shop, almost a year ago, pretty much everyone in the small town of Globe, Arizona, had heard of me...even if they wouldn't personally deign to drop in and buy a spell candle or a set of Tarot cards.

"If you're looking for something in particular...." I ventured, and at once the girl shook her head.

"No, I don't need anything from your store," she said, and gave a brief glance around before returning her attention to me. "It's just that I know you're good at dealing with ghosts, and my apartment is haunted."

She uttered this statement in such a matter-of-fact way that for a second or two, I could only stare back at her, not sure how I should respond. True, I'd had a few dealings with ghosts during my tenure in Globe, but I still didn't think those experiences exactly made me an expert. And in one case, the ghosts—or demons—had turned out to be nothing supernatural at all, only an elaborate ploy to get my mother and stepfather to sell the gorgeous Victorian mansion they'd recently purchased.

"Um...how do you know it's haunted?" I asked.

"Just a feeling," she replied. "Oh, I'm Leah Murphy, by the way. My apartment is in the Freeport Arms."

Well, that made a little more sense. Globe, with a population of barely seven thousand people, wasn't the sort of place that offered a lot of high-density housing. But the Freeport Arms—so named because the apartment building had first been built as a dormitory for workers at the local Freeport Mine—had been standing for a little more than a hundred years, thus giving it plenty of time to have accumulated its own share of ghosts. The place was turned into apartments in the late 1960s and had been pretty much continuously occupied ever since, and yet I'd never heard anyone mention that it was haunted, even it did seem like the sort of place where spirits would tend to hang around.

"If you think it's haunted," I said, doing my best not to sound too dubious, "then maybe you should see if there are any ghost hunters in the Phoenix area who'd want to come out and take some readings. I'm really not an expert."

At the mention of ghost hunters, Leah's expression shut down. She didn't quite pout, but I got the distinct impression she wasn't too keen on the idea.

"I'd really rather have you take a look first," she told me. "If you don't sense anything, then maybe I'll call in some outside help."

For a second or two, I hesitated. Then again, I had the evening to myself; Calvin Standingbear, the chief the San Ramon Apache tribal police...and my fiancé...had to work late, and so I didn't really have any dinner plans. What could it hurt if I headed over to Leah's apartment after I closed the store at five o'clock?

"Okay," I said, hoping the pause before I made that decision hadn't been too obvious. "I can be over a little after five, if that works for you."

"It totally works," she replied, her eyes glowing. "I'm in number 212. It's on the second floor."

I probably could have deduced that bit of information from the apartment's number, but that was fine. And I was definitely glad to hear that Leah lived on the second floor, and not the fourth or fifth. After spending all day on my feet at the shop, the thought of climbing that many flights of stairs wasn't terribly appealing.

Once I'd made another promise that I'd be there as soon as I was done closing up the shop, Leah said goodbye and headed out, her face all smiles.

Well, we'd see if she was still smiling after I gave her my report.

The Freeport Arms felt like a time capsule from an earlier era, right down to the faded linoleum in the hallways. And oddly, I did experience a weird creeping sensation in the lobby, and another on the second-floor landing. Maybe there really was something to Leah's claim about ghosts.

Of course, she'd said it was her apartment that was haunted, while the odd feelings that crept over me in the lobby and again on the stairs were in public spaces. Still, ghosts didn't always have to stick to a particular location. What she was experiencing in her place could have just been those spirits roaming around the building.

She answered my knock immediately, and sent me a smile of relief, as if she hadn't been entirely sure whether I would show up or not. "Hi, Selena. Come on in."

I entered the apartment and took a quick glance around. It was small and spare, with a collection of hand-me-down furniture in the living room and not much else to decorate the space, not even any pictures on the wall.

"I just moved in a couple of weeks ago," she said quickly, as if wanting to explain why her apartment had so little personality. "My cousin Rachel works at the Freeport Mine, and she helped get me a job as an admin there."

Okay, that explained why Leah had seemed so unfamiliar to me, why I couldn't recall even seeing her pass by on the street or at the local Super Walmart. The "Rachel" she was referring to was probably Rachel Murphy, a woman I knew by sight and not much more, since she'd only come into my shop once to buy a couple of candles and had looked as though she'd smelled something bad the entire time.

I nodded, then said, "Can you tell me more about these 'feelings' you've been having in the apartment? Are there any places here where you feel it more than others?"

Leah wrapped her arms around herself as if she'd experienced a sudden chill, even though the heat in the little apartment was ratcheted up pretty high, and I found myself almost uncomfortable in my wrap sweater and boots. "The bedroom," she said in a very small voice.

"Nowhere else in the building?"

"No."

Which seemed odd to me, because if there really were any presences hanging out in the lobby or stairwell, you'd think she would have felt those, too.

But the spirit world wasn't exactly cut and dried when it came to how it affected people, and so I pushed that small inconsistency aside and let Leah lead me into the bedroom. It was even smaller and shabbier than the living room, leading me to wonder exactly how much the Freeport Mine paid its admins. After all, another woman I knew who worked for them, Jennifer Espinoza, had a cute little cottage just a quarter-mile from where I currently stood and seemed to be doing just fine for herself,

Since that disrepancy shouldn't have really been a factor in my current situation, I brushed it aside and did my best to focus on my surroundings.

Nope, not a darn thing.

"Do you mind waiting out in the living room for a minute?" I asked Leah. "Sometimes it's easier for me to pick up on vibrations if I'm by myself. I promise I won't touch anything."

"Oh, that's fine," she said immediately. "And if you do need to touch something, I understand…if you think it will help you focus."

Somehow, I doubted that handling the cell phone currently charging on the rickety bedside table or picking up the scarf Leah had draped on the iron bedstead would help much. I didn't demur, though, only told her I'd be out in a couple of minutes.

Another nod, and then she was gone, leaving me alone.

Although I'd only been telling the truth when I informed Leah that I generally worked better when I was by myself, it still felt odd to be standing in the bedroom of someone who was next to a stranger to me. However, I knew I needed to push my misgivings aside so I could focus on what I was here to do.

A breath in, and out, and then another inhalation, another exhalation. This helped to ground me, to allow me to stand there and reach out to the building that surrounded me, to get a feeling for all the lives that had been lived here over the past hundred years.

And…nothing.

However, I knew that communing with the spirit world wasn't the sort of thing that could be rushed, and so I closed my eyes and made sure my breathing remained rhythmic and gentle, opening me to the vibrations of the space.

Still nothing. While I couldn't shake the impression that something was definitely floating around the public areas of the building, this apartment of Leah's felt absolutely blank. The only energy here was hers and mine.

I kept trying, but after another five minutes or so passed, I gave up the enterprise as a lost cause and returned to the living room, where she was waiting on the dingy beige chenille couch.

"I'm really not feeling anything," I told her, and immediately a wave of disappointment crossed her face.

"Nothing at all?" she asked in plaintive tones.

"Nothing," I said. "I'm really sorry. As I came up to your apartment, I did get the feeling that maybe there's something in the building itself, but there's nothing in this apartment specifically. Still," I added, before she could protest and ask me to try again, "I'm really not an expert. Maybe if you had someone come in with EMF readers and other ghost-hunting equipment, they might be able to find something. As it is, though, I'm just not getting anything."

She blew out a breath and stood up, disappointment still clear on her waifish features. "Well, you tried. Thanks for coming over—I'm sorry I wasted your time."

"Oh, it's fine," I assured her. "And it wasn't a waste of time. I just wish I could have something concrete to give you."

"It's all right," she said. "Maybe it's just me feeling hinky because this is the first time I've ever lived by myself. This building is pretty old, and it creaks a lot."

That made a lot of sense. Even the building that housed my shop and the apartment above it was around ninety years old, and although it had been thoroughly updated and was in much better repair than the Freeport Arms, it could still make some pretty weird noises in the middle of the night.

"Well, if you feel hinky again, just come by the shop," I said. Possibly a hint of guilt at not being able to offer more help spurred me to add, "And if you want, I'd be happy to come over sometime and smudge your apartment for you. Sometimes energies pool in places—we're not really talking about ghosts, but even so, that kind of residue can lead to feelings of being watched or having some kind of spirit hanging around even when there isn't any kind of entity involved."

Her big brown eyes widened, and she sent me a tremulous smile. "Oh, could you really do that for me?"

"Absolutely," I said stoutly. "In fact, I can come by tomorrow at lunch, if you like. Or are you working?"

"No," Leah replied. "It's Saturday."

She made that statement so flatly, I could tell she'd never stopped to consider that not everyone at the Freeport Mine had weekends off, since the facility ran pretty much 24/7.

No point in commenting on that, however. I agreed to swing by a little after noon the next day to smudge the heck out of her apartment, and that seemed to be that.

The smudging went without incident, and I figured that was the end of it. I remembered what it had been like when I first moved out of the apartment I'd shared with my mother, and how, at the tender age of nineteen, I hadn't known whether I was really up to living by myself. Back then, I'd startled awake at every creak and odd sound, and so I didn't think it too strange for Leah to be jumping at shadows. With any luck, the smudging would help settle her down and let her know she was safe and surrounded by healing energies.

And when I didn't hear from her again over the next couple of weeks, I figured that was exactly what had happened.

But then she appeared in my shop one Saturday morning toward the end of February, looking worried and tragic once more.

"What's wrong?" I asked. "Do you need your apartment smudged again?"

"No," she said, and paused to shoot a worried glance over one shoulder. "I mean, it's fine. It's not the apartment...it's the guy who just moved in across the hall."

Considering the Freeport Arms was the cheapest place to live in Globe, it did tend to attract some shady types. More than once, I'd wondered at Rachel Murphy for allowing her cousin to live there alone, rather than trying to find her a roommate situation in a house in a better neighborhood.

"Is he dealing drugs or something?" I inquired then. "If you suspect anything, you should really reach out to the police."

Because, while I'd had my run-ins with Henry Lewis, Globe's

chief of police, I knew he was good at his job. He just didn't approve of me sticking my amateur nose into murder investigations where it didn't belong.

To my surprise, Leah let out a nervous giggle in response to my question. "Oh, my neighbor isn't dealing drugs," she replied, her tone somehow indicating that I was crazy for even asking such a thing. "No, he's a werewolf."

About all I could do was stare at her for a second. "A what?"

"A werewolf," she repeated patiently. "You know, someone who changes into a wolf at the full moon?"

Oh, wow. "Werewolves aren't real," I told her.

Which was true enough. At the same time, though, I knew I was being just a bit disingenuous. Although I knew the werewolves of legend and TV and film weren't real, I also knew that shapeshifting was a thing...mostly because the San Ramon Apache, the tribe Calvin belonged to, were all coyote shifters. No, they didn't live at the mercy of the full moon, and had complete control over their shifter natures, but that didn't change the fact that all of them could assume a coyote's form at will.

For just a moment, I wondered if Leah's new neighbor was from the San Ramon tribe, and whether she'd seen him changing shape when he'd thought he was alone and unobserved. But no, that didn't make sense. Everyone in their tribe lived on San Ramon land, which was located on the eastern outskirts of Globe and bordered the river of the same name. None of them would take the risk of living with regular people like the town's inhabitants.

"Werewolves *are* real," she insisted, her delicate jaw sticking out at a stubborn angle.

"How do you know that for sure?"

Her gaze shifted away from me for a second, and then I knew.

She was lying. Maybe not intentionally, maybe just because she wanted the attention, but she really didn't believe her neighbor was a werewolf any more than I did.

"He's always acting creepy," she said, still not meeting my eyes.

I didn't exactly believe "acting creepy" was a sign of being a werewolf, but I didn't say anything, only stood there behind the counter and waited.

"And it was a full moon the other night," she added, now sounding almost desperate. "He was out all night and didn't come back until almost five. I heard his door slam when he went into his apartment. And then I heard the next day at work that one of Hector Gonzalez's cows had gotten slaughtered. Cows are too big for coyotes to attack, so it had to be a wolf, right?"

None of this was factually untrue. That is, I couldn't speak to the behavior of Leah's neighbor, but I had heard from my fiancé Calvin that Hector had in fact lost a calf a few days earlier, sometime in the very early morning. A pack of coyotes, probably, hungry and desperate at the end of a long winter. They would never have gone after a full-grown cow, but the calf's mother hadn't been nearby, for whatever reason, leaving it vulnerable.

"It was a calf," I said, trying to be as precise as possible with my words. "But everyone is pretty sure it was a pack of coyotes, taking advantage of a vulnerable animal that had been left alone by its mother."

"Do they know for sure it was coyotes?" Leah asked next. There was something almost belligerent about her tone, as though she thought if she kept on the offensive, I'd give in eventually and say, sure, her neighbor was a werewolf.

I shrugged. "I haven't talked directly to Hector. I'm just repeating what my fiancé told me—he's the chief of the San Ramon tribal police," I added, although I guessed Leah probably already knew that. There weren't a lot of secrets in this small town.

"Well, there are wolves around here, aren't there?"

A year earlier, I might have supposed the same thing, since the open land around Globe was certainly wild enough for wolves. After all, we had coyotes and bears and mountain lions, so why not wolves as well?

"No, there aren't," I said gently. "Not in this part of the state. The only wolves in Arizona are way east of here, in the White Mountains."

Leah looked nonplussed by that particular piece of information. "Well, I know what I saw."

Which didn't sound like much, although I held my tongue. I didn't know exactly what was going on with her, why she saw the need to manufacture these stories of supernatural activity where there was none, but I guessed that confronting her openly on the subject probably wasn't a good idea.

"Keep an eye on him," I told her. "And if you see anything else, let me know."

She stared at me for a moment, maybe trying to figure out whether I was being serious or not. I maintained as straight a face as possible.

"I will," she said. "Because I know there's something going on with that guy."

And then she headed out, letting the front door to the shop slam behind her with a discordant jangle of the bells hanging from the handle.

I shook my head and hoped the rest of my customers that afternoon would be a little less difficult to deal with.

"It sounds like that Munchausen's thing," my best friend Hazel remarked as she reached for a tortilla chip.

I'd called Hazel and asked her if she wanted to meet for lunch, since Calvin was working and I really needed to discuss the problematic Ms. Murphy with someone. While I'd met an assortment of wild and woolly types over the years, whether back in Los Angeles or here in Globe, this was the first time I'd ever encountered anyone who seemed so dedicated to spinning wild yarns for no apparent reason.

"That what?" I responded, mystified.

A crunch of a tortilla chip, and then my friend responded, "You know, that thing where people make up stuff about themselves in order to get attention."

Right. But….

"I thought Munchausen's was specifically about faking having an illness of some sort," I pointed out, and Hazel deflated a little.

"Oh, right. I forgot about that part. But still."

I sipped some of my margarita. Most of the time, I wouldn't drink when I had to go back to the store and work all afternoon, but after Leah Murphy's visit, I'd been in need of a little liquid reinforcement.

"But why would she be coming to *me* with all this stuff?" I asked next. "I mean, she doesn't even know me."

"If she moved here recently, she wouldn't know anyone except her cousin and the people she works with," Hazel said reasonably. Her greenish eyes, a perfect match to her name, narrowed a bit as she appeared to think over the situation. "Also, you're the town woo-woo queen. You're kind of the logical person to be coming to about anything supernatural."

I'd made a face at the term "woo-woo," but I knew my friend had a point. It wasn't as though Leah could go to Chief Lewis with these sorts of stories.

"So, what should I do?" I said.

Hazel shrugged. "I'd just humor her for now," she replied. "I mean, it sounds like she wants attention. If it suddenly seems as though she's going to hurt herself or someone else, then maybe that would be the time to reach out to the police or her family or something. But I have a feeling this whole thing is mostly harmless."

"'Mostly,'" I repeated, then shook my head and sipped some more of my margarita.

I sure hoped my friend was right.

The next week or so, I didn't see or hear anything of Leah Murphy, and I found myself crossing my fingers that she'd gotten through her little phase after living in Globe for nearly a month and becoming more accustomed to her new life. After all, it wasn't so strange to think she might have hit a rough patch after starting over in a brand-new place where she hardly knew anyone.

But then she entered the store one Saturday afternoon right before closing, looking so drawn and worried that I couldn't help uttering a sound of dismay.

"Leah, are you all right?"

She sent a furtive look around the store, but that close to the end of the day, I was the only one there. After appearing to assure herself we were alone, she came up to the counter, where I'd been just about to start emptying out the cash register and putting away my receipts.

"It's my neighbor," she said in a hushed voice.

"The werewolf?"

That query got me a scornful look. "Oh, he wasn't *really* a werewolf," she told me, as if such a fact should have been self-evident. "He was just a guy who worked the night shift at the Super Walmart as a stock boy and always forgot to shave." Another pause to glance around the empty store, and she went on, "No, it's the man who moved in down the hall. He says he's a writer, but I *know* he's a vampire."

Oh, boy.

Here we go again, passed through my mind, but I did my best to prevent my disbelief from revealing itself in my expression.

"What makes you think that?" I asked. At least this time, I knew there was no point in trying to assure Leah that vampires weren't real.

She drew in a breath, as though to make sure she'd have enough air to get through all the information she wanted to relate to me. "Well, he sleeps all day. All. Day. I've never seen him up before sunset, and a couple of times when I woke up in the middle of the night, I heard a car engine and looked down into the parking lot, and saw him driving away."

Admittedly, somewhat odd behavior for Globe, most of whose residents were definitely of the "early to bed, early to rise" variety. Still, being a night owl didn't exactly constitute criminal behavior... or the behavior of a vampire, either.

"You said he's a writer, though," I remarked. "They keep odd hours, don't they?"

Leah's nose wrinkled slightly as she pondered that question. "I don't know," she admitted at last. "Aidan is the only writer I've ever met."

"His name's Aidan?" I inquired. That didn't sound like a very vampirish name to me. "So, you've talked to him?"

"Yes," she replied. "He was leaving one night as I was coming home from work after having to stay late. He introduced himself, and told me he was a writer doing some research on local history for a book he was working on."

Again, none of that information seemed terribly suspicious to me. All right, I might admit that the history of Globe had never seemed too exciting—it sounded like the usual expansion into a region in the Southwest because of a silver strike, or whatever—but I wasn't exactly what you could call an expert. And also, I could see why someone doing that kind of research would get a place at the Freeport Arms, since the apartments there were rented on a month-to-month basis and he wouldn't have to worry about signing any kind of long-term lease. So far, nothing about Leah's story sent up any real red flags.

"He's very pale, too," she went on before I could comment. "And he wears black from head to toe."

So do thousands of other people, I thought. In fact, even I'd flirted with an all-black wardrobe for about a year before deciding I needed a little more variety in my life. "I suppose he would be pale if he doesn't go out during the day," I remarked.

Leah was quiet for a moment, her dark eyes studying my face intently. At length, she said, "You don't believe me."

"I didn't say that," I replied, but of course, that was a flat-out lie. How could I possibly let myself believe that a vampire had taken up residence in Globe, Arizona, under the cover of being some kind of author? I would have been skeptical even without the previous stories about the ghost in her apartment and the werewolf across the hall.

"You didn't have to," she retorted. "Think what you want—I know what's really going on!"

"Leah—" I began.

But it was too late. She'd already turned on her heel and stalked toward the door, and then slammed it so the bells hanging from the handle jangled all out of tune.

You know, putting those things there might have been a bad idea.

Almost at once, guilt assailed me. I should have known the exact right thing to say, or should have run after her and told her that of course I believed her story. Not that I did, but she clearly needed support and validation, or she wouldn't have been making up these wild tales in the first place.

Or maybe that would have been entirely the wrong approach. Wasn't it a bad idea to go along with people's neuroses rather than trying to help them get through those issues somehow?

I didn't know; I wasn't a psychologist, although back in the day when I'd still been reading Tarot and performing divination for my clients in Los Angeles, I'd had to do my own form of therapy for some of them. But absolutely none of those people seeking help had come to me with stories of monsters down the hall.

Frowning, I locked the front door to the shop and turned around the "be back at" sign in the window so it showed my customary opening time of 10 a.m.

I really hoped I hadn't just done exactly the wrong thing.

There was no sign of Leah for a few days after that. On Wednesday, though, I saw her start walking out of Cloud Coffee just as I got in line to place an order for a late morning pick-me-up of a cardamom latte and a croissant. She looked drawn and pale, and had a long purple scarf with some silvery threads in it wrapped around her throat.

That scarf set off my spidey sense at once, although I tried to tell myself I was jumping to conclusions. It was late February, after all, and while conditions might have been warm and mild down in the Phoenix area's so-called "valley of the sun," the weather was still pretty cold and raw up here in Globe. As for Leah's pallor, well, pretty much everyone I met these days had that same "I'm totally sick of winter" tint to their complexions.

All the same, I called out to her. "Leah!"

She turned, her expression shutting down as soon as she saw me. Tone flat, she said, "Oh...hi, Selena."

Not the most exuberant of greetings, but I'd take it. "I haven't seen you for a while. How are you doing?"

A small lift of her shoulders under the black puffer coat she wore. "I'm okay. I've been feeling a little under the weather the past few days, so I called in sick today. I just wanted to come in for some green tea and a muffin."

"'Under the weather' how?" I asked, knowing how blatantly suspicious that question must have sounded.

"A cold," she replied at once, although she didn't sound particularly stuffy. "That's all."

And before I could say anything else, she headed out, one gloved hand clutching her paper go-cup of tea. I frowned, but I somehow knew that even if I tried to say something to get her to stop, she'd keep going and pretend she hadn't heard me.

Stay out of it, I told myself. That wasn't even my own inner voice advising me; I'd brought up the topic of Leah Murphy's odd behavior to my fiancé Calvin at dinner a few nights earlier, and he'd said pretty much the same thing, that there were people in this world who wanted attention, and it wasn't helping her any to keep contributing to the false narrative she'd built up for herself.

"You went to her apartment and helped her look for a ghost," he'd said. "That's more than most people would have done for a total stranger."

Maybe so, and yet I couldn't help feeling that I hadn't done enough.

Friday night, I made the unwelcome discovery that I was out of my cat Archie's favorite salmon feast canned food, and there would be hell to pay if I didn't make sure it was restocked before breakfast rolled around the next morning. Since Archie was no ordinary cat, but a man who'd been cursed into a cat's form some seventy years earlier, I couldn't exactly blow him off, either. A cat might have meowed to show its indignation at such a situation, but Archie would talk my ear off while letting me know just how much I'd failed as a cat caretaker.

So, I shrugged on my coat, grabbed my purse, and headed over to the Super Walmart, which luckily stayed open until eleven every night except Sunday. Since I was there already, I figured I'd pick up a few more odds and ends, and so put off another trip to go grocery shopping for at least another four or five days.

As I trundled my laden cart up to one of only two open checkout lines, I realized that the person standing in the queue a few feet away from mine was none other than Leah Murphy.

A radically changed Leah Murphy, that is. While her skin still appeared ivory-pale, her mouth was now coated with dark red lipstick, and she wore black eye liner and either multiple coats of mascara or some very good false eyelashes. Under her black coat, her clothes were all black as well, and long silver earrings peeped out from under her flat-ironed hair.

She must have caught me staring at her, because she said casually, "Hi, Selena. How are you?"

"Fine," I replied, an automatic response. "All over your cold?"

"Oh, yeah," she said. I noticed that the cart she was pushing held bottles of red wine and nothing else. True, they had some good deals at the Super Walmart, but…. "I popped a bunch of zinc and drank a lot of green tea and kicked it right out."

"Well, that's good," I said, and then hesitated. A checkout line wasn't exactly the best place for this sort of conversation, but since the opportunity had presented itself, I figured I'd better go for it. "How's your neighbor?"

Her expression didn't slip even a fraction of an inch. "Aidan's great," she responded. "We've gotten to be really good friends, actually. I was *totally* wrong about him."

"You were?" Not that I wasn't glad to hear such a thing, but all my instincts screamed at me that once again, she wasn't telling the truth...only this time, for completely different reasons.

"Definitely," Leah said. The person in front of me finally finished checking out, and so I had to push my cart ahead and start unloading its contents lest I invoke the ire of the man in line behind me. "But it was nice seeing you."

That sentence was a dismissal if I'd ever heard one. There wasn't much I could do except keep placing items on the conveyor belt, even as I murmured a "nice to see you, too."

My checker, Anita, was chattier than I would have liked, and so I had to hold my attention on her and our conversation rather than being able to keep an eye on what Leah was up to. Once I was done checking out, I realized that Leah had gotten out ahead of me, and was now pushing her cart into the parking lot.

I increased my pace. Maybe she thought our conversation was over, but all my instincts told me something was terribly wrong here.

"Hey!" I called out, and she paused, sending an irritated glance over one shoulder. In a way, I couldn't really blame her; it was pretty damn cold out there.

"What?"

Now that my cart was parallel with hers, I wondered if I'd just stuck my foot in it again. But I'd opened my mouth, and so I knew I needed to continue.

"You're sure everything is okay?" I asked. My glance strayed to all the wine bottles in her cart, and her mouth quirked.

"I'm not an alcoholic, if that's what you're asking," she said. "Aidan asked me if I could pick up a few things for him, and I said sure."

Never mind that she seemed barely old enough to drink. But she must have been, or she would never have been allowed to buy all those bottles of wine.

"It just seems like you've had kind of a radical style change," I ventured. Before, I'd only seen her wearing jeans and sweaters in shades of blue or pink, not the head-to-toe black she was sporting now.

Her eyes glinted in the light from the sodium-vapor lamps in the parking lot, sparking an odd reddish glow in their depths. "Sometimes it just takes a while for a person to find themselves," she said.

A quick flash of a smile, and then she pushed the cart past me, heading to a black SUV parked a few yards away. She opened the hatch and began unloading the wine she'd just bought.

Wait a second....

No, the lighting out here was bad, and I'd be the first to admit that I had a wee bit of an overactive imagination.

All the same, I could have sworn I'd seen the gleam of some *very* pointed incisors as she smiled at me.

"Leah!"

She ignored me, slamming the hatch and hurrying into the driver's seat. A moment later, she started to back out.

I could only stand there, continuing to stare until she'd pulled out of the parking lot and onto the main highway.

No, it wasn't possible...or was it?

A cold wind blew across the parking lot, reminding me that standing out there in near-freezing temperatures probably wasn't a very good idea. I hurried over to my Volkswagen Beetle, unloaded my own groceries, and then climbed inside and turned on the heat full blast. Even so, it didn't seem to do much to dispel the chill that had spread through my body.

I should have listened to her. I should have told myself that this last time, she'd been telling the truth.

Because right then, it sure looked to me like vampires might be real after all.

~END ~

AUTHOR'S NOTE

"The Girl Who Cried Vamp" is set in the world of my Hedgewitch for Hire series, although the story stands on its own. I thought it would be fun to update the old fable of the boy who cried wolf in a universe where the paranormal is quite real, only this time with a story about someone who seems to be seeking attention by seeing something supernatural around every corner. Like Selena, I'm still not sure whether Leah Murphy's vampire was real or not. What do you think?

This story takes place between *Jingle Spells* (Hedgewitch for Hire: Book 5) and *Wandering Monsters* (Hedgewitch for Hire: Book 6), and so has a few very mild spoilers for earlier books in the series.

ABOUT THE AUTHOR

USA Today bestseller Christine Pope is the author of the Hedgewitch for Hire, Witches of Wheeler Park, and Project Demon Hunters series, along with many other books (ninety and counting!). A California transplant, she makes her home in New Mexico with her husband and a rescue Chihuahua she's sure must be a Capricorn. Find out more about her books at christinepope.com.

THE UGLY DAUGHTER

DONNA AUGUSTINE

CHAPTER ONE

"Why does your face look like that?"

The boy tilted his head this way and that as he stepped closer, looking at the jagged scars that ran from my cheeks, down my jaw and then to my neck, until they disappeared behind my shirt.

"I was mauled as a baby," I said, not picking up on the scent of maliciousness. All the adults in my life thought I was crazy when I told them I could smell emotions. It didn't matter what they said. I still smelled them, and this kid didn't smell bad.

"Does it hurt?" He squinted, trying to look even closer. He was probably six or seven, a few years younger than I, and oblivious to how the other children on the playground kept their distance. They usually warned each other off, telling each other how they could catch whatever I had if they got too close.

"It doesn't really hurt, but sometimes it feels like my skin is shrinking." Talking about my scars was better than being stared and pointed at—or worse, laughed at.

Another boy approached cautiously, sidling up to my curious companion. I didn't like his smell at all.

The newcomer whispered in his ear as he kept an eye on me, as if an attack was imminent.

My curious companion's mouth dropped open before he let out a scream in my direction. The two of them took off, running and yelling, as if a game of monster had ensued. It wouldn't last long, since this monster wasn't the type to give chase.

I picked up my jump rope, going back to my solitary amusement as they gathered forces on the other side of the schoolyard. The return bell chimed before they'd decided on a plan of attack. Tossing my rope into the bin, I headed back inside.

It was math class after lunch. Most of the kids hated it, but it was my favorite of the day. Mr. Hackus had told me several times that I was gifted in math. Sometimes after class, when I'd really nailed a test, he'd sneak me some cookies from his snack drawer when none of the other kids were around.

I got settled in, taking out my pencils and getting ready for the quiz, my mouth already watering at the thought of shortbread cookies, when the telephone in the class rang.

"Winni, could you come here?" Mr. Hackus asked as he hung up.

There were a few giggles in the corner as I made my way up to his desk.

"Yes, Mr. Hackus?"

"The principal would like to talk to you in his office." His voice was soft for someone so gruff looking.

"Am I in trouble?" I hadn't done anything, but when bad things happened, I was usually called upon for questioning.

"I'm sure it'll be fine," he said, though his face didn't look so reassuring.

I walked slowly toward the principal's office.

When I got there, the secretary glanced up and looked away fast, signaling me to go in with a tilt of her head. She was one of those people who didn't stare because she didn't want to see me at all.

My mother was sitting in the office already, looking oddly peaceful, considering she'd been called down here. Normally her lips would be pinched and her nostrils flaring. Even her red hair seemed redder when there was a problem, as if her annoyance added a spark to the cheap dye she used.

"Please take a seat, Winni," Principal Eckard said.

I did as he asked, knowing for sure I was getting blamed for something.

He folded his hands as he talked, fixating his stare on the top of my head, instead of my face.

"You're a very good student, but this school, this situation, might not be the ideal place for you. We tried to make it work, but sometimes it's just not the right fit." His smile was real, as if he'd finally gotten a gift he'd been waiting years for.

"Is it because of recess? They were playing monster, but I didn't chase them, I swear." I could feel the tears flooding over my lids, but no matter how hard I tried, I couldn't stop them.

My mother put her hand out, patting the air in front of me in her signal to hush up.

"But––"

"Winni, let the principal speak," she said in that fake calm voice she used in front of the rest of the world.

I dropped my head. No one would listen anyway.

The principal cleared his throat before he continued. "We understand that maybe there are misunderstandings, but we still think it's best if you transition to homeschooling. We're prepared to foot the bill for whatever supplies or possible tutoring you might need."

"That is so very generous of you," my mother said, jumping on board as I still digested what he was saying.

"Of course. We'll send you a check monthly," Principal Eckard said.

"I've felt this might not be the right situation, but her father insisted she try to be"—she glanced at me before turning back to Principal Eckard—"as *normal* as she can be."

They didn't want me here anymore. They wanted me home, hidden away, so no one would have to see the ugliness of my face, feel the discomfort of having to talk to me, knowing I existed.

The principal stood, shaking hands with my mother as they both smiled in agreement before she headed for the door.

I'd always known I wasn't his *favorite*, but him too? Could no one stand me?

I stood, staring at him. The principal quickly shifted his attention to other paperwork on his desk as if I were already gone.

"Come, Winni, let's not waste any more of the principal's time." My mother snapped her fingers, demanding I get moving as she stood by the door. The calmness of her tone wore off like cheap mascara after some fake tears.

I followed her out until she stopped short.

"Claire?" a woman asked. "What a coincidence! I was hoping to run into you. I was wondering if you and your lovely daughter Hannah wanted to come by next week. They could play and we could have some tea..."

The woman's eyes darted to where I was peeking around my mother's skirt as she tried to step in front of me.

"Is this..." The woman leaned around to see me. "*Who* is this?"

Her tone was light and civil but with an edge I recognized. It wasn't *who* she wanted to know but *what*.

"This is Winnie," my mother said, being careful not to claim me.

"She's...*yours*?" the woman asked. "Well, that's...*wonderful*. I thought you only had two children, but..."

She didn't sound overjoyed.

My mother cleared her throat, sounding almost strangled as she muttered, "Winnie tends to be shy. Doesn't like much attention. She's a special situation I can tell you about at another time."

"Sure." The woman glanced over her shoulder, down the empty hall, as if she heard someone calling her name. "Well, I've got to get going. We'll see each other soon." She walked away with extra haste.

My mother turned to me with a sneer. "I don't know why you're always so intent on showing that face of yours." She turned and headed out the door, leaving me in the hall.

I followed. I had nowhere else to go.

My younger sister Hannah walked into my room and dropped onto my bed. She was followed by my younger brother Rickie, who stopped beside us with his arms crossed.

"Heard you scared off Mrs. Gordon today," Hannah said, the braids hanging on either side of her head reminding me of Medusa.

I glanced over the book on my lap. "I didn't mean to."

"Mom said you didn't hide though," Rickie added, his upper lip in a snarl that showed off his braces. "They're all going to know we're related to the monster now. How are we supposed to show our faces at school tomorrow?"

Hannah shook her head, her perfect cheeks bright red with anger. "Look, we know you don't *want* to look like that, but you don't seem to understand what it's like for us to be related to *you*. Every time a friend is over, I have to worry about you making too much noise in your room and them figuring out the monster lives here. No one else has a freak in their house. It's a lot to have to deal with."

"I didn't mean for her to see me. I'm sorry." I'd learned long ago that arguing prolonged these visits. The easiest way out was to apologize repeatedly until they tired of the game and left.

"I can't wait until you're old enough to get out. Mom says we have to keep you until you're eighteen because it's the law, but I don't see why." Hannah got off the bed, clearly bored already.

"Hannah, Rickie, come into the kitchen, please," Mom called from the other room. My siblings left with a last glare in my direction.

I went to the door, intending on shutting it. I'd learned long ago it was a blessing to not hear what was being said about me, but I couldn't stop myself this time. Instead of shutting the door all the way, I left a crack, putting my ear there and straining to hear them in the other room.

"There's nothing we can do about it, so let's not make the situation worse," my mother said. "I don't need her playing the victim again to your father. You know how he falls for that."

"She's such a whiner," Rickie said.

"I'll fix it," my mother said. "I'll talk to Mrs. Gordon tomorrow and tell her that Winnie is a foster child that we took in for a few weeks but that she's leaving soon because she doesn't fit in with us."

"You promise?" Hannah asked.

"I wouldn't say it if I didn't mean it, princess," Mom said. "Just don't get her all riled up. Hopefully she'll stay in her room for dinner and we can all forget about what happened."

I closed the door, holding the knob so it wouldn't click home too loudly.

I went and lay down on my bed, closing my eyes and daydreaming that I didn't belong to these people at all. That I belonged somewhere else. That there was a place for me somewhere far away from here. Anywhere but here.

CHAPTER TWO

Eight Years Later

I WRAPPED THE SCARF AROUND MY NECK, BUT THE SCARRING ON MY cheeks was still visible. No amount of makeup could hide them, and I wouldn't be wearing a scarf when I was working. Still, the sign had said baker wanted, and they weren't usually in the front of the house. They were tucked in the kitchen, out of sight. What I looked like shouldn't matter. Only what I could do—*hopefully*.

As I walked under the red and white awning, Betty's Muffins and More, it didn't have the same inviting feeling it usually held for me. Today it was more like entering an arena as the main combatant in a trial by fire. I'd come in here a few times before, and the owner had been one of the few people who greeted me normally. She hadn't stared with barely concealed horror or looked away so quickly as if trying to make me invisible.

I walked up to the counter, wondering if that would soon change as the owner discovered my purpose. It was one thing to be kind when it cost you nothing, but this was her business. Would she be so brave as to risk her customers seeing me?

Betty walked over. "Can I help you?" She greeted me with a smile. We'd see how long that lasted.

If this didn't work, there was word the delivery company down the street was desperate for people to load trucks in the warehouse. I might have to find out exactly how desperate they were.

"I saw you were looking for a baker?" I pointed toward the sign she'd posted by her door, in case she tried to deny it. If she didn't want me, fine, but she'd have to own it.

She wiped her hands on her apron as she looked me over. "I am, but..."

Here it came. She was trying to figure out a nice way to shut me down. I could feel the burn working its way up my cheeks, adding a great background to the scars to show them off in all their glory.

"How old are you? You seem to be a bit young. I'm looking for someone with experience."

It was probably a lie, the only thing her brain could come up with. Still, I'd play it out. Nothing to be lost now.

"I'm eighteen. I might be young, but I've been baking for years. I don't have a resumé, but I can bake something for you if you'll give me the opportunity."

She leaned her arms on the counter, clearly giving it some thought. Maybe it was just my age that worried her.

"I can make you an amazing pumpkin muffin with a cream cheese center. People go wild over them." Or at least that was what I'd heard.

Her brows drew together. "Anything similar to Madeline's Bakery across town?"

Exactly the same as Madeline's, but I wasn't allowed to say that because Madeline and my mother had some hush-hush deal going on. Until I could get out of my mother's house, I had to toe the line. But that didn't mean I'd use that line to hang an opportunity for myself.

"Maybe," I answered.

"Very interesting." She hummed. "She's been saying she makes those muffins, but nothing else in her bakery comes close to those." She made the face of someone who'd sniffed out a lie but couldn't prove it. "If you can make something like that, we'll talk about wages."

"Give me an hour in your kitchen and I'll show you what I can do." My entire body was buzzing with the real chance of being a paid baker, getting out of my house and out from under my mother's control.

Betty tilted her head, signaling for me to follow her into the back.

It was a small kitchen, but it was perfect, just as charming as the front of house. The harshness of the steel tables was broken up with twirled white and red iron chairs, with gingham-covered seats. The counters were lined with containers filled with nuts, chips, and every sugary wonder in between.

"See you in an hour." She handed me an apron and left.

It felt as if someone had dangled the keys to heaven in front of me. I couldn't waste a minute or I'd get booted back into my life of purgatory.

Flour was flying as I measured, mixed, stirred, and whipped my heart out, keeping an eye on the clock the entire time.

Betty took pity on me, or perhaps got hung up with customers, because she gave me an extra ten minutes before she walked back into the kitchen. I was finishing up the last filling as she did.

She walked over, taking a long inhale as she looked over the muffins. "They smell amazing. I'll give you that."

I handed her one, hoping she didn't see the tremor in my hand, knowing there was a tad too much salt and the cream cheese had been a little lumpier than it should've been.

She took a bite, and her face contorted. My stomach twisted.

"Oh, my..." She took another bite. "This is utterly amazing. You can make other stuff, right?"

"Many things. Baking is my passion." I'd let my mother pretend that the pumpkin muffins were hers, but I'd sabotaged every other item she'd tried to sell. I could justify letting her earn money off my talents while she paid for the roof over my head, but I wouldn't be that woman's slave.

"You're hired. When can you start?" Betty continued to eat while she waited for me to answer.

Something that had been dead and buried inside me seemed to warm in my chest. A glimmer of a feeling that maybe life would be getting better soon. That maybe life could be more than the dread of waking every day to be berated and criticized. That things could get better.

Hope.

It had been so long since I'd felt the feeling that I'd nearly forgotten what it felt like at all.

"Well?" Betty asked, already working on a second muffin.

"As soon as possible?"

"Great."

Did I go for it? Did I dare? "Uh, I noticed there was another sign…" I pointed in the direction of the front of the building. "It was next to the one about the baker position, and…" *Am I crazy?* I should take what I could get.

But after I started baking here, I'd surely be homeless.

"The apartment for rent upstairs?" Betty asked, filling in the blanks with a wide-eyed look, as if she couldn't fathom the reason for my hesitation.

I nodded, still struggling, utterly terrified that I'd blow the one huge accomplishment I'd had today by asking for too much. Baking was one thing—I'd bring value to her business—but would she want someone like me constantly coming and going out of her building? Would it be too much to stomach having me here day and night?

"You want to make it part of the job terms? Sounds great to me if that's what you're trying to ask." She kept eating, completely unfazed.

I nodded, speechless at how easily this was working out.

"If I had a tenant, I'd kick them out for you with baking skills like this. You can move in tomorrow if you want, as long as you start baking sooner rather than later." She walked to a desk along the wall, retrieved a set of keys, and handed them to me. "We'll figure out a rent you can handle."

I wrapped my hand around the keys, trying to keep a wrap around my emotions at the same time, but not doing as well. I hadn't cried since I was ten years old, no matter what had gone wrong, but somehow this moment had undone me.

"You've had a rough time of it, huh?" Betty asked.

The softness in her tone was like turning the spigot on, making more tears fall.

"I'm sorry. I'm fine," I said, hoping she wouldn't push for more details. I tried to swipe away the evidence of my emotions. A couple of deep breaths and another swipe of my arm across my face and I'd pulled it back together a bit. "Do you mind if I bring stuff over tonight?"

"Not at all. Like I said, we'll work out the details."

"Thank you."

I walked from the bake shop with the keys making a permanent indent in my hand and my spirits in the clouds, not caring who saw me, who looked at my scars and who couldn't bear to. It didn't matter anymore. I'd found a way out of my mother's house, and nothing could ruin my mood today.

It took me a half an hour to walk home. I stopped in front of the small cottage we lived in, giving it one last look. From the cheery yellow door to the flowerpots and the happy little welcome flag, no one would look at this place and think it was a living nightmare.

It was quiet inside. My mother was out having her afternoon tea, and my siblings were still at school. My father had left so long ago that no one knew where he was anymore.

The duffel bag was waiting in my closet. It had been on sale at the secondhand store for two dollars. There weren't that many things to take, but I grabbed my pillow and blanket, along with the yoga mats I'd also found on sale. Until I could afford a bed, they'd soften the floor nicely. Truth be told, a bed of burning coals would be preferable to staying here another night.

My bag full of clothes and essentials, I walked out of my room for the last time, knowing I wouldn't miss it at all. In the kitchen, I left a final note.

I'm eighteen. Your hold on me is over. Have a nice life.
Winni

I didn't really care if she had a nice life. I didn't care what her life would be like going forward as long as it didn't include me. Today I turned eighteen, and it was the best day of my life because it would be the last day I'd have to see my family.

CHAPTER THREE

BETTY STOOD IN THE DOOR TO THE KITCHEN, WIPING HER HANDS ON her apron and then wringing them as she looked my way.

Her gaze darted toward the front of the bake shop before returning to me. I frosted another cupcake, waiting for whatever bad news she was about to deliver. You would think after working together for three years, she'd be better at spitting out bad news by now.

"Winni..."

"Yes?" I put the frosting bag down. The last cupcake looked like a five-year-old's craft project anyway.

She walked closer, strangling her apron the entire time. "I hate to do this to you, but can you watch the front?"

Yep, it was exactly what I feared.

The dreaded front. I wasn't front-of-house material and we both knew it, but Betty only asked me when she was really stuck. She didn't want me out there any more than I wanted to be there. My scars weren't exactly appetite-fueling.

"I wouldn't ask, except the school called and Maggie is sick and the babysitter can't go get her." She bit her lower lip.

I nodded and then cleared my throat, trying to kick-start my voice. "Of..." My voice cracked. I coughed, trying to get past the lump. "Of course. Should I..." I wiped my hands on the apron and then tugged at the cap I wore to keep my hair covered while working in the back.

"I mean, yeah, if you could," she said, looking me over.

We both knew there was a limit to how presentable I was going to get, but I nodded and headed into the bathroom to straighten my hair.

"Meet me in the front in a few minutes?"

"Sure."

I ran a brush through the thick golden locks, pulling it forward to hide some of the scars on the sides of my jaw.

It wasn't like I hadn't filled in before. There'd been a handful of occasions in the last few years where it had been unavoidable. That didn't mean I enjoyed it, or the stares.

I made my way up front and watched Betty's back as she departed, knowing there were four more hours until closing.

He walked in wearing jeans that would cost my entire salary for a month and a t-shirt that was snug enough to bunch at the indent between his shoulders and his biceps. His hair was tousled, dark, and shiny, and his eyes had that brightness of health you couldn't fake. He probably attended the college down the street and was one of the new batch of students.

The bright lights of this place showed his perfection off and made me want to slink back to any shadow I could find. But there was no one else here to help him. I was it.

I walked over to where he was approaching, steeling myself for his revulsion. Somehow it was worse when it came from someone who was this attractive, as if there was some weird equation where the difference in our appeals multiplied my humiliation disproportionately.

"Can I help you?" I let my gaze skim over him, unfocused the way so many did with me, so the horrified look wouldn't be as obvious.

"Can I have an espresso?" The tone was pleasant, almost friendly. He was one of those, the types that tried extra hard even as he was disgusted.

Turning quickly, I gave him my back as soon as possible. His stare didn't seem to leave me as I worked on his order.

I put the cup on the counter in front of him, keeping my eyes down. "It'll be five dollars."

He held out a twenty.

"You're very pretty," he said as I made his change.

I glanced up, not realizing someone else had entered.

We were still alone.

I put his money on the counter and met his gaze. "That's not funny."

Usually it was kids who'd give me a hard time. Adults knew better —mostly.

"It wasn't meant to be funny." He tilted his head slightly to the side, the corners of his mouth lifting in a hesitant smile. "I can see the scars, but that doesn't change the beauty."

My gaze dropped, my mouth dry as I stood speechless. No one ever spoke to me like that, not since my father left. He'd been the only one in my life to ever call me beautiful.

"Thank you," I said, darting a glance at him but having a hard time keeping eye contact.

"And it smells wonderful in here." His nostrils flared as he took a deep breath.

"Did you want something else? The lemon muffins just came out of the oven about half an hour ago." It was a good batch. I'd gotten that recipe down to a science.

"It's not the food. It's you. You smell *really* good."

I shrugged. "I do a lot of the baking. The smells cling to you after a bit."

"No, it's definitely you."

My gaze dropped again and I could feel my palms growing sweaty.

"Am I making you uneasy?" he asked, following me as I moved to grab the rag on the other side of the counter.

"No. I'm fine," I said, searching for busywork.

"I'm sorry if I'm freaking you out. My name is Kenny, and I'm really not a bad guy."

"I'm Winni." I tried to smile back but probably looked more like a scared cat hissing. This was exactly why I didn't like to work in front of house. It was always a disaster, and usually for much different reasons, but the final results would be the same.

I moved around behind the counter, continuing to tidy up.

He followed as I went. "Did you grow up around here? I'm not from around here myself."

I'd already guessed that by the slight accent that I couldn't quite place. "Yes, pretty close by."

He hummed, as if that didn't make sense to him. "I know someone that might be able to help with those if they bother you."

He reached out to me, toward my face. It fell short as I retreated, but he'd actually been about to touch my scars.

"I'm sure I can't afford whoever it is."

Betty paid me well, but this place was hardly bringing in the kind of money that could afford big salaries, the kind that would cover plastic surgery. I'd seen the mortgage statements when I helped her with billing. I also knew how much it would cost to fix my skin, and even then, it would never be perfect. That was what several doctors had said, backed up by my research online.

"It couldn't hurt talking to him." Kenny shrugged. "Not that I think you need to. It's just... I can see the way you try to hide your face."

I nodded, scrubbing the counter again. "I understand you're trying to help, but there's not that much that can be done."

"He does lots of pro bono work. Could I give him your information?"

"Sure. Fine," I said, just to shut down the conversation. "I've got to go clean out the refrigerators. Did you need anything else?"

The soft smile he'd had seemed to fade, as if my rejection had gotten to him.

"I'm sorry. I'm just very busy, and..." I ran my fingers over my scars. "I just... I don't like to talk about them that much."

He nodded, staring intently. "I'm sorry to bother you. It's only there's something about you."

I'd thought he'd been mocking me at first, and then, when he brought up his doctor, that maybe he was pitying me. Now I was beginning to think he was just plain crazy.

"I really need to get back to work."

"Sure," he said, and with a quick, forced smile, he took his coffee and left.

CHAPTER FOUR

I LOCKED UP THE BACK DOOR TO THE BAKERY AND THEN NEARLY JUMPED out of my skin. There was a man standing in the alley behind the bakery. Clean-cut, dressed in a business suit, he wasn't the type I'd mark as a threat if I saw him on the street. But he was lingering in the back alley, standing unnaturally still, and was staring at me.

"Can I help you?" I shifted the keys in my hand so they pointed outward, better to stab him if the need arose.

There were three options: scream, run, or do nothing. The traffic on the main drag was loud enough it would drown out a scream. He looked more athletic than me if I opted for running, plus he was strategically blocking the exit, which left me with the third option of doing nothing.

He took a step forward, and I retreated one. He didn't take another. That was something.

"Kenny told me that you might be in need of my help."

His words were almost too well pronounced, as if this weren't his native language. Perhaps wherever he came from, this behavior was normal.

"I'm sorry if I didn't go in the front entrance," he continued, "but Kenny had remarked that you might be a bit hesitant to discuss this in public, and your bakery seemed quite busy."

The place *was* packed. Betty was still helping people in the front. Maybe it wasn't *that* unusual to have sought me out here.

My muscles loosened a tiny bit. I still didn't like something about this guy, or the way he'd waited for me in the alley, but my instincts on Kenny had been solid. He was a good guy, and if this was a friend of his, he couldn't be *that* bad. Problem was, I still couldn't pay for him.

"Thanks for coming by, but I can't afford a plastic surgeon." I would've walked away from him, but he was blocking my way.

"I'm not asking you to pay."

Free? He'd really help me for nothing? The quick spark soon died. What was the point?

"I've talked to doctors before. They say it's hard to fix scarring. That there's not much they can do with damage of this extent."

"You haven't talked to me. I'm using techniques most haven't heard of before. May I look, since I've already come?"

I froze. I didn't like people looking at my scars, let alone getting up close and examining them. But he *had* come all this way for Kenny. Plus, he didn't smell like someone who was looking to harm me. Awkwardness had me nodding even as I was still undecided.

He walked closer, putting his fingers under my chin and lifting my face upward. He stared at my face without the slightest recoil. "They're unusual scars. How did they happen?"

"I was attacked by an animal when I was a baby." I repeated what I'd been told by my parents. I'd been too young to remember, and they were short on details when asked.

He hummed, as if he wasn't quite sure he believed me.

"I believe I can help you, if you are interested," he said.

"Why would you do this for free? You don't even know me."

"I like to help people." He dug into his pocket, taking a card out of a sterling-silver case. There was only one name on it, *Merlin*. With a number on the back.

"I hope I hear from you," he said, and then walked away.

Merlin's card lay on my table. I'd stared at it half the night then tossed and turned the rest of the night thinking about it. Now, as I drank coffee, I was staring at it again.

What if he was right? What would it be like to walk down the street, head held high, the noon sun on my face? Instead of slinking around, waiting for sunset so I could hide in the shadows, or waiting for the first chill in the air so I could wrap a scarf halfway up my face.

Could I really let this chance pass? Today was my day off from the bakery. My next day off wouldn't be for another week, and it was a hard call to make when others might hear, even if it was Betty. If I waited too long, he might change his mind. I dialed his number before I talked myself out of it again.

"Hello," Merlin answered, as if he knew who was calling. He didn't have my number, so of course he couldn't.

"It's Winni, from the bakery?"

"Yes?" he asked.

Had he already forgotten me? No one ever forgot me, and not for a good reason. Had he changed his mind?

"I just wanted to..." To what? Beg for help? Yeah, that pretty much summed it up. I'd been all tough last night, and now I was about to grovel and it probably wouldn't matter. My finger hovered over the end button.

"Are you interested in my help?"

"Yes. If you're still willing." I began to tremble.

"I am. I have an opening this afternoon. Take down this address."

My hand was shaking, but I scribbled down enough of the address to get there—not that I'd forget.

"See you soon," he said, and then hung up before I could ask anything else.

The place wasn't a doctor's office but a town house in the part of town that was so nice that I didn't like walking the streets with my bedraggled sneakers and hand-me-down clothes. Merlin must be an exceptional doctor to live here. He probably didn't want people to see someone who looked like me walking into his office.

The door opened, and he waved me in before I had a chance to ring the bell.

"The treatment you need is more experimental in nature and not something I do in the office," he said as I followed him into his home. "Please, take a seat," he said, waving to his living room area. The interior was just as impressive as the facade.

I bypassed the couch and took the chair. This way I wouldn't have to share my seat as I got another round of cold feet, this time bad enough to cause frostbite.

"You said this was experimental? What is it that you do?"

Was my life so bad that I was willing to take a chance with this person? His answer made all the difference.

"You see, whatever it was that attacked you, it changed you. It kept you from healing. That's why your scars look the way they do." He walked over to a bag sitting on the sofa table and drew out a large syringe before turning back to me.

"What is that?" I asked, getting to my feet.

"This is what's going to fix you." His matter-of-fact reply made it plain he thought the answer was obvious.

"You mean you're not going to do a skin graft or some sort of new laser treatment thing?"

"If I'm correct, I won't need to."

"You know, this is a big decision. I should probably think it over a bit." I edged toward the door as naturally as I could, waiting to see if he'd grab me.

"I won't stop you if you want to leave. I'm not going to force anything on you." He walked to the couch and took a seat.

I breathed deeply again, knowing how ridiculous everyone said it was to trust my scent the way I did. But it had never steered me wrong, and Merlin didn't smell like someone trying to harm me.

If I walked out on him now, without letting him do this, would he be willing to help me in the future? I wasn't sure about that.

"You really think you can fix me with that?" I nodded at the huge syringe.

"Yes. Just know one thing before you walk out that door: no one else can do what I'm going to do for you. If you leave here, you will be forever scarred. And worse, you'll let these scars dictate the way you live until you die having not lived at all. Or are the scars your excuse to not live? If that's what's happening, I understand wanting to keep them. You can leave here with my blessing. I'll never bother you again."

He had the smell of confidence. Whether or not he was crazy wrong, he believed what he was saying.

But he was wrong about wanting an excuse. What I wanted was a full life—and maybe to get that, I'd have to take a risk.

I walked back and sat in the chair, shoving my sleeve up. "Will this be painful?" It was the only question I wasn't afraid to ask. The answer to anything else might make me run out here screaming.

"You might feel ill for a while after, or you might not. I'm not completely sure myself. You will feel tired."

He didn't bother cleaning the injection spot, immediately inserting the huge needle and emptying its contents into me.

He pulled the needle out, and the tiredness immediately hit. I leaned back in the chair, groggy.

"I don't feel right," I said.

"You might want to lie down while I explain everything."

I wasn't sure I could stay upright for much longer. He grabbed my arms, helping me move to the couch, where I felt like a dead weight dropping.

His fingers grazed my cheek. "How old were you when you were attacked?"

"An infant." My voice sounded as weak as the rest of me felt.

"And what type of animal did this to you?"

"I don't know." I swallowed, wishing I had more answers.

He hummed the same way he had last night. "I'm going to explain a few things that you need to know. Your blood is corrupted. It was changed when you were attacked. What happened to you can't be found in any medical journal.

"The marks on you, they weren't made by claws on an animal. They were made by the fangs of a vampire—I suspect several vampires—as they bit your flesh."

"Vampires?" My head was spinning and my legs were weak. I wasn't capable of running because I'd let a lunatic inject me with something.

"You don't believe me, but why would you?" He smiled like a crazy man looking at the poor, sane soul who didn't see the truth.

Don't insult him. He's not stable.

"Why would they do that?" I asked, trying to play into what he was saying, as if I didn't think he was insane. Hopefully the feeling would wear off and then I could get out of here and get the hell away from him.

"Because of what you were and will be again. What happened changed you, but I believe I just undid that."

"And what exactly am I?" I asked, as if his double talk made perfect sense.

"You were Lycan before the attack. A werewolf? Shifter? I believe you were stolen as a baby and then someone paid those people to raise you."

"Oh." I nodded, as if this wasn't the craziest thing I'd ever heard.

"Most people don't know this, but there's a war about to happen."

And it kept getting crazier. "Between who?"

"Between humans and the race you are reverting to. You have no idea how lucky you are that I found you. What I did is going to make things right for you. You'll be able to go to your kind." He patted my hand as he spoke.

Those were the last words I heard before I completely blacked out.

CHAPTER FIVE

MERLIN WAS CARRYING ME OUTSIDE AND THE SUN WAS RISING, NOT setting like it should've been. I was too weak to move, and my body felt like it was a volcano about to erupt.

"What did you do to me?" If this was an improvement, I'd hate to see how I felt if he was trying to hurt me.

"I made you better. I fixed things you didn't even know were wrong," he said, sounding annoyed I'd questioned him.

We were approaching a car, and sick or not, I was going to put up one hell of a fight if he tried to put me in that trunk.

He placed me in the passenger side instead and shut the door. I fell asleep again before he got in the car.

When I woke, the sun was setting and I was beginning to feel like I was going to be okay—if I made it out of this car alive, anyway. I looked around and didn't recognize anything I saw.

"Where are we going? I've got people waiting for me. I was supposed to be at the bakery. My boss is going to call the police if I'm missing." Too bad I didn't tell her where I'd gone.

Merlin didn't seem concerned. "There are people waiting for you where we're going as well. And you can't go back to the bakery without raising suspicions. You'll need to call and quit." He reached over, dropping my visor with the mirror. "Look for yourself."

I didn't look immediately, afraid of what I'd see. Had he made me worse somehow?

"You've made it this far. Don't be a coward now," he said.

I resented his words, even if they were true. I'd come this far. I'd deal with whatever the fallout was, and something was happening. I could feel it throughout my body, including a burning where all my scarring was.

I glanced into the mirror and stared, speechless at what was there. The scars were flattening out and my skin seemed to be knitting itself back together.

I leaned closer, trying to get a better look. "What's happening? Who are you? You're not a doctor, or not any kind I've ever seen."

"I'm the one who fixed you." He pulled the car over in front of a ranch house with nothing else around it. "This is where we part ways."

His previous words suddenly had more weight. "This war you say is coming—whose side are you on?"

"I pick the side that aligns with my interests. Enjoy your new life while you can. It's not going to be peaceful for long."

I should've been concerned about who was waiting in that house, how I'd get home, or what I would do next, but after the risk I'd just taken and the shock of what was happening, nothing seemed as bad.

I got out of the car and shut the door. Merlin pulled away fast enough to kick up dust.

I breathed in the air, smelling all the scents in the area, and recognized one immediately. Before I could second-guess myself, Kenny stepped out onto the porch and walked over to me.

"Hey," he said.

"Hey." I stayed in place, my head held high, the last of the sun catching my new face.

"You look like you had a rough day."

I nodded, grateful beyond words that it was him. Wrong or right, from the moment I met him, I'd felt something good inside him.

"How much did he tell you?" Kenny asked.

"Only the unbelievable parts about werewolves and war. He left the sane and boring bits out."

Kenny laughed. "Yeah, well, I'm sorry I didn't fill you in on those parts earlier, but it's kind of something you have to experience for yourself."

"So it's all true?" A tingle spread down my spine, as if I were seeing reality for the first time.

"Oh yes. There's a lot to learn, but I'll be here to help."

His hand grazed mine, the invitation there, letting me choose.

I took his hand in mine. "Why did you help me?"

"Because I liked you from the first moment I spoke to you. There's something incredibly beautiful about you, Winni, and it has nothing to do with your face or your hair or your skin. It's in here," he said, laying his fingers over my chest. "There's a lot of people who really want to meet you. Are you ready?"

"Yeah, I think so."

"You might be frightened at first, but that's okay. Merlin said it might help finish your transition back to what you really are. Just know I'm here and I won't let anything hurt you."

"Okay."

"Come out," he yelled toward the house.

A monster stepped out onto the porch, huge and muscled with fangs and glowing eyes. And then another. And another, until I lost count as they all stood staring at me, approaching and then circling us.

Kenny was wrong: I wasn't frightened. I was terrified. My skin began to itch all over, and then my clothes shredded off me as a growl ripped through the air. I realized it had come from my chest. I looked down, seeing the muscled form of the creature I'd become.

I looked at Kenny.

He smiled, and then, in a flash, shifted into a similar creature. I inhaled deeply, smelling the love and caring surrounding me.

I was home. Finally, after all these years, I was truly home.

~END ~

AUTHOR'S NOTE

I hope you enjoyed my retelling of The Ugly Duckling. As a lover of underdog stories, it's always been one of my favorites.

ABOUT THE AUTHOR

If you would like to check out my books, including novels set in the same world as The Ugly Daughter, you can find my Torn Worlds books and complete catalogue at www.donnaaugustine.com.

SPIDER TO THE FLY

KATE DANLEY

THE MUSIC HALL SWAYED WITH THE AMPLE-BOSOMED WOMAN'S raucous tune. The flickering candles in the footlights cast her painted face in elongated shadows. Her ruby stained lips growled her guttural song. Though billed as The Blushing Rose, those petals had been plucked long ago and now the audience reveled in her thorns.

The air was thick and yellow with the haze of cigar smoke. Corks popped and the champagne freely flowed. The room rocked with laughter as Blushing Rose insulted the tuxedoed men at their tables and cheered on the goodtime girls who joined them in their booths.

But in this merry party, a slender woman with long, brown, sausage-curls sped like a mouse along the wall to the exit. The chipped plaster faces of gilded cherubs and leering fauns stared down at her, condemning her for her unwillingness to join in the fun.

Her chest heaved beneath the purple ruffles adorning her tight green bodice. She pulled aside her heavy taffeta skirts to dodge the hands that grasped at her and tried to draw her back.

However, a little mouse trying to hide always catches the eye of the hungry.

"Running away, my lovely?" Blushing Rose cackled at her. She ran her hands along her corseted red waist, down her hips that did not need the petticoats to widen her skirts, and lifted her hem to show off her leg. "I'll see you soon enough. Be holding the headlining spot for you!"

As the audience roared, the young woman stepped swiftly to the cloakroom. A painted lady in the closet leaned upon the counter to learn what sort of assistance she could provide.

"My cape," the woman in purple and green murmured, taking her ticket out of her beaded satchel and, with trembling fingers, handed it to the girl.

"Pardon, miss," a low voice rumbled behind her. "May I be of assistance?"

She turned.

His tall form and broad shoulders loomed over her. He smelled of sandalwood and peppermint. His long black hair swept down across his cheek, covering half his face.

Her liquid brown eyes stared up at him, both begging for help and shying away.

He took the velvet cape from the girl in the closet, then draped it as if he was placing angel's wings upon the woman.

"Please excuse me for being so forward," he said. His spindly fingers lingered upon her shoulders, smoothing the silvery cloth. "You seem in distress."

"Yes…" she replied, flustered, clutching her cape tightly and tying it closed. "Yes, I am afraid I… it has been quite trying. I must go home. This place… if I am seen—" She cut off her own words, unable to go on.

He arched a thick eyebrow. "A gentleman would not allow you to walk home in such a state. Allow me to accompany you, my good and virtuous woman. It is no mystery why your sensibilities were offended here! A theatre such as this is not a place for a refined lady such as you."

She looked at him, at the gentle curve of his thin lips, and flushed.

"I was told it was an opera," she confessed, her eyes darting to the Blushing Rose as she shimmied her aging breasts to get the warble in her low notes.

"Ah! A mistake I am sure you found quite shocking. You inno-
cently came to hear the nightingale sing, but found yourself among
the howling wolves."

"He must have thought it was quite the jape," she glowered,
straightening her lacy gloves.

"Or perhaps thought to injure your reputation." He brushed back
a curl from her slender neck, lingering where the blue blood beat
beneath her porcelain skin. "Let me be your protector. Such a pretty
little thing should not walk unaccompanied through these streets on
a night like this."

His eyes were dark and piercing. His bones so sharp and his face
so pale. He took his silk top hat and cane from the girl in the closet,
then slid his long fingers into his calfskin gloves.

Holding out his hand to her, standing too close, he said in a voice
like a scalpel, "Allow me to accompany you home."

As she rested her fingers upon his palm, a strangled affirmation
made a sound within her throat.

He tilted down the brim of his tall hat upon his head and
extended his wooden cane with its silver tip and handle shaped like a
spider.

With the grace of a dancer leading her through a waltz, he slid
them through the press of bodies in the lobby until they arrived
outside the entrance.

The cool night air was a sobering balm to the dizzying chaos
inside.

But the busy street was now abandoned, silent, and cruel.

At once, he shook his head as if he could not believe his absent-
mindedness. "I am afraid my carriage is at my townhome around the
corner!" he confessed as if suddenly remembering. "However, the
night is so lovely and a stroll would not be amiss."

She glanced over her shoulder at the warm masses laughing and
joking in the music hall, and then at the dark and quiet road he was
steering her down. A tendril of white mist snaked down the cobblestones. The golden light of the party that once seemed too oppres-

sive now called like a siren to come back in. It promised the safety of a clutch of chicks beneath their mother-hen.

"I apologize, sir, but I do not even know your name," she stammered, trying to pull away.

Her large eyes stared up at him, piercing his heart with their innocent purity.

He smiled again as he continued on, holding her hand, now tightly in his palm. "Mr. Araignée, but you must call me Salem."

"Thank you, Mr. Araignée, but—"

He cut her off with the lift of a finger. "Salem. I insist. For we are now compatriots, having survived the infamous battlefield of the Blushing Rose's theatre unscathed."

"Salem," she replied, tasting his name in her mouth. Once again, she attempted to draw back. "While I am quite grateful, I should get a hansom cab to take me home. This is quite the inconvenience for you and I would not wish to impose."

But he insisted. "I will not hear of it!" he replied with horror. "Imposition! Allowing a lovely woman with all your charms to go alone into the foggy dark? What sort of citizen do you take me to be to abandon you to the criminal element that haunts the night?" He tucked her hand into the crook of his arm and held her firmly where he decided she belonged. "You are safe, enchanting lady. Know I am a gentleman."

"Thank you, but—"

"Such a generous, sensible woman to worry about troubling me. Not another word," he said, patting her lacy glove and giving her a reassuring smile. "For it is my pleasure to be of service. Especially after a cad sought to damage you for a laugh..." He tsked his tongue against his teeth. "No further damage to your reputation shall I allow to happen to you out alone in this dreadful night. Come! My own carriage is just around the corner. Accompany me and I will take good care of you." His cane continued to strike the walk as the soles of his hard shoes slapped the dirt and stone. He raised an amused brow as he leaned once more toward her. "I have introduced myself, but I do not yet know your name..."

"Miss Volar," she whispered, her throat very dry as they walked down the dark, lonely street. "Miss Lyra Volar."

"May I call you Lyra?"

"I would prefer not."

"Such a woman of manners and delicate formalities you are, Miss Lyra. Your restraint is most bewitching and I can see how you would ensnare a man without knowing the power you hold." Before she could reply, he deftly pointed at one of the buildings. "Now, shall I tell you about the history of this street? I can tell you are an intelligent woman of great learning and curiosity. Now, do not with modesty protest! I can tell. You are a bright candle in a world of faded lights, and I find myself drawn to your sparkling wit like a moth to a flame. Allow me, a dullard as I am, to share the little I know, and you shall correct me if I'm wrong..."

His silver-tipped cane thumped with every step.

Thump... thump thump... Thump... thump thump...

His silky stream of words were a river that did not allow her room to gasp and fight against the current. Every sentence was littered with compliments like breadcrumbs before a dim pigeon, luring her closer just as she wanted to fly.

At last, he drew them to a halt before a dark brownstone. Six marble steps led up to an entrance shrouded beneath the bare branches of a tree in winter slumber. Brass knockers shaped like goddesses forced to hold heavy rings adorned the shiny lacquered doors. The curtains were drawn and only the palest flicker of subdued gaslight came from within.

"Now, will you come into my parlor while I ring my driver?" Salem asked.

Lyra's hand fluttered at her throat like the delicate wings of a dragonfly. "Really, Mr. Araignée, I am sure you should prefer that I wait outside."

A bat dislodged itself from the eaves and with high pitched cries, it spread its leathery wings.

Salem climbed onto the first smooth step and reached out his hand. "'Tis the prettiest little parlor that ever you did spy."

"Please, dear sir..."

With a gentle touch, he placed his white-gloved palm beneath her lacy fingertips. "So cold is the night and the fog is coming in. This way into my parlor. Just up the stairs and inside."

"Please—"

"I have many lovely things I should like your opinion on while we wait. It is difficult, for a widower such as me, to know what holds value or beauty. I can tell by your taste and refinement that you have a keen eye," he enticed. "I could benefit from your womanly touch. It will only be a moment, a distraction, while my driver brings the carriage 'round."

She stared up the slippery steps at the black doors as a wind began to howl. "Sir, I fear if I enter, we shall not come down again."

"You are quite safe," he said, running his hand along the inside of her wrist, drawing her toward the maw of his lair. "A quiet place to sit and talk and recover from the music hall. My fire shall chase away the damp, moist air."

True, it was cold enough that her teeth chattered.

"Come in! Come in! Rest for a moment. I can see you yearn for warmth, and said warmth I can provide."

Lyra shivered once more as the cold bit and tugged at her bones.

"Accept my invitation," he pressed, drawing her upon the next crumbled step. He pressed his hand to his heart apologetically. "If I offend, know it is because you are a good woman of manners and know better the delicate formalities of social interactions than a grieving dullard such as me. I seek your gentle education. Please, grace me with your presence. Please, step inside with me."

And so, she did.

Because, indeed, she knew he was right in his perceptions of her. And she was sure he was right in his perceptions of himself, too.

The doors opened with a creak and Salem winced. "How embarrassing! In need of a little lubrication from disuse."

He bowed and Lyra stepped onto the black-and-white checkerboard flooring of the foyer. He followed and shut the door behind himself. As the room plunged into darkness, there was the sound of the key turning in the lock.

"Mr. Araignée!" she exclaimed with trepidation.

"One moment! Hold this, please, while I fumble for the light..."

She felt his hard wooden cane forced into her hand, then felt his warmth so close to her as he shuffled by. At last, he turned the key to the brass sconce, and bathed the room in flickering gaslight to reveal a hall papered in scarlet red with black lacquer tables and onyx chandeliers.

But in the blink of an eye, he was behind her, his arms reaching across her shoulders.

"Let me take your cloak," he rumbled, his breath upon her neck.

"The cab, dear sir..." Lyra whispered back, gripping his cane with both hands. "I fear I must go home."

But his words were a thrumming hum inside her ear. Even as he murmured, "Of course... of course..." the ribbon round her throat was undone and the heavy velvet of her cape slid down until it draped upon his arm.

"Your driver?" she pressed once again.

A marble statue of Atalanta in flight stood by the door, and Salem hung Lyra's cape on her outstretched arm. Then he took his cane from her and placed it out of reach.

"Allow me a moment," he replied with a slow smile. His eyes never leaving hers until she was forced to cast hers down, he removed his kidskin gloves finger-by-finger, one-by-one. He placed them inside his upturned tall, silken hat and left them on the half-moon table.

His gloves now off, skin upon skin, he took her bare elbow and led her into the parlor. "Come in. I promised you warmth and rest and relief from the damp."

She stepped into the room with its dead tiger upon the floor. Though red velvet cushions on the sofa called for her to sit, she stood, ready to take wing, while Salem strode to the fireplace and stoked the sleepy embers.

But while he worked so focused and diligently, the wariness

faded and her eyes drifted around the room. Indeed, it was a pretty room, though too strong in its masculinity.

She fingered a carved chess set, paused midgame. She stared at the oil paintings of Roman decadence. At last, the flames sprang to life, lifting the room from the shadows and gloom into warmth and merriment.

"Forgive me," said Salem, with a polite cough. "A little ash in my throat. Perhaps a drink to chase it away before I ring my driver."

He strolled to a mahogany sideboard and his fingers touched each of the crystal decanter lids, as if he could taste the rich spirits through the cold, cut glass.

"I do not drink hard alcohol," she stated, though there was a curious longing to her voice.

Salem caught that wavering note. "Of course. What sort of host would I be if I did not offer you something more suitable to your refined palate." He lifted a claret jug and inhaled the odors greedily. "Well, look what my butler forgot to put away. I am sure you will find this vintage most suitable."

"Really, sir–"

"Just a taste. You should." He poured the red wine into two glasses, then held one up to the light and gave it an appraising swirl. "The legs on this are fine."

He swaggered slowly across the room to her, a glass in each hand. He placed one in hers.

She protested, trying to return the goblet. "You do not want me to drink this."

"And why is that?" he replied, raising his cup slowly.

"Perhaps I shall grow sleepy and nod off before your driver arrives."

"Oh, my dear Lyra! Enchanting creature!" he said, taking one step closer until her vision was filled with him. "You're witty and you're wise. Such a jest to say you would fall asleep from one sip! Though fear not if you decide to extend your stay."

"But your staff… your friends… what might they say?"

"No one shall trouble us here. I assure you, we are quite alone." He placed his finger beneath her cup and gently suggested she should lift it to her lips.

"Dear sir," she said, taking a drink. "You do make me blush."

The cloying grapes held a strange bouquet inside her mouth.

Brushing back a brown spiral curl that had spilled upon her bare clavicle, he said, "How handsome you are..."

Casting her eyes down, she lifted her glass much more easily to her lips this time. "Really, sir."

"You do not believe me?" He pointed at his bookshelf, at a round frame beside a small statue of Aphrodite. "I have a little looking-glass. If you'll step over, dear, you shall behold yourself and see the enchantress who is captivating me."

"I thank you, gentle sir," she said, suddenly feeling as if the floor had lurched, "for the compliments you're pleased to say. But if you will call your driver, I'll call another day."

She quickly finished her wine so that, politely, she might leave and placed the empty cup upon the mantle.

But he set his untouched drink on the chessboard. "Come hither, Lyra, my pretty butterfly. Your eyes are like the diamond bright."

But her head now swum and she clung to the cold stone of the fireplace so that she did not slip into the sweet, sleepy call to curl upon the floor like a kitten full of milk.

"I fear I feel quite tired," she said, raising the back of one hand to her forehead. "Please, sir, if you would call for your carriage I shall go home to lie down."

"Nay, what sort of host would I be to let you stumble home when you look quite ill! Lean upon me," he replied, then pressing close to her side. He took her hand. "You should lie down, my dear. I'm sure you must be weary from such a trial to escape the cads and sinners at the music hall," he said, holding her dizzied form. "Will you rest upon my little bed? There are pretty curtains drawn around, the sheets are fine and thin; and if you'd like to rest awhile, I'll tuck you in."

He drew her out of the parlor and across the checkerboard marble in the hall. Toward the swirling mahogany staircase, he led her.

"A spider's web..." she noticed, pointing at the silvery threads decorating the brass and glass of the flickering gaslight as a cold draft blew through.

"A kindred soul, the arachnid," he shushed. "A hunter we all must admire. Now, come up... Come up... I see you grow weary. Come to my very own room where you can rest and recline..."

She gripped the banister and stared up at the shadowy second floor. "I fear if I should go up, we should never come down again!"

He placed her arm around his neck and his arm around her waist. "Such a dear sweet thing you are... my little butterfly..." he murmured into her hair. "Flit up to the heavens with me."

Slowly, step-by-step, he helped her ascend the winding stairs. There were oil portraits of pale ancient ancestors who leered at her, strange, from their gilt frames.

The gaslights in the hall did flicker as he drew her toward his room. Past locked doors and dusty wooden tables and gothic chairs and a covered mirror, they plodded. Musty and forgotten, not a soul was there to hear a cry to halt the barreling doom.

With one hand, he flicked open the door to his suite and now, walking backwards, tried to lead her inside.

"A sweet little room to safely rest your head," he tempted from the darkness.

But Lyra paused, just outside the threshold, to gather her strength and clear her head.

A four-poster mahogany bed sat in the center of one wall, with a strange, long trunk bound in brass at the foot. The floors were covered in thick Romanian rugs with folk art flowers created in the pile. The full moon filtered through a web of lead that wove its way through the stained glass windows. There were fearfully carved wardrobes and cupboards, so large they could have hid a man inside. On the far end was a marble fireplace. Its embers now cold, it cast the room into a chill. A delicate couch upholstered in silk sat before it, giving the perfect vantage point to meditate upon an oil painting above the mantle of Venus in repose, gazing over the shoulder of her unnatural and elongated back at those who came inside.

Lyra rested her hand upon the doorframe. "Please, my dear Mr. Araignée, is there another room?"

"Why, is this not enough room for two lost souls such as you and I?"

"But where shall you lie? I fear you shall not want me here after a turn on the couch…" She motioned to the thin cushions on the far end of the room, then smiled, barely able to keep open her eyes. "Call the hansom cab. You shall save me and yourself."

"Dear friend, what shall I do, to prove the warm affection I'm feeling for you?" he asked, amused. "'Tis a bed big enough for two."

He removed his tails and tie and draped them carelessly on a wooden rack. He placed his cufflinks in the cup of his wooden valet. *Tink. Tink.* Then draped himself upon the scarlet silk coverlet and stroked the space beside him. "Come hither, pretty Lyra. Come lie down and sleep at my side."

"My head swims too much to walk."

"Then fly across the room to me with pearl and silver wing. Ah! In the moonlight, your eyes are like the diamond bright. Come gaze into my eyes, and see mine are as dull as lead."

"You invite me in, dear sir?" she asked, attempting to raise her slumped body tall. "And ask me to gaze into your eyes?"

His vision roved her body, his hunger no longer concealed. "Indeed, I do." He undid the top button of his shirt. "Come lie upon my bed."

But as he presented himself, his body sprawled with invitation… all weariness and wariness was gone from Lyra.

"Look into *my* diamond eyes," Lyra said, her voice shifting from plaintive confusion to command. She drew herself up until she stood as tall as a mountain. "Gaze with fear and let the lead drop from your dull eyes and settle with heaviness in your soul!"

Strangely, he sat up, realizing this was not the frightened butterfly he thought was prey.

Her teeth began to grow into sharpened bone until they glinted beneath her lip.

Her fingers became knives.

The blush of her cheek faded to deathly blue.

And though her chest once more heaved beneath her green bodice, it was not her pretended fear, but the excitement of cornering her quarry that caused her cold heart to beat.

Stepping across his threshold, she licked her lips as his face blanched and laughed as he recoiled.

"No! No!" he cried, frantically looking for somewhere to run.

Even Venus seemed to approve.

"Thank you for inviting me in. I did want to see your parlor and your bed." Lyra removed each of her claws one-by-one from her gloves, that now poor and shredded lace. She clucked her tongue as her eyes glowed red and a smile crept across her face. "My, my, my... What a dismal den... As I warned you, and you would not heed, one of us shall never leave again."

In the shadows of the quiet music hall, as the Blushing Rose smiled on, Miss Lyra Volar returned, wiping the smudge of her blood-rouged lips. She gazed at the pale faces and vacant eyes of those tuxedoed men who now would never leave.

"I see the fly escaped the spider's lair," the Blushing Rose said with a wink of her eye.

"Of course. You saw and understood his dark heart true."

"I told you I would reserve her the headlining act. Come take center stage, my dear, and tell us all what you have learned."

As Lyra stepped into the center of the stage, she turned to the goodtime girls with their gentle fangs. The girls leaned forward, taffeta and tulle rustling, to hang upon her every word.

"Now listen close, my cold and silent children," she said, "and learn the moral of this happy tale. The world may be filled with spiders and their lies... but they make a most delicious meal."

~END ~

AUTHOR'S NOTE

I've never liked vampires.

You wouldn't know it if you look at the body of my work, but seriously. They've terrified me since I was a kid.

I was probably four- or five-years old and a friend decided we were watching this funny show with a guy in a top hat named Svengoolie, and he was presenting Bela Lugosi's *Dracula*. She said I could hide my eyes beneath a crocheted afghan if I got scared. The thing is, she didn't tell me I should close my eyes, too, so I watched the whole thing through the holes of the blanket. Vampires became the monsters that lived under my bed and terrorized my nightmares. It wasn't until the *Buffy* movie that I realized humor could slay this beast.

However, when the theme for this anthology was announced, I was feeling like I would take a pass. I mean, the only thing worse than vampires were werewolves, and I got suckered into writing about *that* bad dream in a different group anthology. (Yes. My entire *Twilight Shifters* trilogy is because of a nightmare I once had. But that's a different story...)

But then this story came to me and, well, I've long since given up trying to tell the muse my thoughts on her ideas.

Have I also mentioned how much I hate spiders?

My muse has a wicked sense of humor…

The thing about fairytales, though, is that they were told to teach people how to survive. And through fairytales and fantasy and, yes, even horror, we can defang our monsters, both imaginary and real. And in doing so, we can create a different story.

So, my wish for you after you have read *The Spider and the Fly* is that if there are folks in your life threatening to capture you in their web and drain your spark, do not fear to grow your own fangs and eat them for lunch.

ABOUT THE AUTHOR

Kate Danley spent five weeks on the USA TODAY bestseller list and was honored with the Garcia Award for Best Fiction Book of the Year (*The Woodcutter*, 47North), McDougall Previews Award for Best Fantasy Book of the Year (*Queen Mab*), and her *Maggie MacKay: Magical Tracker* series is optioned for television. As a playwright, her 1930s screwball comedy, *Building Madness*, won the Panowski Play-writing Award; *Power* won the Renegade Theatre Festival; and *Kings of the World* was voted an audience favorite in the 10x10x10 Festival.

She graduated from Towson University and is a Maryland Distin-guished Scholar in the Arts. She performed her original stand-up at such clubs as The Comedy Store and The Icehouse, and wrote sketch for a weekly show in Hollywood at The Acme Comedy Theater. She currently sits on the national council for the Dramatists Guild repre-senting the states west of the Mississippi. She trained in on-camera puppetry with Michael Earl (Mr. Snuffleupagus) and lost on Holly-wood Squares. www.katedanley.com

PRINCESS OF SALT

ANTHEA SHARP

CHAPTER ONE

THE FIRST LIGHT OF DAWN LAY SOFT OVER THE HILLS OUTSIDE CASTLE Clare, but the forest shadows still held the cool breath of night. Brianne O'Leary made her careful way through the underbrush, her green woolen cloak wrapped tightly about her, the hem dark with dew. Declan waited for her in the clearing where the ancient oak tree grew, and her heart sped at the thought of him.

In the charcoal darkness before sunrise, she'd crept from her room in the bower, where she slept with her two older sisters, and slipped out of the castle. Past the slumbering guard at the gate - and wouldn't her father, the king, have stern words if he were to hear of that dereliction of duty - past the fields and farms, and finally into the sheltering woods. It was the only place she could meet with Declan, away from prying eyes and wagging tongues. For he was a miller's son, and she was a princess, and her father would never allow them to wed.

Indeed, the king was in the midst of arranging marriages for all three of his daughters. Advantageous matches with neighboring lords that would cement his power in the west. Brianne had told him she had no desire to marry Lord Inchiquin, who was nearly twice her age, but the king had only laughed and waved his hand.

"It's not for you to choose, daughter," he said.

"But I don't care for him. His breath smells of old cheese." Brianne prided herself on always telling the truth, though her older sisters had scolded her for it more often than not.

"Must you be so blunt?" Colleen had said, when Brianne told her that her new gown was unflattering.

"It's insulting," Eva had agreed. "Just because we ask for your opinion doesn't mean you have to answer so rudely."

"If you don't want to hear the truth, then don't ask," Brianne had said, a touch indignantly. "I won't be lying to spare your feelings."

Ever since their mother had died—although the king had assured his daughters the queen was going to recover from her illness—Brianne had no taste for sweet untruths. She far preferred the straightforward to the circuitous. Even if it angered her sisters.

"I'll forgive you," Colleen said, tossing her dark plait over her shoulder, "but only if you help make supper tonight."

Brianne lifted one eyebrow. It was true that she'd a Talent for cookery, and she enjoyed her time in the kitchen, but she disliked the extortion.

"I will, at that," she said. "Though not because you ask. Forgive me, or not, I don't care."

In fact, the hunters had brought in a brace of hares, and she had a rabbit stew recipe she was eager to try. The cook was happy for Brianne's help, and the warm kitchen of Castle Clare was where Brianne felt closest to the memory of her mother. The queen had taught her how to bake and blend, fillet and fry, season and salt. She'd had a rare magic that way, too.

Indeed, like their mother, each of the princesses had a touch of the old Gifts. Brianne's affinity for cooking went far beyond the usual, her dishes flavorful and unique even when she only had the most ordinary ingredients at hand.

Colleen had a way with metal, able to polish up silver with the simple swipe of a rag, or find any lost coins that had rolled away. Once a month she spent the day in the local smithy, where the blacksmiths swore they were able to work three times faster and turn out higher-quality work than without her presence.

Eva's water empathy was useful, as well. She was in demand as a dowser when the farmers wanted to dig a new well, and her bath water almost never went cold, no matter how long she chose to stay in the large tub they used for bathing.

The king was pleased that his daughters had such useful skills, although right after the queen's death, Brianne had been banished from the kitchen for over-salting the food with her tears.

Her grief had become more manageable over time. But the second anniversary of the queen's death was fast approaching, sending a shadow of memory over the inhabitants of the castle. Still, Brianne's blossoming relationship with Declan had reminded her that happiness existed in the world, too, hand-in-hand with sorrow.

She'd gone to the mill for a special sack of finely ground barley flour and ended up spending nearly an hour talking with the miller's handsome son. For nearly a year now, they'd snuck out to meet one another in the forest, though Declan's duties at the mill were taking up more and more of his time.

He was waiting for her beneath the oak, his brown hair the glossy color of ripe chestnuts, his hazel eyes like midsummer leaves, his smile warmer than the fire upon the great hearth of the castle. Brianne's heart gave a thump of joy at the sight of him.

"Declan," she called, and ran across the damp grasses to be folded into his embrace.

He held her close for a moment, their hearts beating in one rhythm, then brushed his lips over hers in a kiss that held a touch of melancholy.

"What is it?" She stepped back and searched his eyes.

"I am traveling to Dublin with my father," he said.

It was a journey of well over a week, and her joy faded. "Must you go?"

"Aye. The new burrstones have arrived from England, and he wants me to meet with the importer and stonemasons, so that I might deal properly with them in the future."

"It's a dangerous journey." Her fingers tightened on Declan's arm. "The brigands are bold upon the highway this year."

"My father is hiring two guardsmen. With them along, I've no doubt we'll arrive safely."

Brianne dredged up a smile. "Then I'm glad your father is taking precautions. But please take care. I couldn't bear to lose you."

"Don't worry, beloved." He brushed another kiss across her lips. "I'll return as soon as I may."

She nodded, her throat tight with tears. There was no stopping him. Even if they had been able to court openly, he still would have to go. And in truth, their meetings must remain secret until they convinced the village priest to marry them. Thus far, the priest had refused to do any such thing, for fear of angering the king and losing his position. Rightly so, of course, but the knowledge was bitter.

"Come home safe to me," she said to Declan. "I'll try to convince my father to change his mind during your absence. Perhaps when you return, he'll give us his blessing."

"Perhaps." Declan's expression was doubtful.

Brianne bit her tongue on the argument that they could run away together. They'd discussed it before, in a brief and shining burst of hope. But then Declan shook his head and reminded her that he couldn't abandon his family. He was the only son, and the business would fall upon his shoulders soon enough.

He was a steady, honest man who would never abandon his responsibilities. It was one of the things she loved about him, after all. He would never lie to her to spare her feelings.

She let out a low breath. Yet no matter how true and deep their love, it was entirely possible that they would not be able to marry, nor spend their lives together.

The knowledge twisted in her like a knife, but it was better than the slow poison of lies. So she held him close, and kissed him again, and they spoke of it no more.

Declan and his father departed for Dublin. His absence, along with the fast-approaching anniversary of her mother's death, turned Brianne's mood melancholy.

Well then, she told herself sternly, tired of her own moping about, *do something*.

There could be no changing the fact that the queen was gone. Brianne might be motherless, but that didn't mean she must drift aimlessly in the current of life. It was high time she speak with her father again about Lord Inchiquin—and her staunch refusal to marry the fellow.

The king had brushed her words away the last time. But if she made it clear how very *serious* she was in her opposition to the match, perhaps he'd relent.

And then she and Declan could be married.

Fortified with hope, Brianne went to her father's study the next morning. He and his seneschal were going over the farmers' tallies, but when Brianne knocked, the king dismissed his man and beckoned for her to enter.

"I brought you a bit of something to eat," she said, setting down the tray she'd carried up from the kitchen.

She'd baked a dozen buttery scones, filled with currants and honey to sweeten his mood, and brewed a nice strong tisane of herbs to go with them.

"Thank you, daughter," the king said, smiling as he lifted a scone from the plate. "I can see you've something you wish to discuss. Are you ready to take Lord Inchiquin's suit seriously?"

Not a good beginning. Brianne knotted her hands in her apron.

"I *do* want to speak with you regarding Lord Inchiquin..." She trailed off, waiting for her father to take a bite of the pastry.

To her relief, he did, nodding with satisfaction. "Delicious, as ever. Do go on."

"Well. I told you I wouldn't marry him."

"That you did." The king smiled indulgently and continued eating his scone.

"And I meant it." She straightened and met her father's gaze. "You've two other daughters to do your bidding, but I refuse."

The king's expression darkened with anger. Slowly, he set down the half-eaten scone.

"*All* of my daughters will do my bidding." His voice was hard. "Which includes marrying the lord I've selected for them. It's for your own good, as well as that of the kingdom."

"It's not!" she cried, her dreams withering like flowers in a sudden frost. "What if I love another?"

"Who?" The king's gaze bored into hers, wrath sparking in his eyes. "What lordling thinks to win your hand without my approval?"

"There is no lordling," she hurried to say, though her heart quailed. Despite her insistence on the truth, she hadn't enough courage to tell her father who it was she truly loved.

Such a confession could only place Declan and his entire family in danger. The king could turn them all out of their home, command the mill to be handed over to some other family, and chase them beyond the borders of Clare. All because the miller's son had the temerity to fall in love with a princess.

She couldn't bring such a fate upon them. Brianne swallowed the bitterness of her truth, and faced her father unflinchingly.

"But there might be, some day," she said. "And what then? I'll not be shackled to a man I cannot love, nor will I make a cuckold of him. Will you doom your daughter to such a miserable existence?"

"Enough!" The force of the king's voice shook the mug upon the tray, the untouched liquid trembling. "You are young, and know nothing of life. I'll hear no more of this. And you're banished to your room until tomorrow."

Brianne clenched her jaw and whirled for the door. Tears stinging her eyes, she stalked to the bower room in the turret.

Eva was there, braiding her long hair, so Brianne didn't even have the privacy to fling herself down upon her bed and give in to the storm of weeping roiling through her.

"What's the matter?" her sister asked, looking up from the dressing table they shared.

"Father's commanded me to stay up here until tomorrow."

"What did you do?" Eva turned fully around and studied Brianne closely. "Did you try and tell him you won't marry Lord Inchiquin again?"

Brianne picked up her pillow and clutched it to her chest. "I thought this time he'd listen."

"Oh, Bri." Eva shook her head. "He's too stubborn for argument. You'll have to bring him around more subtly."

"I baked scones."

"Even your marvelous cooking skills aren't enough to change someone's mind when they're set on a thing. You should have asked me and Colleen for help."

Brianne grimaced. Eva was right, she *should* have waited, should've enlisted her sisters' aid. But she'd been so sure, the hope in her heart so strong...

She let out a heavy sigh and sank down on her bed. "What do I do, now?"

"Be patient. We're all on edge these days. Give him until after the morrow."

Brianne nodded grimly. In hindsight, the day before the anniversary of the queen's death hadn't been the right time to try and sweeten her father. But she'd *so* wanted to give Declan good news when he returned.

Instead, she'd only hardened the barriers standing in their way.

"I'll spend all day tomorrow cooking," she said.

Maybe serving an elaborate feast would help make amends between herself and the king. At any rate, it would distract her from the current bog she was wading through.

Eva gave her a wry look. "Just don't cry in the food, all right? We want the meal to be edible."

Brianne wrinkled her nose at her sister, but she felt better. Eva was right; once they moved past the difficult day ahead, surely her father would listen to reason.

CHAPTER TWO

B RIANNE WOKE THE NEXT MORNING ALREADY THINKING OF WHAT SHE planned to make for dinner. She hurried down to the kitchens to consult with the cook, and they quickly set to work. The scullery maid started scrubbing up vegetables, while Brianne went through the spice chest and the cook fetched butter and cream from the cool-room.

The day flew by, the heat of the ovens and cooking fire baking all the misery out of Brianne's body until there was only the simple dance of chop and stir, sip and season.

Finally, the cook chased her from the kitchen, admonishing her to go put on a new gown before dinner—one not dusted with flour and spotted with oil.

As most of the cooking was done, Brianne obeyed. She chose a dark blue dress with a touch of embroidery on the bodice and sleeves. Somber, to honor their grief. But from the trunk at the end of her bed she pulled a red woolen shawl. It had belonged to her mother, and Brianne folded that brightness about her shoulders, a reminder that life went on. Her mother wouldn't want her family to be mired in sorrow forever.

The fire on the great hearth was lit and the castle's two tall golden candelabra shed light over the table as the family gathered for the meal.

The king took his usual place at the head of the table, where a cup of mead awaited. The candlelight sparked golden glints from the circlet about his brow, and picked out the new lines upon his weathered face. With a pang, Brianne realized her father was growing old. No wonder he wanted to secure good matches for his daughters, to make sure the castle passed to a man of high birth.

Although, as the youngest, it wasn't fair that Brianne was expected to marry a nobleman, too. But now was not the time to turn about in her own self-pity. Brianne shook her selfish thoughts away and smiled at her sisters; Colleen at her father's right hand, Eva beside her on the left.

"You're in a fine mood," Eva said. "I expect a delicious feast, judging from the light in your eyes."

"It will be, at that."

They began with a tureen of leek soup, followed by bread baked with the miller's best flour. The taste of it reminded Brianne of Declan, and she hoped he and his father had reached Dublin safely and concluded their business. Even now, they could be on the road home.

"This is wonderful," her father said, taking a bite of roasted pheasant stuffed with buttered turnips. "Did you add a new herb?"

"I did, thank you. There's a bit of tarragon in the sauce, along with sage and thyme."

"Perfectly seasoned." He brandished his fork in approval before proceeding to eat every last bite on his plate.

The servants kept his mead cup filled, and as the meal progressed his manner grew softer toward his daughters. Brianne credited her cooking, of course, but the constant flow of alcohol certainly didn't hurt. She was glad the anniversary was proving less painful than the previous year, when—despite her best efforts—they'd had a grim and woeful meal, and then all gone to bed early.

After the pheasant came braised rabbits served over fresh greens, and then a final subtlety to finish the meal with a bit of sweetness.

Brianne had whipped eggs into a meringue and fashioned a posy of edible flowers. She'd studded the bouquet with plums and gooseberries, then dusted it with a precious bit of nutmeg she'd been hoarding in the spice chest.

Replete, the family sat back in their chairs. The king smiled fondly at his daughters.

"Your mother would be so proud to see what fine young women you've grown into," he said. ""I do love you, children of my heart."

"We love you, too," Colleen said.

The king nodded, a teasing light in his eyes. "Ah, but how much, my eldest girl?"

He awaited her answer with a smile.

After a moment's thought, Colleen smiled back at him. "I love you as much as all the gold in the land."

"A fine answer." He nodded, clearly pleased. "And what of you, Eva?"

Eva pursed her lips, then gave her answer. "I love you as much as the oceans are wide."

"A vast amount, indeed!" He laughed and patted her arm. "Brianne, can you come up with anything better?"

For a fleeting moment, Brianne considered proclaiming some grandiose affection, like all the stars in the sky or blades of grass in the kingdom. But in truth those were foolish things, and she didn't truly *love* them. They weren't essential. Not the way family was.

She met her father's gaze. "I love you as much as salt."

"Salt?" His smile fell and his gray eyes grew cold. "Did I hear you aright, daughter? You love me as much as *salt*?"

"Yes." She swallowed back the sudden knowledge that she'd answered too honestly, too bluntly.

The king wanted lavish things, like gold and seas and stars. Salt was too small. Too common—even though its lack in the kitchen would be disastrous.

Eva turned to her, frowning. "That's a foolish answer. Perhaps you've a better reply to our father?"

Brianne scowled back. If her family couldn't see how important, how *vital*, her answer had been, it was no fault of her own.

"Salt is my answer," she said stubbornly. "And salt it will remain."

"Ungrateful girl!" The king stood, scraping his chair back. His cheeks were flushed with temper. "First you argue with me over marrying, and now to say such a thing in front of your sisters. I'd thought you cared a bit better for me, Brianne. Such a paltry answer insults me. Insults all of us, and particularly the memory of your mother."

"But father—"

"Silence!" There was a wild light in his eyes, brought forth by grief and anger. "If you persist in arguing with me then perhaps you should spend a fortnight sleeping the forest, until you come to your senses."

Her sisters exchanged worried glances, and Brianne tried once more to explain.

"I only meant—"

"There are no words you can say that will undo this. Go." He pointed to the door, his expression dark. "Gather up whatever supplies you can carry, and don't come back until you've an apology upon your lips and are ready to accept Lord Inchiquin as your husband."

Colleen inhaled and sent Brianne a beseeching look. Eva tried to catch her hand, but Brianne ignored her sisters. Very well. If this were the truth of her family, of her father, then she would accept it.

Lips pinched together, half in anger, half to hold back her tears, she stood. "I'll gladly go live in the woods for *years*, if it means I won't have to marry that doddering old lord. And if you're too foolish to understand how much I love you, then that's upon your head. Not mine."

Vision blurring, she whirled and stalked quickly to the door. She'd take what she needed to survive, and nothing more.

"Wait," Colleen cried, but the king's voice overrode hers.

"I meant what I said, daughter," he called after her. "No need to show your face until you've an apology in one hand and obedience in the other."

That will never happen, Brianne thought fiercely back at him. Her pride and anger kept her marching forward, unspeaking. She would take her refuge in the forest, even as frost turned the leaves brown and sharpened the night stars with ice.

But she would never tell a sweet lie to soothe her father's temper. No matter the cost.

CHAPTER THREE

BRIANNE'S FIRST FEW DAYS IN THE FOREST PASSED WELL ENOUGH. SHE constructed a rude shelter of boughs over a nest of rushes, and spent the nights there warm, wrapped in her woolen cloak with her mother's red shawl for a pillow.

Her camp was near a small stream, far enough from the water's edge to not disturb the creatures that drank from its clear current, but close enough that she could fetch water to boil and cook with. She had flint and tinder, a cooking pot, and the sharp dagger at her belt—enough items for a rudimentary kitchen. In addition to an extra set of clothing and her single blanket, she'd had the foresight to bring a length of wire to fashion snares with. She wouldn't go hungry.

Berries hung ripe on the bushes, and there were nuts to glean and cattail tubers to harvest. She found a small patch of wild onions, and managed to catch a hare in one of her snares. And, of course, she'd brought a jar of salt from the castle.

As she sprinkled it into her rabbit stew, her mouth twisted bitterly. Ah, if her father could only taste a meal made *without* salt, then surely he'd change his tune. But even though the cook was her ally and friend, not a one of the servants would allow her to sneak back into the castle to try to prove her point.

The king's word was law, after all.

By the end of the first week, the fall winds were beginning to blow, bringing storms across the land. Brianne's cookfire went out and she'd no dry kindling. She spent a miserable few days huddled in her dripping shelter, eating raw mushrooms and berries and wishing for the sun and Declan's return.

Not to mention the company of her sisters, her soft bed in the castle, the warmth of the fire upon the hearth...

Still, she'd no intention of groveling for the king's approval. And even less taste for the thought of wedding herself to Lord Inchiquin. Better a few uncomfortable weeks in the forest than a lifetime of unhappiness.

Declan would be home any day, surely. And now that the king had cast his youngest daughter out, the village priest must see reason. If all went well, she and Declan could be wed before the last leaves fell from the oaks.

She clung to that hope, even as the days passed. The air grew colder and the leaves abandoned the trees.

Declan, she whispered into the rising sun. *Where are you?*

The berries withered, the last nuts taken by squirrels, and the land settled in for winter. Brianne punched a new hole in her belt to cinch it tighter about her waist. And then another.

She waited beneath the ancient oak, and crept to the verge of the forest, keeping watch. A week passed, and then another, and still her true love did not come.

Finally, she knew she must go in search of him.

She combed the worst of the tangles from her hair, scrubbed herself in the stream, gasping with cold, and donned her spare gown. She'd been saving it for when Declan returned, and was dismayed at how loosely it hung from her shoulders.

At least it was clean, even if it no longer fit. Her blue dress was stained and torn, despite her best efforts. Living for weeks in the forest, it was impossible to avoid smears of berries and lichens, snags from thorns and brambles, mud ground into the skirt. Her cloak was not in much better condition, but it warded off the cold well enough, despite its stains and tatters.

Ready to face the world, she bundled her few possessions into the red shawl and headed for the village. She'd barely set foot past the first few cottages, when one of the baker's boys spotted her.

"Oi, beggar woman," he called. "You can have a bit of bread from my father, if you'll be on your way, after."

Brianne nodded, her stomach knotting at the thought of fresh-baked bread as she followed the lad to the baker's door. There was no point in trying to convince the boy of her true identity, but surely the baker would recognize her.

To her shock, he did not, only handed her the end of a loaf and told her to go.

"Wait," she said, tucking the bread away though her hands trembled with the desire to tear into it straightway, "I'm looking for Declan, the miller's son."

The baker frowned. "We all are, and for his father, too. The flour's not what it was, I'm sad to say, but we make the best of it."

Fear rippled through her. "What happened to them?"

"They went off to Dublin, nigh on two months ago, and no one has seen or heard from them since." He shook his head sadly. "Must have been brigands upon the road. His wife is carrying on as best she can, but when spring comes, she'll be selling the mill. Aye, but that's enough village gossip. You've your bread. Now be off."

Her heart as heavy as a stone, Brianne trudged past the village green to the crossroads.

She'd no money. No food but a few dried berries and mushrooms and the heel of a loaf of bread. But she had her wits, a sharp dagger, and a good woolen cloak. That would have to be enough.

She paused, glanced back at the silhouette of the castle in the far distance, then turned her feet toward Dublin. Though it might be a hopeless task, she would go in search of her true love.

CHAPTER FOUR

Brianne's boots sank into the mud of the road. The constant drizzle weighed down her woolen cloak until it felt as if it were made of iron, but she bowed her head and kept on. When she could no longer ignore the pangs of hunger in her stomach, she took shelter beneath a dripping holly tree and brought out her bread.

The crust was thick and hard to bite through, the texture of the bread heavy. Somehow, it managed to be both dry and soggy at the same time. She held the heel up and inspected it, realizing the flour was so unevenly ground as to have rendered the dough like paste in some places and like coarse sand in others.

The millstones clearly needed balancing. Where were Declan and his father?

I'll find you, she promised, sending her thoughts winging beneath the gray sky.

Meanwhile, she had an inedible piece of bread to make palatable. She cast about for two flat stones, then pulled out her bark-wrapped packet of dried berries. A few hardy stalks of wild anise grew beside the road, and she plucked a handful to add sweetness and flavor.

She crumbled the bread onto one of the flat stones and added the berries and anise, along with a bit of water from her waterskin.

Humming, for the act of making food always cheered her, no matter how simple the ingredients, she began grinding and smashing everything together.

As she worked, she kept her mind turned to happy things: the sun upon her face, the laughter of her sisters, Declan's kisses...

After a short time she had a purplish dough, infused with fortitude and hope. She formed it into three balls, then pressed each one flat into a cake. They'd be best fried over a fire, and second-best left to dry, but she was hungry and ate one of them right away.

It didn't taste terrible, although the consistency was a bit chewy. As she swallowed the last bite, she felt her mood lift. Surely this journey would end in success. She carefully tucked the remaining two cakes into the bark wrapper she'd used to store her berries, then set off once again.

The rain had stopped, and her steps were lighter along the road. She skirted the worst of the puddles and walked on, keeping herself occupied by recalling every detail of Declan's face. Memories of their time together accompanied her until dusk began to shadow the sky.

Belatedly, she looked about for a place to spend the night. She'd passed a few small villages and farmsteads, but there was nothing but open countryside around her now. With a sigh she resigned herself to a night spent wrapped in her soggy cloak beneath a gorse bush.

She was just about to turn off the roadway when she spotted two travelers coming toward her. *Brigands!* Her hand went to the knife at her belt, but her fear quickly faded as she saw that one of the men was limping badly, supported by his companion.

There was something familiar in the younger man's way of walking. Brianne's heart gave a huge thump, and then she picked up her skirts in both hands and began to run. She splashed recklessly through the puddles, and nearly lost her footing in a patch of mud, but the hope in her chest pushed her on.

"Declan," she gasped when she finally drew close enough to make out his features.

The tightness in her chest made it impossible for her to say more.

Their gazes met, and the love and relief in his eyes told her there were no words necessary.

At that moment, the old miller let out a cry and pitched forward. Declan barely caught him, and Brianne leapt forward to help keep the old man from tumbling face-first into the mud.

"Father?" Declan asked as the miller hung limply in his arms.

There was no response, and Declan gave her a panicked look.

"He still breathes," she said. "There—his chest is rising and falling."

Between them, they got the old man to the side of the road and propped his back against a stone, but he still did not awaken.

"He is weak from his injury, and hunger," Declan said.

"I've a bite." Hastily, Brianne pulled out one of her berry cakes and her flask of clear water.

The first piece tumbled from the miller's lips, and Brianne felt despair touch her soul. But Declan coaxed a bit of water into his father's mouth, and the man roused enough to chew and swallow.

"You must eat some, too," she said to Declan. "The village is still a long day's journey away." And that was on two strong legs.

He shook his head. "I'll save the rest for him."

"I've another cake. Take a bite or two, at least."

He did, and a hint of color returned to his cheeks, though he still insisted on feeding most of the cake to his father. Finally, the old man opened his eyes. His gaze went from Declan to Brianne, and he squinted at her.

"What beggar woman is this?" His voice was hoarse. "We've no coin for you, and no food. I'm sorry lass, but our own journey has been a hard one and we've naught to spare."

"Father," Declan said, "do you not recognize Princess Brianne?"

The miller let out a snort and managed to sit up a bit straighter. "That's no more a princess than I am Lord Mayor of Dublin."

Declan looked at her in turn. "Indeed, there's some truth to my father's words. What has happened to you?"

"A great deal." She reached for his hand, lacing her fingers with his, and told them of her banishment from the castle.

"Stubborn girl," the miller said gruffly when she finished her tale. "Who would be so foolish as to throw away the life of a princess? And over what?"

"Over love," she said, sharing a smile with Declan. Now that he'd returned, all her sorrow had fled. "But what happened to the two of you? What of the burrstones, and why were you so long away?"

"The stones will be along as soon as the roads dry. But after we arranged transport, I was injured in Dublin. It delayed our return." The miller gestured to his leg, propped before him on the sodden grasses.

"You nearly died after a careless English lord trampled you beneath his horse," Declan said, his voice hot. "That is no small thing. And I still say we should have waited until you were fully healed before we set forth."

His father grunted. "I won't heal better than this, lad. Time you faced the truth."

"Perhaps, but that's no excuse for pushing yourself past the end of your strength."

"I feel much better now," the miller said. "That bit of food revived me more than I thought possible."

Brianne gave him a gentle smile. "I'm pleased to hear it. And glad beyond words that the two of you have returned."

"I'm sorry I couldn't send word to the castle." Declan brushed his fingers over her cheek. "I did ask my sisters to tell you what had happened, though, and why we were late in coming."

"Your messages went astray," she said, her heart turning over at the thought of all the sorrow their family had suffered. "They believe you dead upon the road."

"Then we must make haste home." The miller tried to struggle to his feet, but Declan set a restraining hand upon his shoulder.

"Night is falling, and the road's treacherous. We'll wait until morning."

The miller sighed heavily but made no further argument. Accordingly, Declan scouted a short distance from the roadway until he found a thicket for them to shelter beneath.

And if, in the star-dusted night, Brianne and Declan held hands and traded soft kisses, the snoring miller was none the wiser.

CHAPTER FIVE

IN THE MORNING, THEY BROKE THEIR FAST WITH THE LAST OF
Brianne's cakes. The little meal sustained them most of the day,
though the miller slowed as the sun began to set, his face twisted in
pain. Declan supported him on one side, Brianne on the other as
they made their halting way down the muddy track.

It was well past sunset by the time the exhausted trio stumbled
into the village. The miller was at the end of his strength, and
Brianne and Declan were not much better. They barely managed to
get to the pub, the nearest building to the road in the whole village.

The moment they stepped through the door, an excited babble
arose.

"It that the miller, himself?" someone cried.

"Looks to be," another man said. "And worse for the wear, too."

The publican hurried over, full of concern as he helped them to
the nearest table.

"We never thought we'd see you again," he said. "What happened
to you in Dublin?"

"I've only the strength for a single telling," Declan said. "Could
you bring us stew and ale, and send one of your boys to fetch my
mother?"

"Aye." Their host turned back to the kitchen.

With a sigh, the miller set his arms on the table and laid his head down. "Home. At last."

"We couldn't have done it without Brianne." Declan caught her hand, warmth shining from his eyes. "I've waited too long to say this, my love. But will you agree to marry me?"

His words banished Brianne's exhaustion, her heart leaping up like a doe over the meadows.

"That I will, Declan. With all my love."

The nearby patrons let out a cheer, then had to explain to the rest of the room what had just happened. Everyone came over to clap Declan on the back and take a look at this stranger he'd just asked to marry him. Their curiosity turned to surprise when they saw it was the banished princess, but no one begrudged Declan his bride. Who wouldn't want to marry a princess who'd saved your life, after all?

The stew and ale arrived, and the miller's wife and daughters, too. While they ate, Declan told the villagers what had happened, and how Brianne had found them upon the road in the nick of time.

"I understand you're joining our family," the miller's wife said to Brianne with a smile. "I fear our humble house isn't what you're used to, but I bid you warm welcome as a daughter."

Her words pricked tears at the corners of Brianne's eyes. "I care not for living in luxury, as long as I'm with the man I love. And I'll be glad of your mothering hand into the bargain."

It was settled that the priest would marry them in two weeks' time.

"Should we invite the king and your sisters?" Declan asked, giving Brianne a worried look.

"We shall," she said. "Though it might be better not to say who it is you're marrying."

The publican's brows drew together. "I'd not want to bring the wrath of the king down upon us. Are you sure that asking him to the wedding is the wise thing to do?"

"I'll wear a veil," she said, then raised her voice and glanced about the pub. "I promise that the king will welcome me back with open arms, once the wedding feast has begun. But until then, we'll need to keep my identity a secret. Can I rely upon everyone in the village to help?"

"As long as we have edible bread once more, we'd even ride into battle for you," someone called with good humor.

"Too bad you can't ride, Liam," one of his companions replied.

"Or wield a sword," another said, but in the end, everyone promised to keep Brianne's secret.

The evening ended with numerous toasts, and a boisterous escort back to the miller's house, where he was tucked carefully into bed with the doctor's supervision. Despite Brianne's protests, the miller's wife made her daughters all move into one bedroom so that Brianne might have a room of her own.

"Truly, I don't mind sharing," she said, but Declan's mother would hear nothing of it.

"Enjoy your privacy," the miller's wife said. "You'll be sharing it with Declan soon enough." She winked, and Brianne blushed and argued no more.

The day of the wedding dawned clear, though one glance at the sky told Brianne it would rain later that afternoon. No matter, for the wedding feast would be held at the pub, with all the tables pushed together in the center of the room and more chairs added along the sides.

She'd spent the last three days preparing the food for the wedding feast. The miller's wife had helped a great deal, and between her kitchen and the one at the pub, everything was at the ready.

"I can scarcely wait to eat it," Declan's youngest sister said, clasping her hands eagerly beneath her chin. "It all looks and smells so delicious."

"Out of the kitchen." Her mother flapped her apron, and with a grin the girl scurried away, though she stole a biscuit as she went.

Brianne surveyed the plates of food and smiled. She'd put her utmost into every dish: the roast meats, the pastries, the pies and vegetables. Everything was exquisitely flavored, if she said so herself. Everything, that was, except one specially prepared meal she'd set aside.

"Let's fix your hair and get you gowned," the miller's wife said, wiping a smudge of flour off Brianne's cheek. "Ah, the first of my girls to be married."

They went into the bedroom, and Brianne donned her blue dress. The miller's wife had helped her take it in, though it still fit a bit too loosely. Luckily, two weeks of good food had softened the jut of her hips and wrists, returned the luster to her hair. And a bit of healing magic infused into her meals hadn't hurt any of them.

Indeed, despite his somber predictions, the miller was able to move about with just a cane for help, and the grim hollows in Declan's cheeks were gone, as was the desperation in his eyes. The burrstones were due to be delivered later that week, and all was settling well in the world, as far as he was concerned.

Brianne bit her lip, thinking of the risk she was taking. Would she be able to win back her father's favor? More than just her own happiness depended on it now. The fate of the entire village was at stake.

Once Brianne was dressed, Declan's mother helped braid and coil her hair atop her head, then affix the lace veil.

"Thank you." Brianne stroked the fine lacework. The veil was like frost upon a lake: intricate enough to hide her features, while still allowing her to see out.

"Made with my mother's own hands," the miller's wife said. "I'm glad you're wearing it."

She kissed the top of Brianne's head, just as the church bells began to ring, summoning everyone to the wedding.

CHAPTER SIX

Brianne looked at the backs of their heads, ringed with crowns of gold and silver, and felt a clutch of fear. So much could go wrong! If her father recognized her, he could put a stop to the wedding at once and wreak his vengeance upon the villagers.

He will not, she reassured herself. Her form and features had changed, albeit subtly, and she must trust the lace veil to do the rest.

Besides, the king would never expect his daughter to be marrying the miller's son.

With a deep breath, Brianne gathered her courage and paced to the front of the church to stand beside her beloved. As she passed the front pew, she heard her sister Colleen inhale sharply, and her sister Eva say *sh* in an almost imperceptible whisper.

So. Her sisters knew her. Despite the danger, the knowledge warmed Brianne. They, at least, had recognized her.

The ceremony began, and all went well until it was time for Declan to put the ring on her hand. Perhaps made clumsy by the fact of the king sitting in the front row, Declan fumbled with the plain silver band. He dropped it. It fell to the wooden floor and rolled to a stop at Princess Colleen's feet.

The villagers whispered, but Colleen bent and scooped the ring up. She closed her fingers over it and murmured softly, and when she handed it back to Declan, it was shining gold. Through the lace veil, Brianne met her sister's gaze. Colleen winked at her, ever so slightly.

Declan slipped the band upon her finger, and Briane felt her sister's love enfolding her.

At the end of the vows given and received, they drank the ceremonial cups of wine and water. This time, it was the priest's turn to let his nerves overcome him. He managed the wine well enough, but most of the water sloshed out of the small goblet as he handed it to Brianne to drink.

She paused, inclining the nearly empty cup toward Princess Eva. With a slight smile, Eva waved her fingers and the goblet was suddenly full again. Brianne took a sip of the cool, clear liquid. It tingled pleasantly against her lips, and when she swallowed she knew she drank of her sister's benediction, as well.

Now she only needed her father's blessing.

The couple kissed and went down the aisle to the hearty cheers of the villagers. Despite the winter rains, it was a merry procession down to the pub. They went slowly, in consideration of the miller's leg, and so that the miller's wife and daughters could hurry ahead and make sure all was in readiness for the wedding feast.

The king and the princesses rode at the back of the procession, and Brianne was glad of the reprieve. Nervous, too; for the moment of truth would soon be at hand. What if her plan didn't succeed? What if the king didn't forgive her, after all?

He must, she told herself.

Still, when they reached the pub she hastened to ensure that the meal she'd specially prepared for the king was set aside—ready to be served to him, and him alone.

She returned to Declan's side just as the king was congratulating him, not only on his new bride, but his safe return from Dublin.

"And warm wishes to your bride, as well," the king said, turning to her.

"Your majesty." Brianne curtsied, keeping her voice pitched voice low. "Thank you for attending our wedding."

"It is our pleasure," he said, then gave her a penetrating look, as if he could see through the lace obscuring her features. "There is something familiar about you."

"My wife has lived here all her life," Declan said hastily. "She used to serve in the castle."

Brianne resisted the urge to step on his foot to silence him. The conversation was veering into dangerous territory.

"Declan, show the king to his place," she said softly.

"Yes." Colleen stepped up, taking their father's arm and gently tugging him away from Brianne. "Doesn't the food smell wonderful?"

Eva gave her a pointed look as she passed. "I'm certain everything will be delicious."

Declan showed the king and princesses to the head table, and Brianne went to tell the miller's wife they were ready. Satisfied, she returned to take her place beside Declan. The tables were arranged in such a way that she could watch her father eat without being in his direct line of sight, and as the feast began, she kept a covert eye on him.

The first course was a soup made of wild onions and mushrooms, accompanied by hearth-baked bread made from the miller's best flour. As everyone around the king happily spooned up their soup, he took a few mouthfuls then, brow furrowed, set his spoon down.

He picked up his bread, took a bite, then, frowning, lifted it to his face and gave it a sniff. Then, with a grunt he put it back on the plate. Next, he turned to his mead, but Brianne had made sure to water down the pitcher he'd be served from. She wanted her father sober.

The next course was braised eels in a savory sauce, accompanied by roast turnips and carrots. Again, as the people around him ate, the king merely picked at his food. Brianne saw her sisters notice that their father was barely eating, and they began to loudly praise the food, exclaiming over how delicious it was. The king's expression grew darker.

The third course was venison—one of the king's favorite dishes.

Although the dish served to him was tender and looked marvelous, Brianne had taken special care with it.

Grimly, the king took a bite. He glanced at his daughters, who were once again remarking on how wonderful it was.

"Enough!" he cried. "What is wrong with my food?"

"What are you saying?" Colleen gave him an innocent look. "It's one of the best meals I've had in quite some time."

"I agree," said Eva, shooting a glance across the room to where Brianne sat. "The flavors are magnificent."

"No, they are not. I can tell the food is spiced, and yet, it is tasteless." The king gestured at his venison. "Even this! I don't understand."

"I do." Brianne stood and lifted her veil. "None of your food contains salt."

"Brianne?" The king rose, peering at her. "You are the bride?"

"I am." She lifted her chin. "And the cook."

Her father glanced down at his plate, then reached over and snagged a bite of venison from Colleen's. The entire room watched in quiet fascination as he chewed, eyes closed.

"Ah," he said. "Delicious. I think I understand."

Brianne swayed, her legs going weak with relief. Declan stood, slipping his arm about her waist to keep her steady. Still, she had to make sure.

"Do you, father?" she asked. "Do you truly know what I meant when I said I loved you as much as salt?"

He paused, looking down at the food before him, then back to Brianne.

"I believe I do," he said at last.

She exhaled shakily. For a moment, she'd thought all was lost.

The king rounded the tables of watching villagers and came to stand before her. He held out his hands. "Daughter, I have wronged you, and I'm sorry for it. Will you forgive me?"

The room held its breath.

"Of course," Brianne said, clasping his outstretched palms.

The villagers cheered, and Colleen and Eva shouted the loudest of all. Declan hugged her close, and the king nodded.

"Now," he said, "will you *please* serve me some of this delicious meal everyone has been praising?"

The celebration went well into the night. After the feasting, they pushed the tables back against the walls and there was music and dancing and revelry until everyone got hungry again. They ate, and then the children were put to bed under the tables while the dancing started up again, followed by toasts and tales until dawn was near.

Despite her father's pleas for Brianne and her husband to come live at the castle, she declined.

"Who would help the miller and his wife, if we left?" she asked.

"But we miss your cooking," Eva said, lacing her arm through Brianne's.

"Then you'll have to come visit, and I'll make you dinner." Brianne frowned, "Although the miller's house is a bit small."

"Then let a new one be built beside the mill, at my expense," the king said. "With a large dining room."

"And a larger kitchen," Colleen said, laughing. "Oh, Bri, I'm so glad for you. No matter what Eva says, we missed more than your cooking."

"Then, once the new house is built, you'll have to come for supper once a week," Brianne said.

"That we will," the king declared, and the matter was settled.

As dawn filled the sky, Brianne and Declan went home, hand in hand. Rose and gold painted the clouds overhead, but nothing could match the glow of contentment in her heart. At last, she had everything she'd ever wanted: her family, her true love, and the promise of a kitchen of her own. She would stock it with all the finest herbs and spices.

And, of course, plenty of salt.

~ END ~

AUTHOR'S NOTE

When the theme for this anthology was announced, I could not manage to embrace my inner vampire. The past year (or two!) have been tough the world over. Some people deal by facing their dark inner demons, but I found I had to go light, light, light. So how could I write a Bite story, I wondered. What else could possibly fit the parameters? Why, food!

The Princess of Salt is based on an old folktale—some say from Italy, others from England—but the message is truly universal. Love the small, prosaic things that improve our lives immeasurably even when we don't notice them. They are the most important things in the world.

ABOUT THE AUTHOR

USA Today bestseller Anthea Sharp writes fairytale-inspired fantasy. Her current series, The Darkwood Trilogy, is a lush and vivid retelling of *Snow White & Rose Red*. Discover more at antheasharp.com, and join her newsletter for a free fairytale!

THE HUNTRESS

SARA C. ROETHLE

I CLOSED MY EYES, BREATHING IN THE NIGHT AS I SENT MY SENSES outward. Strands of my long, ruby red hair tickled my cheeks, most of it tied back into a single braid. I could sense vampires out in the night, but none were near, and I wasn't sure if they were my prey regardless.

I opened my eyes and started walking. This hunt was like any other, nothing remarkable about it at all. An old woman had been killed, someone's grandmother, and I was to find the killer. I had been sent to the small village to hunt a vampire, only this time, I wasn't sure that was what I was hunting.

There had been too much blood left in the body. The kill was sloppy, leaving the woman hardly recognizable. Ghouls perhaps, though it was rare for them to venture so close to civilization.

I stalked quietly through the darkness, nothing but my sword to protect me. I had left my horse back at the village in favor of stealth. The night air was crisp, the first hint of what would surely be a harsh winter. Leafless trees towered overhead, the light of the full moon casting strange eerie shadows from their boughs.

I took another step, then froze as every tiny hair on my body stood on end. I drew my sword in one smooth movement, my eyes scanning the shadows.

I sensed him as he neared my back, and I lowered my sword as I turned toward him. "What do you want?"

My greatest enemy, but also the reason I was still alive. Asher gave me a small smile, his lips covering his fangs. His long white hair seemed to absorb the moonlight. His pale skin glowed with it. "You are far from home, Lyssandra."

"I know exactly where I am," I snapped, sheathing my sword. I was a hunter, even speaking with a vampire went against my oath to the Helius Order, but I couldn't help myself. As much as he irritated me, I was his human servant. He was my master. "Tell me what you want, then leave me alone," I continued.

His smile remained in place. If I wanted to, I could shove my blade through his heart. It would kill us both, but I could do it. Unlike most human servants, I still had free will. My hunter blood saved me from being a slave for all of eternity.

He tilted his head, draping long hair across the shoulder of his black coat. "Your thoughts play across your face."

I wrinkled my nose. "If you could truly read them, you would take the hint." I turned away and started walking. There was something out here, another monster besides Asher. Something had killed that old woman.

Though I couldn't hear Asher's footsteps, I sensed him as he neared, then he was walking at my side as if he belonged there. "It is not a vampire you hunt this night."

I stopped walking and turned toward him. "What do you know?"

"I smelled the blood of the death in the village, but no vampires roam this territory. Something else keeps them away."

I crossed my arms. "Stop speaking in riddles and tell me."

His eyes lifted toward the full moon.

I stared at him. "You cannot be serious."

"The scent is unfamiliar to me. It is one possible explanation. And there have been other messy deaths left unreported to your order."

I rolled my eyes and continued walking. "Werewolves are mere myth. A werewolf didn't kill that grandmother."

"Then what did?" he asked, catching up to my side.

"It doesn't matter. Whatever it is, I'll kill it."

"And if it's too strong for you?"

I sucked my teeth. "It is useless to think that way. I have to hunt it, no matter what it is."

He sighed dramatically. "I could help you."

"Why?"

"Would you truly rather face an unknown enemy alone in the night than accept my willing aid?"

I turned to look at him, but his expression gave nothing away. He was always doing this. Showing up when he pleased. Asking me questions, but giving no answers in return. I still didn't truly understand why he had saved me that night, and it was the only thing that kept me from killing us both.

But that was a problem for another time. Tonight, I hunted a killer, and as much as it pained me, it was my duty to do everything in my power to enact justice for the dead.

"Fine," I decided. "But this means nothing. I owe you nothing in return."

He gave me a knowing smile, because he knew it wasn't quite true. With that unbreakable bond between us, it felt *good* having him near. It felt right.

But it was all a lie. It wasn't how I really felt. It was just a result of the magic binding us.

I started walking again, allowing my senses to guide me. If the killer really was a werewolf, as Asher had implied, it would be in beast form with the moon high overhead.

At least, according to the legends. Never mind that more recent texts said werewolves had never existed to begin with.

Asher kept pace at my side, a hint of that mocking smile still in place. "Do you truly think you'll find it sticking to the path?"

I glanced down at the footpath I had been following. "Werewolves and vampires are still partially human. It's instinctual for us to follow paths. If the old woman was killed by ghouls, then I would stray from the path."

"If the creature knows you're hunting it, it might not make things so easy on you."

A dark puddle in the middle of the path halted my footsteps. I crouched down. The hunk of meat seeping blood into the earth could have been anything, but I was betting it was human, and I was also betting it was still warm.

"The trail leads off the path," Asher said behind me, laughter lightening his tone. "Imagine that."

I gazed across the tall grass bordering the path. My senses were better than a human's, I could smell the blood, but not as well as Asher . . . and he knew it.

I crossed my arms as I turned toward him.

He lifted a brow. "Yes? Would you like to ask something of me?"

"Would you like to be useful, or not?"

He stepped closer, sending a shiver snaking up my spine. He was a full head taller than me, and that was saying a lot, as I was taller than most women. He angled his head downward, draping his white hair around us. "And what will you give me in return?"

"I won't kill you."

"You won't do that anyway."

I clenched my jaw. He was impossible, a total thorn in my side. I turned away, glancing once more at the hunk of meat and searching for its trail through the tall grass. I smelled blood, and underneath the scent of damp fur.

Curse it all. Maybe it really was a werewolf.

I started walking, following my own senses as well as I was able.

Asher followed behind me like a shadow, utterly silent. Despite his teasing, he corrected me whenever I took a wrong turn, and I grudgingly accepted the directions.

I was beginning to think our prey had eluded us when a faint yellow light became visible beyond the withered trees.

I tensed as Asher put a hand on my arm. "There is a small cottage ahead."

I narrowed my eyes. Even with the full moon, it was difficult to make sense of the shadows surrounding the yellow light. When I looked hard enough, I thought I could make out a window with a lantern shining through it.

"Does the scent lead to the cottage?" I asked.

"You tell me."

My jaw tense, I took a deep inhale. Wet fur and the slightest hint of blood. A trickle of wood smoke reached my senses. Whoever lived in the cottage had just gotten home, and they were building their fire for the night.

I wondered if they would be cooking something unsavory upon it.

Asher watched me. "How would you like to proceed?"

"We go in, kill it, and bring its head back to the village."

"And what if it's in human form? It seems to have built a fire."

I shook my head. "It's still a monster."

"And if you have the wrong person?"

I smiled. "Don't fret, I will make sure I have the right person first."

I started walking toward the cottage. Despite my bluster, I hoped the creature was still in its alternate form. I didn't like the idea of killing anything that looked too human unless it was directly attacking me. Perhaps the creature would ambush us while we walked, saving me the trouble of my conscience.

I reached the cottage with no incident. The wood smoke was stronger now, the glow of the lantern in the window almost comforting. I lifted my hand to knock on the door, but hesitated. Would a wolf leap out at me? Could it be something worse?

Most witches had been killed off over the centuries, but there were legends of some being able to wear the skins of different beasts. I could protect myself physically, but I had no magic—no defense against spells and curses. I could hear a fire crackling inside, but nothing else.

"Rethinking your plan?"

I jumped, turning to find Asher leaning near my back.

"Strategizing," I whispered.

"Should I go around back?"

I shook my head. "Just watch mine." I knocked on the door, then waited.

After a moment of silence, slow, dragging footsteps sounded within. They were lighter than expected, not the hulking mass of a werewolf.

The door creaked open, and a small old woman stood framed in the light. Her eyes wide, her gaze drafted up from me to Asher.

She clutched the tattered red cloak she had haphazardly thrown around her shoulders. "May I help you?"

I blinked at her, unsure of what to say. She was the last thing I had expected.

"We are weary travelers," Asher said behind me. "My wife and I were hoping to warm our hands by your fire."

I stiffened at his words. I had never expected to hear *anyone* call me wife, let alone an ancient vampire.

The old woman scrutinized us, her eyes lingering on my sword. "Are you mercenaries?"

"It is her father's sword," Asher explained. "He passed away in the spring. She carries it for sentimental reasons." He laughed. "I assure you, she doesn't know how to use it."

The old woman seemed unsure, but finally she stepped back out of the doorway. Perhaps she had considered that if we were bandits, we would have simply forced our way in.

She hobbled across the creaking wood floor, back toward the fire. "I'll make us some tea. You both must be chilled to the bone."

I met Asher's gaze as he closed the door behind us. He shrugged. He had no idea what to think of the old woman either. The scent of blood and wolf had led us here. Was the creature perhaps lying in wait outside?

I took a seat on a threadbare chair near the small hearth, watching as the old woman positioned her kettle on a hook above the fire. She looked over her shoulder at us, seeing Asher still standing. "Please forgive the lack of seating. I've been alone here for a long while." There was only one other chair, piled up with blankets like a little lumpy throne. "I'm sure your wife won't mind you keeping her warm," she said to Asher. "No need to be shy in front of me."

He gave me that annoying smile of his, then easily draped himself over the arm of my chair, loosely embracing me.

I stiffened at his touch, inhaling the rich scent of turned earth that always seemed to cling to vampires. Even after the centuries he had lived, the scent never went away.

I realized I was barely breathing, and tried to relax. Asher usually avoided touching me, other than a few times when he had carried me while I was near death. I sensed no discomfort from him, but he knew how to hide his emotions. It was a skill I had never mastered.

He gently tapped his fingers one by one on my coat clad arm, and I almost had to smile. He was usually still as a statue. He was ... fidgeting.

His small display of nerves made me feel more confident. I settled more comfortably against him, and it was his turn to stiffen.

My smile grew. I turned toward the old woman as she used a rag to remove the kettle from the fire. "Don't you get lonely living out here all alone? Or frightened?"

She laughed. "This place is as safe as anywhere. No one ever bothers me. You're the first visitors I've had in quite some time."

She poured us each a wooden mug of tea, then walked them over to us. Despite her limp, her hands never trembled. I took the mug slowly. She was hunched in an awkward position that should have been difficult to maintain for an old woman, but she seemed like she could stand there forever. It was ... strange.

Asher must have noticed it too, because as soon as she turned away, he gave my arm a squeeze.

I waited until the old woman sat with her mug of tea and took a sip. As I watched, she took another.

We were all drinking from the same kettle, it should have been safe enough, but I found myself reluctant to try it. I lifted my mug and took a fake sip, letting the hot liquid burn my upper lip for a moment before lowering my mug.

"Are there many beasts in the woods around here?" I asked. "We could have sworn something was stalking us."

She waved me off with her free hand, the movement once again easy and fluid for someone who limped like she was stiff with age. "A few foxes maybe. You probably just sensed the ravens watching you. They like to flock to the old tree behind my cottage."

Asher's fingers played up and down my arm. I frowned at the excited tingle creeping across my skin. He was my master in title and bond only. I liked to pretend that even those two facts were not true, but it felt a little too nice to have his arm wrapped around me. If the other hunters of my order could see me now, they would kill me on the spot.

The old woman yawned. "My, it's late for me. You both should rest here for the night. It's never wise to be out in the dark." She stood and turned toward the fire.

I took another fake sip of my tea. "I thought you said there were no beasts around."

Her shoulders might have stiffened, just a touch. "Well you know, better safe than sorry. Things aren't always as they seem."

You've got that right, I thought. As soon as she went to sleep I would take a look around her property, especially the tree with the ravens she had mentioned. Ravens were clever birds, and if there was a desirable food source, they would flock to it. There just might be more hunks of . . . *meat* lying around.

"I do not have an extra bed to offer you," she continued. "But you are welcome to my fire." She finally turned toward us. I didn't miss how her eyes went to my sword before my face. "It's actually quite nice to have company. I shall rest well tonight." With that, she excused herself to the small adjoining bedroom, shutting the door behind her.

I stood abruptly, putting space between me and Asher. "Husband?" I mouthed with a sneer.

His face lit with silent laughter. He nodded toward the front door, and I followed him outside.

Once we were alone in the night, we walked a short distance from the house.

"You noticed how she moved?" Asher asked. "If it wasn't for the limp, I would have thought her a spry young woman with skin aged beyond her years."

He crossed his arms and I couldn't help but glance at his long fingers, remembering them playing across my arm. I clenched my jaw. As soon as I had completed my mission, I could return to my order, the one place he could not reach me.

I forced my gaze down toward my boots. "Can you smell anything out here? It all reeks of wet dog to me. I can't pick out any individual scent."

I watched in my peripheral vision as he closed his eyes, his pale face seeming to glow with the moonlight, then he took a deep inhale. "I smell blood and flesh, both old and new. Perhaps we should take a look at the old tree she mentioned, the one where the ravens flock."

It irked me that we thought so much alike, but now wasn't the time to complain about it. I nodded in the direction of the back of the house. "Let's go."

He led the way. As we reached the tree in question, a raven flew up into the night.

I looked up at the twisted boughs, cutting across my view of the full moon. "Anything?"

"The scent is the same here as anywhere else. What exactly do you think is going on?"

I lowered my gaze to find him suddenly standing closer. I hated how fast the dead could move. "Something is suspicious. I wonder what was in that tea."

He shrugged. "If it was a sedative, perhaps we should play along. Force her into unveiling her plan so that you may complete your . . . mission."

"You mean so that I can hurry up and kill her." I didn't say it like it was a question. He had expressed distaste before at how easily I killed vampires and other monsters.

In truth, some of the deaths bothered me. Young vampires couldn't control their bloodlust like the older ones. They often couldn't feed without killing their victims. And when they killed, the Helius Order came for them. *I* came for them. It was never pleasant to kill someone who was begging for their life, even a vampire. Or maybe I was just growing soft.

"Your face once again betrays your thoughts," Asher said.

I turned away from him. "Let's go inside and pretend to sleep. We'll see what she does."

I didn't wait to see if he agreed with me. I simply walked toward the house and went back inside. He followed without a word, but no words were needed.

I knew how he felt, and it didn't change a thing.

I laid my cheek against Asher's chest, the coolness of his body seeping through his shirt. If he had fed recently, he would have been warmer. His heart was beating, though it didn't always. He could survive without air or a heartbeat for a frustratingly long time.

One of his arms curled around my back, holding me close.

I wasn't sure which one of us was more uncomfortable. I wondered if shared in my feeling of torture. If my nearness was as delectable, but at the same time intolerable. I had sworn an oath to kill vampires, and to never cavort with them. Did he feel just as conflicted being close to someone who had slain so many of his kind?

I doubted it. He was, after all, the one who had suggested we cuddle up, keeping up the ruse of a young married couple.

The fire had died down to embers, leaving us in near darkness save the moonlight shining through the curtained windows. Fortunately, as a human servant, I had excellent night vision, and Asher's was even better. He was a nighttime predator, after all.

I tensed at the sound of a door creaking open, then forced myself to relax. The old woman's light dragging footsteps came near.

"Are you awake?" she asked from just above us, her voice taking on a calculating tone.

If the tea had been a sedative, she wouldn't expect us to reply, so I kept silent.

She stood watching us for a while, then eventually walked back toward her room. I waited as her door shut behind her, then I heaved a frustrated sigh. Perhaps we were wrong. Maybe she really was just a harmless old woman.

I was about to sit up when Asher's arm clamped around me, keeping me still. I froze, listening for whatever had alarmed him. Then I heard it. Footsteps outside approaching the front door.

A knock sounded a moment later, but the old woman did not stir from within her room.

I pushed away from Asher, reaching for the sword beside me, but before I could rise he was already out of the blankets we had laid upon the floor. I could make out little more than his white hair as he went for the door and opened it. Moonlight flooded into the room.

I stood, catching a glimpse of the man standing outside. He wore a long tan coat over a white shirt and dark colored pants. His hair was cropped close to his scalp. It appeared pale in color, but it was difficult to tell. Beyond that, I paid more attention to the scars.

The moon was bright enough for me to see all of the scars cutting across his scalp and face. I was betting beneath the coat there would be more of them. He wore a sword at his back and rested a small crossbow across one shoulder.

He looked Asher up and down. "I have no quarrel with you, vampire. Step aside." His voice was deeper than I had expected, but weak, like he had sustained injury to his vocal cords.

Asher stepped back out of reach, then glanced at me for instruction. The old woman still hadn't come back out of her room, but we knew she was awake. She must have heard us.

I strapped my sword to my back and approached the doorway.

The man's eyes followed my movements. "Ah, a hunter. Have you beat me to my quarry?"

My steps faltered. I wasn't wearing my usual armor. He shouldn't have been able to tell who I was.

"You move like a hunter, girl. I've seen others with your training. But you're a little more than that, aren't you?"

I stood there staring at him. My status as a human servant was a well-guarded secret.

He smiled with one corner of his lips dragged down by scars. "Wondering how I could tell? I could smell it on you. My name is Maxim, by the way. What's yours?"

I narrowed my eyes, wondering what manner of beast this man was. "What do you want? Why are you here?"

"We both want the same thing. Well, almost the same thing. You want whoever killed that old woman in the village. I want the bounty placed upon the killer's head."

I stepped past Asher into the doorway. "And you know who the killer is?"

"Scented her all the way here. And I imagine you did the same."

I frowned. No normal man could have picked up such a scent.

Maxim lifted a brow. "I will keep your secret if you keep mine."

"Which is?"

He smirked. "Where is the old woman?"

I resisted the urge to glance back toward the bedroom door. "I think you need to leave."

"Are you protecting her?"

"No, but I don't know who you are, and my instincts tell me not to trust you. Leave, now."

He stepped a little closer. "Or wha—"

Asher was suddenly there, grabbing Maxim's wrist before he could reach his free hand toward me.

The bedroom door creaked open behind us. "I must ask you to stop harassing my guests."

All three of us froze. I don't think any of us had expected the old woman to emerge, but now she was aiming a lantern our way, watching us all like we were misbehaving children.

Asher released Maxim's wrist, and we both stepped back into the house, glaring at him.

He barely noticed us, all of his attention now on the old woman. "I know what you're up to, but you've bitten off more than you can chew. Can't you see that?"

She put her hands on her hips. "I don't know what you're talking about, young man, but I must ask you to leave."

He started to aim his crossbow, but Asher tsked at him.

The crossbow went back to his shoulder. Asher had already proven how fast he was. Maxim wouldn't be able to fire off a single bolt before the vampire crushed his wrist. "You're both going to regret this. She'll eat your hearts and wear your skins."

Wear our skins? Maybe she really was a witch, but I couldn't just let Maxim kill her. I had to be sure.

Asher seemed to feel the same way, because he shut the door in Maxim's face.

I turned back toward the old woman. She looked like a tiny rumpled star with the lantern light shining around her in the dim room. "Who was that man?" she asked breathlessly.

If she really was a monster, she put on a good show.

"You should get some rest," I said. "We'll make sure he doesn't come back."

Her eyes still wide with fear, she nodded. "Would you like some more tea before I retire?"

"I can make it."

My offer made her hesitate, but finally she nodded. "The herbs are in a satchel near my chair. Do help yourself." She turned and hurried back into her room.

Asher stood just behind me. "This is perhaps the strangest night of my life," he muttered.

"That's saying a lot, coming from someone as old as you."

"Did you notice Maxim's scent?"

I nodded, keeping my back to him.

"What are you planning?"

I smiled as an idea came to me. "I think I'm going to go for a little walk."

I shivered as I stood alone in the dark, keeping an eye on the cottage. A light rain had started, deepening the scent of fur and blood. I had left Asher alone on the floor, an empty mug beside him with traces of wet herbs lining the interior.

I hoped I was giving our gracious host exactly what she wanted. An *unconscious* vampire, and her true prey left vulnerable.

I backed further into the trees as the front door to the cottage opened. I caught just a glimpse of a large beast, nothing like the old woman, before I turned tail and ran. Not toward Asher, but deeper into the trees. Not away from the smell of damp fur, but toward it.

I heard the scrape of claws as the beast gave chase.

I depended on my secondary senses to guide me through the trees, their sharp branches whipping by almost too fast to avoid. Speed was just one of the many gifts of a human servant. I was hoping the monster chasing me wouldn't be prepared for it, but maybe I was the one woefully unprepared. A low huffing growl sounded just behind me. I dared a quick glance over my shoulder, spotting a massive silver wolf.

No, not a wolf. There was something not quite right about it. The glance back had slowed me down. I felt just as much as I heard the massive jaws snapping just behind me. Hot breath steamed across my back.

At least I had proven the old woman wasn't what she seemed, though now I was probably about to die for it. My only hope was the scent I now followed. The scent the old woman was hopefully too preoccupied to notice.

Sensing her about to leap, I dove to the ground, rolling painfully across visible roots and stones. I looked up just in time to see another massive shape colliding with her, knocking her off course.

The whole world became snapping jaws and flying fur. I scrambled to my feet, darting behind the nearest tree. I drew my sword, watching the ongoing battle with a sense of awe.

Both wolves were twice the size of a normal wolf, with forearms too long to be truly canine. The muzzles were too long as well, and opened far too wide. I witnessed just how wide they could go as the silver wolf clamped her jaws around the neck of the darker one—the one who'd knocked her off her path.

My instincts screamed at me to run while I could, but I wasn't about to repay the other wolf's aid with abandonment. And so I drew my sword and did the bravest thing I had done in recent memory. I approached the silver wolf.

Her eyes lifted to watch me, startling me with their deep yellow glow. Blood seeped around her teeth from the darker wolf's neck. If I didn't hurry, I would be too late.

I aimed my sword at one of those glowing yellow eyes. "Let him go, now. I'm the one you want."

She seemed to consider my words, then her jaw unclenched. The dark colored wolf slumped limply to the ground.

The silver wolf got to her feet and growled, sending goosebumps up and down my arms. I held my sword in front of me, already regretting my actions.

She stalked me across the forest floor. I continued backing away until I hit a tree. No, not a tree. A tall angry vampire.

He placed his hands on top of my shoulders. "Is this all still part of your magnificent plan?"

"Well I got her to reveal her true form, didn't I?" It would have been a better comeback if my voice wasn't shaking.

He stepped in front of me, his attention on the silver wolf. "You perhaps should have killed me while you thought I was unconscious."

The wolf's fur began to flow like liquid. The transformation was impossible to follow. One moment she was a wolf, and the next she was once again a little old lady wrapped in her tattered red cloak. "I have seen ancient vampires react in their sleep. I was not foolish enough to get so close, and I would have been gone before you woke. *If* you had actually consumed my tea."

I moved to Asher's side. "It was blackthorn, wasn't it? Harmless to humans, but for vampires, debilitating. You disguised the flavor with licorice and clove. But how did you know to have it on hand?"

"She has all manner of herbs," a raspy voice said from within the trees. Maxim stepped into view, his crossbow aimed at the old woman's back. Blood seeped down his throat, but already his skin was reknitting.

"Where does the crossbow go when you're in wolf form?" I asked.

He moved closer, his crossbow unwavering. "The change is more magical, less physical. Both forms always exist, but only one touches the earth at a time."

"That doesn't answer my question."

We all turned toward the old woman as she took a step back.

I aimed my sword in her direction. "I don't think so. You killed that old woman and took her form. That's why you mutilated her corpse. You didn't want any hunters to recognize you."

She gave me a sweet smile. "Hunters are strong and quick. A form I would be glad to collect."

"She has enacted this ruse many times," Maxim explained. "She kills a villager, then leaves a trail. But whoever hunts her finds only a harmless human. She gains their trust, and then she steals their skin."

"You're one of her kind," Asher observed, "and yet you hunt her."

Maxim smirked. "She used to be my wife, until she went against the ways of the pack."

As soon as our attention was off of her, the old woman had started backing away again.

"Show them your true form, Merriam," he said without looking at her. "I'd like to see it one last time."

Without warning, she ran, almost too fast to follow. She only made it a few steps before Maxim's crossbow fired, dropping her to the earth.

I instinctually started in her direction, but Maxim held up a hand. "It was a killing shot."

I stopped walking.

He watched us both curiously. "Aren't you worried that I'll kill you too."

I crossed my arms and shook my head. "Sometimes things aren't what they seem." I nodded in Merriam's direction, then locked my gaze with Maxim's. "And sometimes they are exactly what they seem."

He lifted a brow. "Meaning?"

"Only a wolf's nose could smell what I am."

He grinned. "You knew what I was from the start?"

"There was also the wet dog smell."

He laughed. "Alright, then how did you know I would fight with you?"

"You have an excellent nose. You could have gone through her window and killed her. You wanted proof that she meant me harm. You hoped that a frontal assault would force her hand, then you could kill her without remorse." I resisted the urge to glance at Asher. "I know what it's like to execute someone. It always makes it easier when they are attacking you or someone else. When you don't actually have a choice. I can only imagine it's even more difficult when it's someone you know." I gestured to the woods around us. "Your scent is everywhere. You've been watching her for some time, waiting to see if she would commit a killing offense."

"Well you just have it all figured out, don't you?"

I shrugged.

"Not afraid of the big bad wolf?"

I glanced again toward Merriam. "I wouldn't go that far. She was pretty terrifying."

He laughed again, his sadness leaking through. He looked down at his boots. "That she was, little girl, that she was."

We left Merriam's body for Maxim to see to. She had once been his wife, after all. Asher accompanied me back to town, where my horse waited.

The entire village was asleep when we arrived, and soon Asher would be too. Dawn wasn't far off. Its looming presence felt like a heavy ache in my bones.

I turned toward him as we neared the stables. "I suppose you're expecting me to thank you for your help?"

He smiled down at me. "I *did* go as far as playing the role of your husband."

I snorted. "You enjoyed it."

"Didn't you?"

I was starting to feel uncharacteristically tired. I'd spent many full nights on hunts, and this one wasn't overly arduous.

I realized exactly what had happened as his lips brushed mine.

I pulled back a fraction, my lips tingling from the brief kiss. "You invaded my dreams again, didn't you? I've been avoiding you and this was your way of drawing me back out."

He pulled me close and smiled against my mouth. "Did it work?"

He kissed me again. The intelligent part of my mind screamed at me to pull away, but the other part, that dark hidden part, kept me in place.

Finally, I managed to pull back. "Yeah," I said breathlessly. "It worked. As soon as I wake up, I'm going to come kick your ass."

He stepped away, his laughter following him as he melted into the night.

Just like that, he was gone.

I woke up cursing in my chambers at Castle Helius. Asher couldn't reach me here physically, so he had invaded my dreams.

But why the elaborate mystery?

I sat up and threw my pillow across the room. Did I even need to ask?

It was all his idea of having fun.

I glowered at the first rays of dawn trickling in through my window. Plenty of time for packing up and having a hot meal before I rode off to beat the blood out of a certain vampire.

I got out of bed, then froze, remembering the final moments of my dream . . . and our brief kiss.

I could admit, if only to myself, that I'd had fun too.

Curse it all, I really was going soft.

~END ~

AUTHOR'S NOTE

Little Red Riding Hood has long been a favorite fairytale of mine. While the themes of *straying from the path* and *things not always being what they seem* can be found in many of my books, I knew Lyssandra was the perfect character to embody these two themes in particular. And of course, where Lyssandra goes, so goes Asher . . . even when his servant is hunting werewolves instead of vampires.

If you'd like to read Asher and Lyssandra's story from the beginning, Reign of Night can be found here: http://mybook.to/reignofnight1

To learn about my other books, including the best selling Tree of Ages series, please visit my website at: www.saracroethle.com.

YELF REVIEWS FOR JAQUELINE'S BEANSTALK CAFÉ

KAY MCSPADDEN

MARYANDLITTLELAMB (3 STARS)

Once upon a time, FairyTale Land needed a place for vegetarians to get a meal. Then Jacqueline's Beanstalk Café opened, and be still my bleating heart! As someone with lots of student loans (I'm STILL in school--ugh), I'm glad that the food is tasty AND affordable, and as a committed animal rights activist (you can follow me on Insta at #LovesLambs), I appreciate how all pets are welcome. The Beanstalk Café offers fresh water and organic treats for our snowy, fleecy friends in a special outdoor dining area. The owner, Jackie, is a committed vegetarian whose narrow escape from a man-eating (person eating?) giant showed her the true horror of biting into anything with blood. Thank goodness she used the gold she won from the giant (I'm a little fuzzy on the details about that) to start this terrific café.

Jackie Beans
Business Owner

Thanks so much for the review, MaryandLittleLamb! I'm so glad you are enjoying the "no blood" safe space I've tried to make with the

Beanstalk Café. FYI, I wasn't a vegetarian before my unfortunate altercation with that bloodthirsty giant! Listening to him yell about smelling blood while he hunted for his next meal (me!) made me love beans forever!

Which Witch in the Woods (3 stars)

If you have a sweet tooth, check out the desserts here. A recent storm blew several icing shingles from my roof and Jaqueline's Beanstalk Café made a timely delivery of just what I needed for repairs.

Jackie Beans
Business Owner

Glad we could help! You can now get delivery through Door-Mash, Grubadubdub, and Ogre Eats, too.

C. Dracula (2 stars)

I like tapas, but the Small Bites menu just doesn't do it for me like I was expecting. Limited hours are also a disappointment.

Jackie Beans
Business Owner

I'm so sorry your experience at Beanstalk Café hasn't lived up to our standards. We are refining our Small Bites menu to include some items you might enjoy, including blood orange sherbet and lady fingers. I hope you will give us another chance to become your evening destination. We are now open past midnight Fridays and Saturdays!

TheBeast'sBelle (1 star)

Not sure if the marketing is working for this place. I assumed the café's name was a reference to that architectural fail a few years back when a beanstalk crashed near here, but apparently "beanstalk" is code for "vegetarian." Ugh, and what's this love affair with BEANS on the menu?! So. Many. Beans. Anyway, wish someone had tipped me off before I insisted that my boyfriend take me here for dinner. He was super disappointed that the "lamb" kebobs were tofu or something just as inedible. Won't be back.

Jackie Beans
   Business Owner

My staff and I are sorry that you couldn't find anything on our vegetarian menu to please both you and your boyfriend. We are currently taste-testing some meatless recipes we hope will appease even the most veg-hesitant "beast." Check our website soon for an updated menu.

Snow White (2 stars)

After being out of commission for the past 24 months—witch's spell, pandemic—I was really looking forward to my first meal out. Jacqueline's Beanstalk Café didn't disappoint. I've always been a sucker for good apple dishes and her Dutch apple crumble is to die for. Food is definitely three stars, but I'm putting two because I'm upset that this business is not more socially conscious, in particular in their lack of diversity in the wait staff. Wake up, folks! It's not "long, long ago" anymore. Little People make great employees if you give them a chance.

.   .   .

Jackie Beans
Business Owner
Thank you for the positive shout out for our apple pie! Nothing beats a good apple! And that's what you are, too, for advocating for a more diverse staff. I hear you and am currently interviewing some terrific candidates. Check back soon!

Hans Brinker, Amsterdam (1 star)
I come to town pretty regularly to inspect the local water systems, and when I'm here at lunchtime, I usually try to patronize a local business instead of one of the hamburger chains like Old MacDonald's. However, the service at the Beanstalk Café was really slow. Really. Really. Slow. I felt like I waited forever for my food. I'm usually pretty patient and don't mind waiting, but an hour before I was even served a glass of water is ridiculous.

Jackie Beans
Business Owner
Hi Hans, I completely agree that the service you received was inexcusable. The next time you are in town inspecting the dikes, please stop in for a free meal and an apology.

Sleeping Beauty (3 stars)
If you are looking for something "out of the box," you can't go wrong with Jackie's homemade nettle pie. I admit I was skittish at first to try it (I mean—nettles—ouch!) but they were cooked to perfection.

Jackie Beans

Business Owner

Thank you so much for the positive review! You prove that not every princess is a spoiled diva!

RedHoodie (1 star)

So, the only reason I'm leaving one star is because they won't let me leave zero. It might be unfair to compare a café to the cooking of my mother and grandmother, but if you're gonna pay good money for a meal, it ought to be worth the danger, right? I went here on my birthday with a friend I met recently on Tender and it was awful, to say the least. First of all, my friend is a strict carnivore, and this place serves nothing he could eat. He's a gentleman, though, so he insisted I order (blackbean burger patty with garlic aioli and micro-greens….blah). Poor thing! He had to sit and drool in hunger while he watched me eat!

Jackie Beans

Business Owner

Dear RedHoodie, I'm so sorry that your recent visit to the café made for an awkward Tender date! Hopefully you and your friend will visit again to try our new faux-meat entrees. I'm betting they would even fool your grandmother!

Bluebeard's Fiancée (3 stars)

Full disclosure: I've known Jacqueline (Jackie) since we grew up together in the same little hamlet raising cows for mad money. I'm planning on having Jackie cater my wedding. Went to a tasting today and had the Blueberry Surprise. Or maybe it was the Bluebeard Surprise? Whatevs. Tasted great. Look forward to serving it to all my guests soon.

. . .

Jackie Beans
Business Owner

Thanks, Girlfriend! Can't wait for your big day! Hope you and Bluebeard live happily ever after!

Hansel (2 stars)

When this place first opened, my sister and I stopped in at least once a week to try whatever sweets were on the menu. However, lately the selection seems less appealing. In all fairness, that might not be Jacqueline's fault. I recently had a catastrophic consumption of way too much gingerbread and candy that changed how I feel about sugar (sorry—TMI).

Jackie Beans
Business Owner

Hi Hansel, I'm sorry to hear about your recent bad experience with sugary treats. Not to minimize what you went through, but as a trauma survivor myself, I know that sometimes the best thing to do is to go right back up that beanstalk and see what other gold is there for the taking, so to speak. In other words, hopefully I can tempt you to try again with one of our new desserts. Doesn't a scoop of blood orange sherbet sound scrumptious?!

Li'l Mermaid (2 stars)

Pescatarians still don't have a place to eat in this town. That said, the seaweed salad was okay.

. . .

Jackie Beans
Business Owner

I'm so glad you enjoyed the seaweed salad. I understand your concern about finding good seafood, but alas, after my experience (TLDR: bad giant-induced trauma), I'm just not willing to "bite" anything that can bite back—including our fishy friends in the sea!

Cinderella (3 stars)

I was looking for a place that stays open for that necessary midnight snack run and stumbled on this café. The slice of pumpkin pie was humongous and the pumpkin spice latte was a good accompaniment. The owner says the pumpkin harvest was particularly good this year—which explains so much.

Jackie Beans
Business Owner

So glad you found the Beanstalk Café! The next time you stop in, check our Community Bulletin Board. Someone (*wink wink cough* Prince Charming) left his card and number for you. You go, girl (but only if that's what you want, of course!)

UglyDuck (3 stars)

Don't let the outside of this café fool you. It might look shabby and run down, but inside you will find beauty and delicious food. I highly recommend the wheatgrass smoothie.

Jackie Beans
Business Owner

Hi UglyDuck, I opened Jacqueline's Beanstalk Café on a shoestring budget cadged together with a few gold coins and a golden egg. I always planned one day to upgrade the existing siding and window treatments, but unfortunately, my cash flow stopped after the famous beanstalk crash of '09. Thank you for seeing past the cosmetic flaws and appreciating what really matters in life: food.

PrincessPeaved (1 star)

Finally, a restaurant that focuses on veggies. I had such high hopes, but the peas were WAY overcooked. I've heard of mushy peas, but here in FairyTale Land we like our peas with more definition.

Update: (2 stars) After a second visit, I'm giving the Beanstalk two stars. The green peas are still too soft but the edamame pea pods are a fun appetizer.

Jackie Beans
Business Owner

Hooray for second chances! This means a lot coming from someone as sensitive to taste and texture as you are!

Pinocchio (1 star)

While the dedication to woodland animals is admirable, what about respect for wood itself? Toothpicks, really? At the register? I would expect such a display at an old diner, but a vegetarian café? Have some sensitivity, will you?

Jackie Beans
Business Owner

I'm always glad when someone takes the time to help me learn to be more aware of others, and that's what you have done for me here.

My sincere apologies that our toothpick dispenser upset you. Rest assured that it has been removed.

Goldilocks (1 star)

I really wanted to love this restaurant, but after three visits, I can't recommend it in good conscience. The first time my food was too hot to eat. On my second visit, everything was stone cold! Third time was a charm, I guess, because the temperature was okay. However, the problems with consistency make me hesitant to try again.

Jackie Beans
Business Owner

Hi Goldi, here at Jacqueline's Beanstalk Café we are always striving to improve. As you noticed, consistency has been an issue in the past. However, we are currently hiring more waitstaff (with more diversity!) and believe this will improve our service. To help you overcome your justified hesitancy, I'm sending you a family voucher for four! Come with your family (or three friends) and give us a chance to win your loyalty!

Bad.Rap.from.Rapunzel (1 star)

So, this café is NOT near me at all, but after reading a glowing review in Feyland Gazette, I wanted to give it a try since I like the idea of supporting independent businesses. For the record, I traveled more than 35 minutes for a disappointing meal. The A train was delayed so I missed the connecting crosstown bus and ended up having to pay for a cab (I tried calling a Flyt and an Ogre but apparently this part of town isn't hip enough to attract the gig drivers—go figure). After all that, I found a hair in my soup. Never again.

. . .

Jackie Beans
Business Owner

Hi Bad, thank you for making the effort to eat at Jacqueline's Beanstalk Café. I apologize that your meal was subpar. Please know that your criticism is taken seriously and we work hard to correct any mistakes on our part. Side note: in the future, you can order take-out delivery instead of making such a long quest for dinner!

PiperNinja (1 star)

I'm not saying this place has a rodent infestation, but I'm NOT not saying it, either. For a BETTER meal, head to Wonderland instead and check out Pied Pies, the best bakery in all the land.

Jackie Beans
Business Owner

Our health rating is A+, and any accusations otherwise will be met with legal action. Furthermore, I am petitioning Yelf to remove your post for violating the non-compete clause. My reviews are NOT the place for you to advertise your own family's business (don't try to deny it! The business license for Pied Pies lists YOU as the primary owner.)

Thumbelina (3 stars)

Glad to see a menu for Small Bites. Still too much for me, but the waitress was good about packing up a puppy bag.

Jackie Beans
Business Owner

You might be interested to hear that we are adding a Teeny Tiny Bites menu soon to better serve our miniature patrons. Stay tuned!

PrincelyFrog (3 stars)

It isn't easy being green, but the Beanstalk Café makes it easier! Lots of veggies to choose from. My only complaint is that it is too clean—not enough flies! Just joking! This place is great!

Jackie Beans
　　Business Owner

Dear PF, thank you for the great review! Someone should KISS you for that!

Peter Pan (2 stars)

You know how when you were a kid everything tasted better? Back when cooks used real butter and sugar and not the imitation stuff they use now? The first time I ate a piece of Jacqueline's cherry pie, I crowed in pleasure! If they added something to pull in young people, like karaoke or trivia night, this place would attract the Tick-Tock crowd for sure.

Jackie Beans
　　Business Owner

You've spoken, and we heard you! Look for an announcement soon about coming events, such as our new open mic night with live music (featuring my own golden harp!)

Al's Best Bud Genie (3 stars)

I confess I don't have a chance to get out very often, but when I do, the Beanstalk Café is the answer to all my culinary wishes. If you haven't tried the jasmine rice, what are you waiting for!? It's magical!

Jackie Beans
Business Owner

It's always a treat when you appear! At your last visit you mentioned our lack of adult beverages. You'll be pleased to hear that since then we have gotten our liquor license and can now serve spirits. Our bartender is ready to make you a special Jinn and Tonic!

PigBros (2 stars)

We are three brothers who live together (not by choice, btw) in one small brick bungalow, so the Beanstalk is our go-to hangout place after we get off work. All three of us work in construction and come home HANGRY! It's fair to say that Jackie's food (and some elbow room) has kept us from blowing our tops at each other! Only complaint: portions are sized for runt piglets instead of hearty eaters like us!

Jackie Beans
Business Owner

Thanks for being such loyal customers, boys! I hope you will consider renting out the café for that long-awaited double housewarming party once the hay is harvested and the twigs are collected!

Scheherazade (3 stars)

Full confession time. My husband and I eat dinner at Jacqueline's

Beanstalk Café. Every. Single. Night. Her extensive Persian food menu means there's always one more thing to try! The salad-e Shirazi and bademjoon are better than my mother makes (sorry mum!) With food this good, I'll be talking about this place forever!

Jackie Beans
Business Owner

I can't thank you enough for such a ringing endorsement! Small independent businesses without a marketing budget really depend on reviews and word-of-mouth praise. Keep talking! You are keeping us alive!

~ END ~

AUTHOR'S NOTE

"Happily ever after"? Worst ending ever! Who doesn't want to know what happens next? That's my inspiration for "Yelf Reviews for Jacqueline's Beanstalk Café." In my reimagined version, the least adventurous part of the famous ascent up the beanstalk is Jackie's tangle with the giant or her theft of his gold. Far more interesting is what happens after she returns to FairyTale Land. After all, she's flush with cash, so what does she do with it? Open a café, of course, to serve all the residents of her magical community. Except magical beings aren't so different from the rest of us after all. Some are fans, but some are cranks, and their online Yelf reviews offer peeks into their personal lives.

ABOUT THE AUTHOR

Kay McSpadden writes short stories, one-act plays, and newspaper op-eds. Her collection of essays, "Notes from a Classroom," chronicles her career as a high school English teacher in the rural South. She was a finalist in several fiction competitions, including the Norman Mailer Fiction Award, the Novello Festival, and the

Tennessee Williams Literary Prize. She is a contributor to several Once Upon anthologies and has published short fiction in Kestrel, Chautauqua, and Cobalt. You can message her at kmcspadden@comporium.net.

MARUSIA AND THE MONSTER

JAMIE FERGUSON

Sand squished between my toes as I walked along the beach, flip-flops in one hand. The warm, golden glow of the sun hung low above the ocean to the west, and a soft breeze ruffled the skirt of my light cotton dress. I stopped next to a palm tree and watched the sun change to orange, then red, then crimson, and then it sank below the horizon and was gone.

I took a deep breath of the salt-scented air and smiled. I'd been living in the little town on the Mexico coast for almost six months, but watching the sunset never got old. If things went well, maybe I could make this place work out. Maybe I could stay here for good.

I couldn't, of course. Things never worked out.

The monster inside of me was asleep, but it was still there.

It would always be there.

Music and laughter spilled out from the bar at the end of the beach. Normally I'd turn around at this point, head back to my villa, and spend the rest of the evening reading a book. But tonight I felt restless. I decided to get a drink and do a little people-watching instead. The town was maybe an hour north of Puerta Vallarta, so there was always a steady stream of tourists. I'd have to walk back up the hill later in the dark, but I'd be safe. The monster would make sure of that.

I paused at the edge of the patio, slid on my flip-flops, and tugged my hair free from its ponytail. I grinned as I spotted Tør, my favorite bartender. He was funny, made excellent margaritas, and spoke Spanish with a Norwegian accent, which was oddly charming as well as amusing. But most importantly, he never asked personal questions. I walked across the flagstones to the bar and gave him a little wave.

"Hola, Kara," he said. "What'll you have?"

"A margarita with Patrón silver, please," I said. I turned and looked at the large, festive group that took up most of the nearby area. There were fifteen, or maybe twenty, in the party, all of them dressed in white.

"Oh, your hair is lovely," one of them said to me. She waved a hand in the air, almost spilling the cocktail she held. "I tried dying my hair red, but it looked better in my imagination. Yours is simply scrumptious."

"Thanks," I said. "What's the occasion?"

"Our friends Jim and Jayden got married yesterday."

"They're off on their honeymoon now," said another. "A bunch of us decided if we were going to fly to Mexico for their wedding, why not stay for another week?"

"We don't normally color-coordinate our outfits," said a dark-haired woman. She grinned, her smile so bright and infectious I felt my own lips curving up. "The guys asked us to wear white for one of the events before their wedding, and we decided to get all dressed up one more time while everything is still, well, white."

"Seems reasonable," I said.

"It's a good thing tequila doesn't stain," the bearded man said with a chuckle.

"Or at least not much," said a short, curvy blonde.

"Why don't you join us?" the man asked me.

"Yes, do!"

"The more the merrier, when you're merry-making!"

Join them? Could I? Should I?

The monster inside of me stirred, but did not awaken.

"Thank you, but..." I began.

The dark-haired woman took a step toward me, and then another. She stood so close I could smell her soft vanilla scent. Her lacy white dress framed her tanned cleavage in a tasteful, yet enticing, way. Silver bracelets jingled on her wrists. "Please, I'd—I mean, we'd all love to have you stay. My name is Marusia."

She reached out and touched my forearm, just for a split-second, and then her eyes widened, and she pulled her hand back. My skin tingled where her fingers had touched it. I couldn't tear my eyes away from hers. I knew the others were still standing around us, but it was as if my world had narrowed, and all I could see or hear was her.

"Then I will stay," I said. "I'm Kara."

Marusia's face brightened. An unfamiliar sense of joy coursed through my body, and my pulse quickened. I swallowed and told myself to keep it together. She was just an attractive woman, that was all....but I felt drawn to her as if I were being pulled by a magnet. Her long eyelashes framed warm brown eyes, and a splash of freckles ran across the bridge of her nose. Her figure was a little curvier than mine, and she had tiny laugh lines at the corners of her eyes. I felt an almost uncontrollable urge to reach out and touch her skins, to run my fingers through her long, dark hair, to press my face into her neck and inhale her sweet vanilla scent.

I forced myself to turn away from her and wave at the bartender. "A round for everyone, on me!"

Dancing and revelry commenced. All the partygoers danced well, but Marusia the best of all. I danced with everyone: two charming young men who told me they'd just gotten engaged earlier that very day; a bubbly woman with bright red lipstick that never seemed to smudge; a super-hot man with short dreadlocks and a tattoo of the solar system on his left arm; and all the others.

But I kept coming back to Marusia.

As the night grew on, I stopped pretending I was interested in dancing or talking with anyone else. I'd never felt this aching, burning need to be with someone before. I wanted to touch her, to kiss her, to hold her. I wanted to watch her sleep, and then make breakfast for her in the morning. I wanted to hear her tell me her hopes and dreams, and do whatever I could to make them come true.

I wanted things I knew I could never, ever have.

Sooner or later the monster would destroy everything, just like it had every other time I'd tried to have a normal life.

But I couldn't bear to leave.

So, when she asked me to walk her back to her room at the resort, I smiled and said yes.

I slipped out of Marusia's room in the wee hours of the morning while she was still asleep, leaving a note on the hotel stationary containing only the words *marry me*, followed by a somewhat lopsided heart.

I intended to stay away, to accept my one amazing, wonderful night with her as all I could have.

But as the day progressed, my need to see her again grew until it was a raging fire inside my veins.

I watched the sun set from the deck of my villa, and then stared out at the stars twinkling in the sky above the ocean. The sun would be back tomorrow, but soon Marusia would head back to her home, and I'd never see her again.

I knew I shouldn't do it, but I had to see her. Just one more time.

I threw on a blue-and-white polka dot dress, fluffed up my hair, and pulled on my sandals. I walked down the hill and made my way back to the bar at the end of the beach.

Marusia and her friends were at the same bar as the night before, although this time no one wore white. She sat in a chair near a few of the others, her hands clasped together. Our eyes met as I walked across the flagstones toward her.

"Kara!" She leapt up, ran over to me, and took my hands in hers. Her soft vanilla scent enveloped me. It took all my willpower to not take her in my arms and kiss her rosy lips.

"Hi, Marusia." I squeezed her fingers, and then dragged my eyes away from hers and nodded at her friends. "Good evening, everyone."

They greeted me with warmth, but I could tell they were filled with curiosity, and watched us even after they turned away and resumed their conversations. I couldn't blame them. Marusia was their friend, and I was the stranger she'd hooked up with while on vacation in Mexico.

"I'm so glad you came," Marusia said. She took my arm and led me to a quiet corner. "I saw your note when I woke up, but I didn't know if I'd ever see you again. We're only here until Saturday."

"I couldn't stay away," I said. I kissed the back of one of her hands. "I thought of you all day."

"I thought of you too. I couldn't get you out of my head. Your dress is lovely, but you're beautiful even without anything on." She giggled, and then blushed.

"As are you," I said. We grinned at each other for a minute.

"Oh Kara, I'm so, *so* glad you came tonight. Although it's too bad you missed dinner—the food was amazing."

I wouldn't have been able to eat whatever they'd had, of course, even as hungry as I was, but I smiled nonetheless.

"Where are you from?" she asked. "Are you on vacation too, or do you live here?"

A chill ran down my spine. I should have expected her to ask questions I wasn't prepared to answer.

"From such and such a place." I shrugged and tried to ignore the cold lump of fear that had formed in my middle. "I'll be right back. I'm going to grab a couple of margaritas."

I hurried over to the bar and placed my order. I couldn't give Marusia the real answers to her questions. If I told her where I'd grown up, she might research me and find out some of the things the monster had made me do in the past. If I told her I lived in a place for a while, then moved on when it began to feel risky, she'd want to know what that meant—and there was no way I could possibly tell her. I could lie and make up a fake life story, but then I'd have to remember exactly what I'd said lest I get my made-up facts mixed. No, it was better to just avoid answering entirely.

I took our drinks back to where she sat, handed her hers, and then raised mine in a toast. "To us."

The corners of her eyes crinkled as she smiled. "To us."

I took a sip, raising my eyebrows as the zing of the lime juice hit my tongue. "Did you and your friends do anything fun today?"

"We did," she said. "We went to a museum, and then wandered around and looked at art galleries. But...I'd really like to know more about you. I really like you, Kara. A *lot*. I told you last night that I grew up in Seattle, and live in Colorado. You know what I do for a living, where I went to school, and what toys my cats like to play with. But I don't know anything about you other than you're beautiful, and amazing, and I can't stop thinking about you. I want to know all about you."

I sat frozen for a moment, hoping my face didn't show the terror I felt inside. I set my glass down and took a deep breath.

"I don't feel like I'm from anywhere in particular. I—I haven't seen my family in a long time. I try not to think about them, or about where I used to live, because it's just too...too hard. So many bad things happened, and it...it hurts to remember. I'm a clerk at a merchant's, and I've been living here for about six months."

I bit my lip. Everything I'd said was true, but it still felt like I'd lied because I'd left out so much.

Marusia squeezed my forearm. "I'm sorry, Kara. I didn't mean to stress you out. You don't need to talk about all of this right now. I just... I've never felt this way about anyone before."

"Marusia, sweetheart." I brushed a lock of dark hair away from her forehead. "Neither have I."

We looked into each other's eyes for a minute, and then she stood up and pulled me to my feet. "Let's make this night even more fun than the last. It's time to dance!"

We joined her friends, and dancing and revelry commenced yet again.

And again I spent the night in Marusia's room.

I left a few hours before dawn. This time my note read: *See you this evening.* I drew another heart; it was a little crooked but was noticeably less lopsided than the last one I'd drawn, which pleased me. I would never be an artist, but Marusia deserved the best hearts I could draw.

I tiptoed out of her room, pulling the door shut behind me as quietly as I could.

I knew I should stay away, and never see her again.

But I knew down to the core of my being that I would see her that night.

Stars twinkled in the cloudless sky, and the soft, ever-present shush-shushing of the waves on the nearby shore was familiar and comforting. The sun wouldn't be up for a while, so I had plenty of time. I headed down the cobblestoned street and turned left, then right, then right again. As I moved further inland the cobblestones changed to dirt, and the sound of the ocean diminished until I couldn't hear it at all. I paused next to a clump of bougainvillea and looked at the little mortuary that stood in front of me. I walked around the side of the building, picked the lock as easily as always, and entered the building.

The moonlight streaming in the window provided enough illumination for me to see the coffin was right in the middle of the room, exactly where I'd seen it earlier in the day. But then it had been empty. Now an old man lay inside of it, a sheet of plexiglass placed over top.

The monster inside of me awoke, its glee at what I was about to do so strong I shuddered.

I pushed aside the plexiglass, wrinkling my nose at the sweet, fruity smell, and reached in and took the old man's hand in mine. I gritted my teeth and then, filled with both revulsion and need, brought his hand to my lips and bit off the tip of his little finger.

The monster forced me to do this. I did not want to eat people.

But the monster would not allow me to eat anything else.

And I was hungry.

Mexico hadn't been the best place for me to try to settle down. I had come here knowing nothing about the local funeral traditions, and hadn't realized how important it was for family and friends to attend to the deceased—and therefore how few opportunities I'd have to access the dead before they were buried. Not that I was above digging up a grave—I'd had to do that a couple of times over the years when I was starving and had no other options. But it's a lot of work, plus it's hard to do without being noticed.

It's also hard to hide the fact that a dead body is missing pieces, much less disguise the toothmarks left on its flesh. But I'd learned long ago that people almost never inspect corpses once they've been placed into coffins.

After sating my hunger, I rearranged the man's clothes to hide the parts I'd eaten, and then slid the sheet of plexiglass back over him. I stared at the body, filled with the usual mix of relief at having assuaged my hunger, and disgust and regret at what I'd become.

Marusia deserved better than me.

And yet, I went to the bar again that evening.

She wore a dress of green linen, and her long, dark hair had been plaited in French braids. I watched her from afar for a few minutes before making my way through the crowd. Seeing her captivating beauty made my heart soar. But when I reached the area where she and her friends sat, she looked alarmed to see me, not happy.

I didn't understand why at first, but I made the best of the situation. I chatted with the two charming young men who'd gotten engaged the other day. I danced with the bubbly woman with bright red lipstick that never seemed to smudge. I learned that the super-hot man with short dreadlocks and a tattoo of the solar system on his left arm was an astrophysicist. But I kept coming back to Marusia. And she kept ignoring me.

"Go on," one of her friends said finally. "You're upset with Kara about something. Talk with her about it!"

"Yes!" said another. "This is ridiculous. Go make up!"

Marusia rolled her eyes, but rose from her chair nonetheless. I followed her across the patio.

"Let's go for a walk on the beach," I said. I glanced up at the sky. A tiny puff of cloud floated in a sea of stars.

"Fine," she said, and glared at me. "But I'm not going out of sight of my friends."

"Okay," I said, my brow furrowing. What was going on?

We walked along the waves, the sea foam sparkling in the moonlight. A growing sense of dread began to fill my body. I could only think of one reason for her to be acting this way.

One logical, horrible, reason.

"What is it, Marusia?"

She shook her head. "Nothing."

I stopped, grabbed her shoulders, and turned her so she faced me. "Did you follow me this morning?"

"No," she said, her voice wavering. She shook her head. "Of course not. No."

Her nose wrinkled, and her eyes darted around.

"Did you see what I did?"

"No. No! I didn't see anything! But—*what are you?*"

The monster sprang to life and took over.

"Very well!" it said. It spoke with my voice, and sounded just like me, but with the addition of the raspy timbre I'd come to detest. I watched as it clenched my right hand into a fist which it then shook at Marusia. "Tomorrow one of your friends will break an arm!"

It relinquished control of my body, and went back down, burrowing deep inside of me.

And, just like all the other times, I was left to deal with what it had done.

I trembled as I stared at my dear, sweet Marusia. Her mouth hung open, and her eyes were wide with shock and horror.

"Oh, Marusia… That wasn't me. It wasn't… I am so sorry!"

I turned and ran down the beach as fast as I could go.

I knew I shouldn't, but I went back to the bar the next evening.

I expected Marusia to be gone, but to my surprise she was there. Sitting next to her was the bubbly woman, now lipstick-free, her right arm in a cast.

As always, the monster was true to its word.

I walked over to them, my flip-flops making soft scuffing sounds on the flagstones. Marusia glanced in my direction, but wouldn't meet my eyes.

"What happened?" I asked, although of course I already knew what had happened. I didn't know *how* the monster had done it, but I knew why. This was all my fault. I told myself to leave, to spare Marusia any more pain, but my feet felt rooted to the ground.

"Oh, it's really silly," the woman said. She laughed, as bubbly as ever. "I still don't know how it happened. I was walking down the steps in the hotel lobby, and I slipped and fell and broke my arm. There are only three steps—and I *swear* I had my hand on the banister at the time."

Marusia scowled at me, her eyes narrowed. "Why do you care?" she asked.

I fiddled with the strap of my purse. "I don't want anyone to get hurt."

She stood up, patted her friend's non-broken arm, and then stormed off the patio toward the beach. I caught up with her right before she reached the water.

"Marusia, I'm really sorry. I didn't mean for—"

She spun around. "You're *sorry*? You weren't even there when it happened. How could this possibly be your fault?"

The sharp tone in her voice made my heart ache.

"I know you followed me the other day," I said, then pressed my hands to my mouth. Why, oh why had I said that?

"No," she said. She took a step backward. "I didn't follow you, and I didn't see what you were doing, and I don't ever, ever want to see you again. Get out of my life!"

To my horror, the monster took over once again. "Very well! Tomorrow one of your friends will break a leg!"

Marusia stared at me, open-mouthed, and then she ran back toward her friends.

I clasped my hands together and sank to my knees in the sand. I knew not to get involved with anyone. I knew not to make attachments. I knew not to fall in—

Love.

Tears trickled down my cheeks.

I'd fallen in love.

And now my dear, sweet Marusia was paying the price.

The next evening I paced back and forth on the deck of my villa. I watched the sun set. I stared at the moon. I did jumping jacks. I tried to read a novel, but the words all swam together. I closed my eyes and tried to focus on the sound of the waves.

No matter what I did, no matter how hard I tried, I couldn't stop thinking about Marusia. She was going back to Colorado tomorrow, and I would never see her again.

Finally, even though I knew I shouldn't, I grabbed my purse and headed back to the bar.

She sat in a chair near a few of her friends, one of whom had a cast on his left leg. There was a sad, pensive look on Marusia's beautiful face.

I tried to force myself to leave, to spare her having to even look at me again, but I couldn't make myself do it. I crossed the patio to where she sat. Her friends greeted me, but with noticeably less warmth than they had a few days ago.

"What happened?" I asked the man with the cast. He was one of the men who'd just gotten engaged. His partner gave him a tender look, then spoke.

"We were by the pool, and he slipped and fell."

"I have no idea what I could have slipped on," the man with the cast said. "Everything was dry as a bone."

"You're just klutzy," said the other man, then raised his eyebrows. "But you're *my* klutz."

They grinned at each other.

"I'm really sorry," I said. I glanced at Marusia. To my surprise, she met my gaze. But instead of the angry glower I expected, she looked calm and serene. "Marusia, I came to say goodbye."

"I'm not leaving yet," she said with a laugh. She rose to her feet. "Let's go for a walk on the beach."

This didn't seem like a good idea considering how things had gone on our last two walks on the beach, but I couldn't say no. Just being near her, even though this was the last time I'd ever see her, was worth any price.

We walked side-by-side in the moonlight. Marusia's soft vanilla scent mingled with the smells of the sea and the sand. The sounds of merriment from the bar diminished, and the shush-shushing of the gentle waves on the sand was soothing. If things had been different, I would have reached out and held her hand. But I would never hold her hand again.

"Marusia, I want to—"

"Shhh." She patted my arm, and then gestured at the empty tables and chairs of a beachside restaurant that had closed for the night. "Not yet. Let's go sit over there."

"Um, okay."

We sat down at one of the tables. She took off her sandals, shook the sand out of them, and then slid them back on.

"So, I—"

"Shhh," she said again. She looked up at the stars.

I bit my lip. I didn't know what to say or do.

On the other hand, it wasn't as if I'd had a plan other than to see Marusia again.

"I love looking at the night sky," she said, then turned to me and smiled. Her eyes sparkled. "And I love looking at you, Kara."

"But...*you saw me*," I said, my voice wavering. "You know what I did."

She nodded. "I followed you. I don't really know why. It just seemed like something about you was off, and I didn't understand what."

The monster stirred. "Very well!" it said. "Tomorrow *you* shall break your ankle!"

It sank back down inside of me, leaving me to look at my beloved Marusia in horror. I could feel the monster's pleasure at what it had done, and its glee at my reaction. Now it was going to hurt Marusia, and it was all my fault for not staying away from her. I shivered.

"Then I will cancel my flight back," Marusia said, her expression calm and unruffled. "Kara will care for me until I've recovered. Won't you, Kara?"

She rested her hand on my forearm, her skin warm against mine. I blinked at her, confused, and then nodded.

"And Kara will be free of you," she said, her voice suddenly as stern and as cold as the depths of the ocean. "For I know what you are, and I know what you've done to her. You are a ghoul, and you're living inside of her. But you are done here. Be gone!"

The monster clenched my hands into fists and raised my arms. "I am not done!" it rasped.

"Yes, you are," Marusia said. She looked brave and beautiful. "For there is one thing you cannot defend yourself against."

She squeezed my arm.

"Love."

The monster cackled, the sound so horrific I could scarcely believe it came out of my mouth. It forced me to stand up. I tried to resist, but it was stronger than I was.

"Love," it said, curling my lips into a sneer. "She doesn't love you. *I* am in charge of her. *I* am all powerful. *I* am—"

"Stop it," I said, my voice so faint it was a mere whisper. And then, more loudly: "Stop it!"

I looked into Marusia's eyes, and knew she was right.

"I love you, Marusia," I said. I felt the monster inside of me tremble. "I've only known you a handful of days, but I love you."

"I love you too, Kara," Marusia said.

She took my hands in hers and slowly, tenderly, uncurled my

fists. The monster tried to curl them back, but I wouldn't let it. For the first time since it took over me all those years ago, I felt strong.

A horrible squealing sound erupted from my throat, and then abruptly stopped as the monster left my body. It floated in the air before us, a dark, writhing mass.

And then it turned into mere dust and ashes and was swept away by the soft ocean breeze.

Marusia did not break her ankle the following day. But she did cancel her trip back home, and stayed with me at my villa for another week. And then we both went back to her home, now our home, in Colorado. With the monster no longer inside of me I became a normal person once again, the compulsion to eat people thankfully just a horrible memory.

And from that time forward Marusia and I knew neither sorrow nor separation, but lived together long and happily.

~END ~

AUTHOR'S NOTE

My story is based on "The Fiend," a Russian fairy tale about a young woman named Marusia who meets a handsome, wealthy, charming man who wants to marry her. But, as is often the case with fairy tales, there's more to this mysterious gentleman than meets the eye...

The main message in the original tale is "don't get swept away by a handsome stranger without knowing anything about him." This seemed easy enough to work with until I actually started writing. It was hard to write an engaging story because Marusia is pretty passive—most of the actions she takes in the original tale are because other people tell her what to do. I finally decided to switch things up and write the story from the mysterious suitor's point of view, which turned out to be a lot of fun.

ABOUT THE AUTHOR

Jamie focuses on getting into the minds and hearts of her characters, whether she's writing about a saloon girl in the Old West, a man who discovers the barista he's in love with is a naiad, or a ghost who haunts the house she was killed in—even though that house no longer exists.

Jamie lives in Colorado and spends her free time in a futile quest to wear out her two border collies, since she hasn't given in and gotten them their own herd of sheep. Yet.

You can find Jamie at jamieferguson.com.

TWISTED CINDERELLA

JULIA CRANE

As soon as Ella saw Henry dismount from his horse without her father, she knew he was gone. There could be no other reason her father's most trusted advisor would arrive at their house unaccompanied, carrying a branch ... that Ella requested from her father. It was a game between them. The others—her stepmother and daughters—always demanded fine silks or anything that glittered. Ella found it more exciting to have her father bring back something from the land when he was out for business. Such as a rock he found while traveling, or perhaps she would ask for an unusual herb from the area. This time it was the first branch that snagged his cloak.

Henry's face clouded over. He didn't speak for a moment, "I'm sorry, Ella, your father was shot by an arrow in the back by a bandit. He did not make it. "

With a shaking hand, she reached for the thick branch. It was beautiful, knotted, and shaped like a U at the end. Her eyes welled with tears. She could feel the hum of energy in the branch attempting to soothe her broken heart. She swallowed to ease the tightness in her throat. "I must tell my stepmother. I'm sure she will be devastated."

Henry locked eyes with Ella, and something passed between them in that glance. Both knew the woman would only be upset about

losing money and not love. She felt her eyes stinging as she fought
back the tears.

"I wish there was more I could do for you. He loved you dearly."
Henry tilted his head before returning to his horse.

Ella made her way into the manor house, her heart screamed out
in anguish. First, her mother and now her father. All that was left
was her wicked stepmother and daughters. Why had the Heavenly
Father allowed such a thing to happen? Had she not been good
enough? She always worked to uphold her mother's request before
her death to be pious and good. Not an easy feat after her father
brought home his new wife.

She set the branch in the entranceway. Her wretched stepmother
would surely make her throw it out if she saw it.

Walking slowly, she searched for the unthinkable words as she
made her way into the parlor.

Not knowing what to say, Ella blurted the truth. "Mother, Henry
has been by. Bandits killed Father."

Her stepmother's cup of tea dropped to the table before it rolled
and shattered on the ground.

They both stared at the mess.

"What are you looking at? Clean it up."

Cinderella glanced behind her, expecting to see the housekeeper,
but there was no one. She ran off to the kitchen and returned with a
broom and towels. Unfortunately, that was the first of many tasks.
Now that her father was gone, they took delight in treating Ella like
her only purpose was to care for them.

Her once calm exterior began to boil on the inside. While she
wished more than anything to keep the word she'd given her mother,
she found that the desire slipped further and further away each day
that passed. Throughout the years, she imagined doing terrible
things to her stepmother and sisters in her mind. She considered
running away, but she knew not where she would go. She'd been
kept sheltered after her mother's death, and she knew little about the
world outside of their walls. Beyond their land was the dark woods,
where monsters lurked.

Often, she found herself wandering the grounds, talking to herself and the animals. Even their delight at seeing her was beginning to wear thin. Misery settled like a black cloud over her thoughts. There must be a way for her to escape the prison she'd somehow found herself. No longer a child, she would soon be married off, which did offer a little hope in the darkness. Perhaps, there would be a perfect match for her, a man as kind and giving as her father had been. She began to imagine her ideal mate. He would be handsome, have lots of lands, and of course be incredible and not awful like her stepfamily.

Later that afternoon, Cinderella decided to speak to her step-mother about her future. She walked tentatively into the parlor room. Her stepmother primly sat as if she were center stage at court. She was alone with no one to entertain her ... what a sad existence. Not even her daughters enjoyed the woman's company.

"Mother, isn't it time for us to begin to have suitors? The right match would help your standings. I know it has been hard since Father has gone."

Her stepmother glanced up at her and laughed. "Who would want you? No one, my dear, other than a peasant. I prefer to keep you here to tend to the house. You will remain a maiden all your days. But you are correct. It's time to find the girls a match. Perhaps you can assist me with the selections since you know the family lines well."

Cinderella's heart sank. How could this be? Filled with anger, she made an excuse to exit and ran deep into the woods. The brush scraped at her legs and snagged her dress, which she ignored. When she finally reached an opening of grass, she tossed her slender body onto the ground in a heap, sobbing.

Emotional exhaustion took over, and soon she drifted off to sleep. While deep in slumber, a woman appeared. She wore a long, black dress, her hair so blonde it was nearly white, her face impossibly perfect, lips so red they seemed to be bloodstained.

"Why do you allow them to treat you like that?" the woman inquired as she moved around Ella, soaking in every inch of her with disapproving eyes.

Startled, Ella pushed herself up to sit before rising to her feet. Nervously she brushed away the leaves and dirt on the front of her dress.

"Speak, child."

"There's nothing I-I can d-do," she sputtered, eyes downcast.

"Nonsense. There is much you could do to free yourself from the pathetic existence you've been living. You are far more powerful than any of those wretched women that have displaced you in your own home."

Shame washed over Ella. Her parents would be disappointed in her.

"Inside, there still lies a tiny amount of cinder which only needs stoking for the flame within to be reignited. No fairy godmother is going to come to save you. You must save yourself."

Ella's face grew hot. "I don't know how," she cried out.

Eyeing her, the woman sighed. "You must break free from the chains that you have accepted. Raise yourself back to your true standing. Stand firm, and you will overcome the obstacles laid before you, but you must hurry before it's too late. We wouldn't want you to turn into a pumpkin now, would we?"

Confused, Ella's nose crinkled.

"It was a joke, my dear, but time is ticking. If you don't meet the prince soon, you may have missed the boat."

When she awoke, she was startled to see the sun setting. The strange dream was already fading from her memory like mist. She did recall the woman's mention of a prince. *If only*, she thought, sighing.

There was not much time if she were to make it back to the manor home before nightfall. They would be expecting dinner. She pushed herself up with one hand before she dropped back down, staring up at the sky. Her whole body felt heavy with despair. The last thing she wanted to do was return to the hell that awaited her. But what were her choices? A rotten twist of fate. Her life that once held so much promise, long ago, shattered.

Oh, get on with it, she scolded herself.

Standing up, she dusted the grass off her simple blue dress. That of hired help, not a member of a highly regarded family. How had she allowed herself to play the role of the victim just because her stepmother willed it? When had she become so weak? *Unacceptable.* Both of her parents had been powerful and never backed down from a challenge. And yet here she was cowering to a woman who was horrible and never cared one whit about Ella.

Thinking of what her life had become, rage bubbled inside.

After a glance behind her, Ella made her way forward, determined to see what was on the other side of her estate. If there indeed were beasts in the dark woods, she doubted they could be worse than the ones that resided in her home. Suddenly, a wave of excitement overcame Ella. Perhaps the tales had just been made to keep kids from getting lost, and there was nothing more than more woods, a place she'd always felt quite at home.

With new resolve, a lightness returned to her heart. The music of the birds once again lifted her spirits as they had years ago. *Good-bye, old life.* She was off to remake herself. Ella would be brave, and it would be an adventure like she'd imagined many times as a child. She was going off to see the world.

Eventually, she reached the edge of her property. There was a stone fence, not high enough to keep anything out, but enough to make it known one land had ended and another began. She reached up, grabbed ahold of the crevice between stones, and began climbing until she was able to pull herself up to sit on the edge. The woods appeared no different than her own. There was a shaft of darkness due to the sun setting, but she saw no frightful creatures.

Taking a deep breath, she jumped down to the ground. A pile of leaves softened the landing. She'd done it. She was free. Now she just needed to make her way through the woods and into the next village, which couldn't be too far. If she hurried, she might be able to make it before nightfall arrived. She was grateful for her nap and that she always carried a small ration of dried meat and fruit in her sachet. Reaching into the bag, her hand scrapped the small section of the wood branch her father had left her. Running her thumb over the groves, her heart tugged. She'd left the branch at home; she should have been more prepared and brought it with her. But long ago, she'd cut a small section of the wood, so she'd always have a reminder of a life that once was.

She took a bite of dried meat before moving forward with renewed vitality. A new life awaited her, one she would be in control of. Perhaps she could work at a bakery. She was good at baking, which was probably why her stepmother was unwilling to let her go. Maybe if she had been terrible at all the tasks handed down, she would have grown bored of tormenting her.

Allowing her mind to wander helped keep her fear at bay.

After a while, Ella realized something peculiar about the dark woods. True, there were no monsters, nor were their birds or any other kind of wildlife that she could see. Not once had she seen a squirrel or even a butterfly. This realization caused a chill to skitter down her spine. Ella strained to see beyond the thick branches for any sign of life. Nothing. She held her breath and listened intently. The only sound was her breathing. Ella quickened her pace. She must hurry.

The woods darkened, but there was still a slight gloomy haze while the moon rose, and the sun dipped farther below the horizon. How much farther did she have? It was impossible to know. At least she knew she'd been going in one direction. In her mind, she chased the sun, which kept her heading west. It would be more difficult now, but her father had trained her in the way of the woods since she was a young girl.

However, the resolve she felt earlier had long vanished. What had she been thinking? She should have at least waited until morning. What if she died in the woods? No one would even know … not that anyone was left to mourn her.

A branch cracked, causing Ella to spin around. Her body froze as she stared into the red eyes of a dark figure. She couldn't make out details of the being, other than it stood on two legs, was hairless, and the creature's arms hung low to the ground. Despite her vow of fearlessness, fear encompassed her. He smelled rancid. She nearly gagged.

She scrambled, turning to run. Ella crashed through the branches. The once silent woods were now loud with her panting and footfalls. *Breathe*, she willed herself through gasps. Her side ached from the effort of running. Was the creature nearby? Had she lost him?

Suddenly, she tripped over something hard. Pain shot through her foot as she collapsed on the ground. Her left elbow slammed into the dirt, breaking her fall. She strained to listen through her ragged breathing.

Maybe I escaped?

No sooner than the thought left her did her nostrils flare at the disgusting scent of the creature. Of course, she'd not been that lucky. Good fortune was not her friend these days.

"You are a brave little girl." The voice of the monster was low and sounded more like a snarl.

"Leave me alone!" Somehow her voice remained firm and did not crack even though her insides trembled. Why had she not thought to bring a weapon? Her eyes darted to the sides, but it was too dark to see if any stones lay close. Was this the end?

She skittered backward; her hands stung from the fallen branches indenting into her skin, but that was the least of her worries. Knowing she couldn't outrun the monster, she decided to demand answers. Perhaps she could survive this encounter if she distracted the beast while concealing her fear. Her father had said people would respect you when you demanded respect. It was as if his spirit was reminding her of those words she'd long forgotten.

Rising to her feet, she glared at the monster. "How much farther until I reach the edge of the forest?" Her voice dropped to a cold whisper. She was struck by how much she sounded like her stepmother.

With a tilt of his head, he snarled. "You are still a day's trip. The woods are deep and full of malice. I am surprised to find you still alive. Perhaps you are full of malice yourself."

The creature was on her in an instant, binding her hands behind her back. So much for that plan! She struggled with all that she had, but it was no use—his icy grip was too firm for her to break free.

"I wish I could feast on you myself, but I need to bring you to my master. She will have the pleasure." His gross breath lingered on her neck. "I do not recall the last time someone with a scent like yours has entered the forest."

Ella twisted; her heart hammered in her chest.

Oh, what a fool she'd been. A stupid fool.

The beast pushed her forward, and Ella attempted to fight him off. Unfortunately, it was too strong. She screamed, but that only made the creature laugh. "Be careful. You might call forth something you are not prepared to deal with."

That made her snap her mouth closed.

They eventually made their way down a narrow path between pushing and dragging her. A small, run-down cabin stood before them. When the beast opened the door, Ella was shocked to see what lay behind it. It was no simple shack. Inside were soaring ceilings, exquisite artwork hung on white walls, pillars going as far back as she could see. Relief washed over her. It was a dream. What she was seeing was impossible. When had she fallen asleep?

"You are not dreaming; you have merely walked through a portal into another dimension."

Confusion settled over Ella when she saw the woman from her earlier dream. "What do you mean, another dimension? There is no such thing."

"You are a fool, aren't you?" Her eyes narrowed. "There are worlds beyond your wildest imaginations, hovering all around the simple sphere you call Earth. But that is neither here nor there. I am glad to see you made your escape. It would appear you do have a spark left in you after all. Bring her forward."

The beast pushed her, causing Ella to fall to her knees.

"You have been marked as a daughter of the dark."

Ella's head snapped up. "What are you talking about? I am not dark; I am known for my goodness."

"Were known. Now your heart is black ... hatred fills you,

consumes your thoughts."

Ella realized the woman spoke the truth; she'd long ago lost the innocent child she'd been.

"Join forces with me, and you will have your revenge on the family that stole your happiness. You can make them suffer as they made you."

While tempting, Ella was not going to trust a stranger in the middle of the dark woods. "I don't need to make them suffer. I just want to be away from them so I can start a new life."

"Very well, but know this, you will not survive the woods. What I am offering you is your only chance of redemption. However, you must make a choice willingly. I cannot make it for you. There is no magic wand to wave that will create a happily ever after that you've spent your early years dreaming about."

Perhaps she'd gone mad. Whatever this strange woman was talking about could not possibly be true, and yet Ella found herself curious ... wanting to know more. What if she spoke the truth?

Ella knew she needed to find a way to get out of the dark woods, even if it meant going back to her pathetic life. She was not ready to die.

Maybe she should at least listen to what this woman had to say. The thought of dying in the woods alone was not pleasant.

"If I agreed, would I have to stay in this dimension, or whatever it was you called it? Or the dark woods?"

She shook her head. "No, you would have to go back to your life and reclaim your place. You will grow in your power and be feared. All that mocked you will bow to you once you're mated with the dark prince, and together you will rule the kingdom."

Dear Lord, the woman was off her rocker. A dark prince? Rule a kingdom? "I believe you are the one that is mad and not I. Which is somewhat relieving."

"Look around you, child, does this look like madness? Rise to your feet and come to my chambers."

The woman shot eye daggers at the monster, and it skittered

away, leaving through the doorway without opening it. As if it indeed were a portal.

Ella followed the woman down the expansive hallway. Any other day, she would have been distracted by the beauty surrounding her, but Ella was so confused that she used all her energy to keep up with the woman before her. At the same time, her mind whirled, attempting to make sense of the senseless. Her knees and elbow ached from her falls, but she pushed the pain aside.

They walked through an enormous double door into an open ballroom. Everything inside was black, including the marble floors and walls. Red drapes billowed even though there was no wind. It was oddly stunning, in stark contrast to the white walls before.

"I am going to show you your fate, and then you can choose. You will only have this one chance." Spinning her hand in an anti-clock-wise pattern, a scene hovered in the air. "You can either be a dimwitted woman who can't even keep her shoes on her feet or a woman who will bring people to their feet just by your very presence."

"I don't understand why this is happening. Why me?"

"Because you were born of the light and marked by the dark. Someday you will understand the significance of that statement."

Ella watched the scene as she ran through the woods crying. Her misery had left her aged and ragged. A handsome man on a horse dropped to the ground to see if she was okay. She pushed him away. The man hesitated and returned to his horse without a glance back. Eventually, Ella stood up and chased after him, but he was long gone. As she ran, one of her shoes fell off.

She was alone. Defeated, she sat down on a fallen tree and sobbed. The scene ended and changed to the man on the horse throwing a grand ball. Her stepsisters were there amongst countless other beautiful women, waiting for the man to notice them. It was a pathetic scene. The man seemed to pay no attention to anyone, just cast his gaze around as if looking for someone he could not find.

The next scene showed Ella walking tall and regal. She was stun-ning in a red dress, her hair perfect and her face flawless. She walked toward a man who turned before she reached him. Ella gasped when she saw it was the same man from the woods. Smiling, he tilted his head toward her before reaching for her hand, which he grabbed. He pulled her into him and they shared a kiss.

Ella blinked. "I'm not sure what to believe. You must understand how absurd this all seems."

"Your world is one of duality. You can pick the weaker side of the light or the powerful side of the dark. The light has failed you. You lost your parents, your home, and your dignity. What do you have left?"

Nothing. Ella had nothing left. Certain death awaited her in the woods if she believed this woman. After meeting the creature, she did.

Something in her snapped, and Ella knew it would never go back into place. The idea of power and other dimensions, while hard to grasp, was enticing. For years she'd been begging for someone to save her, and no one had shown up until now. Not exactly what she'd dreamed of, but she fooled herself into believing there was still goodness in her when the truth was, she had lost the faith required to believe in happy endings. Perhaps making her stepfamily as miserable as they had made her would make up for the empty hole left inside of her heart.

"What do I have to do?"

The woman smiled. "It's simple. Give me your wrist."

Ella hesitated briefly before holding out her arm.

The woman turned her hand over. She ran one of her sharp fingernails across her delicate wrist. "It will not hurt. We will be bound by blood. Blood is our elixir. We need it to survive. You will have access to my power."

Alarmed, Ella attempted to pull her hand back, but the woman's grip was like a vice.

"You will be immortal. Your beauty will never fade, only be enhanced. Your power will be intoxicating to all those you meet. Do you wish to change your mind?"

Images of the life she would be leaving behind her filled her mind, the way her stepmother and sisters had treated her. Ella's eyes flashed. "Do it."

"As you wish." The woman pulled Ella's wrist close to her lips. The hot breath caused chills throughout her body.

When her teeth sank in, Ella's body sagged. There was no pain, only bliss. Exquisite euphoria filled her body, and suddenly she felt as though she was a part of everything. She no longer felt like a body but like an expansive vibrating light. No sooner had she embraced the feeling than it shattered. The wholeness now felt like shattered glass. As if pieces of her were flying in all directions. Fear consumed her. What had she done?

"Now, now, don't let the fear control you. It is you who controls the fear." The voice echoed in her mind but seemed to come from so far away. "Call the fear back to you. It must abide by your command."

That sounded like a horrible idea, but she could feel she was losing herself as the pieces became smaller and smaller, scattering farther away.

Inside of her mind, Ella screamed, *Make me whole again.* No sooner were the words released than all the shards came slamming back into her being, the power pulsed throughout her, flashes of red light vibrated in her head, and once again she felt the bliss so strongly that it bordered on pain. Too much to bear.

"There we go, excellent. You did well. Now you must rest as the molecules of your body reformat to hold the energy. You will sleep for three nights, and when you awaken the process will be completed."

All feeling faded away, and Ella plunged into darkness.

When she awoke, she felt larger—like herself but as if she were a giant, although she appeared the same size when she looked at her body. Her vision was crisp. Colors seemed brighter, her body electrified. She felt as though she could take on anyone or anything. Her mind flashed to the creature in the woods. Ella wanted him to pay for the fear he caused her.

"Welcome back, Cinderella."

"Cinderella?"

"I told you, the cinder still burned like embers within you. Now you have reignited the fire, your source of power. From this day forth, you will be known as Cinderella. The world will always remember your name. You will become a fairytale told to children for ages to come."

Cinderella found that hard to believe ... nor did she care. She was starving.

"Yes, you need to feed. There is nothing to sustain you in these woods, so you'll make your way back to your home and reclaim it. There is a ball tonight, that you will attend and be paired with the dark prince."

The man from the vision seemed a lifetime ago. That fantasy was of little importance anymore. "I don't wish to be paired with him or anyone else."

"Some fates cannot be sidestepped. No matter which side you would have chosen, eventually you would end up with the prince. The two of you are entwined. You'll just have to deal with it."

The next thing Cinderella knew, she was standing before her home, in the stunning red dress from the vision, her shoes made of glass. How they didn't break was beyond her.

The hunger was so intense now that if she didn't find something to eat soon, she wasn't sure what would happen. Cinderella strode through the front door.

Her stepmother glanced up and her eyes widened in surprise.

Tunnel vision consumed her. Cinderella could only focus on the vein pulsing on her stepmother's neck. One minute she was in the doorway, and the next, her mouth was clamped on her stepmother's neck. She fed ravenously. Once she was finally satisfied, the body dropped to the ground. Cinderella glanced down and was surprised to feel no remorse or even disgust in herself for the blood dripping down her mouth. Nothing. She wiped the blood away and stepped over the dead woman on the floor.

Suddenly, her stepsisters came in and screamed.

Lifting her hand, she sent a blast of energy out, and the two of them went flying. They hit the wall and crumbled to the ground ...

their bodies splayed out, bones crushed. Well, she no longer needed to be concerned with that nonsense. Curious, she glanced down at her hands. It seemed her power was something to be reckoned with.

Cinderella made her way to her bedroom. In the room, she noticed the branch her father had given her. When she reached for it, her hand glowed.

The air shimmered, and a woman appeared. She looked very similar to the woman from the woods, except for her black hair. She wore a glittering white dress. "Cinderella, I see you have chosen your path."

"Who are you?" By now, it was not alarming to see someone arrive from nowhere. Strange how quickly her life had changed in a matter of days.

"I am the Goddess of the Light."

"Yeah, well, where were you when I needed you? You left me to fend for myself."

"I've never left you. You just could not see nor hear me." She continued, "Tonight, you will meet the prince. You will find he's not as easy as you were to turn toward the darkness. There is a lightness in him that even you cannot destroy."

"Again, where were you when I was marked for darkness?"

"Did my sister explain to you how that came about?"

"Sister? No, she did not. Does it matter?"

"Your father marked you."

Anger rose within Cinderella. She wanted to lash out at the woman, but the power once there seemed not to be accessible. "How dare you tell lies about my father? He was a great man."

"Indeed, he was, but it does not make it any less true. When you asked for the branch, the branch caught onto him was a Rowen tree in the dark woods. A tree of great power."

Cinderella glanced down at the branch now in her hand.

"His blood spilled, seeping into the wood, merging your bloodline with the darkness. You have carried a piece of that wood with you every day since. If you look back, you will see day after day that the darkness did indeed begin to consume you. The once bright light had dimmed beyond recognition. And yet even in your withering state, the prince could not get you out of his mind. The ball tonight is to find you. He searched everywhere for the woman who had lost her shoe in the woods. You have haunted him since he was a child."

"The vision was true? I don't understand. I've never met this man before."

"Yes, it was true, at least to the prince. There are things about your world that you cannot possibly understand. Much of what you think are dreams are more real than the waking life you take for granted. My sister has manipulated your thoughts repeatedly. Along with the prince's, mostly through dreams."

"I do not wish to go to a ball. Now that I understand what is needed to feed, I will be leaving. This home no longer has the pull it used to have. It can crumble into ruins for all I care."

"Oh, Cinderella, you have lost your light. I see I am too late, but I want you to know that you are not only of darkness. My sister likes to bend the truth. I have as much darkness in me, and she has as much lightness in her. We share the same blood. We each choose which side we want to be on. I know you felt the power of the light when you were bonded with her. That always comes first, so you will remember where your true home is, and you will crave it, that much I promise you. Spend as long as you wish playing in the darkness, killing innocents for their lifeblood, but eventually, you will fall to your knees and beg for redemption. I only hope you don't take too long."

Confusion settled over Cinderella, fueling her anger. Nothing made sense.

A strong urge to destroy overtook her.

"What you must remember is fear and anger is what fuels the darkness. Joy and love sustain the light. The more you feed off others' fear, the longer you will remain in the darkness. I wish I could do more, but unfortunately, I do not have a magic wand. You must make your own choices." The very same words her sister had said to her.

The woman before her faded out. Cinderella was left with three dead bodies and not an ounce of remorse. One thing she wasn't going to do was go to the ball. The thought of being around a crowd of people was not her idea of pleasure. She wanted to be alone while she sorted through the changes that had taken place in a flash.

Impatience filled her as she paced the house. It was infuriating. Once again, she felt she'd put herself in prison. She would go into town. Maybe something would catch her interest.

As she strolled down Main Street, Cinderella was surprised to see all the shops were closed. *What in the world?*

A woman was outside of a shop sweeping.

When Cinderella asked her why the shops were closed, the woman peered up at her. "Ella, is that you? I haven't seen you since your father passed."

"I've been kept pretty busy at the manor house."

"So, we heard. That woman—"

"Where is everyone?"

"The same place you must be heading in that dress—the ball. Everyone was required to attend. At the king's demand."

"Then why are you here?"

"Everyone under a certain age that had daughters. I never had any children. I could attend if I wanted, but I decided it was best to make use of the quiet and catch up on chores."

Cinderella started to feel the hunger return. No. She would not harm this woman. She'd done nothing wrong. A thrilling sensation flowed through her. Cinderella did not trust herself, so she said goodbye and hurried off. Maybe she wasn't beyond redemption if she didn't take the blood of the woman. She wondered how often she would have to feed to sustain herself. A little more instruction would have been nice. The feelings intensified, pushing her forward, seeking, searching for lifeforce.

Indeed, there would be someone who had pissed her off over the years at the ball. The town was small, and the castle was not very far to travel from where she was.

As she walked, she heard laughter. Turning, she saw a group of dressed-up women walking toward her. They appeared to be immensely enjoying the evening.

It had been so easy with the others. Cinderella found her consciousness bothered her at the thought of taking lives, yet she was starving. She would wait and see how long she could make it before the urge became too strong.

She quickened her pace, wanting to put distance between herself and the women.

The music could be heard as she rounded the corner. The castle was in view. She'd never been this close before. How unusual that the whole town was commanded to attend a formal event.

There was a line outside of the massive doors. Whatever patience she once had was no more. Skirting around the group, she made her way to the front. Some mumbled, but no one outwardly questioned her. They probably assumed she was with a party upfront.

She pushed her way to the front of the line. The knights at the door took one look at her and stepped back, waving her through. Cinderella found she enjoyed the power that radiated throughout her body. She truly could have anything she wanted. She just had to take it.

Her arrival seemed to cause quite a stir. Many were glancing her way and whispering. The crowd parted as she strolled through the grand foyer. Her eyes rose and caught the gaze of the prince sitting, watching those below. Jumping to his feet, he hurried down the staircase straight toward her. Cinderella was surprised to feel eager anticipation. Her earlier protest vanished. If possible, he was even more attractive than the visions. She felt an undeniable pull toward him.

"You're here," he exclaimed, excitement shining in his eyes. "I wasn't sure I would see you again. Even the dreams had stopped."

Cinderella felt the eyes of all watching the exchange.

"Dance with me." He reached for her hand.

As she glanced down at his hand, her throat constricted at the sight of veins. She could hear the blood pumping through his body even over the music. She must learn to control these impulses, or she would murder everyone she crossed paths with. Her hand shook slighting when she placed it in his, not from nervousness but desire. The hunger inside of her became exponentially more potent than before. She could drain his life force before all these people, but she knew that would not be wise.

The next thing she knew, she was twirling around the room in the stranger's arms. Their eyes locked. Her chest heaved, and she attempted to pull away. She needed to escape before she did something she could not take back. A part of her didn't care, but there was a slightly annoying buzz in the back of her head as if a warning.

The prince pulled her closer. "You got away from me once. I will not allow it again."

"I think you have me mistaken for someone else." Cinderella cast her eyes, seeking a way to escape. She would have to find someone to feed on, or she would not have the ability to compose herself. This had been a terrible idea. She should have never come.

"There is no other, although your beauty far outshines my visions."

Despite her resolve, Cinderella felt a longing. How long had she waited for someone's attention, anyone's? Ever since her parents died, she'd been in a black hole. And now, this prince was shining the brightest of lights on her. "I'm not who you think I am."

It was taking all of her control not to latch her teeth onto his neck and drain his blood. She'd been turned into a monster, and yet she still hesitated. Why? Maybe she wasn't as dark as the woman had claimed. Perhaps there was hope for her after all.

"No, you are more. I do not just speak of your beauty, that is obvious, but your bearing, as if all around you dim in comparison. You were born to be a queen. We will be wed, and my father will be pleased."

Her body stiffened. "Have you lost your mind? We've only just met. You don't even know my name."

"Arranged marriages happen all the time between those that have never met. You should not be so surprised. This ball was set with the intention of me finding a princess. My father's patience had worn thin of my endless search for you. You have no idea how relieved I was to see your face. Please, will you at least consider?"

Cinderella thought of what the woman had told her in the woods about their fates being entwined. It was an extraordinary coincidence that she came back just in time for this selection process. "I will consider it, but I must have some time to think."

She pulled away. The prince grabbed her hand.

"At least tell me your name."

"Cinderella." Oddly, the new name rolled quickly off her tongue, not at all awkward, as if she'd been born with the name. She hurried off, brushing past the throngs of couples dancing to the lively tune that began as soon as she turned away.

She did not feel very upbeat. Closing her eyes, she attempted to control the madness that raced through her. Was there anything else that could calm the desire other than blood? She should have asked the sister who called herself the Goddess of the Light. There had to be another way.

When she reached the back doorway, it opened into a garden seating area. She rushed forward, beyond the enormous shrubs. She was running toward the gardens. She needed to be away from people before she did something she would regret. And yet a sea of red surrounded her vision. All she wanted was blood. Running faster, she rounded a corner. A young woman was sitting on a bench crying.

No. No. No. Why couldn't she get away from people? Cinderella licked her lips when the woman glanced up, wiping away her tears.

"What has you so upset?"

The young woman wiped her nose with a handkerchief. "I've recently been widowed, and my family forced me to come to this stupid ball. All I want is my husband back. Why would a prince want a widower? He would not, yet my family has no sympathy for me. They just want me to be married to anyone to get me out of their home. I've lost everything, and they won't give me a moment's peace."

Cinderella understood the woman's pain, but at the edge of her mind, she thought, *If this woman misses her husband, I could send her back to him beyond the veil.* They would be together, and she would finally be able to get a reprieve from the uncontrollable craving.

Chest heaving, Cinderella took a couple of steps, lessening the gap between them. Maybe she didn't have to kill her? What if she could stop herself? Perhaps she'd wanted to kill her stepmother, and that's why she died. Why hadn't she been instructed better on how to handle her return?

While she had some sympathy for the woman, she mostly felt the intense craving. Cinderella knew the woman would not be leaving. It seemed fate had brought them together, and her life would be ended. No sooner had she thought the words than her mouth was on the woman's neck in a flash.

Startled, the woman attempted to push her away, but it was useless once her teeth sunk in. Bliss flowed through Cinderella. She could have sworn she heard the woman sigh right before the woman's body dropped lifelessly. As if staring through someone's eyes, Cinderella glanced down at the woman. Her earlier sympathy was long forgotten. She felt full of power and once again no remorse.

"Cinderella, my god, what have you done?" The prince stood staring down at the woman and then back at Cinderella, who wiped a drop of blood from her mouth. His mouth was agape.

"I told you I wasn't what you thought. I am a monster. This," she pointed down at the woman, "is who I am."

"I don't understand. I mean, I've heard stories, of course, of the immortals that live off blood, but I didn't know they were true."

Immortals? She liked that sound and found herself wondering how many more there were.

"What have you heard of them?" she asked, surprised that he'd not run off screaming. Why was he still standing there? It would only take a flick of her hand, and he would be dead like her sisters. Of course, he didn't realize that.

He glanced at her, but his gaze went back to the dead woman. "That they wield power from the abyss."

"The abyss? What does that mean?"

"I don't know, the darkness, the space beyond what the human eye can see. I have seen books on the occult, but I thought it was myths. How long have you been like this?" he asked, running his hand across his jaw. Finally, the despair became apparent on his face as reality sunk in.

She laughed bitterly. "I woke up like this today."

"Today? My god, what happened? Were you hurt?" His eyes cast up and down her body.

Why was he concerned about her when he knew she'd killed another?

The Goddess of the Light appeared the air wavered around her.

The prince jumped back, surprised. "Azure, what are you doing here?"

"You called for me," she said simply.

Cinderella glanced between the two of them, surprised. "You know her?"

"Yes, yes, of course, I do. Azure's been my guardian since I was a child."

"Your guardian?" Cinderella raised a brow. This world was much stranger than she'd ever realized. Why hadn't she had a guardian?

"Azure, how could such a thing happen to her? We need to help her."

Cinderella's eyes widened. He wanted to help her.

"She has made her choice, and she must deal with it. I'm afraid there is nothing I can do."

"There must be something! Why would we be brought together if we weren't meant to be together? I can't believe— You know how long I've waited for her. I am not going to give up this easily."

"You have a good heart, but she will continue killing innocents. Until she can get herself under control, there is nothing I can do, and that sort of control could take decades. Very few can fight the darkness and return to the light."

"You said few, so that means it is possible."

"All things are possible. But Cinderella has to want it."

The more they talked, the angrier she became. "You have no idea how I feel or what I've been through. You all keep saying I have options, yet I've been pushed into impossible corners. Let me ask you this, is there any other way that I can survive other than ..."Cinderella's hand flew out toward the woman on the ground.

"I'm afraid not. Blood fuels you now. As long as you are entangled with the darkness, this is how you must live. And live you must because you cannot die."

"Never?" the prince asked, shocked.

"Not in this world. She can leave this sphere for another, but as long as Cinderella is on Earth, she is immortal."

"What do you survive on?" Cinderella asked the woman.

"I merely visit this world when I am called. I do not need the nourishment of your world. In my world, I survive on the energy of joy."

"And your sister?"

"The same, but she survives on fear energy."

"I don't understand why you are bothering with our lives at all?"

She smiled. "It's our job. We are both guardians of this world. She for the dark, and I for the light. She is now your guardian."

This was all way too much to take in. Only days ago, she'd been miserable but not a killer. In the back of her mind, it bothered her that she didn't feel guilty about the dead woman.

"You will always be drawn to those that are in lower states. I'm assuming this woman was upset when you came across her?"

Cinderella nodded. "She was a widower and did not want to be here."

"You will also be drawn to those that are angry or afraid. It fuels your power. It's intoxicating. My sister should have gone over this with you."

"Well, she didn't. She just tossed me out and told me to go to the prince."

"This is a battle my sister will lose. She wants you to turn him to the dark. However, his love for you is too strong. What she thought would be her biggest weapon is actually what will keep him in the light."

"I don't understand why you both keep saying our fates are tied.

What does that even mean? And how can he love me? He doesn't even know me." She looked at the prince, and he shrugged.

"There are some souls that always find their way back to each other. It's preplanned before their births. It's truly written in the stars, you could say. How will it work out?" she smiled, "no one ever knows. There is always a fine line between love and hate with strong links. Sometimes they destroy each other, sometimes they find true love, but it is never easy no matter how it goes. Charming could never hate you. As he has said, he's loved you since a boy. Since he was five years old, he's dreamt of you and searched for you always." She paused. "I told you, Cinderella, my sister has been messing with your mind ever since you got ahold of the branch. It's all manipulation."

Now her anger was focused on the Dark Goddess. She appeared before them.

"You called?" She smirked.

Cinderella threw up her hand to send out a blast of power, but nothing happened. She glanced down at her hand.

"Your power does not work against either of us."

"Why did you do this to me?" Cinderella demanded.

"It's my job, nothing personal. But I do have to say it's been quite delightful, and I look forward to watching you through the ages." She looked over at the woman. "You should dispose of the body." With a flick of her wrist, the body evaporated.

"How?" Cinderella's mouth hung open.

"It's easy. You can do it as well. Once the body has perished, that is. I've already cleaned up the mess you made at your house."

"Is there a way I can live and not kill?"

The dark woman tilted her head. "Not likely. Not with your lack of control. It's nearly impossible to stop once you begin to feed."

"You said nearly," the prince said eagerly. "Explain."

"Our kind feeds on fear, pain, and hatred … all potent emotions."

A thought clicked in Cinderella's mind. "But why the blood?"

"The blood carries emotions in humans. It's encoded in the system."

"What if she fed on someone whose emotions were pure? And not tainted with hate?" Charming asked.

The Dark Goddess shook her head. "Impossible. There is no draw ... like attracts like. It's a universal law."

Cinderella knew she'd been drawn to and wanted to feed off the prince's blood when they danced. So, there was some untruth being spoken. As the Goddess of the Light said, her sister manipulated the truth often."

Her eyes locked with the prince's, and he nodded. Both were thinking the same thing, but how could she control herself and not drain him of his lifeforce?

"You would never kill me," he stated as if he heard her thoughts.

The two goddesses exchanged glances.

"It is possible," the Goddess of The Light spoke slowly, "that you could find balance within each other. But it would be dangerous. A soul connection leads to the attraction, the magnetic pull you both feel. If Prince Charming allowed you to feed on him and you could stop yourself, you could sustain, but you would have to leave this world behind until you gain control, which could take a very long time. You would have to go into a space where you would not be influenced or drawn into the emotions of the outside world. Cinderella, you would truly be in a prison of your own making."

"But she would be with me," the prince exclaimed. "I can bring her back to the light; I know I can. My feelings for her are pure and true. It would not be a prison but a haven."

"And if she kills you?" the Dark Goddess asked.

"Then I will die with a smile on my face. Please, Cinderella, we must at least try. I know you are good."

Cinderella was unsure. She did not trust herself enough to know for sure if she could stop. She honestly did not think she could. And yet a stirring of hope could be felt emerging.

He turned toward the Dark Goddess. "How much longer until she needs to be nourished again?"

The Dark Goddess sighed. "I can give her a reprieve for one moonrise and set. After that, it will vary. With the newly turned, they are unsatiable. Eventually, the desire wanes, and they can feed less frequently."

She held out her wrist to Cinderella.

Startled, Cinderella asked, "Why are you doing this?"

The goddess locked eyes with her sister. "We've been doing this a very long time. This Earth sphere has been out of balance for centuries, which is why we were brought in. Knowing the planet would either destroy itself in the dark or renew itself in the light. The push and pull have never strayed too far. You are the first glimmer of hope we have seen. You will fail, or you will succeed. The choice has always been yours."

Cinderella's mouth clamped onto the goddess' wrist. Her eyes closed in pleasure. It surprised her that the energy she received was that of light. It was ecstasy. When the brightness began to fade, Cinderella released her arm.

Cinderella gazed into her guardian's eyes. "Thank you. We will not let you down."

"We shall see." A portal opened, and the Dark Goddess pushed them through. "Both of you can call us with your thoughts. Good luck."

If it didn't work out well, at least they had one day together, where Cinderella would be able to resist the darkness.

~END ~

AUTHOR'S NOTE

Why did I pick Cinderella as my retelling? As a child, I never understood why she was treated so poorly or why she wouldn't stick up for herself. I wanted Cinderella to take back her power and find her happy ever after, not just because she was beautiful but because she knew she was worth it. Even if it meant she had to fight to be true to herself.

ABOUT THE AUTHOR

Julia Crane dreamt of elves and teen androids long before she captured them and put them on paper. She's written and released over fifteen young adult and new adult titles. You can find more about Julia Crane at www.juliacrane.com.

FAEFROST

JENNA ELIZABETH JOHNSON

A PALE SLICE OF MOONLIGHT WINKED BETWEEN THE TREES AS AIDEN and I rushed along the narrow trail leading to the edge of the Weald. It was the morning of Solstice Eve, and we had woken long before dawn to make the most of our day before the festivities began later that night. Normally, Aiden only visited in the summer months, and only for a few weeks at that, but this year he had begged his mortal family to send him to the Otherworld to celebrate the Winter Solstice, and they had complied. Yet, instead of being tucked away in the heart of Erintara with his mother, the high queen Danua, he had been secreted away to an even safer location. The Morrigan may have been defeated nearly a year ago, but her dark magic still stained our world and it sometimes seeped into the walls of the queen's castle. But as long as we remained within the magical boundary of the Weald, nothing evil could harm us.

"What exactly do the unicorns look like again?" Aiden breathed, picking up his pace.

I hurried to keep up, the light of our glamour dancing in our palms just bright enough to illuminate a few feet of the trail stretching out before us.

"They're not unicorns," I panted, "they're dhadarca. But I guess they look enough like the unicorns you told me about in the fairy books of the mortal world."

The dhadarca were horse-like, amphibious creatures with shimmering white bodies covered in scales. They had tails and manes of wispy, fine hair, and foreheads that sprouted two or more curved, spiraling horns. The Winter Solstice was the time of year they most often traveled between the immortal worlds.

"I bet that's where our unicorn legends come from! I bet the, um, *darka*, came into our world, like the faelah, and people saw them."

"Dhadarca," I corrected. "And you're probably right."

A few minutes later, the trees grew sparser, the path passing between two large stones and disappearing down a wide sloping field. The newly risen sun sent beams of light cutting through the misty morning, and a pale gray shimmer flashed just above the guardian stones.

I grabbed Aiden's arm and pointed. "The boundary to the Weald. We can't go beyond it."

He nodded grimly, his aquamarine eyes serious. Unlike the boastful boys of my village, Aiden had actually experienced what the Morrigan was like firsthand. Although she was gone from Eile for now, those loyal to her still lurked in the shadows, waiting to claim the power she once held. Neither Aiden nor I needed to be told of how important it was that we stay within the bounds of the Weald.

"If we are to see any dhadarca, it will be in the next hour or so," I mentioned. "They spend most of their time in the water, but they like to graze along the shoreline at dawn and dusk."

We headed toward one of the guardian stones and sat behind a holly bush to wait. The dark leaves and berries of the shrub appeared nearly black and storm cloud gray. Wanting to see their true colors, and not just the muted tones my eyes registered, I reached out and placed my fingers against the inch of exposed skin on Aiden's wrist. Instantly, the smoky screen clouding my vision evaporated to reveal deep, glossy green and red as bright as blood. I almost sighed at the beauty of it, but Aiden hissed and pulled his hand free, taking the vibrant scene with him.

"Your fingers are like ice!" he complained, grabbing his wrist.

I shrugged and said, "Sorry."

Just a few months ago, Aiden discovered one of my secrets. The other children of the Weald had found a large spider and were in the process of killing it, but Aiden had come to its defense. We had saved the creature, but in the struggle one of its legs had been crushed. My glamour, still as much a mystery to me as anyone else, has healing capabilities, and I fixed the spider's leg with Aiden as witness. He is the only other person who knows about this side of my magic. But there was one secret I could never tell anyone else, not even him. I was colorblind. I perceived the world in shades of gray and black and white. Before meeting Aiden, I didn't realize this was a defect. I never really knew what the names of colors meant when people described them. It wasn't until I saw Aiden's eyes for the first time that I realized there was more to the world than the dull palette I was granted. For some reason, I could see the true color of his eyes, and later I discovered that the closer I was to him, the more the colors of the world bled into my vision. And if my skin touched his, I could see even more. But, he couldn't know. No one could. It was my biggest fear because maybe that was the reason my true family, whoever they were, had abandoned me.

"Tegan, look!"

Aiden's hushed but fervent voice snapped me out of my reflection, and a flash of color spilled into my field of vision as he wrapped his fingers around my wrist. I glanced up, blinking against the beautiful but shocking sensation, my eyes following the direction of his finger. He pointed beyond the edge of the tree line, out into the frost-dusted fields along the edge of Lake Ohll. There, like drops of pearlescent moonlight, stood three dhadarca. A stallion and two mares, if I was correct in my judgement. The male was larger, his twisting, curved horns longer than the females'.

"Wow!" was all Aiden could say. Slowly, he stood up and began to creep around the holly bush to get a better look.

"Aiden!" I hissed as quietly as I could. "Don't go past the trees!"

"I won't," he replied, waving me off with a hand. With the other, he reached up and took hold of a branch, pulling himself up onto a large boulder.

"Ow!" Aiden yelped, ripping his hand free of the limb and almost tumbling off the rock.

I bolted to my feet and rushed forward. "What happened?"

He had slid off the stone, his right hand clutching his other wrist. The sun had risen enough to chase the shadows away, and as I squinted at the base of his thumb, it was impossible to miss the two puncture wounds scoring his flesh. They weren't large, but they stood out against his pale skin like two drops of blood.

"I think a spider bit me," Aiden said, hissing through his teeth.

"Does it hurt?" I asked, reaching out to gently touch the wound. Perhaps I could heal this, too…

"Don't!" he snapped, something vicious underscoring his tone.

I stepped back, slightly stunned.

"It's fine," he panted. "Doesn't really hurt. Just feels kind of cold."

Giving him a wary look, I stepped around him and climbed up onto the rock. With a sinking heart, I realized the branch he had grabbed stretched past the protective wall of glamour surrounding the Weald. Had crossing the barrier somehow hurt him? But that didn't make sense. People passed in and out of the boundary all the time without suffering any ill-effects.

Movement out of the corner of my eye drew my attention back to the tree. A small insect-like creature scuttled along the limb. It resembled an ant, but was the size of a mouse and had four legs, two on each side. I couldn't tell its true color. Aiden was too far away, but I thought there might be a hint of red or brown pushing through all the dark gray. The ugly creature twisted its head, the jaws splitting apart to reveal two swollen bulbs tipped with sharp curving fangs.

I let out a gasp and scrambled off the rock. What in Eile was that thing? I'd never seen the likes of it in all my excursions into the forest. And something about it felt off, my skin prickling with a sudden sense of icy dread.

"Aiden, please let me see the bite mark."

I approached him, my own hand out. For all I knew, that bug

could be carrying deadly venom in those fangs. Or something worse. When I was only a foot away from Aiden, he snarled and slapped my hand away. His reaction caught me so off guard, I fell to the ground.

"Leave me alone!" he growled.

Before I could form another question, or any sort of response, the sound of soft music drifted to my ears. Aiden noticed it, too. His head jerked around and he peered out over the stone he had climbed before. It was strange, but it was as if suddenly the only thing in the world that mattered to him was the source of that song.

"Aiden!" I called out, not worrying about scaring away the dhadarca any longer. Aiden was acting strange, and another wave of dread shivered over my skin.

I got up, not bothering to dust myself off, and went after him. If he attempted to leave the Weald, I'd have to do everything in my power to stop him. He was the son of the high queen. If any of her enemies recognized him, they would harm him or take him to control her. Fortunately, Aiden only climbed to the top of the boulder. Keeping a wary eye out for more venomous bugs, I joined him, though was careful to keep my distance. The beautiful song grew louder. I suddenly realized it was a solstice tune and the voice that carried it belonged to a woman.

"Aiden?" I asked tentatively, glancing over at him. But his attention was trained on something beyond the edge of the forest. Something that was so arresting I might as well not be there beside him.

Along the edge of the lake, a tall figure dressed in a pale cloak all but glided through the mist. The dhadarca were long gone, but a horse, just as pale as the stranger, stood off a short distance from her. Her song grew stronger as she followed the edge of the water, and she reached up to lower the hood of her cloak. The woman's hair was so light blond it appeared white, her gown and robes like shimmering winter stars. I clutched the back of Aiden's cloak, fear spiking through my heart. Something wasn't right.

"Who is that?" Aiden breathed, inching forward.

"No!" I hissed, my fingers digging deeper into the wool. "We can't go past the boundary! The Weald's magic can't protect you if you move beyond it."

Once again, Aiden reacted sharply, ripping his arm free and nearly tearing my fingernails away with the action.

"Aiden! What is wrong with you?!" I cried as I fought back tears and reached for him again.

But he jerked back. "Get away from me, you little freak!"

Those harsh words lashed at me like bramble vines. Despite the hurt blooming within my heart, I tried stopping him again, but he easily pulled away, biting out nasty curses and names as he remained out of my reach. He was taller and stronger than me, and as I attempted to hold him back one last time, some of my fingernails now torn, he shrugged free of his cloak. I collapsed back off the stone, the wind rushing from my lungs as pain burst along my spine. Gasping, I rolled over, becoming somewhat tangled in the heavy fabric.

I scrambled up the rock, adding more abrasions to my palms, and watched as he slid down the other side and began walking towards the singing woman with purpose.

"No," I choked out, clutching his cloak to my middle.

As I nursed my injured fingers, I kept my eyes on my best friend. What had overcome him? Why had he called me those horrible names? Why was he going to the woman like a moth hypnotized by flame? I glanced back up at the tree. He only started behaving strangely after that odd litterbug had bitten him. My mind raced. Could it have been some devious creation of the Morrigan or one of her followers? Ignoring the ache of my bruised pride, I climbed to my feet and peered out across the field. Aiden was only a few feet from the woman now, and she had stopped singing. Instead, she stood tall, her hood pooling around her shoulders, her arms held wide. Fear and panic pierced through my heart. The woman had to be Daormorrig, one of those still loyal to the goddess of war.

"AIDEN!" I screamed.

But, I might as well have been whispering. He did not stop pacing toward the elegant figure at the edge of the lake, nor did he falter.

Torn between chasing after him and running back for help, I went with my instincts. It would take too long to go back to the village. Or, he would be dead. I was no match for this woman, but I would not abandon my friend.

Taking a deep breath, I leapt from the top of the rock, passing through the invisible barrier of magic keeping all within the Weald safe from those intent on evil, and began running through the tall grass. I had no idea what I was going to do when I reached Aiden and the Daormorrig, but I had to try something. As I drew nearer, the figure reached down and took Aiden's face in her hands. My heart almost stopped altogether as she leaned in and kissed him on the forehead. I watched in horror as my friend collapsed, the woman gathering him in her arms, then lifting him up onto the waiting horse. My cry of terror was nothing more than a gasp, and I pushed harder, my lungs burning with the effort.

I was only yards away when, with Aiden tucked in the saddle before her, the sorceress wheeled the horse around and kicked it into a hard gallop.

"No!!!" I cried out again as I pulled every last ounce of strength from my body. I made it another fifty yards before collapsing from my efforts.

Sobbing, I drew in long, ragged breaths, the beat of horse hooves fading in the distance. I had failed. Danua's son, the high prince of Eile, was once again lost to the enemy.

The sharp, urgent chirps of a sparrow drew me out of my haze of despair. I was lying in the icy mud, a few feet from the lakeshore, my legs and arms numb, my eyes swollen from tears. How long I'd lain there, I couldn't tell, but by the angle of the sun, it was still morning.

Stand up, child. Stand up!

The thoughts flittered through my head, not unlike the small sparrow hopping around in the branches of a blackthorn a few feet away.

What? I thought, my mind muddled.

Get up! I can show you where they went. Follow me!

The sparrow darted off to the north, following the shoreline. I blinked, and made to stand up, hissing a little at the stiffness of my muscles.

"Wait," I croaked out, stumbling after the bird. "Wait!"

Quick, quick, quick! the tiny creature sent.

My progress was slow, but eventually, I caught up with the bird. It was now perched in the bare branches of a willow, its dark eyes glossy and bright.

Your friend was taken by a fae woman we call the Frost Witch.

Frost Witch? I thought.

The bird let out a few sharp chirps. *She makes our blood run cold when she is near. She has taken many of us to harvest our glamour.*

I shivered at that. The Morrigan had done as much, while she still lived.

I cannot help you get him back, but I can show you where to start. The bird ducked its head, indicating a small brook that flowed into the lake. *Follow that stream. Others will help you along the way.*

"Thank you," I murmured quietly, then faced the small sparrow. He was light gray with a black cap on his head and dark stripes running down his back. I wondered if any other colors adorned his feathers, but I did not have Aiden's glamour to aid me now.

With a deep breath, I pushed forward, forgetting my sore muscles and sorrowful heart. I had always been able to pick up on the thoughts and emotions of those living around me, but this was the first time any of the creatures held a conversation with me. Unfortunately, I didn't have time to ponder what that meant. I had to find Aiden.

The stream, it turned out, meandered for miles through rolling hills dotted with more blackthorn, holly, and heather. The somewhat rugged terrain slowed my progress, but I refused to stop. My fingers and toes were numb from the cold, but I had Aiden's cloak and that kept me mostly warm as I scrambled over large stones and pushed through tangled shrubs. Every half mile or so, a small animal – a shrew, a pair of thrushes, a rabbit, a badger, a quartet of rooks – pointed me in the right direction, all agreeing the Frost Witch had taken Aiden and that they would do all they could to help. I hoped that, by the end of this journey, I'd be able to repay them in some way.

Eventually, the stream grew so thin it was barely a trickle of water dripping down a narrow canyon cut between a range of hills. Finally, I stopped and took a moment to study the world around me. The rolling fields were behind me, and ahead oak and birch, their branches bare for the winter, crowned the low hills like thorns.

You must go into the canyon, a voice pressed into my head, the cracked, aged words scraping against my conscious.

I blinked away my weariness and glanced over my shoulder. An ancient crow, its feathers ragged, its bones protruding through emaciated skin, sat upon the bough of a nearby oak.

Cautious alarm trickled through my blood.

I know what you think, child, the bird sent, *but I am no minion of the Morrigan, nor am I a keeper of her memory, nor a boon to her followers. She preferred my cousin, the raven, and even then, we corvids all harbored a healthy fear of her.*

The old bird shivered, his black feathers trembling. *She took more of us than she spared, so I mean you no harm.*

"Where is Aiden?" I asked aloud, my own voice raspy.

The crow cawed mournfully, spreading his tired wings. *She has taken him to her cave. It's where she takes them all. Follow the canyon another half mile. Go beyond the winter roses that bloom blood red on their bare, thorny branches, and then you will see the entrance.*

Before I could nod my thanks, or even take another step, the hair on the back of my neck pricked. Two, three, five more spirits, bright with purpose and violence, approached. My breath caught in my throat as the old crow cawed in warning.

Silence, ancient one!

The words cut through my fear as a snarl broke out behind me. Slowly, I turned to discover a small pack of wolves slipping from behind thick bushes. Their colors could have been a beautiful pattern of brown and white and gold, but only varying shades of gray registered in my field of vision.

Be calm, fae child, the largest one, a female, sent into my mind. *We come with the same purpose. The Frost Witch must be destroyed. She threatens not only the male child, but our family, and all that is good and sacred in Eile.* Sorrow filled her eyes as she continued, *She has already taken my mate from me. I will not let her take my pups. Now, step aside and let us do what we came here to do.*

I glanced up at the crow. He remained wary, but he nodded his old head once. *She speaks truth.*

"No," I said, stepping into the middle of the path. "I need to go into the cave alone."

The large female bared long, white teeth. *You do not stand a chance against her.*

I know. But I cannot risk my friend. I have to make sure he is safe, first. However, I have an idea that might serve us both.

Swallowing back my nerves, I shared my plan, my mouth held in a tight line, but my intent bright as firelight. I hated the thought of death and pain being brought down upon another, but this woman, this Daormorrig, would take my best friend away from me and harvest his glamour, just as the Morrigan had done with her countless victims. Nothing, not even this impending violence, would sway me from doing what I must to keep Aiden safe.

As the wolves stood down, the alpha female gave me a look of pure purpose. *You will alert us should your portion of the plan fail.*

I nodded once, then turned to the crow. He remained hunched on his branch, his eyes clear despite his age. As I studied him, I noticed one wing drooping more than the other.

You should leave, I sent to him. *It could be dangerous for you now.*

The crow blinked once, ruffling his neck feathers. *I would, but my wing has finally given out on me. I've been waiting here for death to claim me for several days now.*

A fresh sadness washed over me, and in response, my healing glamour, that second well of magic nestled beside my soul, rose to mend my sorrow. I gave it free rein and golden light pooled in my palm.

Can you hop down here so I can reach you? I asked gently.

The crow eyed me warily. *Why?*

I wish to offer you a token of gratitude. I lifted my hand and the crow, unable to resist his curiosity, made his way down the tree. It was slow going, but eventually, he was within reach. Spreading my fingers, I let my magic flow over his left shoulder. He let out a quiet grumble, then ruffled his feathers and stretched his once-damaged wing.

You are a gift beyond measure, he sent, his words warm with reverence. *You cannot go into that cave. The witch will surely destroy you.*

I must, I repeated to him as I drew back my hand. *She has something that is worth more to me than my glamour.*

As the words faded from my own mind, I turned and started down the canyon, praying to the spirits of Eile to bless me and give me courage.

The cave entrance was nothing more than a narrow slash in the rocky hillside, but the space widened as I moved deeper into the earth. Flickering light reflected off the curved walls, and as I went along, the scent of death and pain, terror and sorrow, filled my nose and seeped into my soul. Every instinct in my body screamed at me to turn and run. *No,* I told it. *NO.* I would not forsake Aiden. I inched around a corner and almost gasped. A fire burned, small but bright, within a ring of black stones. Above it, a cauldron hung from a chain. In one corner stood a table, the dark wood scarred and stained, all manner of pottery and herbs scattered upon its surface. And directly ahead, between me and the Frost Witch, Aiden sat slumped against the grimy wall. His head lolled to the side, but his eyes were cracked open, the only fleck of color in the entire space. Their aquamarine hue sparked as those eyes fixed upon me. As subtly as possible, I shook my head once.

No, I sent, though the two of us had never tried to establish a shil-sciar connection before, *don't move. If you can sense these words, Aiden, and if you are lucid enough to understand them, please, remain still.*

His eyes flared again and a string of words in the same brilliant color scrolled into my mind. *I am fully conscious, but thought it best to play dumb.*

A strange joy burst into my heart. He understood me.

What ... happened? How did I end up here?

Dark magic, I returned. *I have a plan to get you out of here, but I need you to trust me.*

His response was immediate: *Always.*

The upwelling of delight following his answer gave me courage. Perhaps my friend wasn't entirely lost after all. Closing my eyes slowly, I drew in a long breath and let it out in complete silence. Then, I allowed my foot to scrape across the rough floor, the sound amplified by the curved walls of the small cavern.

The Daormorrig, who had been absentmindedly stirring the contents of her cauldron, froze, then stood with graceful speed and turned to look at me. Surprise made her eyes go wide, but she hid the emotion as quickly as it had appeared.

"What do we have here?" she asked in a sing-song voice.

"Pl-please," I managed, not needing to feed the thread of fear into my words. "I've come for my friend."

The woman placed her hands on her hips and laughed. It was a low, rolling sound that any living thing with a speck of sense would recognize as impending death.

"Have you now?" she said once her spout of humor had dried up.

"Let him go," I pressed, standing tall with false bravado. "T-take me instead."

The sorceress arched a pale brow. "And what makes you think I would do such a ridiculous thing? Surely, the son of the high queen has far more glamour to offer than an unwanted foundling."

I let the insult crash against me like a wave upon stone, but the mention of Aiden's identity shook my foundation.

"You are wrong," I replied, pulling up the shard of rock I'd picked up from the cave floor. Before I could lose my nerve, I drew the sharp edge across my arm, wincing as pain and blood welled up.

The Frost Witch hissed, but I ignored her. Making a fist so the blood surged even more, I drew up my uninjured arm and called forth my glamour, that warm magic I had used to heal so many wounded animals. I spread my fingers wide, the raw power flowing over the large gash. Slowly, as the blood stopped and the wound reknit, the Daormorrig's eyes grew wider.

"Gods and goddesses of Eile," she murmured. "Such power …"

One foot slid forward, as if she'd fallen under a spell. I took a small step back, unwilling to be touched by her evil hand, yet afraid she'd snap out of her haze of greed and see through my guise.

"You must let him go. I offer you a trade, that is all."

"Are you one of the Fandhi?" she breathed, ignoring my request.

I frowned at that. The Fandhi? I wasn't familiar with that term, but I needed to keep her focus on me. I let my uninjured arm fall to my side, weaving just a small flicker of healing glamour between my fingers. And my ruse worked. She stepped forward, slowly, carefully. I mirrored her, moving in the opposite direction.

The woman smiled and reached out a welcoming hand. "Come, child. I'll let the boy go as you asked. Just take my hand."

Her pace quickened ever so slightly, and I put all my energy into keeping just out of reach. We were mere feet away from the cave's entrance when the façade of hospitality cracked and fell away.

"Come now, girl! You cannot escape me. Why do you try to flee? What about your friend? With your glamour added to his, I'll be unstoppable. I will destroy the Tuatha De and take my rightful place as high queen!"

She lunged for me, but with quick feet, I skittered back, slipping through the narrow fissure like a sleek fish. The loose gravel of the cave floor tripped her up, and the witch caught herself on the rough wall. She spat a curse at me, her anger boiling over. The frosty air of the outside world stung my nose, the landscape now cast in the deeper tones of early twilight. Just before the Daormorrig regained her footing, I bolted down the canyon, as fast as I could. I took a sharp turn too fast and crashed into the patch of winter roses the crow told me about, their drab, nodding heads trapped beneath a layer of ice. Trapped, as I would be if I didn't move. Wicked thorns tore at my skin and snagged my cloak, and struggle as I might, I couldn't pull free. The Frost Witch burst out into the open, her face twisted in an evil snarl as her eyes snapped to mine.

"Now, I will make it as unpleasant as possible for you, fae strayling!" she spat.

A black slash of feathers and claws streaked from the branches on the left, slamming into the side of the witch's face. She screamed her outrage as the crow raked her with his claws and drilled her with his beak. With little ease, she batted him aside.

"No!" I cried, but he righted himself in midair and flapped up to the topmost branch.

Cawing mournfully, he rose above the treetops and disappeared from sight. I breathed a small sigh of relief. At least he had escaped.

"Now you die, girl. And all that delicious glamour will be mine!"

She lifted a hand, prepared to draw her nails across my face. But the blow never landed. Between one heartbeat and the next, the wolves leaped from the shadows, the alpha female's teeth clamping down on the Daormorrig's raised arm. The limb twisted at an odd angle, the scream of pain overridden by the snap of bone. I put a hand to my mouth and shed the cloak, slipping beneath the melee of white-gray robes and snarling wolves to run back into the cavern. It took mere seconds to reach Aiden this time, and as I slid to a halt, I noticed my friend was no longer conscious.

"Aiden! Aiden, please, you have to wake up!"

I shook his shoulders, but his head only lolled to the side. He was so pale. With a sob, I brought my hands together and summoned my healing magic. The glamour pooled in my palms, and I waited a bit longer before overturning my hands and pressing them against his chest. I willed the magic to seep into his skin, his marrow, his soul.

Please, please, please ... I pleaded with no one in particular. I drew on that well until I nearly passed out, sensing more than knowing that my efforts had somehow purged all that poisonous magic from my friend.

"Aiden," I whispered, tears streaming down my face. "Aiden, please be okay. You are my best friend. Please don't leave me."

In the distance, the growling of wolves ceased, the screams of the witch long since faded. What seemed like hours passed, but slowly, ever so slowly, Aiden's face lost its pallor, the colors of the world blooming and overtaking the gray. I knew then he would be okay. Whipping my head around, I caught myself laughing. The fire was no longer just bright, but a vivid orange and yellow and red. Aiden was coming back to me.

A moan returned my attention to my friend. His eyes were open, the aquamarine irises not dull, but vibrant and lucid.

"T-Tegan? Where are we? What happened?"

I leaned in and hugged him, forcing the air from his lungs. He returned the gesture weakly.

"No time to explain," I said. "We need to leave now. Before her friends discover she has been defeated."

The look on his face would have made me laugh, if I wasn't so exhausted.

"Come on!" I insisted, standing up and offering him my hand. He took it, and I pulled him to his feet. Although he was taller than me, he felt surprisingly light. Not letting go of his hand, I pulled him down the cave tunnel. We stepped out into a landscape further darkened by dusk, and not a trace of the wolves or the witch could be found. Thank the gods and goddesses of Eile. They must have killed her after all, dragging her remains off to some unknown location. I couldn't feel sorry for her, though. She would have done worse to us.

We jogged to the end of the canyon and were halfway down the hill before we stopped to rest.

"How are we going to get home?" I panted. The Solstice festivities would begin soon, and we would be missed.

Aiden shrugged. "We'll just have to walk, I guess." His eyes met mine, his expression serious. "We cannot tell anyone about this," he whispered.

I could only nod. If his mother or sister found out about what had happened, they would never let him come back to the Weald again.

"Pinky swear," I said, offering up my littlest finger.

He smiled, though it held little humor, then linked his small finger with mine and we shook.

"I guess we had better start walking," Aiden suggested wearily. "We can work on a believable story on the way back. We'll have enough time."

Before either of us could take a single step, however, a large pale shape pushed out from a grove of young beech trees. My gasp was silent, but Aiden seemed to melt with relief.

"The witch's horse," Aiden said breathlessly. "She was a member of Epona's herd before she was kidnapped."

I turned to face my friend. "How do you know that?"

Aiden's turquoise eyes held no wariness as he said, "She told me." He tapped a finger to his temple. *The same way you spoke to me earlier,* he finished using shil-sciar. *I think I was able to speak to her and to you because I learned how to do it when Meghan and I were ..."*

He didn't finish the thought, and as his words faded away, I glanced down at my muddy boots. I knew of what he spoke, and I wasn't going to press. When he was kidnapped by the Morrigan, his sister, Meghan, had gone to save him, and they had been trapped together for a time. The exact details of how they had escaped were still unknown by many, but I didn't need to know. He and his sister had escaped and defeated our world's greatest enemy. That was good enough for me.

As if unsettled by the shift in topic, Aiden straightened his shoulders and thrust out his jaw. "You are free," he told the horse. "The Frost Witch is dead."

The horse shook out her mane and snorted. Aiden blinked a few times, then said, "But, don't you wish to return home?"

"What is she saying?" I asked.

"She said she owes us a debt of gratitude and has offered to carry us back to the edge of the Weald."

A smile broke across my face. Perhaps we would make it back in time for the start of the festivities after all.

"Where have you two been?!" Fiadh, one of the Faelorehn women in charge of keeping an eye on the younger children, insisted as Aiden and I jogged into the center of the village.

The bonfires were roaring, music was playing, and the scent of roasting meat and simmering spices infused the cold air. The village of the Wildren was alive with activity and color. Oh, all the wonderful colors! I had held onto Aiden's hand as we'd raced through the trees, telling him I couldn't risk losing track of him again. He'd rolled his eyes and told me not to be ridiculous, but I had insisted. It wasn't entirely a lie. I wanted the reassurance that he was okay, and being able to see the brilliance of the world around me, even though night had fallen, was just another reminder of that fact.

"Sorry!" Aiden answered breathlessly. "We were trying to find twigrins and lost track of time."

Fiadh eyed us suspiciously, and I quickly let go of Aiden's hand to shove mine into my pockets. I feared they might start shaking again and give us away. The color swiftly drained from the world around me, but there were still a few muted tones to brighten my Solstice. Besides, Aiden and I were once again within the safety of the Weald. We hadn't spoken of what had happened during our entire journey back, and part of me didn't want to. What I had done to save my friend, while justified, still left me feeling cold and empty.

With a soft snort, Fiadh shook her head and waved her arm in the direction of the festivities. "Fine, but you're lucky you two didn't get lost out there. Go, find yourself some dinner and join the celebration."

All we could do was nod. Aiden grabbed my arm and pulled me away before Fiadh could change her mind. We didn't seek out the other children, but we did eat plenty of sweets and played the games, acting as if Aiden had never been bitten by that strange bug and that the Frost Witch hadn't dragged him off to harvest his glamour. When we grew weary, we grabbed mugs of hot cider and found a spot in front of one of the many bonfires.

As the adults and children laughed and chattered around us, my mind wandered back to the events of the day. I shivered and set down my spiced cider, taking Aiden's hand in mine.

"What's the matter?" my friend asked with mild surprise.

Ignoring his complaints, I turned his hand over in my own. The bite marks were gone, the swelling all but vanished.

"Just making sure," I mumbled, letting him go.

He placed his other hand on my shoulder, forcing me to look into his eyes.

I can't remember what happened, he sent using shil-sciar, the words tainted with a sense of apology, *but I imagine it wasn't pleasant.*

The worst part was believing, if only for a few minutes, that you hated me, I thought to myself. But I did not share that with Aiden.

I shrugged, the motion shifting his hand from my shoulder. *Don't worry. It's over, and we are both safe. It won't ever happen again,* I vowed, not knowing if what I spoke was true.

The rest of the evening passed in a whirlwind of cheer and good tidings, and we all stayed up until the first light of dawn stained the eastern sky with blush and rose. Many of the children, and adults as well, had fallen asleep around the bonfires, and I didn't even realize Aiden and I were included among them until a deep voice broke through the fog of exhaustion.

"Prince Aiden," someone said.

We sat up straighter, blinking away sleep. A small party of armed soldiers stood before us, their breath steaming in the air, a thin, sparse blanket of snow coating the ground around them. The fire had burned down to coals, but it had been hot enough to leave us warm and to keep the worst of the frost at bay.

"It is time for you to return to your mother," the soldier standing apart from the other four said.

The Faelorehn man didn't mention any news from Erintara, good or bad, and Aiden didn't ask. He simply nodded, his eyes drooping, then replied, "I'll need to get my things."

The soldier ducked his head once. "Take your time."

Aiden stood and I made to follow him, but he held out a palm. "I won't take long. You stay where it's warm, and I'll come back before I leave."

I fought the urge to follow him. After what had happened, I was reluctant to let Aiden leave my sight. But the village was slowly waking up, and there would be chores to attend to. I allowed myself to rest a bit longer, doing my best not to dwell on the fact that my friend would be leaving again for the gods and goddesses knew how long.

By the time Aiden returned, dressed in fresh clothes and a traveling cloak, his pack secure to his back, I had been put in charge of handing out bowls for breakfast.

"Can I borrow Tegan for a moment?" he asked one of the adults stirring the large cauldron of porridge.

The young Faelorehn man nodded once, his eyes kind, and said, "Go ahead. Mirra can take your place for now."

Handing the bowls over to a girl with a flurry of curly hair that looked to be red, I followed Aiden to the foot of the path that would take him and his royal escort to the far-off palace in the heart of Eile.

"Here," Aiden said, holding out a simple wooden box. I took it, surprised at how light it was, and flicked my eyes to my friend's. They were still that brilliant aquamarine blue, a good sign the poison was truly gone. "I'm sorry I didn't give it to you earlier, but it was in my cabin all day and," he paused, eyes flicking up to the soldiers, then added "I wasn't able to get it before." He shrugged. "Don't open it now. Wait until I'm gone."

I furrowed my brow at that. Why?

Before I could put my thoughts into words, Aiden reached out and pulled me into a tight hug.

"Until the summer," he said quietly, as if those months were decades away. Strangely, I felt the same way.

He let go and smiled, then turned to walk away with the queen's guards. I watched as he followed the Faelorehn men and women in silence, my eyes fixed on Aiden until I couldn't see him any longer. I stood there facing east until the cold of the winter morning numbed the tip of my nose.

Drawing in a deep breath, I let it out in a billow of steam. The wooden box was warm in my hand. I lifted it and removed the sprig of holly garnishing the top, then undid the simple twine bow. The lid slipped off with little effort, and the small gasp that escaped my throat was as delicate as the frost crackling beneath my shoes. A silver ring with a band of dark color running around the middle sat atop a piece of folded paper. Stamped across the band in bold letters was the word *BEST*.

With shaky fingers, I pulled the note free. In Aiden's neat, elegant script I read:

I meant to give this to you yesterday, but I got a little sidetracked. It's a mood ring, something from the mortal world. It isn't real magic, not like Faelorehn glamour, but I thought you might like it. The colors change depending on your mood, and it reminded me of your eyes. Anyway, it came as a set. My ring says FRIEND, but I wanted you to have the one that says BEST because that is what you are. Thank you, Tegan, for saving my life. And for being the only friend I have ever had, both in Eile and the mortal world.
—Aiden

The writing grew wavy as tears filled my eyes. I clutched the beautiful ring to my heart and drew in a deep breath, letting it out with a sigh. I had almost lost him, but now I knew the value of what could be gained by facing your fear.

"Until the summer months, then," I said to myself, slipping the ring onto my thumb, the only finger it would fit. Casting one last glance at the path leading out of the Weald, I turned and strode back towards the heart of the village to wait until my friend came back to me again.

~END ~

AUTHOR'S NOTE

Faefrost is a retelling of The Snow Queen and is set in my Otherworld universe. The story features Tegan and Aiden, two of my younger characters from that series, and is told from Tegan's perspective. I chose The Snow Queen as my fairytale for two reasons. One, I really wanted to tell another story with Tegan and Aiden as the focus, and The Snow Queen features a young girl who embarks upon a quest to rescue her close friend. In my retelling, Tegan must leave the safety of her home to save Aiden from a dangerous adversary. A second reason I chose The Snow Queen is that the plot of this fairytale meshes well with my Otherworld universe, and it gave me an opportunity to offer my readers a glimpse into what has been going on in that world, as well as a fore-shadowing of books to come. Whether you are familiar with my Otherworld series or not, I hope you have enjoyed this small tale of adventure, sacrifice, and enduring friendship.

ABOUT THE AUTHOR

Jenna Elizabeth Johnson is a bestselling, multi award-winning author of contemporary and epic fantasy. She has written multiple books in the Otherworld, the Draghans of Firiehn, and the Legend of Oescienne series.

For contact information, visit the author's website at www.jennaelizabethjohnson.com.

CAT IN COMBAT BOOTS

C. GOCKEL

TENRYU WAKES IN HIS HUMAN FORM, TIED TO A METAL BED, WITH PAIN like fire in his chest, and a woman shouting so fiercely it cuts through his agonized haze. He can't understand what she's saying; she is speaking in a barbarian language, maybe English or German? He can't reach his magic so he can't translate her words. Have they sliced the shard that gives him the bulk of his power from his chest? He should have *some* magic without it, yet feels none.

There is an ear-splitting crack, a thunk, and then another, and another. Gunshots? Have they shot her? He can imagine the brutes who'd captured him and bound his magic shooting a woman. If he had his magic, even just a little bit he'd ...

He feels magic then, as though his mental wish had summoned it —though that is impossible, he's been wishing for his magic since he arrived here. The magic is just a trickle, just the slightest thread, but he seizes it.

The woman is silent; there are no more sounds of struggle. He can do nothing for her, not tied down, not in so much pain. The men are talking, and the flow of magic is strong enough that he could translate it if he wished, but he must heal his injuries first. If he heals himself, he might be well in time to save the woman, too.

He uses his magic to cut off the pain and surveys his wound not with his eyes, but with his magic. He still has *most* of the magical shard that gives him the bulk of his power. They've only sliced off a tiny sliver of it. If he has the shard, why doesn't he have *more* magic? There must be some other binding, but first things first. He mends the flesh they cut through to get the shard that resides beneath his sternum, next to his heart; heals the muscles, tendons, and ligaments; and last, heals his skin. It's slow going with so little magic to work with, an hour, maybe more. He's afraid he'll be discovered, but the men are intent on whatever they are doing. When his wounds heal, he turns his attention to their language.

"It worked!" says one.

"She's healed the incision above the sliver. I think you were right. I think she has maintained human consciousness even in this new form!"

"The sliver we implanted may have accelerated normal healing without her conscious effort. We can't be certain yet."

There is a snort. "Whatever. I'm ready to cut another sliver out of our friend's chest and place it in mine right now." From the sound of the man's voice, Tenryu knows the human is looking at him. Fortunately, Tenryu's eyes are closed.

The other man grunts. "Be patient."

The man who wants to rip Tenryu's chest open again says, "Damn, it looks like the bitch damaged the Promethean Wire with her bullets. Do you think he'll be able to use his magic?"

Promethean Wire? Is that how they are binding his magic? Tenryu keeps his eyes closed, despite his desire to open them, to see this wire, and the weak point.

The other man replies, "He's still human, so no, I don't think we have to worry."

Tenryu begins working on his bonds. Telekinesis is among the most difficult of all magic tricks to do, but the bonds are simple buckles, not locks. He slips the one around his right wrist loose and then the other three. Wiggling his fingers and his toes, he does his best to test his muscles without attracting attention. Half opening his eyelids he surveys his surroundings. There are lights above him, but they are not on. On the ceiling there is a strange octagonal wire—perhaps that is the Promethean Wire they were talking about. He lets his gaze slip from side to side. The strange wire is on the walls, and on the floors, too. But two of the octagons are damaged—one to his right and one directly across from it on the left, shredded in both places, as though by a human bullet.

"Keep running the experiments," one of his captors says. "Before he wakes up, I'm going to seal that wire."

He'll never have another chance. Tenryu leaps from the bed, knocking over some sharp and shiny instruments as he does.

"He's awake!" shouts the man.

The other man shrieks, "She bit me!" holding up a hand from which a slender, white cat briefly dangles.

The shiny instruments could be weapons. But Tenryu might not get another chance at this, and he can't risk recapture now, even if it may mean losing his life later when the weyr of dragons finds him. He races to the side of what is his cage and their operating theater and presses his newly healed chest to the gap in the Promethean Wire.

One of the men, dressed in a long, white formless coat, runs to a cabinet beyond the wire, tripping over the white cat as he does. She hisses defiantly, he kicks her, and she thuds against the wall and is quiet. The man then pulls what looks like a pistol from the cabinet. The other is running to join the first.

Tenryu smiles sharply. The cat has given his shard just enough time to pull magic into itself. "Too late," he says to the men and transforms into his dragon first-form. The Promethean Wire rips from the inside out, and he has one large claw crushing the first man and a talon through the second. They are both dead, the blood and gore make the mouth of his first-form water.

An alarm goes off, reminding him that he still isn't safe. He has to get out of this place. He also has to get out of this form. If he doesn't, the weyr will surely have word of his presence. Looking at the heavy double doors at the entrance to the room he can't bring himself to change back to a human. Men are shouting on the other side.

Undoubtedly they have more firearms. In this form he is immune. First, he must get to safety, and then he'll worry about the dragons of the weyr.

But before he does anything else ...

The tiny unconscious cat is insect-sized compared to a dragon, but dragon talons can be as delicate as human hands. Tenryu picks the cat up, feels the rapid beat of her heart, and the thrum of magic from the splinter of the shard they stole from his heart. The splinter is so tiny that he has to touch her to sense its presence clearly. Without a better idea, he puts her in his ear. It is the perfect size for a cat, tucked behind one of his fins so she will not be blown away. Satisfied she is safe, he almost rushes through the double doors ... but then he thinks of the steep cliffs that surround his horde on this continent and scans the room for her clothes. They're wet and bloody, but there is a pair of boots that at first he doesn't think can be hers—they look like the boots of the Meiji Era army. He has been asleep since just recently—his children in Meiji Era Japan going to war with his children in China had been too much—he'd had to pull back from human affairs. Also, Longue Croc's ... attentions ... had begun to get serious. He isn't sure how long he slept, but surely women can't be in organized combat? Perhaps they are work boots? Though why was she wearing them with a black and white polka-dot dress? The boots are the only footwear he sees, so he loops the laces together and wraps them around a claw. The shouts outside the double doors grow louder. Tenryu rushes through them, past men with weapons that fire on him and hurt as much as pinpricks, and then he is outside, and there are more shouts below, and more gunfire, but he is high above them all and rising into the clouds.

It is tricky business getting the cat out of his ear. She is still unconscious and unable to help. In the end, he presses the flat of his claw to it, turns his head, and then shifts bringing a comfortable yukata with his human form. She winds up on his arm. Tenryu isn't a judge of cat beauty, but he thinks she is very pretty, with a lithe dainty body and white fur.

He finds another yukata in his horde and spreads it out on a bed of coins from a long-dead empire. He tucks her in so that just her head is showing. He sets the boots at the bottom edge of the yukata, so she'll be sure to find them, even if anything happens to him. There is a moan outside the cave, and for a moment he freezes, expecting the rumble of dragon voices at any moment. None comes. It was just the wind.

They will come. But he has been delaying the inevitable long enough. Maybe it is his time ... although ... he looks at the little white cat who saved him thrice over, with her Promethean Wire shredding bullets as a human and then with her teeth and her body as a cat. He will help her. It will be his dying gift.

Sitting cross-legged beside her, he rubs his chin. It is obvious that his captors were trying to master instantaneous transformation. Why they didn't kill him and remove his whole shard is only conjecture—perhaps they thought its magic would die with him? He should be grateful for their ignorance.

Instantaneous transformation is the most power-robbing of magical tasks. It's not so much that one transforms, as it is that one keeps another form in stasis in the In-Between, a plane of existence not part of the universe. He has never known any creature to be able to maintain that stasis, except those with the magical shards like the one he has tucked just beneath his sternum, right beside his heart. He touches his chest. His shard is now a sliver smaller—that lost piece is in the little cat before him. He could take the sliver back ... but he is going to die soon anyway, and any sliver that won't go to his enemies is a victory.

He needs to find her human form. Stroking the cat between the ears, he lets his magical senses move between the tiny sliver by her heart and into the In-Between. He frowns. The humans who transformed her have made a mess of it. He finds not a human in the In-Between but a mass of cells in stasis around a tiny echo of the shard on the Earthly side. He rubs his brow. Since he'd awoken he'd learned that humans were again aware of magical beings. He'd thought humans becoming aware of magic and the other realms would make relations between them and himself safer; instead, they have just become more dangerous for him and for this woman.

With his own shard to give him power, he reads the DNA and telomeres within the woman's cells. He finds some oddities—magical matter in her nervous system. He's heard that some humans have become magical of late, too, but not yet met one. What is more striking is that there is not a single tumor cell in her body. There should be some cellular trash as of yet to face her body's immune system, but as hard as he looks, he finds none. Also, all of the bacteria and viruses within her DNA are beneficial symbiotes. He can only explain it by her youth, mid-twenties going by her telomeres. He gradually puts the woman back together, cell by cell, tissue by tissue. When he is satisfied, he opens his eyes to the cat, presses gently upon her chest ... and finds his hands on the sternum of a young barbarian woman, her heart beating beneath his fingers, her chest rising and falling, the thrum of the sliver noticeable but so small it is difficult to pinpoint. She has too-pale skin and hair that is such a light gold it is almost white. She looks like a ghost, but at least she doesn't have the typical, enormous, barbarian nose. He tilts his head. She might even be beautiful in her ghostly way. He's sure she'll have a long magical life and magical children. He'll have to find a way to see her back to her people ... should really take her now ... but he's sleepy. Putting her back together again took a lot of concentration, even if his shard gave him the power.

His yukata is only cotton, and he's beginning to feel quite cold. Finding a quilt stuffed with silk, he lays down beside her, pulls the quilt over them both, and, promising himself he'll only rest a little while, falls asleep.

The lumpy mattress under Beatrice chinks every time she rolls over. It's also slippery, too hard, and altogether uncomfortable. It's probably the reason for her strange dreams. She opens her eyes and finds herself staring at a man she's never seen before. He has tan skin, and long dark hair, black and smooth as a raven's wing. Even with his eyes closed, she can tell he's probably of East Asian descent by their shape and his full lips. He is also magical and more than that, the area around his heart is *more* magical; it thrums with power. She struggles with the urge to reach out and touch it. All of this is disconcerting, but for Beatrice, the most disconcerting thing of all is that he's sharing the same quilt that covers her. She gasps and doesn't quite manage to stifle it.

His eyes flicker open and widen slightly. He speaks in another language—she doesn't know which—but she does understand the words. She's unusually good at magical translation, probably because she was trilingual since she was an unmagical child. "Your eyes are very blue," he says in his foreign tongue. Which is an odd thing to say.

"Yours are brown," she says, thinking at the same time that they are also flecked with gold, quite startling, and if she thinks on it, attractive.

He shakes himself and rises. "We must get you to your people." A sardonic smile touches his lips. Under his breath, he adds, "Before mine come for me."

Rising beside him, she finds she is wearing a loose cotton robe. It's similar to one he's wearing, but hers is adorned with a flower print, while his is a rather drab blue, striped with a slightly paler drab blue. She's naked under the robe, but as an elderly woman, it's not her first worry. Yes, of course, some men molest old women, but she feels instantly that isn't what's happened here. Still, she doesn't know *what* happened. Exploring the back of her skull, she finds no lumps. "How did I get here?" she asks.

He gives her a smile that makes the edges of his eyes crinkle. She can't help noticing how handsome he is. She is elderly, with a few magical enhancements, not dead. "You saved my life three times," he replies.

That explains ... nothing. Squeezing the bridge of her nose, she closes her eyes. "The last thing I remember is being captured." She'd been sent to investigate a magical disturbance in the Sierra Nevada range. She'd told Rush that they shouldn't split up. He'd ignored her and told her to wait with the car while he and Park checked out the nearest rise. The ground had literally opened up as soon as they were out of eyesight—mechanically, not magically—she'd been grabbed and tasered. She'd regained consciousness without her captors noticing, and fired her pistol ... and then ... and then her memories got hazy. Had there been a jab in the neck? After that ... "I dreamed I was a cat."

"Not a dream," he says.

"That's impossible," she replies. There are all sorts of things that are possible in the universe now that magic is real, but changing into an animal is impossible, or at least, very slow, and very painful. To transform, every part of the body has to be painstakingly regrown, with emphasis on the "pain." It would take months ... or years ... or ... "It hasn't been decades, has it?" she asks, alarmed by the possibility of a Rip Van Winkle scenario.

His brow furrows. "No, it was ... a few hours ago. I ... " He bows slightly, maybe nervously, then rolls his hands, "Put your body back together."

He's not lying. Detecting lies isn't Beatrice's magical strength. But some of her associates can, and she's picked up some things. This man is telling the truth.

He rubs the back of his head, and she notices how tall he is, and well proportioned. She finds herself blushing, as though she were a girl. Looking away her eyes take in the chamber around them for the first time. Her body goes cold and her stomach sinks. "We are in danger."

"How do you know?" he asks, eyes going wide.

"This is a dragon horde," Beatrice whispers. Her "mattress" is a bed of coins. And the chamber they are in is stuffed full of weapons, armor, porcelain vases, and bones ... none human, but she's pretty sure she sees a horse head picked clean, and what was once perhaps a bison, but she didn't think they were that big, or their horns were that wide.

Rummaging through a pile of coins, he mutters, "Why didn't I bring shoes when I transformed," and then looking up at her, says, "In my human form, you don't have to fear me."

Beatrice blinks at him. "Human form?"

He says something that must not translate into English, Russian, or Ukrainian, and pulls a sandal that is falling apart from the coins. Slipping it on, he says, "I have a dragon form like you have a cat form. I would show you, but then I would want to eat you. Also, it will draw unwanted attention. Would you please put on your boots? We need to leave."

Her mind spins. Obediently going to her boots, because her mind is spinning too fast to do anything else, and it's a practical suggestion whatever is going on, Beatrice says, "Cat form? But how is that possible?"

"You wouldn't ..." He looks up at her sharply, and says what sounds like, "Eh toe," and then, "Your language has a word for it." He begins digging frantically through the coins again. "A long time ago, millennia, before even the Xia Dynasty, a dragon named Tiamat got hold of a World Seed."

Pulling her socks from her boot, Beatrice murmurs, "Oh no." World Seeds are essentially "baby universe eggs." When they hatch they can destroy the current universe. Also, the only one she knew had an unpleasant personality.

Waving a hand, her new companion says, "No, it was fine. Tiamat broke it up into little bits and gave a shard to all of her children. Dragons that have a shard of it next to their hearts can transform into, well, anything. You have a tiny sliver of my shard and you can turn into a cat."

The laces of Beatrice's boots are tied together, and she begins worrying them loose. Still digesting everything he's told her, she falls back on practicalities. "I don't know your name."

"Tenryu, and yours?"

"Beatrice."

"Nice to meet you." He pulls out another sandal. It looks worse than the first. He sets about putting it on anyway.

"Nice to meet you, too. Tenryu, if you are a dragon and this is your horde ... why are we in a hurry?"

From outside the chamber comes a roar that reverberates through the stones and makes some of the coins slide down the pile. The roar is echoed over and over. Beatrice doesn't have to be told that a whole weyr of dragons has gathered outside.

Tenryu doesn't so much sit as fall on his butt. "That's why."

Outside his inner chamber the roars continue, and then there is the scrape of claws on rock, and the rumbling voice of Longue Croc, "Tenryu, you can fly but you can't hide. Not forever. Come out now, my love."

He presses his hands to his head.

Beatrice sits beside him. "I take it you are having problems with an ex-lover?"

He is being stupid and childish. Yes, he is going to die like a dragon, but Beatrice can live like a human if she hides first.

Dropping his hands, he turns to her. "Beatrice," he whispers, "You can turn into a cat. They won't notice you, you can get away."

Her brows draw together. "I thought you said you can turn into other forms. Couldn't you turn into a cat, too?"

He gives her an indulgent smile. "You are clever." He sighs. "But my shard is too large. No matter how small I am, they will feel it. They'll catch me."

She glances at his chest, and raises her hand, as though to touch it. "I understand." She drops her hand self-consciously and he sighs again. He'd welcome even a platonic touch from the ghostly, but beautiful barbarian before he dies.

Outside the chamber, there is a rumble and a few roars. Of course, Longue Croc would bring witnesses; and of course, no dragon would dare not join her, no matter how distasteful they find the proceedings. A moment later, a giant yellow eye surrounded by green scales peers into the chamber. Longue Croc rumbles. "Another human wife? Tenryu, you are so boringly predictable. Come out and *live* like a dragon."

Another voice rumbles, "And die like a dragon."

The eye vanishes and is replaced by a side of green scales that completely blocks the chamber entrance that is just large enough for a male dragon's long serpentine body but too small for an adult female dragon. Longue Croc's voice is muffled by her girth when she replies, "Oh hush now, Sharp Claw. You know I'll make it worth it."

Beside him, Beatrice shivers. "Die like a dragon?"

She understood that dragonese? She is more talented with magic than he presumed. Strange for someone so young. Tenryu shakes his head; that doesn't matter. "We must teach you how to turn into a cat."

She stares at him. Her eyes are very wide, blue, and strange. He says what he *means* wondering if that will make it easier for her to understand. "We must teach you to switch your cat body, that resides in the In-Between, with your human body here."

She looks away. "The In-Between ... I can't walk through it, like my grandson-in-law." He must have misunderstood that last word; she must have meant brother-in-law.

She scowls. "He's always using it to walk in and steal food from my kitchen."

Tenryu blinks. Her husband doesn't put a stop to that? She must be unmarried. Perhaps living with a widowed mother? Certainly, she wouldn't live alone.

She turns back to him. "I have a cat body there? How do I access it?"

"It is very easy; think of a white cat."

She closes her eyes. "Nothing is happening."

"Try touching your breast bone, you'll feel it—"

She does as he says and vanishes. He glances down to find a small white cat sitting pertly beside her boots.

Tenryu glances at the door. Longue Croc is still blocking the entrance with her scales. The dragoness is telling the story of her last paramour now, and how their coupling lasted for seven days and seven nights. Longue Croc's trying to entice him. The total time he spent in bed with his last human wife was far more than seven days and seven nights, but spread out over decades, and he lived to see his grandchildren. He pushes the thought aside and focuses on the human woman in front of him ... who is now a cat.

"Do you still understand me?" he asks.

The cat nods, and he is pleased. She is still accessing her human faculties in the In-Between. He doesn't have time for explanations even if she's curious. "We should practice changing back into a human," he says. He holds out his arm, and she hops onto it. He is touched by the trust and rubs a hand between her ears. "You don't tickle my arm as much as you tickle my ear."

Beatrice the cat raises her nose in question.

He explains, "I put you in my ear to keep you safe from the wind and cold when I flew here."

The cat meows and magic translates. "Dragons have ears?"

He chuckles. "How do you think we hear?"

The cat's ears go back and her tail flicks. Magic translates again. "I suppose that was a silly question."

"It is no problem." On impulse, he walks her over to where a mirror hides behind a tapestry. As he does Beatrice kneads her claws into his arm and purrs. "I can work with these." She licks her lips. "And these teeth are sharp, too."

He smiles despite himself. She's adapting very quickly. Reaching the mirror and pulling away the tapestry, he holds her up to the glass so she can see herself as a cat. "Here you are," he says, "and if you want to change back think of your human—"

She changes back; she's not just magical, she has obviously *used* magic before. His hand is now on her lower back, not beneath her feet. Also, she is naked. He should have expected that. He didn't, and now he has a view of her from her pale white hair to her toes. He thinks he has heard somewhere that barbarians are more prudish about nudity, but for a moment he is mesmerized by her beauty that is both exotic and familiar and cannot turn away. His eyes rise to Beatrice's in the mirror. She isn't looking at him. She isn't looking at her naked body. She's looking directly into her own eyes. "You made me young!" she shouts, the same sort of angry shout he'd heard when he was a captive.

He nods. "Yes, you are young." He is confused, wondering what concept between their languages doesn't translate.

"I am a grandmother!" she says. "I'm over ninety years old. My hair is white, not blonde!" She pulls on her cheeks. "I have wrinkles on my wrinkles."

Tenryu holds up his hands in surrender. Obviously, there has been some terrible misunderstanding, and he's somehow made a horrendous mistake, one that has robbed her of her status as an elder. "Forgive me. You had no trace of cancer in your cells, and your telomeres, those are the—"

Beatrice puts her hands over her face and groans. "I know telomeres are the time clocks of the cells. My granddaughter is the doctor of all doctors."

Tenryu swallows, and says carefully, "You must be very proud?"

She looks over her hands at him and narrows her eyes. "She needs me to be *old* to protect her."

He blinks. "The practice of medicine must have changed a great deal in the time I was asleep."

She tilts her head, and her pale hair goes over one shoulder. He can't help following it with his eyes. "You're cold," he says, regretfully holding up the tapestry for her. She's cold, and he has no time for the thoughts that just flitted through his brain and other places.

Her cheeks go charmingly pink as she takes the tapestry and wraps it around her shoulders. "I was given younger telomeres so I wouldn't age anymore, and a healthier immune system, and stronger muscles and bones so I could protect Amy, my granddaughter. She is always getting herself in trouble." She adds in a small voice, "I don't have time for feelings." At the last word, she glances at him, and as their eyes meet he knows that the attraction he'd felt earlier isn't one way.

Her cheeks go darker still. He dips his head. "You are very beautiful, even for a barbarian."

"For a what?" she asks.

He rolls his eyes. "We don't have time."

Outside the chamber, Longue Croc finishes her grisly tale. Beatrice's eyes go wide and she looks between the scaly wall blocking the exit and him.

"Tenryu ... is that dragon going to ... mate with you and then ... eat you?"

Tenryu's face flushes and he paces a few steps. His eyes flash with anger, but he shakes his head and says, "There's a pool at the back of the chamber. There are fish and insects there. In your cat form, you won't mind eating them. When I'm ... when the dragons are all gone, you leave. We're in the place you know as ... Gold Country ..." He blinks. "Oregon."

Putting a hand on her hip, she demands, "You're just going to let yourself die?"

He barks a short laugh. "I'm not going to *let* myself. I'm going to wait here until I am so hungry I change back into my real form in delirium, and then she will release her musk. I will go mad again, and then ..." He shakes his head and gives her a crooked smile. "Not all female dragons eat their males, but some dragons are even more barbaric than Europeans."

Beatrice decides to ignore the last barb. "You can't fight her?"

"Female dragons are twice as large as males, but, yes, of course, I can fight her. I can't fight the musk."

"Can't you ..." Beatrice looks around helplessly, "Put something in your nose?"

He gives her a glare. "I'm sure I could, and that she could rip it out."

Beatrice frowns. The only thing she sees that might remotely qualify is fabric, and she knows that doesn't keep odors out very well. "You can't just make yourself bigger than this ... Crock of Dragon?"

"I could. But then she would make herself bigger," Tenryu says. "And that wouldn't solve the problem of the musk."

"Why not make yourself into a female dragon?" Beatrice supplies. "That would—"

Tenryu's head whips around fast. "That would ensure the female dragons ripped me limb from limb."

Beatrice's eyes widen in shock.

He looks away. "Although female dragons are allowed to become male dragons for a lark, male dragons aren't allowed to have female dragon forms. Females control *everything*." He raises his chin and sits very still.

He's already defeated. Beatrice isn't ready to admit defeat. Tapping her lip, Beatrice surveys the weapons in his horde. Most look more ceremonial than effective. Obviously, if they'd been effective, they wouldn't have wound up in his horde. As her gaze roves more carefully through the piles of gaudy gleaming dragon stuff, she sees some things that are out of place. Here and there, tucked into nooks in the rocks, high above the treasure are faded objects made from wood, faded fabric, straw, and porcelain. They're dolls of people, and animals, and little wagons with wheels. "You have toys in your horde," she declares in surprise.

"Of all the human children I've eaten," he says flatly. Again, Beatrice isn't terrific at spotting falsehoods, but this one is obvious. "Liar," she says.

His face flushes again. Still not looking at her he mutters, "They're mementos from my human children's childhoods."

Her brow furrows. So he's spent extensive time as a human. Her eyes go to a doll made of disintegrating straw. He probably lived as a peasant to escape notice. He's married and loved humans, which explained Longue Croc mistaking Beatrice for "his wife."

Tenryu continues, "And the mementos of my children's children from two continents. I always keep something. I *am* a dragon. We horde."

She has baby blankets from both her daughter and her grand-daughter. Beatrice understands that.

He has feelings for his family, which doesn't explain why she's here. "You saved me because … ?"

He shrugs. "I've had better experiences among humans than my own kind. You might be a barbarian, but you're still human."

She snorts but isn't really offended. She'd spent most of her child-hood in Ukraine. When she'd come to America in the 1930s, it was less diverse than modern times, but it had still been shockingly diverse to her. She'd brought to America a lot of prejudices born out of the isolation she'd grown up with. It is easy to mythologize and pathologize those you've never met, harder to do that to your neighbor.

He looks at her, eyes blazing. "You saved my life. I saved your life. We are even. Turn into a cat now, hide, and save yourself."

He is a decent fellow, racism aside. "Can't you do anything?"

"The only way out of it is if a female declares herself my champi-on," Tenryu says, staring at nothing. She recognizes the look on his face. She's seen it on men's faces before. Stoicism in the face of death, which is sometimes admirable. However, this situation is beginning to get under her skin. He's being treated like an object, as less than human, or less than a dragon, because he's small. Beatrice had a loving husband, but she's been treated as "less" by others because of her gender, and later because of her age. "Damn telemarketers," she mutters, earning a curious eyebrow rise from Tenryu.

Beatrice nods to herself, mind made up. "I'm female. I'll be your champion." A part of her knows she is acting in anger, but nearly a century of being seen as less is a *long* time to build up righteous rage.

He doesn't look at her. He looks at her boots. "Those don't make you a warrior," he says.

"Of course not. My brain does," Beatrice replies, lip curling in irritation. He snorts and looks off into the distance again.

"I've taken on bullies larger than me before," Beatrice counters. Technically, everyone Beatrice has ever fought in earnest has been larger than her. She's tiny. She folds her arms. "And I always win."

He levels a glare at her.

She shrugs. "I cheat. It's only fair." Most of the enemies she's fought have been male and stronger than she is.

Rolling his eyes, he looks off into nothing. "You think Longue Croc doesn't cheat?"

Tapping her chin, Beatrice considers that. "Then it will be a battle of wits and I'm bound to win." Longue Croc has mommy deceptive skills, but Beatrice has *grandmother* skills. Age isn't always the measure of maturity.

"You're mad," Tenryu says.

Picking up her boots, still tied together by the laces, Beatrice gestures at the wall of green scales. "I'm mad at *her*."

Before she can lose her nerve, she strides over to Longue Croc's hide. Beatrice swings the arm with the boots back and hits the dragon's hide with all her might, which isn't, admittedly, very mighty. So she makes sure her words hurt. "Hey! Long and Full of Crock, I'm his champion!"

For a moment, Tenryu is too shocked to do anything.

The next moment he is on his feet, furious that Beatrice would throw away the gifts of life and freedom he's given her.

Before he reaches her, Longue Croc moves to the side, and Beatrice steps out into the main chamber. Tenryu follows just behind.

Longue Croc is the only dragon in dragon form. To fit into the cave, the others have taken the form of other animals, mostly large cats of the independent sort: tigers and panthers, which most dragons feel have a natural affinity with dragons. There is also one griffon and one lioness. They're all female, of course. Most dragon parents only give shards to females; not all are as progressive as Tenryu's mother. They crouch on ledges above Longue Croc. Any of them could have slipped into his smaller chamber, but of course, hadn't. To have done so would have been to challenge Longue Croc's claim to him, and Longue Croc is the biggest, most powerful dragon in all the weyr. Longue Croc could have made herself smaller, too. He can only presume that she has too much pride to make herself small.

"What? Do I hear right?" Longue Croc asks, pinching Tenryu between two talons to prevent him from grabbing Beatrice and pulling her back into the chamber. Leaning in close to Beatrice, peering at her through one enormous eye, she says, "Did you declare yourself Tenryu's champion?"

"Yes, and that you're full of crock," Beatrice replies. The room goes silent.

Longue Croc throws back her head and laughs. After a beat, all of the other dragons nervously join in. Still laughing, mouth ajar, Longue Croc brings her head down and snaps her jaws shut, engulfing Beatrice in a single bite. There is another beat of silence. That is not how a challenge works. There are *rules* to these things. Longue Croc didn't even officially accept the challenge.

Tenryu looks hopefully around the corners of the cavern. Maybe Beatrice escaped at the last moment, but he sees no small white cat. Also, Longue Croc is chewing, obviously, and loudly. Tenryu deflates. Beatrice had seemed clever … even for a barbarian.

A tigress hops down next to Tenryu and whispers, "That was cruel of you, you know. Letting a human die for no reason." Tenryu isn't the only dragon to like humans as more than a culinary diversion.

Tenryu doesn't have the heart to respond. He contemplates just remaining human. Perhaps Longue Croc, known for *all* her appetites, will get bored waiting for him to return to his first form and just eat him as he is.

Clunk, clunk, clunk go Longue Croc's teeth. She spits, and the tapestry and the boots land at Tenryu's feet.

"Well, that settles that," says the pantheress with a sigh. "Tenryu is yours, Longue Croc."

"You got her, Longue Croc," agrees the griffon, but her voice is stiff and disproving.

It's at that moment that Tenryu realizes the boots and the

tapestry are not bloody. From above him comes a cat's purr, oddly amplified, as though coming from a tube. Magic translates the purr. "Indeed she has got me," says Beatrice the cat. "Full of Crock, I am in your ear, and if my granddaughter's anatomy lessons have taught me correctly, this is your eardrum."

Longue Croc screams and a puff of steam comes out her nostrils. She thrashes her head side to side, making the cave shake, and rocks fall from the ceiling.

One of the rocks nearly knocks the griffon from the ledge. "That is enough!" the griffon roars, shifting into a dragon, and pushing all the other big cats off the ledge and onto Longue Croc, pinning down the larger dragon.

From Longue Croc's ear comes another amplified purr. "Were you shaking your head, Longue Crock? I barely felt it. Probably all the fat in here. Tenryu, do I have to kill her to win this championship? Her brain is just up ahead and ... oh, my ... this cat form would love to knead its claws in it. It looks delicious."

Longue Croc squeaks. "I submit!"

"But how can I trust you, Longue Croc?" Beatrice purrs.

"Because we'll kill her," replies the formerly-a-griffon, now a dragon.

The tigress beside Tenryu rumbles. "Yes." There are echoing rumbles throughout the chamber, and dragon and cat smiles. It's as though all the weyr had just been waiting for an excuse to unify against Longue Croc. Tenryu knew that the other dragons hadn't been pleased with Longue Croc's "bullying", not every female dragon took the loss of a father, son, or brother gracefully, but he hadn't realized the depth of their anger.

Longue Croc sinks to the ground, releasing Tenryu, and lowering her head.

"Shall I come out, Tenryu?" Beatrice purrs.

Some of the dragons look at one another askance. It isn't normal for a female to ask a male's opinion among dragon kind, at least not in public.

But Longue Croc squeaks. "I accept defeat! You are the victor! My life is forfeit if I ever take action against you ... ahh ... I don't know your name."

"Because you never let her announce it before trying to eat her," rumbles the tigress beside Tenryu. "Contrary to the rules of combat."

The lioness and a pantheress knead claws into Longue Croc's scales, and more steam comes out of the dragon's nostrils.

"It's Beatrice," Beatrice replies.

"Beatrice is champion!" declare the dragons, chanting it three times over.

Clearing his throat, Tenryu says, "I think it is fine to come out, ma'am," being as polite as possible, and not using Beatrice's name in front of the other females, lest he seem disrespectful. Longue Croc whines and Beatrice hops out of her ear, shaking her paws, flicking her tail, ears back, fur stained with blood and wax. She gingerly walks over to Tenryu, and then sitting with her back to him, she gazes up at the dragons with her sapphire blue eyes. "Any others?" she asks, and Tenryu holds his breath because there is no way that will work twice.

The dragon-formerly-griffon laughs. "Female to female we respect your claim, Beatrice."

There are growls of agreement and assent among the dragons. Longue Croc hides her snout under a claw.

Beatrice flicks her tail. "Very well. I wish to bathe now, and *not* with my tongue."

The tigress beside Tenryu huffs. "Take care of her, Tenryu!"

"Yes, ma'am," Tenryu says, bending down and lowering an arm. Beatrice springs into it, and he walks her back into the inner chamber.

That didn't go as he'd expected. He doesn't know Beatrice well, but he does know she is brave and clever. And sometimes without an extended prior history in these situations, there are more realistic expectations. He does wonder what Beatrice expects.

🐐

"You're sure you can't age me?" Beatrice asks Tenryu, emerging from the pool of water he heated with magic, and pulling on a garment he calls a yukata. He is sitting with his back to her, stoic again.

"I know you may not believe me, but rearranging you, and putting you back together, based on your cellular code was difficult because it took concentration ... but shaving your telomeres down, creating an older-looking version of you without a blueprint, is beyond my skill."

"It sounds quite reasonable, actually," Beatrice replies. Is he saying she wouldn't believe him because of the attraction they seemed to share? That she suspects ulterior motives?

"I'm dressed," she says, and Tenryu turns around.

His expression is still stoic. "You will want to be reunited with your granddaughter immediately."

There seem to be no ulterior motives in that statement. She is relieved. "You're right. She is a magnet for trouble. I blame my grandson-in-law."

The corners of his eyes crinkle when he smiles. "We must never blame our own children."

Beatrice would blame her own child; her daughter has caused heartbreak to so many people, most of all Beatrice's granddaughter, Amy. But Amy is different. "I won't blame Amy," Beatrice says. "She's a doll." And her granddaughter's goodness makes Beatrice believe in her own goodness, and makes her set aside her guilt about her daughter.

Tenryu's eyebrow rises almost imperceptibly. She thinks he's caught all that. Her gaze flicks nervously over the assortment of toys around the room; there are dozens of them. He probably has *experienced* it.

He says nothing but beckons her toward a corner of the cavern, and gestures to what turns out to be a litter, half-buried in coins. "It's over a hundred years old, but it's still sound. I thought you might find it more comfortable than riding in my ear."

Beatrice laughs in relief. "Your ear was much cleaner, I'm sure, but yes, I'd prefer not."

"If you don't mind ... would you turn into a cat? Having you be human ..."

"Is it like having bacon under your nose?" Beatrice suggests.

He laughs and then grimaces. "Yes."

Beatrice walks over to the litter. There are wooden screens on all sides. When she opens one, she finds the seat is dusty, and the fabric fragile, but the wood does seem quite sturdy. She takes a seat inside. She hesitates, not turning into a cat, and not knowing why at first. And then she realizes that she hopes he'll say they'll see more of each other or ... or ... something. It's foolish to have any such expectation. He thinks she is a barbarian, as he's pointed out more than once, and she doesn't have time to prove otherwise.

He doesn't say a word, and she changes into a cat. Tenryu changes into a dragon, a long sinewy dragon, smaller than Longue Croc but definitely not small. He has shimmering blue-green scales that remind her of the reflection of the sky on water. His eyes are still brown flecked with gold, like speckles of sunlight on a river bottom. He lifts her out of the coins, litter and all, and although he has no wings, soars up into the evening sunlight.

It's nighttime when they land in the Sierra Nevadas. Because Beatrice doesn't want to cause a panic with an approaching dragon, they land a ways away from where the organization Beatrice works for has created a perimeter around the compound where elicit magical experiments have been going on. It's good that it is night because Beatrice has no boots—Longue Croc had hopelessly wrecked hers—and the nighttime pavement is cool beneath her feet. They start walking in near silence and Tenryu moves ahead of her. When she skips to keep up, he walks even faster. She is almost jogging when he turns around and says, "I'm sure it will be fine if we slow down."

Beatrice pants. "I'm just trying to keep up with you."

He blinks. "But I'm trying to keep three paces ahead so that if there is danger, they attack me first, and you can get away." He grins. "Or organize your attack."

Beatrice's lips purse. "It's not a bad idea ... in dangerous situations ..." He is bigger after all, especially as a dragon. "But I think in this situation, where we are approaching people I know, it might be better if I walk with you so you don't get shot."

Tenryu shrugs. "Ways change all the time. I can adapt."

He falls into step beside her, and they walk briskly the rest of the way, side-by-side. The sentries on duty are Rush and Park. "Ma'am," Rush says when they're still a distance away. "This is a restricted area and—"

Beatrice waves a hand in annoyance. "It's me, Beatrice. I've de-aged."

Park tilts his head like a confused puppy.

"Nah," Rush says, but then he hums, something he does to access his magic, and his eyes bolt wide. "Beatrice, you're hot!"

Rolling her eyes Beatrice tries to step past them. "Is Amy here?"

Inclining his head in Tenryu's direction, Park puts a hand on her shoulder. "Yeah, but *whoa*, who is *this guy?*"

Huffing in exasperation, Beatrice says, "He's a dragon."

"What?" blurt Park and Rush.

Eyeing the hand Park has on her shoulder, Tenryu says darkly, "And her husband."

Beatrice, Park, and Rush spin toward him in unison. "What?"

Tenryu's eyes go wide. "What?"

~ END ~

AUTHOR'S NOTE

Thank you for reading my (very) loose retelling of *Puss in Boots*! Beatrice, Amy, and the "annoying" grandson-in-law are from I Bring the Fire, my USA Today bestselling series about Loki, Norse God of Mischief and Chaos. The first book is free—check my website for details. I also have a new release in a completely different fantasy universe called *Snow So White*. It's a retelling of Snow White in the modern era with a Princess Charming. For more fantasy, sci-fi, new releases, and free books, sign up for my newsletter here: https://www.cgockelwrites.com/sign-mailing-list/.

BLOOD AND WATER

ALETHEA KONTIS

LOVE.

Love is the reason for many a wonderful and horrible thing.

Love was the reason I lived, there in the Deep, in the warm embrace of the ocean where Mother Earth's loins spread and gave birth to the world. Her soul was my soul.

Love is the reason she came to me in the darkness, that brave sea maiden. I remember the taste of her bravery, the euphoric sweetness of her fear. It came to me on wisps of current past the scattered glows of the predators.

The other predators.

Her chest contracted and I felt the sound waves cross the water, heard them with an organ so long unused I had thought it dead.

Help me, she said. *I love him.*

The white stalks of the bloodworms curled about her tail. We had a common purpose, the worms and I. We were both barnacles seeking the same fix, clinging desperately to the soul of the world. Their crimson tips brushed her stomach, her breasts. They could feel it in her, feel her soul in the blood that coursed through her veins. I felt it too. I yearned for it. A quiet memory waved in the tide.

Patience.

My answer was slow, deliberate. *How much do you love him, little anemone?*

More than life itself, she answered.

She had said the words.

I had not asked her to bring the memories, the pain. There is no time in the Deep, only darkness. I could but guess at how much had passed since those words had been uttered this far down. Until that moment, I had never been sure if the magic would come to me. Those words were the catalyst, the spark that lit the flame.

Flame. Another ancient memory.

The empty vessel that was my body emptied even further. I held my hands out to her breast, and there was light.

I resisted the urge to shut my inner eyelids to it and reveled in the light's painful beauty. It shone beneath her flawless skin like a small sun, bringing me colors...perceptions I had never dared hope to experience again. Slivers of illumination escaped through her gills and glittered down the abalone-lustered scales of her fins. Her hair blossomed in a golden cloud around her perfect face. And her eyes...her eyes were the blue of a sky I had not seen for a very, very long time.

She tilted her head back in surrender and the ball of light floated out of her and into my fingers, thin, white and red-tipped, much as the worms themselves. I cupped her brilliant soul in my palms and felt its power gush through me. So long. So long I had waited for this escape. I had stopped wondering what answer I would give if I should ever hear the words again, ever summon the magic. When the vessel was full, when my dead heart beat again, would I remember? Would I feel remorse? Would I have the strength of will to save her, to turn her away?

You will see him, I told her.

She smiled at me over the pure flame of her soul.

I was a coward.

I pressed her soul into my breast. The moment the light filled me I became her. I could see my body through her eyes—translucent white skin marred by jagged gills, blood red hair tossed up by the smoky vents and tangling about the worms, black eyes wide, lips parted in ecstasy.

I could see him in the back of her mind, the object of her affection. He was tall and angular, with sealskin hair. There had been a storm and a wreck, and she had saved him. She had dragged him onto a beach and fallen in love with him as she waited for him to open his eyes. She had run her fingers through his hair, touched his face, traced the lines of the crest upon his clothes. He was handsome and different and beautiful. When he awoke, he took her hand in his and smiled with all his heart. And when he kissed her, she knew she would never be able to live a life without him in it.

In that small moment, as the glow of her soul dimmed into me, she told herself it was worth it.

Once the transformation began, the pain pushed all other thoughts out of her head. Water left her as suddenly as her soul had left her, her gills closing up after it. The pressure that filled her chest made her eyes want to pop out. She clamped her mouth shut, instinct telling her that she could no longer breathe her native water. She beat furiously with her tail, fleeing for the surface.

Halfway there, the other pain began. It started at the ends of her fin and spread upwards, like bathing in an oyster garden. The sharpness bit into her, skinning her, slicing her to her very core. Paralyzed, she let her momentum and the pressure in her chest pull her closer to the sky. Part of her hoped she could trust the magic enough to get her there. Part of her didn't care. It wanted to die, and knew it could not.

That price had already been paid.

Her head burst above the waves and she opened her mouth, letting the rest of the water inside her escape. Her first full breath of the insubstantial air was like a lungful of jellyfish. She coughed, her upper half now as much in agony as her lower half, not wanting to take that next breath and knowing that she had to.

She lay there on the undulating bed that was once her home and let it heal her. She stared up at the sky until it didn't hurt so much to breathe, until her eyes adjusted, until rough hands plucked her out of the sea.

She was dragged across the deck of a ship much like the one from which she had rescued her lover, right before it had been crushed between the rocks and the sea. The man who had pulled her up clasped her tightly to him. He was covered in hair, more hair than she had ever seen in her life, and in the strangest places. It did not reach the top of his head, but spread down his face and neck and onto his chest. Perhaps it liked this upper world as little as she did and sought a safer, darker haven beneath his clothes. She reached out a hand to touch it, and he spoke to her. The sounds were too high, too light, too short, too loud. She did not understand them. His breath smelled of sardines. She ran a finger through the hair on his face, and he dropped her.

Misery shot through her and she collapsed on the deck. Her hair spilled around her…and her legs. She stared at her new skin. It looked so calm and innocent, but every nerve screamed beneath it. Another man stood before her now, wearing more clothes than the hairy man and shiny things on his ears and around his neck. His bellow was deeper than the first man's but still as coarse and profane, and still foreign to her. He crouched down before her and brushed her hair back from her face. He cooed at her. She touched the bright thing around his neck that twinkled the sun at her, and he grinned. His teeth were flat. She wasn't threatened. Braver now, she pulled at the necklace. He let her slide it over his head and put it around her own neck.

He picked her up and carried her to a place that hid her from the sky and set her somewhere softer than the deck. She liked this place and this man who now worshipped her. He had given her a gift, and now he would take care of her. If only there was a way she could tell him why she was there. She was sure he would help her. Perhaps he could see into her heart and just know.

The man removed his shirt, and she relaxed even more. He wanted to put her at ease. By looking like her, he would make her feel like she belonged. He took off the rest of his clothes and came up beside her. He patted her head, ran his hands down her hair. He touched her breasts, her belly and her legs. Still sensitive, she brushed his hand away. He put it back. She tried to push it away again, but he was stronger. She frowned. He smiled all those flat teeth at her once more. She wondered if she might have been mistaken. He moaned, parted her knees and entered her.

The misery she had felt before was nothing compared to this anguish. She inhaled the excruciating air and screamed a hoarse cry. She clawed at him, pushed at his weight on top of her, but she could not move him. Agony ripped her body apart again. A tingling sensation washed over her and the light in her eyes began to dim. Somewhere in that darkness, through the pain, she could feel his heartbeat. The emptiness in her cried out. He had something she needed.

She reached up, pulled him to her, and sunk her pointed teeth deep into the skin of his neck. She drank him down, consuming his soul, filling the barren places inside her. He collapsed on top of her and still she drank, until there was nothing left.

The door burst open and the hairy man entered. He pulled the naked man off of her. He could tell what the man had done from the blood between her legs. He could tell what she had done from the blood she now licked from her lips.

"Siren," he whispered.

She gasped. In her brain there was an avalanche.

Words flooded her, images and thoughts, smells and sounds. Knowledge. She cried out again and slapped her palms to her head. She had taken the man's soul, and his life right along with it. She watched as the shafts of her golden hair turned deep red, filled with the captain's blood.

The first mate had named her. He knew what she was. She was death, the shark, the thing to be afraid of. She lured men to their graves with her beauty.

In one swift motion he pulled the knife from his belt. She did not flinch as he approached her. There was nothing left to fear.

The knife swept down and split the captain's throat open, hiding the teethmarks in the cut. He stared deep into her eyes as he pulled a large ruby ring off the dead man's finger and put it on his own. The knife, streaked with what little crimson was left in the captain's body, he brandished at the crowd of men gathered at the door.

"Eddie Lawless, what's goin' on?" the man in front asked. The men behind him whispered low, words like "magic" and "evil" and "witch" catching in her ears.

"It's Lawson, Cooky," the hairy man responded. "Cap'n Lawson. An' don't ye forget it."

"Yessir," the men mumbled. "Yessir, Cap'n."

"Leave me," Lawson ordered.

"But sir, what about Cap'n—"

"*I* am the cap'n," he told them. "Ye can collect the carcass later. Leave me now." He slammed the door in their faces.

The mattress shifted under his weight as he sat down across from her. She did not want to look at him, concentrating instead on the ends of her new hair and the line across the dead man's throat.

Lawson shoved the body onto the floor. "Siren."

She looked up.

"So. Ye can understand me then."

She nodded once.

"Good." He pulled the sheet down and wiped his knife blade with it. "Understand this. I know what ye are, what ye need and what ye do. If ye do exactly as I tell ye, I won't kill ye."

If she had known how to laugh, she would have. It was unsettling. She knew what laughter was, what caused it and why someone did it, but she didn't have the slightest idea of how to make her body perform such a feat. It was the same with the words – she could understand them, but she couldn't get her tongue around them and speak back. She would have laughed at the thought of this man killing her, for she would have welcomed death. But there was one task she meant to accomplish before that happened. She had to find her lover.

She nodded her head once more.

"Excellent." He left the bed and went to open a trunk on the other side of the room. He rummaged through it for a moment, and then tossed a bundle of burgundy material into her lap. She stared at it, marveling in the slight difference between it and the color of her hair. She reached out and stroked its softness, drawing patterns on it with her finger.

His chuckle brought her out of her state. "Ye 'ave no idea what to do with it, do ye?" He took her by the hand and gently eased her off the bed. "Come on, stand up."

She placed one foot flat on the floor, then the other. Then she pushed up with all her might, locking her knees and propelling herself forward into him.

He caught her before she hit the floor. "Whoa. Easy. Ye 'ave to get yer sea legs." He helped her balance enough to stay upright. Surprisingly her feet held her without too much trouble.

"Now," he said, grabbing the bundle off the bed, "ye're lucky I 'ave a daughter an' I'm used to doin' this." He spun her around so that she faced the wall. "Six years ago I only knew 'ow to *un*dress a woman." He pulled her hands up above her head and eased the material down around her. He moved her hair to one side so he could button up the back.

"There." He turned her back around. "It's a bit large an' it'll probably be a tad warm. But it'll keep the sun off ye, and the...my...men away from temptation." He looked her up and down. "Not that they'll need much warnin', mind. But ye get enough rum into a man...well... stranger things 'ave 'appened."

He looked down at the former captain's body. "Ye won't need to... eat...again for a while then?"

She shook her head.

"Right. Best if ye only do it when I tell ye." He shoved the knife back into his belt.

Her eyes widened.

"Oh, don't worry," he chuckled. "Ye're aboard a pirate ship, darlin'. If there's one thing we've always got more than our share of, it's blood."

He wasn't wrong.

They encountered a ship three days later. There were blasts from cannons spread amidst the cries of men. She lost her footing when the ship lurched sideways, hooks pulling the losing ship close enough so that men might cross over. She peeked through the windows at the smoke of the guns, swords clashing as the blood flew.

Lawson came back to her room when the battle had died down. He opened the door and threw a man down at her feet. His clothes were ripped and his face was a bloody mess. Gray eyes looked up at her from the red-stained face and filled with terror.

"No…oh, God, no" were the last words he spoke.

His fear was intoxicating.

She closed her eyes when she was finished and let the magic wash over her. It wasn't just the blood she craved; it was everything. She needed the senses and the feelings, the emotions and the pain, the good and the bad. She needed his life, his soul.

Rejuvenated, she tossed her hair back and peered up at Lawson. He cupped her cheek and wiped a spot of blood away from the corner of her mouth. "There's my girl." He threw open the door and kicked the man's body over the threshold. "There's yer cap'n, men," he bellowed. "Seems 'e got into a spot of trouble. Any of ye want the same trouble, just cross me."

Crews were mixed and booty was swapped, and then they were off in search of the next victim.

The second ship they burned. It was spectacular. She ran to the railing and held her hand out to the beautiful, live thing that danced on the sea as it consumed sails and timbers and bodies alike. She had seen candles and lamps, but this was a beast, wild and hot and bright as the sun. Hands grabbed at her clothes to keep her from falling over the rail, and they pinned her down when the magazine finally exploded, taking the rest of that ship's crew with it.

On the third one, she found him.

The battle this time was a long one, and by the time Lawson brought her the captain of the other ship, he was half dead. She drank him anyway. And somewhere in the memories of this man was the someone she had been looking for.

She gasped when his face came to her. She drew back, her teeth disengaging from her meal, blood running down her chin and staining her dress. This man knew her lover. Not well, but he knew him. She tried to make sense of the jumble of images that flowed through her, but nothing connected. She searched his body for a sign, a hint, something. She found it on the smallest ring he wore, a gold band stamped with the crest she had traced over and over on the beach that day.

When Lawson returned, she pointed at herself and then held up the ring. He smiled and patted her on the head. "O'course ye can keep it, darlin'. Ye can 'ave all the trinkets yer little 'eart desires."

He didn't understand. How would she make him understand? She slid the ring over her red-tipped thumb. She would save it until she thought of a way.

The fourth ship was a long time coming.

She spent most of that time at the bow of the ship. The crew didn't grumble much about having a woman on deck. Most of them apparently didn't consider her a woman. Lawson made it plain that he enjoyed having her there. Word was getting around about Bloody Captain Lawson and the Siren. They struck fear in the hearts of men and made quite a profit as a result, so if anyone had disagreements, no one made mention of them.

Lawson called her their figurehead. It was an apt description, based on what she had seen on the prows of other ships. She would lean against the rail, arms spread, red hair trailing behind her in the breeze. She liked letting the wind slip through her fingers. It reminded her of home. The currents of air were not that different from the currents of water. Men did not have the freedom of movement that her kind enjoyed, but the principles were the same. They walked among it, breathed it in, let it give them life. It brought sounds and smells to them. They did not see it or think to taste it, but it was always there in them, touching them, surrounding them.

She stood there, day after day, until the salt encrusted her lips and her hair was a burnished orange. What little red appeared in the tips of her fingers had been burned there by the sun. The men avoided her and prayed hard for another ship. They tread lightly around the captain. No one wanted to be the Siren's next meal.

Lawson finally bade her return to the stateroom, and she was too weak to disobey. The table was covered in maps and charts. She walked past them on the way to the bed and glanced down at the area Lawson was plotting. A symbol caught her eye, and she jumped back. She waved at Lawson. She pointed to herself, and to the ring around her thumb. She pointed to herself, and to the same symbol down on the map.

"There?" he asked her. "Ye want to go there? Why?"

She could not answer, so she just kept pointing to herself and the map.

"That's 'ome," Lawson told her. "Where Molly is. I promised never to go back until I 'ad a ship full o'riches. She deserves no less." He shook his head. "No, darlin', we can't go there. Not yet."

Frustrated, she closed her eyes. Disjointed thought flashes skipped through her mind. She tried to remember the man with the ring, tried to bring his soul to the surface. But it had been so long, and she was so weary...and there was a port...

Her eyes snapped open. She moved her finger on the map to an island just off the coast of the country bearing her lover's symbol. She pointed at Lawson, and then stamped her finger back down on the map.

"There? What's there?"

She threw her hands up in exasperation and scanned the room. She held up the medallion of her necklace to him.

"Gold?"

She nodded and kept searching. She found his knife on the table, picked it up, and then shook her head.

"Swords?"

She shook her head again.

"This?" He removed the pistol from his belt and held it out to her. She nodded emphatically.

He cocked his head and grinned. "Siren, if ye're right about this,

I'll take ye anywhere in the world." He strode out of the room and hollered to his first mate. "Hard to port, matey!"

"Cap'n?" the first mate asked.

Lawson hooked his thumbs in his belt. "We're goin' 'ome."

The greatest tale of Bloody Lawson and the Siren is the Massacre at Windy Port. Legend has it that their ship, cloaked in dark magic, slipped by the watchmen unnoticed. Once docked the crew cut a gruesome swath through the town, led by Lawson and his Sea Witch. Lawson brandished a rapier in one hand, a pistol in the other. The Siren, dressed in fine burgundy velvet, marched through town before him, seducing men to their grisly deaths. Her eyes were as black and cold as a shark's, her hair a mass of ebony fire waving about her. They left none living in their wake, took what they wanted and stole back into the night as invisibly as they had arrived.

Like most legends, not a word of it was true.

They sailed into Windy Port under a royal flag they had appropriated from a previous hunt. They docked without incident, the crew scattering to the winds to pick up intelligence, hefty bar tabs, and the occasional whore.

The moment Lawson set her down on the dock, she fell. The hollowness inside her throbbed. She could not believe anything could have been so still as land. There was no life in it. The air was not strong enough to keep it fluid. It was rock. Still, empty, dead rock. She was but a shell, a humble reconstruction of the world upon which man walked every single day. How did they survive without a connection? She hugged her stomach, doubled up and gagged, only emptiness escaping her dry heaves.

"You okay, honey? Take it easy. It'll pass soon."

The words spoken to her had a cadence she had never heard before, and it surprised her so much she didn't understand them at first. The hands that pulled her hair back away from her face were small and delicate. The woman had on a black dress. Her hair was pinned up on her head and decorated with shiny black beads. She smelled...soft and nice. And she was gentle when she accepted the Siren's embrace.

"It's all right," the woman said as she patted her back. "Everything's going to be all right."

She didn't scream when pointed teeth pierced her flesh.

Everything was going to be just fine.

Suddenly conscious of her appearance, she pulled her dress over her head and began tearing at the woman's clothes. Lawson knelt beside her and motioned for his men to surround them so as not to draw attention to the scene. "Discovered vanity, 'ave we?" he chuckled as he helped her undress the woman's corpse. Once she had changed, the men weighted the body and rolled it into the ocean.

Lawson helped her stand. He tossed a dark cloak about her and covered her hair with its hood. She was glad he didn't force her to wear shoes—it was hard enough enduring this much separation from the water. She didn't know how much more she would be able to bear.

The inn they went to almost pushed her sanity over the edge from sensory overload. The room was filled with people of all shapes and sizes. There were smells from the food, the ale, the dogs in front of the fire, the fire itself. Men and women talked and shouted and joked and laughed. A scrawny youth crawled up beside the dogs at one point and sang for his supper. She was mesmerized. These were so different from the songs of the water, the flash of fish in the currents, the mating of whales in the deep. Some were slow and soft; some were fast and loud. And when the rest of the room joined in, she clapped her hands in merriment.

The crew dropped in one by one to report and consult with Lawson throughout the night. There were nods and low whispers. She watched as papers were signed and money changed hands. Thus Bloody Lawson conquered Windy Port, without ever leaving his seat. When the festivities ended he paid for his meal, tipped heavily and left, dragging his cloaked companion behind him. It was the sailors and merchants that returned to their vessels the next morning and found them empty or missing who took their anger out on the citizens of the port. Lawson and his crew were miles away before the massacre even began. Bloody Lawson and the Siren were never heard from again.

Several months later, Edward Malcolm opened a waterfront inn in the capitol city named The Sea Lass. He purchased the house next door as well. It had a master suite and a nursery and a very large kitchen that could be used to supplement the inn's in case of over-flow. One of the rooms in the house had a door with seven locks. They were installed the day before Molly's return from school.

Molly's homecoming was a grand event. Lawson, now called Edward, had covered every flat surface in the house with sweets and cakes and flowers. He had hired a seamstress to take Molly's measurements for a whole new wardrobe, the only one that didn't seem overly preoccupied with the Prince's upcoming wedding. Paper-wrapped packages of all sized littered the largest of the tables. A doll and a rose waited on the chair for his princess.

The Siren sat on a stool in the corner, cut off from the sun and the earth, the water and wind. She waned as she watched the minia-ture cherub-faced human run through the door to embrace her father. Her mop of dark brown curls disappeared in her father's coat as she hugged him, right before he picked her up and twirled her around the room. There was something about this strange appari-tion, this child, and she could not decide what it was.

Molly giggled as she snuggled her doll. She reached out to the rose.

"Be careful," her father warned her.

"Yes, Papa," she said smartly. "I will watch for the pricklies and the thornies." She buried her nose in the crimson petals and took a deep breath. When she opened her eyes, Molly saw the Siren there in the shadows.

The child set her doll down carefully on the table. "Who is she, Papa?" Molly whispered.

"She's..." he started, twisting the ruby ring on his finger. "I saved 'er," he said finally.

"She's so pretty," Molly said. The child came around the table and held the flower out to her. "She's just like the flower."

"Yes," he said. "Just like the rose. She's got pricklies and thornies too, Molly. You have to be careful around her."

Molly took another step forward, still offering the flower. The Siren took it and grinned, being careful not to show any teeth. Before her father could stop her, Molly launched herself into the Siren's arms.

The child's skin was softer than the woman's at the pier. Her hair smelled of sugar and...something...indescribable. She took another deep breath. There was life within this little bundle, so much life she all but vibrated with it.

Edward wrenched her away. He took her by the arms and held her tightly. He sank down to his knees, so that he could address Molly eye to eye.

"Don't ye *ever* go near 'er again," he said sternly.

"But Papa, she's so sad," Molly cried.

"She is dangerous," he admonished. "Just be a good girl and do as yer papa says."

Molly bowed her head. "Yes, Papa."

"We'll even call 'er Rose, okay? So ye don't forget." Edward chucked her under the chin. "Now, what are ye gonna name yer dolly?"

Molly's eyes brightened again and she rushed back to the table for her doll.

The Siren sunk her nose into the flower and inhaled sugar and sweetness while she watched the child open the rest of her gifts.

That night as he escorted her to her room, he said to her, "Ye touch my daughter, I'll kill ye." Then he shut the door and turned seven keys in seven locks.

Each day after that was much the same. She was not allowed to leave the house, and the third time Edward caught her staring out the windows, he forbade her that too. Each night he would take her to her room and give her the same warning about his daughter before turning the seven keys of her prison.

She would sit on her bed and stare into the darkness, wondering what she had done wrong. Had she not given him the riches he desired? Had she not paved the way for him to return home to be with his daughter? She had made him happy—why should she suffer as a result?

She edged closer to the window and watched the moon move across the sky. Somewhere not far, the reflection of that same light was skipping across the waves. Somehow, she would escape from this prison. Someday, seven locks would not hold her.

Every few nights he would bring her someone, long after Molly was asleep. He would wake before the dawn and take the body away. She learned all she could from these poor souls, but it was never enough. They were whores or cheats or liars, people whose absence in some way benefited Edward and whose minds were such a jumble of unreliable information she could never discern anything that could help her.

She waited. She waited while he scolded her every night. She waited as he shoved each of the seven bolts home. She waited as he fed her, sparingly, enough to survive. She waited for him to get comfortable, to slip, to let something get by him.

Like the snitch.

Edward bent over and the unconscious man fell from over his shoulder and onto the bed before her. "Small, but 'e's all ye'll get, understand?"

She opened her mouth, throat contracting. "Yeth," she managed to say.

"Good. 'Cause if ye touch my daughter, I'll kill ye." He shut the door. She counted slowly to seven before pulling the man into her lap and feasting.

Her heart pounded with a foreign pulse.

He was there.

Her lover.

He was everywhere inside this man's head. He sat at the head of a table, talking sternly to a group of older men dressed in black. He sat in a large chair at the end of a hallway. He rode a horse down the path through the garden and along the beach. He rode in a carriage beside a beautiful, golden-haired maid and people threw flowers in the street before them.

He was the prince.

And he was getting married in a week.

Edward fell ill the next day. He did not come to let her out of her cell. The first two days of isolation weren't bad. The third day, the snitch's body began to smell. The fourth day, she tried to feed off it again and gagged. There had not been much in him to begin with, and whatever was left in him now was gelled and rancid. The fifth day, she began to shake. She pounded on the door and the walls and the window until the skin of her fists shed. The sixth day, she began to scream. It came out of her as a long, keening wail. It echoed her hunger, her desperation, her emptiness. Her voice gave out as the sun rose on the seventh day, his wedding day.

She spent the hours curled up against the door, hoping to hear something. Any sign of movement at all would have been welcome. She played with the ends of her faded hair, teasing them in and out between her toes. The shadows moved, lengthened, and eventually, the sun's light died. Her hopes went right along with it. She placed her palm flat on the door beside her head.

It was warm.

She closed her eyes and could feel the energy radiating from the other side. She could hear small, shallow breaths. She could taste sugar on the air.

Molly.

She knocked two times on the door.

"Rose?" the tiny voice called hesitantly.

She knocked two times again.

"Daddy's sick and he had to go away." Skirts rustled against the floorboards. "I'm lonely. Are you lonely?"

Two knocks.

"Do you want to play with my dolly?"

She spread her fingers against the door. "Yeth," she croaked.

The warmth faded, and there were sounds of a heavy chair being dragged across the floor. One, two, three, for, five, six, seven keys were all slowly turned in their locks. The chair was pushed aside, and the door opened.

Molly flew into her arms, the momentum pushing her back onto the bed in her weakened state. She cradled the frightened child in her arms, felt the porcelain head of her dolly poking into her side. She soaked up the child's energy, willing it into her empty body. She bent her head and smelled the sweetness of her. She nuzzled her nose in the softness of her, like burrowing into the petals of a newly-opened flower.

She shouldn't. She knew she shouldn't, but he had caused her so much pain, and she had nothing left to lose.

Molly screamed and fought, but every bit of her gave the Siren the strength to hold her down, to fill the abyss inside her with this soul of pure innocence. It was so beautiful. The sensations did not wait until she was finished. They exploded into her mind every second. There was fear, yes, sweet fear, but then came sadness and betrayal. There was happiness and laugher, anger and tears, but most importantly, she finally realized the whys. She knew why a person felt joy and why they felt pain. She learned the elation of seeing something for the very first time, and the despair in losing it.

Loss. She knew now what she had been dealing out all this time. There was no way she could have ever known the impact of death without knowing what it was like to live a life. The weight of all the souls she had consumed pressed heavily upon her. She learned consequences. She realized that the things she did affected people other than the person she was killing. She understood that all the pain she had felt before was nothing to the pain these people would feel for the rest of their lives. She felt regret, and love.

Love.

It spread through her. Unconditional love tickled her down to the red tips of her fingers and toes. Love was trust. Love was faith. Love was believing in the impossible. The rainbow of Molly's soul filled her with love until the last drop. She held Molly's limp body in her arms…and she laughed.

She laughed and laughed, her voice echoing through the dark, vacant house. She laughed until she cried, tears flowing unchecked down her cheeks. She cried for Molly, for all of them. She cried for all the things she had done. She cried for herself, for everything she had lost, for nothing.

Or was it nothing?

She had to hurry. She had to leave this place and never come back. She gently laid Molly's body out on the bed and curled her arm around her dolly. She smoothed back the dark curls and kissed her forehead. She covered herself in the black cloak and fled into the night.

She was glad again to be in the air and running over the earth, despite what little support they gave her. She followed her heart and the dim memories of the snitch up to the castle gates.

She strode up to the guards there and threw her hood back. Those that knew of her let her pass. Those that didn't know of her learned.

The myriad halls and stairs and rooms made the castle a giant labyrinth, but she knew where she was going. Up and up and up…to the balcony suites of the Prince's bedchamber. She did not stop until she was at the foot of his bed, staring down at his sleeping body. She wanted to shake him awake, wanted to explain everything to him, wanted to scream her love for him to the rafters.

But she couldn't.

If he awoke now, he would know what she had become. He would see the evil inside of her, the mark of it in her hair and on her skin. She had saved his life, true, but how many others had she taken on her path back to him? With love came regret. She knew what she had to do. She knew that the only thing she had to offer him now was her absence. If she could just touch him one more time…she reached out a hand to him and stopped herself.

No.

It would not stop at a touch, she knew that from what had happened with Molly. She could never be with him, truly be with him, because eventually she would consume him. His soul was not bright enough for her to survive alone outside it, nor was it strong enough to sustain him once she had consumed it. If she stayed beside him, it would mean his death.

She was a monster.

She forced her hand back to herself and placed it over her heart. She hoped that it spoke enough in the silence for him to hear it, to feel how much she loved him. If it had been water and not air between them, she knew he would have felt it.

He stirred and opened his eyes.

She gave herself one moment, one tiny, blessed moment of looking into his eyes before she turned and ran.

She tripped down the stairs and cut her feet on the stones. The cloak caught on something and she unfastened it. She was sure that soon they would come for her. They would hunt her like the beast she was. She tasted the tears that streamed down her face and knew there was only one refuge.

The cold beach sand kissed her feet like a prayer. The salty spray mixed with her tears, chasing them away. The first tiny wave reached up and licked her toes. Waves rumbled in a cadence she had almost forgotten how to translate.

Come, they pulled.

Home, they crashed.

She took small steps forward. The sand slipped out from beneath her if she stayed too long. The force of the waves pushed her backwards in opposition to the call she felt.

Come, they pulled.

She stumbled, and the tide ripped her sideways along the beach. Gasping, she managed to regain her footing and continue walking out to sea. The current grabbed at her clothes, and she tore them off. The tips of her hair mingled with the foam. Flotsam swirled around her waist.

Home, they crashed.

She walked until the undertow took her and dragged her out to sea.

.   .   .

I lost her sometime before that, back when the moon shone off her white skin and blood red hair. But I didn't have to live inside her anymore to know where she was headed.

She would grab the first sharp object she found – maybe a crab's claw or a clam's shell – and rip gills into herself so that the water could flow through her again. The first one might have been straight, but the rest would be ragged and flawed. She would make her way to the Deep, her body drawn to the neverending call of the soul of the world. She would make a home there among the bloodworms and the warm vents and the other predators.

She would take her love and regret with her. She would heal in the balm of the ocean, away from the complexities of mortal life. She would tell herself that if the day came, if the words were spoken and the magic came to her, she would turn them away. She would not let evil back into the world. The suffering would end with her. She would stew in the self-affliction until it became a dim memory, tucked away in the recesses of her mind like sight and sound, air and fire. Time would fade her lover's face, his name into nothing, and then time itself would melt into darkness. She would ebb and flow and never die.

And when that day did come, ages and ages from now, she would choose the light. She would choose the escape. She would let the evil out one last time just to feel it all again, to live.

As I had.

Strong arms wrapped around me, brushing my satin bedclothes against the small jagged scars on either side of my chest. I leaned back against him, feeling his heartbeat through his chest.

"I just had the strangest dream," he said. I felt his deep voice rumble through the skin of my back. "You came to me while I lay in bed, only your hair was red and your skin was different. You stared at me like you wanted to say something, and then you ran. You looked so…sad."

He turned me around to face him. "The day you saved me was the happiest day of my life. And this day should be the happiest day of yours. Don't be sad."

I smiled and shook my head.

"Good." He kissed me then, long and slow and deep. He hugged me tightly before pulling away. "Come back to bed?"

"Yeth," I whispered, the words still foreign to my tongue. He kissed me once more and left me. I looked out over the moonlit water once more and said my goodbyes before following him, my prince, my soulmate, my love.

Love.

It was the reason I lived.

~END ~

AUTHOR'S NOTE

I used to travel with a small notebook in my car. My friend Brandi once flipped through it. She pointed at two words I'd written down independently of each other and asked, "What's a vampire mermaid?"

As a Marine Chemistry major obsessed with the hydrothermal vents, my mind went wild. "Sirens" preyed on humans, but "mermaids" were usually benign. How would either one think, knowing only the ocean as a frame of reference? What would their life cycle look like? Vampires need blood, right?

The tube worms at the hydrothermal vents have bright red plumes filled with blood. The thermal vent clam is so abundant with hemoglobin that its meat looks like a dark red tongue. Down there, energy doesn't come from the sun, it comes from the earth. Chemical interactions *without* radiation. Chemosynthesis, not photosynthesis. But blood is still required for circulation. Warmth. Life.

Like fish, humans probably wouldn't be able to tell one mermaid from another. The difference between mermaids and sirens might be like clams: the one down at the hydrothermal vents is just filled with blood. And if mermaids' hair shafts are hollow like polar bears', that's the perfect place to store ingested blood. Voila, red-headed mermaids! (Wink.)

In 1989, Disney gave Hans Christian Andersen's "The Little Mermaid" the happy ending she deserved. Up until then, her tale was one of love and tragedy and a jaded sea witch who somehow knew far too much.

But what if the sea witch *was* the original little mermaid, spurned by her lover and returned to the water, soulless and doomed to the hydrothermal vents? After enough time in exile, would the siren give in to temptation and seize the opportunity to escape?

What would *you* do?

ABOUT THE AUTHOR

New York Times bestselling author Alethea Kontis is a princess, storm chaser, and Saturday Songwriter. She has authored over 20 books and 40 short stories, including *AlphaOops: The Day Z Went First* (Candlewick), *Enchanted* (HMH) and *Prince Phillip's Birthday Waltz* (Disney). Alethea is the recipient of the Jane Yolen Mid-List Author Grant, the Scribe Award, the Garden State Teen Book Award, and two-time winner of the Gelett Burgess Children's Book Award. She has been twice nominated for both the Andre Norton Nebula and the Dragon Award. She was an active contributor to *The Fireside Sessions*, a benefit EP created by Snow Patrol and her fellow Saturday Songwriters during lockdown 2020. Alethea also narrates stories for multiple award-winning online magazines and contributes regular YA book reviews to NPR. Born in Vermont, she currently resides on the Space Coast of Florida with her teddy bear, Charlie. Find out more about Princess Alethea and her wonderful world at aletheakontis.com.

BREADCRUMBS

SARRA CANNON

NOT UNTIL TONIGHT

EVERYONE THINKS IT WAS A WITCH WE FACED IN THOSE WOODS, BUT SHE wasn't a witch. She was a vampire. And we didn't push her into the oven the way those children's stories will have you believe. We burned her to death in the light of the sun.

I dragged her out there with my own bare hands at the age of eight.

It wasn't a house made of candy that lured us in, either. It was a simple mouthful, handed to us by a man we trusted.

A man I hadn't seen in nearly two-hundred years.

Not until tonight.

At first, I wasn't even sure if it was him or just another shadow inside my brain. My mind had been playing tricks like that on me for as long as I could remember. I would be sitting in a restaurant, laughing with my friends when the tilt of someone's head would catch the corner of my eye, and my entire body would stiffen. My heart would race, and my mouth would fill with cotton.

But then I would gather the courage to actually turn my head and look, only to find, every single time, that it wasn't him at all. Just some random person who'd moved in a way that had once been so familiar to me.

It must have happened a thousand times over the past two

centuries. So much that I'd become numb to it, sometimes not even bothering to confirm his non-existence, because some part of me was so damn tired of wanting it to be him.

And at the same time, I was terrified that someday, it would be him.

That he'd be there, the man with all the answers, and I would be too scared to demand them.

Too scared to even face the truth.

"Mags? What's wrong with you? You look like you just saw a ghost." Landy touched my arm playfully.

If she only knew. Was he a ghost? Or was he immortal, like me?

"Maggie?" She grabbed my wrist this time, shaking it back and forth. "Hello. Earth to Maggie."

Maggie.

I hardly recognized that name. I'd never been Maggie back then.

Margarete Anne, though my mother had always preferred the nickname Gretel. That's who I had always been. Two hundred years as Gretel, but I'd stopped using that name the day my brother Hansel disappeared, almost two full years ago now.

Had it really been that long?

Without him, I wasn't myself anymore. After six months of wandering around, completely lost, I decided the only way to save my sanity was to become someone new. Someone without a bloody past and the skills to take down an entire hive of vampires in a single evening.

That's when I'd decided to call myself Maggie and live my life as if I were a normal human.

And so far, it hadn't been half bad, if I was being honest.

But the past and its shadows always followed me.

The past didn't care if I'd changed my name or dyed my honey-blonde hair black as a raven. The second I saw that man—Wolfgang —I'd become Gretel again. An eight-year-old girl being led through the woods with the promise of a big surprise.

Without even thinking, I reached for my dagger, only to remember I didn't carry weapons like that anymore.

"Holy shit, Maggie, are you even hearing me?" Landy asked, shaking my shoulders now and motioning to someone nearby.

For a second, I'd forgotten she was talking to me. All I could think about was the man who'd just disappeared into a hallway near the back of the club. Could it really be him this time?

"What's she on?" Vick asked, lifting his fingers to my eyes. "She didn't eat any of that candy they were passing out, did she?"

I grabbed his wrist so quickly, he jumped about a mile high before pulling away, a terrified look on his face.

"What candy?" I asked.

Landy gave me a questioning look as she reached into the pocket of her tiny black shorts.

"You got one, too, remember?" She held out a large piece of candy wrapped in glittering gold foil. "That girl was passing them out as we walked in."

"Please tell me you didn't eat one of those things," Vick said, rubbing his wrist. "Because I heard from one of my friends that it's laced with something weird. Like, she took one last week and woke up three days later with a massive hangover and literally no memory of what happened to her."

"That's just an urban legend," Landy said, rolling her eyes and unwrapping the candy. "No one is giving out free drugs that make you forget your life. People pay too much for that kind of trip. It's probably just pure sugar."

She started to put the purple candy in her mouth, but the sight of its shimmering surface made my stomach lurch. I knocked it to the floor and stomped it to pieces with the heel of my boot.

"What the hell did you do that for?"

I stared down at the broken candy and shuddered. The wrapper had certainly gotten an upgrade, but the candy itself was nearly identical.

"If that's actual free drugs, you owe me big time," she said. "You know what kind of a week I've had. I deserve to have a good time tonight."

"No good time to be had down there, I can promise you that," I said.

It had been a long time since I'd seen candy like that, but the kind of betrayal that followed sort of made it impossible to forget.

It was meant to be a treat, he'd said. A treat for being such good kids. It wasn't until afterward that I remembered how nervous he'd seemed. How he kept looking over his shoulder as he led us into the woods.

And we'd trusted him with all our hearts. We loved our Uncle Wolfgang and Aunt Lydia as if they were our own parents. We'd been happy in their home after our mother died. We felt like a real family.

In my mind's eye, I could still remember the cottage we lived in on the edge of the village like it was yesterday.

I shook the memories out of my brain as a strong, warm hand clasped my own and gently pulled me forward.

"Hey. Are you okay?"

Cole. Back from the bar with two drinks cradled in his other hand as he pulled me closer.

"What's going on? How can I help?" he asked, his warm brown eyes searching mine as I looked up.

The concern in his voice was so sincere, it nearly knocked the breath from my lungs. Despite the fact that we'd been dating for months, I hadn't realized just how much he cared until that moment.

Or maybe it was the fact I cared that surprised me so much.

No one but my brother Hansel had ever cared about me, and when he disappeared, I assumed no one ever would again.

Part of me wanted to rest my head against Cole's chest and tell him it was nothing. To forget the past and the man who'd betrayed me.

But I knew better. Peace was not possible for someone like me.

I shifted my weight and a piece of candy crunched under the heel of my boot.

Purple, shimmering candy. What were they doing passing it out in a club like this? And what did my uncle have to do with all of it?

I looked around the club, seeing beyond myself and my questions now.

This was bigger than me or Hansel. Everyone in this club was in danger, including my new set of friends. None of them were qualified to figure it out, though. Not like I was.

So, I had a choice.

I could grab Cole's hand, leave this club, and never look back. I could just be Maggie, a normal woman trying to live a normal life.

Or I could follow the shadows that still haunted me, searching for answers to the questions I knew damn well I'd never stop asking.

And maybe I'd manage to save a few lives in the process.

If Hansel were here, there wouldn't even be a question of what to do. He'd have already tracked Wolfgang down and had him nailed to the wall.

"I'm fine," I managed, squeezing Cole's hand before pulling away. "I just have to go talk to someone real quick. I'll be right back."

"Maggie, wait," he called, his voice fading as I slipped between the bodies packed on the dance floor.

Now that I'd made up my mind, I moved quickly, zeroing in on the spot where I'd last seen the man who looked like Uncle Wolfgang. Part of me hoped I'd find the guy only to realize it wasn't him at all. Just some rando with a familiar face.

But it was different this time, and I knew it in my ancient bones.

Hansel and I had always suspected Wolfgang was immortal like we were, but there was, of course, no way to prove it. By the time we'd killed the vampire and stumbled back through the woods to find our way home, Aunt Lydia, our mother's sister, was dead and Wolfgang was long gone.

No one in the village knew what had happened to him. He'd simply disappeared.

We'd spent centuries looking for him, and it wasn't fair that I may have just found him when Hansel was gone.

As I reached the dark hallway where I'd seen him last, though, I cursed my own hesitation and doubt. I should have run after him right away. How could I have been so dumb?

I searched the area, realizing soon enough that there were only two ways out of this back room and hallway. He could have either come back through to the dance floor area, which I would have noticed, or he went through a door labeled Do Not Enter.

Without hesitation this time, I pushed through the door, realizing too late that it led to the alley beside the club.

The door slammed behind me, locking before I could catch it, and suddenly, the darkness seemed to close in. Shadows moved around me, despite the fact that I seemed to be completely alone.

Without a weapon.

Good going, Gretel.

I mean, I knew I was out of practice, but this was embarrassing. Seeing Wolfgang here had obviously rattled me, but now I wondered if that had been the plan all along.

A shadowy figure to my right began to materialize, and I prepared my stance. Weapons or not, I was in it now. I'd survived worse.

My body tensed, ready to fight, when the door behind me opened and the encroaching shadows dissipated in an instant. Cole stood there, concern in his dark eyes. He shook his head.

"What's going on with you, Maggie?" he asked, holding the door open. "There's no one out here."

"Not anymore," I muttered as I slipped under his arm and pulled him back inside the club before the shadows could follow us.

I shuddered as something brushed against my bare leg just before the door closed us off from the darkness of the night.

WHO I WAS BORN TO BE

I couldn't sleep.

Instead, I must have sat in bed just twirling that golden-wrapped candy in my fingers for a straight hour.

It had no identifying marks. No logo. Nothing that would indicate who created it or where I could find them.

It had been nearly two hundred years since I'd seen our uncle. Two centuries since I'd held a candy exactly like this one in my hands. And yet, it was so familiar, I could almost taste it on my tongue.

So, an identical candy to the one Wolfgang gave us that night and a man who looked just like Wolfgang disappearing into a dark alley that was obviously occupied by vampires?

There was no way this was just a coincidence. But why now?

Hansel and I had spent most of our immortal lives looking for any sign of our uncle, and though we had captured and interrogated many vampires along the way, no one had admitted to knowing him or who he worked for.

In the end, we'd simply given into the fact that our uncle must have worked for the vampire who'd tried to kill us in that house in the woods. How he'd met her or why he'd betrayed us that way was still a mystery, but we'd run out of breadcrumbs to follow.

We'd spent a month in that vampire's house, living through unspeakable horror my young mind had mostly managed to block. We were her prisoners, and for a while, we'd thought that was going to be the worst of it.

Spoiler Alert. It wasn't.

We'd overheard her talking to a visitor one afternoon about plans for our blood. That we were special in some way. She planned to sell me to another vampire for an outrageous sum of money and keep Hansel there for herself.

Living through the horror of that house was bad enough when we had each other, but Hansel and I knew we'd never survive it if we were separated. It would have been unbearable. So, we came up with a plan to trick the old woman, making our move the next time she dared to approach our cage.

Hours later, when she was nothing more than ashes on the ground, we got our first real look at the inside of that house. The vampire had been making candy like the ones Wolfgang had given to us. Like the one I now held in my hands.

Back then, we'd taken what we thought we could use from that house and burned the rest, destroying what was left of the candy.

But apparently someone else knew the recipe. Someone who'd resurfaced after all this time so they could start drugging innocent people again.

It had to be Wolfgang, and for some reason, he was working with those vampires.

I could only imagine what a group of powerful vampires with access to an unlimited supply of blood could do to this world. They would be unstoppable and more dangerous than any hive my brother and I had ever faced.

The question now was whether I was strong enough to face them alone.

Tonight's little alley incident proved just how out of practice I was these days. And not just out of practice but out of sorts. Back when Hansel was alive, I never would have just followed a suspected enemy into a dark alley without a weapon. It was stupid and reckless, and if it hadn't been for Cole, I might have died.

Or worse.

Beside me, Cole rolled over. I used the movement to slide out of bed without waking him and carefully tiptoed toward the closet.

I glanced back at him, just to make sure he was still sound asleep, and when I was certain he had settled, I disappeared into the large closet and removed a panel along the back wall behind a row of my dresses.

A long black box hid in the shadows of the makeshift hiding place, and my hands trembled slightly as I reached for it, flinching as the strange symbols lit up on the keypad. I had hoped to never need this stuff again. Hell, maybe I didn't need it now. Maybe I didn't want to get back into this after all this time.

I had a great guy in there, who, despite my awkwardness and mostly distant attitude, really seemed to care about me. I had friends for the first time in my life. I had a decent-paying job that, admittedly, was torturously boring.

Somehow, though, there was a level of comfort in the boring parts.

I'd never had a normal life before this, and despite missing my brother more than words could express, I was starting to get used to normal.

And how do you see that playing out in ten or twenty years, Gretel?

Hansel's voice popped into my head, as if he were standing right here. I swatted him away, like that was going to make any difference.

"I'll figure it out when we get there," I muttered.

But it wasn't like I'd never thought of that before. Of course, it crept into my thoughts almost daily. Any time Cole mentioned us having a future beyond this weekend, I clammed up.

He seemed to think it was because I'd been hurt before and was scared of commitment. What he didn't have any damn clue about was the fact that in fifty years, he'd be an old man, but me? I'd be exactly the same. Never aging. Never dying. Not by any natural causes, anyway.

I ran my hand across the black leather of the case.

Who was I kidding? There was no normal future for me. I'd managed to play this role for over a year. I'd tried on an identity like trying on a piece of clothing. Maggie Miller. But I was delusional if I thought it would last or that I could ever really be anyone else but who I was born to be.

Besides, my life had been messed up since that day Uncle Wolfgang had given me a piece of strange candy and lured me into a vampire's lair. I was never meant to come out of that house normal.

But there were a lot of people in this city who still had a chance at a good life. People who'd been handed a piece of candy just like this one lately, thinking it was relatively harmless. And then what? Vick said his friend had woken up with no recollection of what had happened to her, but I had a pretty good idea of what must have happened.

Vampires were having more and more trouble surviving in the modern era of the internet, where literally everyone held a news camera in their hand. It was difficult to murder en masse and get away with it for long.

So, despite the fact that there were more humans on earth than ever before, the vampires were hungrier than they'd ever been. Reduced to road kill and blood banks, they were having to get creative with their food supply.

I twirled the golden-wrapped candy in my hand, trying to piece it all together.

Unsuspecting singles in the club, already prone to overindulgence and reckless behavior, get a free piece of luxe candy. Hearing that it might be a free way to get high, they eat it.

Once the drug takes over, they're taken to a vampire's lair here in the city, where they become temporary vamp food. A few days later, before they die or get too weak to recover, they're taken home and left to wonder what trouble they got into along the way.

As far as plans go, it wasn't half bad. Truth be told, it was a lot more humane than the old school vampire plans of feeding until every human around was dead. Still, vampires weren't exactly known for their ability to hold back when it came to feasting on human blood. Even if they intended to keep the humans they kidnapped alive, they were bound to go too far every once in a while.

No one was safe while this candy was being distributed in our city.

And no one had the ability to take care of it the way I did.

I entered the code into the backlit panel on the black case and winced as it popped open. It was louder than I remembered, and I leaned over to peek into the bedroom, just to be sure it hadn't woken Cole up.

I definitely didn't want to have to explain why I had a black case full of guns, daggers, and pointy objects in my closet.

It didn't seem like he'd moved, though, so for now, I was still safe. I should have had him sleep at his own place tonight, but truth be told, I didn't want to be alone. I actually loved having him around, though I hadn't gotten up the nerve to admit that to him yet.

He had a calming influence over me that I liked. He made me feel safe.

So, what exactly was I doing here, sitting in my closet in the middle of the night staring at a cache of weapons?

I ran my hand over the blades of my daggers with a soft touch, as if they were precious. Sacred.

I realized with a start that I'd missed them. I lifted a silver dagger into my hand and wrapped my fingers around its hilt, closing my eyes as the memories of all those years of hunting with my brother came rushing back. I'd managed to do a better job than I thought of blocking it all out over the past year and a half, but in an instant, those same feelings were back.

Gretel was back.

And as I thought about the innocent people in those clubs and the malevolence out there preying on them, I knew that while Maggie was enjoying her somewhat normal existence, Gretel could never turn her back on this.

"Babe?"

Cole's voice from the next room. The rustle of covers.

"Shit," I muttered, throwing the dagger back into the case and snapping it closed. I quickly pulled a dress down from the hangers above and threw it over the top of the case as I stood, my body blocking the closet as Cole appeared in the doorway.

"What are you doing up so late?" he asked, rubbing his eyes and looking into the closet.

I put my hands on his chest and urged him backwards.

"I don't know. Just couldn't sleep," I said.

He narrowed his eyes, glancing behind me and shaking his head. I caught the start of a curious smile on his lips before he turned around and started toward the kitchen.

It couldn't be more than four in the morning. "Wait. Where are you going?"

"I'm making tea," he said. "That's the only thing that ever helps you sleep."

My heart literally melted in my chest. Why, after everything, did he have to be so good to me?

Why was it always that we found something wonderful just as we realized it could never be ours?

I turned back to the closet, shoved the case back in its hiding place, and went to join my boyfriend in the kitchen, knowing that as soon as the sun came up, everything would change for us.

I was going back to my old life, which was the one place he could never follow.

A TRAIL TO FOLLOW

OVER THE NEXT WEEK, I WENT TO THE CLUB EVERY NIGHT. NOT TO dance or to party.

I went to watch.

No one offered me any strange candies the first five nights I was there, and I caught no sign of the man who'd destroyed my life all those years ago. Nothing unusual at all, in fact, and I went home each night feeling frustrated and slightly insane.

Had I invented this whole thing? Was I stepping back into an unhealthy obsession after nearly two years of fighting for a new life?

Cole had been calling me for days, and I'd basically told him I needed some space. Distancing myself from him had nearly broken my heart, and if I didn't find some sign of Wolfgang or vampire activity soon, I was going to pick up that phone and tell Cole I was sorry.

One more night, I told myself. If there was no sign after that, I would give it up. Try to go back to the normal life I'd at least temporarily carved out for myself in this crazy world.

But my destiny wasn't about to let that happen. On the sixth night, a young, beautiful woman in a skintight black dress came up to me at the bar and slipped a golden-wrapped candy into my hand with a wink.

"Wait," I said, touching her arm as she turned away.

Her skin was ice cold, which should have come as no surprise.

She pulled away quickly but kept a smile on her face.

"Just try it," she said softly, leaning in.

"What is it?" I asked.

An eyebrow popped up and her smile brightened. I could practically see her incisors grow as she thought about the blood fest waiting for everyone she convinced to try that candy.

"It's a gateway to the best night of your life," she said. "Trust me."

I wanted to ask her more, but she'd already moved onto another woman further down the bar, and I didn't want to draw too much attention to myself. Not yet, anyway.

I turned the candy around under the light a few times, searching for any kind of mark or logo, but again, there was nothing. No clue or sign of who had created it or where I could find them, but that was okay. I had what I needed now, anyway.

I smiled as I thought of my brother and his trails of white breadcrumbs, so he wouldn't get lost in the woods without a way home.

Our mother had given him a magical pouch one year for his birthday, the summer before she died. That pouch contained one hundred smooth, white pebbles, each with the letter H engraved in gold on one side. They'd replaced his breadcrumbs, and we'd used those pebbles for years as we explored the woods outside our village.

I no longer had Hansel or his magic pebbles, but what I did have was a trail to follow.

I looked at the woman as she slid another candy in the hand of a handsome guy standing at the edge of the dance floor.

It took a few hours for the action at the club to slow down, but the mysterious woman continued passing out candies all evening. She seemed to mostly target singles out alone. Every once in a while, she'd give the candy to all the women in a small group of friends or a man on his own, but most of the candy went to young women standing by themselves.

I watched carefully, waiting for someone to take the bait and actually eat the candy. A surprising number of people, despite being promised the night of their lives, just threw the candy into their bag or pocket without a second glance. The smart ones left the candy on the bar top or threw it in the trash.

But one young woman in a purple dress sat at the bar moving it between her fingers for a few minutes before shrugging, unwrapping it, and popping it into her mouth. Her eyes widened and she nodded, so I took that to mean it tasted as nice as it looked.

My own mouth watered slightly as I remembered the taste of that purple candy. Sweet, yes, but it was more than that. It was exquisite. Perfection.

Seductive, even though that's not a word I would have understood back then.

The woman in the purple dress closed her eyes, as if to savor it. My stomach tightened, and I had to look away for a moment. It had been almost two decades since I'd tasted that candy, and yet I still remembered it so acutely, I could smell the sickly grape scent of it in my nostrils.

When I finally collected myself, the woman had made her way to the dance floor, hands up and dreamily slow dancing despite the fast house beat. People bumped into her, moved past her, stared at her, and none of that seemed to penetrate the euphoria she was experiencing. She'd left the club and entered her own little world, it seemed.

I knew that feeling, only I hadn't been a twenty-something adult back then. I was only eight years old. One minute I was dancing just like that in the forest, twirling around and feeling certain that snow was falling onto my cheeks. The next, I was waking up, who knows how much later, trapped inside a wooden cage in the basement of a vampire's lair.

I took a deep breath, hoping to calm my racing heart. I'd come here for exactly this, but now that I was seeing her reaction and knew what was planned for her, I felt like that child again, reaching for my brother's hand in solidarity. Only, this time, he wasn't there.

A tear ran down my cheek, and I brushed it away quickly, glancing around to make sure no one had been paying any attention to me. Hansel would have been ashamed of me, standing here feeling sorry for myself.

Over the years, we'd taught ourselves how to feel nothing but anger and to focus only on justice and revenge.

Maybe it was because I'd loosened my grip on who I used to be. Because I'd allowed someone human and normal into my heart and my bed. I'd gone soft.

And soft was not going to get me anywhere with the vampires I was likely to face later tonight.

I had to be strong. Determined. Fearless.

I straightened my shoulders and pushed back any emotion that had risen to the surface.

I was this close to finding answers about this candy and why our uncle had ruthlessly handed us over to a vampire all those years ago, and I wasn't about to screw it up.

Would I have rather had my brother by my side for this moment? Of course. But being here was like finally finding closure for him. For both of us.

But it suddenly wasn't Hansel's face I saw flash in my mind when I thought about the choice I was about to make.

Instead, I had a vision of life with Cole. He'd gotten under my skin, for some reason, and even though I knew I had to deal with this threat, I was more disappointed at the thought of losing him than I expected. Maybe once I'd closed this chapter of my life, I could come back. Try it all over again.

It couldn't last forever because of what I was, but we could have decades together, if we were lucky. What would that be like? To truly walk away from this life of revenge and sorrow? To have the answers I'd been seeking for more than a century?

Would it bring peace? Or was the quest for answers the only thing holding my sanity together all these years?

There was only one way to find out.

I followed the girl in the purple dress out of the club a few hours later, keeping to the shadows the way only Hansel and I could. She managed to stumble her way down the sidewalk a block or two before the mysterious candy girl caught up to her.

To any normal observer, it looked like a couple of BFFs taking care of each other after a little too much to drink.

I followed them carefully, watching as they got into a dark blue SUV that appeared to have a few other victims inside.

Multiple clubs.

No wonder I hadn't seen them for a few days. They must have been hitting up multiple locations here in the city.

Unfortunately, the windows were too dark to tell exactly who was in that vehicle. Was Wolfgang in there with them? Was he the leader of all this? Or just some lackey passing out the candies?

And why had he come back into my life now, after all these years of searching?

I quickly ran to my own car and followed them, something I was pretty good at, especially since I had ways of making my car practically invisible.

The SUV made two more alleyway stops before finally pulling into a gated warehouse on the outskirts of the most dangerous neighborhood in the city. The whole area looked like a dumping ground, which I'll admit made it the perfect hideout. It looked like it had been abandoned except for the five expensive SUVs currently parked outside and a handful of lights shining from some of the windows.

What kind of operation were they running here?

And, more importantly, how many vampires were hiding out inside?

There were at least five victims and five vampires inside the SUV by the time they pulled up to their final destination. Assuming the other four parked outside the loading dock had gone on a similar hunting trip tonight, that meant potentially twenty more vampires inside and twenty more victims to try to save before the night was over.

But what if I was underestimating? What if an entire hive of vampires was in there feeding on the club victims?

I shuddered and reached for the black case. I entered the code and reached for the weapon I knew I had to use tonight.

Hansel's favorite dagger shone in the light from the lamppost overhead, and I lifted it from the case without a second thought. No, it wasn't my normal choice, and I hadn't practiced as much with this weapon over the years, but it was his, and I wanted some piece of him to be here with me tonight. He deserved that.

This is for you, brother.

And with that, I crept toward the warehouse and back into the world of vampire hunting.

THE HIVE

Vampires carried the limp bodies of their club victims through the back door of the warehouse. I had no way of knowing if they'd been given something else inside the vehicle, or if the candy had finally made them pass out, but they were definitely better off that way.

I knew from experience.

When the entire group from the SUV had disappeared into the warehouse, I sat on the ground behind one of the vehicles and took a moment to center myself and connect to my energy. I no longer had access to all the tools Hansel and I used to have, but I still had the most important thing.

My magic.

I connected to the fire within me, like sparking a match in the center of my heart. It had been nearly two years since I'd fully given into the power inside like this, and I gasped as it filled me.

Damn, I'd missed this.

My entire body lit up with the magic of my ancestors. Mages who'd lived for hundreds of years, fighting to maintain the balance between good and evil. For all I knew, I was one of the last mages alive in this world.

I never should have abandoned this duty, but tonight, I would do whatever it took to make it right again.

When I opened my eyes, my vision was sharper. My hearing was more acute. Every movement of my body felt different. Stronger. More graceful and precise.

I cloaked my appearance, vanishing from sight, at least for anyone who didn't know how to look. Since mages weren't exactly commonplace these days, I was hoping none of the vampires inside would be tuned into the type of magical energy I gave off, anyway.

I didn't want to just walk straight through the door, because while my body seemed invisible, the door itself would still move if I opened it. I needed a more hidden entryway, and it took me a good ten minutes to find it.

I slid in through a broken window on the east side of the building. There were no lights on in the room or the adjacent hallway, but I could see well enough to get around. Besides, I'd placed a magical trace on the woman in purple back at the club, and in here, it was like a beacon to me. A kind of magical compass inside told me exactly where to go and how far away she was at any given moment.

She hadn't moved at all since I first stepped foot in the building, which likely meant they were holding her and all the other club victims in a room somewhere near the center of the warehouse.

I cringed at the thought of what I might find when I got to that room, but I had no doubt I was going to have to my work cut out for me before I made it there.

It didn't take long to find the first group of them in a room, hovering over a set of documents spread across a table.

From the hallway, I quickly went through the motions of a powerful battle rune I'd learned from an ancient mage about a hundred years ago. It was the best spell I knew for paralyzing vampires so they couldn't make a sound or move a muscle.

As long as I had the element of surprise on my side, it worked every time.

This one was no exception.

The entire group of eight men froze, and I entered the room

quickly and quietly, ending each of them with a single stab to the heart.

I worked my way through the warehouse, quickly and methodically, taking out smaller clusters of vampires in the various rooms but seeing no sign of the victims just yet.

The largest group of vamps seemed to be gathered in the warehouse entrance area. This must have been where they'd come in after arriving in their SUVs, and I caught sight of the woman who'd been passing out candy standing next to a larger man in a suit.

There was still no sign of Wolfgang, which was starting to piss me off, but at least I was making progress.

I counted fifteen in all. Not exactly a cake walk, but it wasn't the largest group I'd ever faced.

I needed to act fast, though, because if I'd missed some along the way or anyone discovered the trail of dead vampires I'd left behind me, they'd be hunting me, instead of the other way around.

I cast my rune spell one last time, covering an area large enough to trap at least eight of the fifteen. That was going to have to be good enough.

I kissed the H on the hilt of the dagger and said a little prayer before sneaking into the room, triggering the spell, and going after the remaining seven vampires who were still mobile. My biggest mission here was to kill those seven before anyone managed to get away or warn more of their kind that I was here.

At first, my reactions were too slow as I tried to mix defensive moves with spells. One particularly nasty vampire with the strength of at least ten brought me to the ground and nearly made a snack of my neck, but something inside me lit up as he lunged for me.

"That's not how this works," I said, casting a barrier spell to protect my skin as I gathered fire in my palm and burned the shit out of his arm.

He screamed and sat up, a look of shock crossing his face as my dagger plunged into his heart.

After that, I was back to the old me. The Gretel that knew how to kick vampire ass since she was just a little thing, hiding in the woods.

I tore through that room, spells flying as I downed them all, one by one.

When I was done, blood dripped from the edge of my dagger. I casually wiped it across the skirt of my black dress as I stared at the carnage. Thankfully, once a vampire was dead, it didn't take long for their body to decompose and turn to ash. It happened in a matter of seconds if they were exposed to the sun, but a dagger through the heart usually meant half an hour until their bodies were dust.

Plenty of time to go searching for my woman in purple and the other victims from the clubs.

I focused in on her energy and practically ran toward a door in the back of the large room. I whispered an incantation and placed my hand on the door, just in case someone had set it with a trap, but there was nothing here.

Strange for a hive of vampires not to at least put some kind of trap on the doorway where they were hiding their most precious treasures.

I closed my grip tighter on my weapon.

Something didn't feel right, but nothing could have prepared me for what I saw when I stepped into that room.

More than fifty people, all dressed in club attire, lay passed out on grimy tables, their arms hooked up to lines that drained their blood into clear, plastic bags. Coolers lined the walls, and I could only imagine how many of those bags were stored inside.

But it wasn't the sheer number of victims that made me nearly drop my weapon.

It was a single person chained to a chair in the center of the room. His mouth was covered with a dirty piece of cloth, but his eyes met mine, and I knew that kind of terror.

Like an idiot, my heart took over, and I ran to him without thinking.

"Cole," I shouted, but he shook his head violently, looking past my shoulder.

I didn't even get close enough to touch him before something sliced through my calves. I'd run straight through some kind of trap.

I fell to my knees and then tried to stand again, failing miserably as pain consumed me.

Behind me, a woman laughed.

This was not good.

I slowly turned to her, my palms on the floor as I tried to push myself back up, nearly sliding on a pool of my own blood.

"This was so much easier than I thought it would be," she said, her eyes practically glowing in the dim light. "The last of the mighty duo finally brought to her knees."

I didn't recognize her, but she obviously knew who I was.

And she also knew that Hansel was gone. If I found out she had something to do with that, I was going to have fun putting an end to her life.

The hive queen, if I had to guess. Somehow, she'd known I was going to be here tonight.

I'd been too careless. Sure that no one around knew who I was.

"What do you want with me?" I asked.

"Well, first, I'd like you to put that weapon on the floor and kick it toward me," she said.

I didn't have much choice about that, seeing how I was literally on my knees with no ability to cast magic in this state, so I obeyed, feeling a little bit of my hope slip away with the dagger.

She smiled, her fangs showing as she met my eyes. "And people said it would be hard to bring the two of you down."

Every muscle in my body tensed.

"What's that supposed to mean?" I asked.

Hansel had disappeared nearly two years ago on an entirely different continent. The way his room had looked when I found it made me believe there was no way he'd survived. I'd searched for him for months, but I'd eventually given into the truth.

If this vampire had been any part of that, I wanted her dead.

And I wanted it to hurt.

"Unfortunately, I don't have time to go into all the details right now. Since you took it upon yourself to kill half my hive, it's time for me to get the hell out of this city before someone a lot more dangerous than you figures out what we've been doing here," she said. "But don't worry, you'll be coming with me. I can't wait to tell you all about what your brother went through that night."

I couldn't tell yet if she was bluffing about Hansel, but she'd at least admitted she didn't plan on killing me tonight. She wanted to take me with her. But why?

What use could a mage be to a vampire?

And more importantly, what did she plan to do with Cole and the others when we left?

I'd basically been on borrowed time ever since I lost Hansel, but Cole? I'd never meant to drag him into this world. I couldn't let anything happen to him.

"Who are you?" I asked, hoping to stall her long enough to think of a way out of this.

She narrowed her eyes and shook her head, as if she could read my mind. And with vampires, you honestly never knew.

Either way, she wasn't about to answer any of my questions here.

"Come along without a fight, and I will promise not to harm your boyfriend or any of the people here," she said.

"And how do I know I can trust you not to light this whole place on fire as soon as we're out of it?" I asked. "I may not know who you are, but you're a vampire. And vampires can't be trusted."

"What choice do you have?" she asked, raising an eyebrow. "If you try to fight me on this, I'll kill every human in this room. And the man you seem to care about so much? I"ll make him suffer beyond anything he's ever imagined. While you watch. Those are your only choices, so I suggest you come with me now, and I'll tell you everything you want to know on the way to our next location."

I shrugged.

"Or I could just kill you and save everyone, including Cole," I said, glancing at the dagger and wondering if I had enough power to take this vamp on my own. Queens were never easy, and there were more than a few that nearly took Hansel and me down when we were working at our best.

But she was right. What choice did I have?

She laughed again, and as her head was tilted back, I fought against the pain and gathered my magic inside my belly, ready to make my move.

Only, I never got the chance.

Hansel's dagger flew through the air, and before I could wrap my mind around what was happening, the silver tip of it pierced through the vampire's chest from behind.

She stumbled forward, eyes wide, hands clawing at her chest as she fell to the floor in front of me, revealing the man standing behind her, his eyes locked on my face in pure shock.

"What the hell are you doing here?" I asked, standing to wrench the weapon from the queen's dead body. I winced at the pain but didn't want him to see my weakness.

Wolfgang threw his arms wide, lifting his hands up in surrender. There were tears in his eyes.

"My dearest Gretel," he said, shaking his head. "You have no idea how long I've been searching for you."

I swallowed and kept the dagger raised, completely confused.

"What are you talking about?" I shouted. "You drugged us and left us for that vampire to torture us. We were just children. We trusted you."

He put a hand on his heart, his eyes never once leaving mine.

"I swear to you on my life, I did no such thing," he said. "The candy I gave you was meant to mask your powers, so that the vampires who were looking for both of you would never find you. They were coming there that night for me, Gretel. As an alchemist, they knew I could help them lure and control humans, but I didn't want them to have you and your brother. So I took you out into the woods, far from the village, where I thought you would be safe. You should have been okay, but you came back. Somehow you found your way home too soon."

I shook my head, trying to make sense of the mixed-up fragments of memory in my mind.

The pebbles? Had we used them that night?

"No, that's not how it happened," I shouted, but I wasn't so sure anymore. "You gave us the candy and then took us to that vampire's house."

"Gretel, you have to believe me. I never would have done that to you," he said. "Leaving the two of you behind after I'd promised my sister to look after you was the hardest thing I've ever done in my life. You have no idea how much it nearly killed me when you reappeared at the house so soon. The vampires took you, and I thought they'd killed you both all those years ago. But then, I started to hear about the work you were doing. Your mother's work. You were following in her footsteps, even though you had no idea about her life back then before she was taken from us. She would have been proud of you both, Gretel."

I closed my eyes, and suddenly a piece of memory that had never made sense to me came rushing back to me. It slid into place like a puzzle piece, turning my whole life upside down.

He was telling the truth. Hansel and I had come back to the village. We'd followed the white pebbles from Hansel's magic pouch. The one mother had made for him before she died.

The vampire had grabbed us there, at the edge of the village near our home. I'd forgotten it until this moment.

"You never betrayed us?" I asked softly, tears stinging my eyes.

Uncle Wolfgang stepped forward and threw his arms around me.

"Gretel, I have always loved you," he said. "I have spent my whole life trying to find you again and make it up to you after what happened that night."

I stared down at the decaying corpse of the vampire queen.

"Then what in the world are you doing working for these guys? I saw you at the club the other night, and I know this is your creation," I said, pulling a candy out of my pocket. "Why are you making this for them?"

To my surprise, he smiled through his tears as he put his hand over mine.

"Because they caught me following you," he said. "They promised not to harm you or even interfere in your life as long as I made them the candies. I didn't want to do it, but I hope you can see that I would do anything to protect the people I love."

Which suddenly made me remember that I had someone else I loved who was currently chained to a chair behind me, most likely freaking out about everything he'd just witnessed in this room.

I quickly turned to him and ran, muttering a simple spell to free him from the chains.

I pulled the cloth away from his mouth and put my hands on his.

"Cole, I never wanted to drag you into this," I said. "I know what you must be thinking right now, and I promise I'm going to explain everything, I just—"

But before I could say another word, he pulled me into a kiss.

"I love you, Maggie. Gretel. Whatever your name is," he said, a partial smile tugging at his mouth as he searched my eyes. "And yes, you have a lot of explaining to do when all this is over. You never even told me you had a brother."

I laughed.

"Out of all that happened tonight, that's the thing you're shocked about right now?"

"I hate to break up this lovely reunion, but we need to get out of here before more of those vampires arrive and see what we did to their leader," Wolfgang said.

He tossed me a clear vial and told me to put it on my wounds. The salve acted fast, and though I had a feeling the cuts from the trap might leave scars, the pain was gone for now.

"What are we going to do about all of these humans?" I asked.

There were way too many of them to get them all home, and we couldn't very well just leave them here.

"We'll have to call the local police," Wolfgang said. "Hopefully, they'll arrive before any of the other vampires."

I sighed. Not exactly ideal, but maybe we could stick around outside and watch the place until the cops arrived.

"Okay, you call them. I'm going to look around for a minute and see if I can find any clues here about this hive and where their headquarters are," I said. "Do any of the other hives have access to these candies of yours?"

Wolfgang nodded.

"I'm sorry, but yes," he said. "They've had me making batches for at least three other hives. If we can find their headquarters, I'm sure we can hunt down those other hives, as well."

"Okay, then call the police and clean up any evidence of magic," I said. "Cole, you're with me."

He smiled and grabbed my hand.

"What are you smiling at?" I asked as I led him toward the room where I'd seen those documents earlier. "You found out your girl-friend is some kind of magical being, that vampires are real, and you literally almost died tonight. You shouldn't be so happy right now."

He laughed.

"I always knew there was something special about you, but you were always hiding from me. No matter how hard I tried, it was like you would never let me in," he said, pausing to pull me into his arms again. "Vampires and death aside, it's just really nice to see the real you. You're even more amazing than I imagined."

We kissed again, and I realized it was the first time in my immortal life I'd actually kissed someone I loved who knew the truth of who I was.

He was right. It was nice.

But we would have plenty of time later to talk. I needed to search this place and get us both the hell out of here.

I led him to the room where I'd killed those first vampires, and as I was going through the documents, Cole crouched down on the floor and came up with something white and shining in his fingertips.

"What's this?" he asked.

One glance at it, and I felt as though the entire world had come alive again.

I brought a hand to my lips, suddenly finding it hard to breathe.

"Let me see that," I said, holding out a trembling hand.

Cole placed the smooth pebble in my palm, and I turned it over twice, laughing through my tears when I saw the letter H engraved on the side.

There was only one way a stone like that could have made its way into this room.

My brother was still alive, and somehow, he'd managed to leave a trail for me to follow.

"What is it?" Cole asked.

I smiled and held the pebble to my heart.

"A breadcrumb."

~ END ~

AUTHOR'S NOTE

If you enjoyed this story, you might love Sarra's Shadow Demons Saga. You can download the first three books and see the complete reading order here: https://sarracannon.com/books-2/reading-order/

Join Sarra's thriving fan community on Facebook, YouTube, or Discord. Find all the links here: https://sarracannon.com/sarra-cannons-coven/

Hansel and Gretel was always a favorite of mine as a child, because I also grew up in the woods. I frequently got lost, though, and probably should have taken notes on how to leave a trail of pebbles or breadcrumbs to find my way home. The original stories are much darker than the one we read as children, which is often the case with these fairytales, and I wanted to bring a little hint of that into this story by introducing vampires.

To be honest, I really enjoyed this story world so much I feel like it deserves its own series. But that tends to be the way I am with all stories. There's always more to tell. Thanks for reading.

www.ingramcontent.com/pod-product-compliance
Lightning Source LLC
Chambersburg PA
CBHW050508110726
47899CB00005B/1369